Precious-In-His-Sight

(Red; Brown; Yellow; Black; and White)

A Novel

MARVIN V. BLAKE

(Author of "Why" & "E.Pluribus Unum…")

Library of Congress Control Number: 2023918048
Paperback: 979-8-9886071-6-8

Contents

"You have to be carefully taught."
        —Oscar Hammerstien II

****

"It is easier to build Strong Children, than to repair broken men."
        —Frederick Douglass

****

*"The Ultimate tragedy is not the oppression and cruelty by the
bad people, but the silence over that by the good people."*
        —Martin Luther King, Jr.

****

*"They made us many promises, more than I can remember. But they
kept but one-they promised to take our land...and they took it."*
        —Chief Red Cloud

****

With the exception of historical figures, all characters
in this novel are fictitious, and any resemblance to
living persons, present or past, is coincidental.

For... *Jannifer; Dana; David; Jason & Miles*

CHAPTER 1

Richmond, Virginia— July 29, 1861 July 29, 1861

The Rosewood Plantation's carriage bounced along on the narrow path. Approximately two miles from Richmond's city limits, the path gradually widened to the extent that two vehicles, one moving in either direction, could traverse the road.

The attractive, petite, twenty-three-year-old young woman, Eleanor Leary, who when standing stood five feet-five-inches, sat forlorn, slouched in the corner of the jostling carriage.

Eleanor's reddish, chestnut brown hair, was parted down the middle, drawn back into soft folds that accented and flattered her pale, round, oval face.
Eleanor's usually bright sparkling brown eyes were red-rimmed from crying.

Pee Wee, the Rosewood Plantation's, black slave liveryman, kept his head bent forward, his eyes staring straight ahead.

Although Pee Wee religiously adhered to the slave tenet...— *"don't cha go gettin yo self mixed up in da white fok bizzness* —, Pee Wee felt genuine pity and sympathy, for the pretty little white *"teecha"*.

Eleanor Leary sat up in her seat. She stuffed her damp handkerchief into her rattan-handbag, and sighed.

Although, intellectually and realistically—especially during these turbulent times of increasing tension between the North and South, over the issue of slavery —, the fact that she was leaving the South, instilled in her a definite feeling, of relief.

Eleanor was experiencing remorse, regret from her abrupt, unceremonious, departure, following her being summarily, discharged by Henry Billings, the Master of the Rosewood Plantation. Discharged for her having allegedly, violating Virginia law, by teaching a slave, to read and write.

Despite her depression, a satisfied, wry-smile formed at the corners of her lips.

While Eleanor's inclusion of Shakespeare's 16th century, classic play Othello, into their reading-list, play that told of a black man, a black general, married to a white woman, commanding an army of white men—had undoubtedly been a contributing factor, that helped to instill in the slave girl Mandy, a sense of racial pride and self-esteem—Eleanor did not doubt..., not for a moment, that her decision to include that particular literary classic, had also contributed to her abrupt, dismissal.

Ironically, Eleanor mused that, she was completely innocent of the crime that her employer, Henry Billings, Master of the Rosewood Plantation, had accused her of committing..., of violating the Southern Law, which prohibits; *"The Teaching of Slaves..., to Read and Write"*.

Eleanor remembered how impressed she had been, when Rebecca, Henry's white daughter—Eleanor was convinced that her clandestine, black-pupil, the slave-girl Mandy…, that Rebecca and Mandy are sisters—had proudly stated, that she…, had taught the slave-girl Mandy, to read and write.

Mandy, had actually been taught to read and write, by her young mistress Rebecca.

Eleanor had long suspected that, because of the remarkably, striking physical-similarities between; Rebecca; Mandy; and Rebecca's father, the Master of the Rosewood Plantation—that Henry Billings, had literally "planted the seed(s)", albeit in different gardens, that had blossomed into two, practically inseparable, beautiful girls…, one white, the other black.

There was little doubt in Eleanor's mind, that Henry Billings, had fathered both girls.

Eleanor especially regretted that she had not been given time to seek out the girls. Time to have at least said goodbye to Rebecca and Mandy.

Eleanor up to that point in her career considered these two remarkable young women, to have been her most intellectually gifted and promising, students.

Eleanor knew that she would never forget them…that she would always remember them—that she would always think of them as; *"The Brilliant Billings Sisters"*.

****

Pee Wee reigned in the mare at the train-depot. He jumped down from the driver's seat, and straw hat in hand, opened the door of the carriage.

Eleanor extended her gloved hand to the black slave-coachman. Pee Wee assisted her in stepping to the ground. With her feet firmly on the ground, Eleanor, gave a gentle squeeze of appreciation, to the black slave's hand.

Pee Wee's instinctive, reflexive survival reaction to the white woman squeezing his hand, a reaction ingrained in him from over two hundred-fifty years of enslavement, was that as if he had touched a hot stove.

The black slave immediately, jerked his hand from Eleanor's grasp. He then sprinted up the two steps that lead to the porch of the train-depot. Again, hat in hand, Pee Wee held the door open.

"Mizzy...Ise be fetchin yu bag frum da buggy".

Eleanor managed a smile of gratitude. "Thank you Pee Wee". Eleanor approached the ticket agent. She reached into her retinue, removed several bills, and asked for a one-way ticket on the first train, whose destination was one of the northern states.

The ticket agent accepted her money, and gave Eleanor a ticket. "Train'll be leaving in ten minutes lady".

Pee Wee, with Eleanor's suitcase in hand, followed Eleanor to the train, where a black porter waited; he placed a stool on the ground, and assisted Eleanor, in the boarding of the train.

Pee Wee handed Eleanor's suitcase to the porter.

Pee Wee climbed aboard the Billings' carriage, turned the mare's head in the direction of the plantation, relaxed his grip on the reigns, and allowed the mare to slowly plod her way, back towards the Rosewood Plantation.

****

Although it was the beginning of October, the weather had been unusually hot.

Pee Wee remembered Massa Prentiss, the Rosewood Plantation's Overseer's, instructions to him, prior to his taking the white-teacher, to the train depot this morning.

"Pee Wee, I wants you to get your lazy black-ass back here in time for you ta help ta pick the cotton. It's harvest time I need all you bucks and wenches, field hands and house-niggers, out picking in the fields."

"You hear me Nigger? You get your lazblack-ass back here soon as you takes that teacha, to the train".

Pee Wee, as usual, had bowed his head. *"Yassuh Massa Lucuss, Ise be comin' back lik-ah-di-split."*

As he allowed the mare to leisurely transport them back to Rosewood, Pee wee reflected upon what he had been thinking this morning, when he was receiving, the Overseer's instructions:

"Dis cracka Massa Lucus, mus think dat dis niggah bees powafull-dum. I shoo-nuff ain't in no hooree ta break mah back ah pickin, an ah packin cotton, till it bees to dark ta see. Me an dis here hoss, we buff smart nuff ta taks our time, getting bac."

Pee Wee wrapped the plodding horse's reigns, around the carriage's brake- handle. He reached down below his seat, and removed a jug of luke-warm water.

Pee Wee took a long, satisfying drink, and then replaced the jug under the seat.

He stood, and slowly removed the damp, sweat encrusted shirt, that was clinging to his body.

Pee Wee draped the shirt, over the back of the buggy's driver's seat, and slowly, gingerly, lowered himself onto the seat.

****

Eleanor, after having removed her hat and gloves, while still holding her damp handkerchief, with a relieved sigh, leaned back in the surprisingly comfortable, train-seat.

As the train monotonously, chucked along, leaving a thick-cloud of black smoke, in its' wake, Eleanor's thoughts were of the wondrous times that she had spent at Rosewood. The time spent teaching…as well as learning from her highly literate, precocious, students, Rebecca and Mandy Billings.

Eleanor knew and appreciated the fact that, to her white student, Rebecca, the name Billings, represented familial pride. Pride of her heritage... pride of her ancestral, lineage.

As for Mandy, Rebecca's black sister, the name Billings, was not so much a name... as it was a proprietary **BRAND**.

The word *Billings*, was for Mandy... for her mother Ruth, for her brother, Jason, an ugly word, a label; a legal label that connoted ownership…, *property of the Billings family*.

Eleanor had been told by Mandy, that for her, the name Billings proclaimed to the world, at least to the Southern world, that she, Mandy *Billings*, as indeed was the *Billings'* horse, that was hitched to the *Billings'*-carriage, that *had* this morning, brought Eleanor to the train station.

As she gazed out the window, Eleanor saw a black man leisurely plodding along, seated on a carriage, no more that thirty yards from the train.

Instantly she recognized that the black man was Pee Wee, the Rosewood Liveryman.

Pee Wee was standing, balancing himself in the moving carriage, while removing his shirt, exposing the network of ghastly-scars, red.

The path that the mare was taking, on its' own—as if from instinctive memory —, angled off onto a rutted, dirt-path, leading away from the train tracks.

Eleanor sat up in her seat. She gasped in horror, at the sight of Pee Wee's mutilated back. The black man's back was crisscrossed, by a multitude of raised-hideous, scars.

From her time spent at Rosewood, Eleanor knew that those scars had been inflicted by one of the bullwhips, routinely used by the Rosewood overseer, to punish the black slaves, for perceived... often imagined, plantation, rule- infractions.

A piteous, moaning, sound escaped from Eleanor's lips. She hastily stifled the sound, by placing both of her hands, over her mouth.

****

Precious In His Sight

The many fond memories of her time spent in the South, were quickly supplanted, by the numerous times that she had seen… seen with her own eyes, white-men and boys, routinely subjugating their fellow human beings… black- men, women and children, to brutal, inhumane, corporal and often-times, capital punishment.

As the Rosewood carriage, disappeared in the distance, with tears once again flowing down her cheeks, Eleanor began to rummage through her bag. She pulled her journal from her bag, turned the pages to her last entry, and silently read…

Well, perhaps for me, it's for the best.

I have learned a great deal about the South and its' piteous, feeble attempts to justify,
and to preserve Slavery.

I will miss Rebecca and Mandy, the two of whom act like, and I believe are truly, in every sense of the word, sisters. They are indeed two of the most engaging and intelligent students that I have had the privilege, and the honor to teach.

My hopes and my prayers, for their future, will always be with them. My time here at Rosewood, is at an end.

Eleanor opened her bag and replaced her journal. As she was closing the bag, she noticed the unread, railroad ticket, that she had just purchased.

In her haste to board the train... to leave the South, *when the ticket agent asked; "Where to Lady?" Her response had been immediate.*

Eleanor had asked for a ticket, on the first train leaving the South.

For the first time, she gazed at the ticket's destination. The ticket read;

Destination: Gettysburg Pennsylvania.

****

****

CHAPTER 2

Gettysburg, Pennsylvania - Thursday, October 18, 1860

When Eleanor arrived in the bustling town of Gettysburg Pennsylvania, it had been her intent to procure a room, to rest overnight. And to in the morning, continue her northwestern journey, to her family's farm, in the small town of O'Fallon, located in the U.S. Territory of Nebraska.

The next morning when she arrived at the depot, Eleanor was informed by the railroad ticket agent, that due to the need to repair and replace damaged rail road tracks, it would be several days, possibly weeks, before train service to the northwest, would be resumed.

After a week had passed, and rail service had not been restored, and with her meager funds, beginning to rapidly, become depleted, Eleanor applied for and obtained a teaching position in the English Literature Department, at the local, institution of higher learning..., the Pennsylvania College.

****

Eleanor, deliberately chose to include the Shakespearean classic play, **_'Othello'_,** for their reading and comprehensive analysis, by her first year, Pennsylvania College, English Literature-Students.

In addition to broadening and expanding, the education of her current students, Eleanor's intent was to dispassionately, and intellectually, collect _a small snippet of data... data that she planned to use, to_ compare and contrast, these students—her now all white, politically-progressive leaning, students' thoughts and reaction, to Shakespeare's 17th century classic Romantic Tragedy —, with the 19th century's vitriolic, racist views and words, that had been so vehemently, spewed forth by her former student, seventeen-year-old, Jesse Billings, the heir-apparent to, one of the state of Virginia's, largest and wealthiest, Cotton Plantations. During her time teaching in the South, Jesse Billings, the son and heir, of Eleanor's then employer, Henry Billings, the Master of Virginia's Rosewood Plantation, had been her lone white-male, student.

Eleanor vividly recalled, Jesse Billings' violent reaction to Othello. Jesse's exact words, as told to her, by Jesse's sister Rebecca, had been;

"Miss Leary, Jesse is offended by "Othello". He says that the play is malicious fiction. Yankee Abolitionist propaganda.

Jesse insists that the premise of the play, a black military general, commanding white troops, is ridiculously, unbelievable".

Rebecca had gone on to say that following his reading of the scene, when Othello kills his white wife, Rebecca said that Jesse's reaction was so severe, that she thought, that her brother might be having a _"fit"._

Rebecca said that she actually, feared for his life.

Twelve- year-old Rebecca, had thought that her seventeen-year-old brother, was on the verge of having a stroke.

"Jesse, fuming with anger, had ripped a page from the book and shouted; *"That black nigger bastard, Othello kills his white-wife. That nigger kills a white woman!"*

Still, despite young Jesse's beliefs and practices…; the sanctity of slavery…of human bondage, Eleanor did not think of Jesse, as being an evil person.

Instead, Eleanor tended to attribute Jesse's warped, racist beliefs, to his having been raised a white male…, in the White-Supremacist, slave-holding, South.

After all, Eleanor had reasoned, Jesse Billings, was a young white-man, born, raised, and indoctrinated to believe, and to embrace, the values, and the white-privileges, of the South's aristocratic, slave-holding, Planters Society.

****

Eleanor was seated, sipping coffee, in Pennsylvania College's crowded, faculty lounge.

She was totally engrossed, deep in thought, after having meticulously read…, and in the case of three outlier-student essays…, reread the written, critiques, of her fifteen freshmen-students analysis, of Shakespeare's **_'Othello'_**.

Although the majority of her fifteen, Northern college students —— thirteen of her students, representing (80%) of the class—had written essays that where albeit, simplistic, obvious, analysis, they were at least marginally consistent with, and reflective of her more in depth, personal interpretation and critique of Shakespeare's play.

Eleanor was surprised…, a bit shocked, and dismayed, after having read the essays submitted by three, (20%) of her students.

Those three students had presented principally, racially biased, negative criticism of *the main character of the play, Othello, as well as the author of the classic romantic-tragedy,* William Shakespeare.

Those students appeared to be put-off… obsessed with what they considered, the amoral miscegenational-marriage of the Venetian-General, Othello…, a black man, to a white woman.

After reading those three papers, Eleanor concluded that those students had fixated… viewed their critique of Shakespeare's 17th century classic tragedy, through the foggy-lens, of the prevailing 19th century white-supremacy, societal filter, that especially abhorred racial integration, and thus, endorsed and promoted, "Anti-Miscegenation", bias.

Eleanor readily acknowledged, that the sample size of her little experiment, was just that, *little*…, too small, therefore lacking statistical significance.

Still, she was disappointed to discover that three, of her fifteen— *"Northern Born and Breed"*— upper middle-class, white students, apparently held stereotypically, negative, opinions of blacks, based upon their birth…their race…, and the color of their skin.

Two of the three students (66%), that had, expressed negative racially biased, critiques, were male students.

Those two-male student's, expressed outrage, based upon the white-male, chauvinistic, *"knee-jerk"*, reflexive objection; at the thought of a black man, being married to a white woman.

Eleanor silently mused; "These two white-male student's views, are strikingly similar, compatible, with those of the many southern, white-males, that she had encountered, during her time teaching, in Richmond Virginia.

This attitude, she found to be especially prevalent among those southern, white-males, who belonged to the Aristocratic, Slave-Holding, Planters Class."

Those *"white-gentlemen"*, had *"metaphorically"*, "placed the white-female, on a pedestal". And tended to ascribe to unmarried white females, of the "Planters Class", the allure of chastity, and of universal, virginal purity.

Of the three negative essays, the essay that most alarmed Eleanor, was a well written, obviously researched, reasoned paper, submitted by, Miss Loretta Watkins.

Now annoyed, and becoming increasingly exasperated, Eleanor sighed as she dutifully, reluctantly... for the third time, forced herself to reread, Miss Watkins's essay;

I thought that Shakespeare's Othello, for its' time (written in the early 17ᵗʰ Century), to be an insightful, entertaining play.

The play is insightful for its' depiction, its' portrayal of the consequences that sometimes, result from destructive human emotions, such as jealousy and deceit.

However, I found Shakespeare's premise, his "Promulgating the belief that, a black man, could and would, have the intellect, the mentality, the ability to rise in the Venetian Army, to achieve the rank of General", to be both fanciful, and extremely misleading.

Modern 19ᵗʰ century science... theories, lectures, and publications, put forth by prominent scientists, believe that polygenism, not monogenism, accounts for the existence of the different races of man.

And while the descendants of each group share... to a degree, common attributes, e.g., creation of unique languages; the ability to make tools; and the ability to effectively utilize fire; the quantity and quality of those attributes, differ markedly in each separate and distinct, race.

These prominent members of our 19ᵗʰ Century Scientific Community, are in agreement; that among the races, in terms of the quantity and quality of intelligence, we the white race, occupy the top rung of the ladder, and conversely, the Negro occupies the bottom rung.

References:

1. *Agassiz, L.: Principles of Zoology For Use of Schools and Colleges (Boston, 1848)*
2. *Gobineau, A.: An Esssay on the Inequality of the Human Races (1853-1855)*

    Precious In His Sight

It was this..., this well written, obviously researched—Eleanor thought, racist, *"White Supremist"*, negatively-critical—essay, submitted by one of the class's three female students, that gave Eleanor the most reason, for concern.

Eleanor thought of Loretta Watkins as being…if not the brightest, she was certainly, one of the brightest of her fifteen students.

In her paper, Miss Watkins had criticized Shakespeare for..., as she had written:
"Promulgating the belief... the possibility, that a black man could possess the requisite intelligence, and the military knowledge, to be a leader of white men, and thereby ascending to the rank of General, in the Venetian Army".

Additionally, in her essay, Miss Watkins had… if not proclaimed…she most definitely had implied, that, modern science supports the doctrine of racial *"White Supremacy"*.

Eleanor was surprised…albeit impressed, that Miss Watkins, had found... and had cited references… ostensibly, scholarly references, in support of— what Eleanor considered, as being—her student's racially-biased, critique, of Shakespeare's ***'Othello'.***

Loretta Watkins had footnoted her paper;
References:

1. *Agassiz, L.: Principles of Zoology For Use of Schools and Colleges (Boston, 1848)*
2. *Gobineau, A.: An Esssay on the Inequality of the Human Races (1853-1855)*

Although her brightest student's assessment of the play, was diametrically opposed to her own, intellectually…as an educator,

Eleanor was none-the- less, impressed with her student's initiative, and with the scholarly, manner in which Miss Watkins, had attempted to support her analysis... her critique of Shakespeare's classic Tragedy, **_'Othello'_**.

****

The students' papers were scattered over the table. Eleanor's concentration was abruptly interrupted by a well-modulated, slightly high-pitched, but definitely, male voice;
"Do you mind, if I join you?"

Startled, Eleanor looked up into the soft *("put you at ease"),* brown, comforting, eyes, of Professor Paul Winslow.

Eleanor's immediate reaction to, what she would later describe as, those cute, sorrowful, little puppy-dog eyes, was that of annoyance.

Fully intending to politely but firmly, deny the intruder's request, for some inexplicable reason, she smiled.

The frown that had been covering her face, dissolved, and was replaced by a sincerely warm, friendly, smile.

Standing in front of her, awkwardly shifting his weight (142 lbs), from foot to foot, was the diminutive, unquestionably brilliant, Dr. Paul Winslow, an acclaimed, Full Professor—on track, to becoming chairman —, in the college's Department of Sociology.

Paul Winslow, in his stocking feet, stood 5' 7". However, in his mail-order shoes... shoes that he had had made in, and transported by rail, from Philadelphia, Dr. Winslow had managed to gain an inch and a half of height.

Professor Winslow's ordering and purchasing of the *"elevated-shoes"*, was not out of vanity, it was instead, out of necessity.

When Paul gave lectures— especially in large, cavernous auditoriums…in front of large audiences, those attendees in the rear of the auditorium—, although they could hear, they simply could not see, the 5'7", distinguished, erudite, scholar.

Professor Winslow, in his soft, calm, well-modulated, tenor, voice, repeated;

"Do you mind… if I join you?"
Eleanor was momentarily, speechless... caught off guard. The world-renowned social scientist, Dr. Paul Winslow, was asking permission to sit with her.

Eleanor "froze". She stared as if in a trance, at the multiple student essays, that were cluttering the table.

When she regained her composure, her initial thought was… *"Oh heavens, "**Thee**", Professor Paul Winslow…, wants to sit with me."*

To her surprise and dismay, for the first time in her adult life, Eleanor Molly Leary, was experiencing a sensation... that same long ago, vaguely, remembered, giddy, tingling, adolescent-sensation, that she had felt, when at the age of twelve, her mother had insisted that she *"get her nose out of those books"*.

Her mother had cajoled…and insisted, that she attend a birthday party, at which she had succumbed to "peer-pressure", and had participated… played, *"Spin the Bottle"*.

Eleanor, as mandated by the rules of the game, was obligated to kiss— her first kiss, a boy— thirteen-year-old, Melvin Baxter.

During her second week as a new member of Pennsylvania College's faculty, Eleanor and six of her colleagues were told—actually they had been politely ordered—to attend the college's, *"New Faculty Orientation Dinner"*.

It was at that semi-social gathering, that Miss Eleanor Leary had been formally introduced, to Dr. Paul Winslow.

On that occasion, when Professor Winslow shook her hand Eleanor had inexplicably , almost immediately, experienced an undeniable, increasingly, strong intellectual…and for her…an unnervingly, physical attraction, towards the relatively short, prematurely balding… distinguished, academician.

For the past several weeks, following that brief, innocuous meeting, and her having been formally introduced to the professor, Eleanor, when she could find a free moment, had researched and reviewed, as many articles, and scientific papers, that she could find, that were either written by... or written about, Professor Paul Winslow.

Like a shy, frightened school girl, she had gone out of her way, to avoid being alone in a social setting, with the most intelligent, schlarly, and interesting man, that she had ever met.

****

Dr. Winslow impatiently, swept his eyes across the lounge, looking for a vacant chair. With the exception of the chair at this table…every chair in the Faculty-Lounge, was occupied.

Nodding his head in the direction of the vacant chair at the table, Paul asked once again…this time with a trace of irritation his voice;

"Do you mind if I join you?" Eleanor was flustered…she felt trapped.

Frantically and clumsily, she began to nervously stack, the numerous student essays that cluttered the table, into a non-to-sturdy pile.

Embarrassed... and though her throat was dry, Eleanor managed to mutter; "Please Professor... please, be seated.

Paul estimated that prior to his being given permission to be seated, that he had stood, nervously shuffling his feet, patiently waiting—at least for a good thirty-fifty seconds —, for this very attractive, obviously studious young woman, to acknowledge his presence.

****

Paul placed his tray on the table in the space that Eleanor had cleared. The two faculty members sat silently on opposite sides of the small table.

Dr. Winslow cleared his throat, and broke the awkward silence. "Please excuse, my manners. He leaned over and extended his hand. My name is Paul Winslow".

When Eleanor placed her hand in his, Paul gently squeezed her hand.

Eleanor involuntarily, blushing... gasped. Paul reacted by immediately disengaging, releasing her hand, breaking contact... that ended their momentary, societally approved, initial-physical, contact.

Eleanor was mortified. Paul seeing her discomfort, attempted to put this delightfully charming, and nervous, young lady at-ease.

"I hope that you won't think that I'm being forward...or heaven forbid, that you think, that what I am about to ask, is either rude or presumptuous... however, that not-withstanding, I must ask...have we met before?"

Regaining her composure, Eleanor relaxed. "Indeed, we have Professor Winslow. Two weeks ago, we met at the "Welcome New Faculty-Dinner".

"I was one of the new faculty members, that was being introduced to our distinguished-tenured, faculty. I had been recently honored, by Pennsylvania College's, favorable acceptance, of my application to join the faculty.

I was appointed to the rank of "Instructor", in the college's English-Literature Department."

****

Long after the faculty lounge had emptied… the corner table was once again cluttered, covered with student papers. However, while the essays were being graded by Eleanor…now, instead of the papers being reviewed by a single educator, the, student essays were now being reviewed and discussed, by both Eleanor, and Dr. Paul Winslow.

"Miss Leary… may I call you Eleanor?" Eleanor looked up from the student essay that she was grading. "Yes, yes. Please…please do. "

"Well then … I shall. I would like to ask a favor of you. Now that we are no longer merely colleagues… now that we are friends, it would please me Eleanor, if you would call me… call your new friend… Paul".

Not waiting for her response, Paul continued. "If I may Eleanor…I have a couple questions.

"Eleanor, I am curious. While I enjoy… and believe me, I do enjoy, and I am, a fan of, …and an avid reader of Shakespeare, I'm a bit curious, especially during this time of sectional-tension between North and South… I'm curious as to why you chose to include in your student syllabus, the assignment to read and submit to you, a written critique, of this particular classic, Shakespeare's… 'Othello'.

Eleanor placed the paper that she had been grading on the table. She hesitated, marshalling her thoughts, before speaking.

Instead of an immediate response to his question, Eleanor raised her hand, as would have one of his students, and spoke;

"Professor Winslow?"

Upon seeing the raised hand—the gesture that to all teachers, since antiquity, was the universal signal—that signified: "I have a question".

In a deferential, yet steady voice, Eleanor began to speak; "Dr. Winslow…"

Before she could articulate her thoughts, Professor Winslow interrupted. "Paul… remember. I thought that we had agreed. Paul and Eleanor…

Eleanor and Paul."

Once again, Eleanor was flustered; she felt the blood rushing to her face.

Awkwardly, she turned her head, picked-up her coffee cup, and sipped the, now cold coffee.

"Pau.. Pah…" Eleanor was stuttering…she was mortified. Her voice had betrayed her. Eleanor's precise and concise, diction had failed her.

She attempted to cover her embarrassment, by taking yet, another sip of her luke-warm coffee.

"Pah... Paul, in order for you to understand my motivation, for choosing this particular classic, 'Othello', I think that it would be helpful, if I shared with you... a little of my history."

"The last teaching position that I held, prior to my joining the faculty here…here, at Pennsylvania College, was in the South, at the Rosewood Plantation."

"Rosewood is a huge, sprawling, fabulously wealthy Cotton Plantation, located in Richmond Virginia."

"Rosewood's human population... excuse me, I misspoke. Let me rephrase."

"In the words of the Owner/Master of that huge cotton- plantation, Henry Billings, the human population of Rosewood, consisted of but five people…himself, his wife, his two children, and the plantation's white- overseer, Mr. Lucas Prentiss."

"Consistent with the "*Master's*" assessment, in total, not counting myself, according to Henry Billings, the white population five humans… now six… since my arrival, the white population… despite the nearly one hundred, black slaves, living and toiling on the plantation… Henry Billings held firmly to… was adamant in his belief that, the aforementioned white people, were the only "*humans*", living on the Rosewood Cotton Plantation."

"In addition to, and totally subservient to, the five whites… in the words, thoughts, and actions of the Master—excluding *the* horses, pigs, chickens, and mules—Rosewood was also inhabited, by ninety-eight, "*nonhumans*" who, as he did his livestock, he owned. His property… his "*nonhuman*- property, the "*black slaves*"."

"I had answered a newspaper advertisement, that I had come across, in my home-town's, one room library. The advertisement had been placed in the Richmond-Virginia, Gazette".

"Mr. and Mrs. Henry Billings, the Master and Mistress of Rosewood were seeking to obtain the services of *"A College Trained Female"*, to tutor the couple's two children".

"Mr. Billings…more precisely I suspect, it was his wife Margaret Billings, hired me to teach their two children… specifically to expand their children's education and to teach, their daughter Rebecca, and their son Jesse, the classics."

Paul, with a genuinely perplexed expression on his face interrupted.

"Eleanor, before you continue… if I may ask…. how, and why, in today's factional climate, why in the world… did you decide to go South, to teach."

Eleanor hesitated. "It's a long, boring, story Paul. I really doubt, that you'd find it interesting."

Paul, with a mischievous glint in his eyes spoke, "Au contraire", Miss Eleanor Leary, I am very interested".

Eleanor looked deeply into Paul's eyes…she hesitated. Then she shrugged her shoulder, and resumed speaking.

"Alright Profess... I'm sorry. All right Paul, but don't say I didn't warn you.

"I'll give you a short, abbreviated history, of the life, thus far, ... the life of Eleanor Molly Leary."

"Let's see... where should I begin?"

****

"In 1847, when I was thirteen, during the height of the Irish Potato Famine, in an attempt to save us from starvation, to feed the five of us, to feed his family; my father, Sean O'Leary, packed up our family's meager belongings, and we, the O'Leary family, of Cork County Ireland, immigrated to the "New World"… to the United States of America."

"After struggling for six months, in New York City, and not being able to find steady employment; tired of trying to ignore, but being forced to live amongst the ubiquitous signs and slurs, that boldly proclaimed and announced;"

"Irish Need-Not Apply"

And/Or

"Niggers, Dogs and Irish, Keep Off the Grass"

"Tired of being constantly hungry, and being subjected to…and forced to endure, senseless-blind, prejudice against the Irish, Daddy once again, made the decision to move the family."

"This time instead of traversing the vast Atlantic Ocean, the five of us, my father and mother… my two younger brothers Patrick and Timothy, and I, the O'Leary family— Daddy dropped the O', from our family's surname, he thought that that, would help us to blend-in; to assimilate… to melt-in, the "Leary" family, joined a wagon train, bound for the Northwestern, frontier."

"I won't bore you with the details of our western-emigration, but eventually, we… the Leary family, settled in O'Fallon, a little town, in the Nebraska Territory."

"My father, his father… his father's father, were all farmers. Because farming was in Daddy's blood, and because our land, our Nebraska homestead, was extremely fertile, after two years of back-breaking work, after expending copious, amounts Daddy and my brothers', blood, sweat and tears, the Leary Family-Farm, had become very… some might and did say, extremely, successful. So much so, that when I turned eighteen, my father agreed to my request. He consented, and arraigned for me, to attend Ohio's Oberlin College."

"Immediately, and I suspect because I graduated magna cumlaude, from Oberlin College, with a Bachelor of Arts Degree. Oberlin's faculty encouraged me, to broaden my education.

Oberlin extended to me, an offer that I declined, of a scholarship, to continue my studies, as a postgraduate student."

"Because I was eager to begin… to start my teaching career, eager to begin teaching, I decided to postpone graduate studies, and to instead, begin teaching."

"I received several offers to teach in my home town, O'Fallon Nebraska. I was prepared to accept an offer, when an interesting advertisement in our local newspaper, caught my attention."

"The advertisement was to tutor two young children, the son and daughter of Mr. and Mrs., Henry Billings the Master and Mistress of Rosewood, a cotton Plantation, in Richmond Virginia."

Paul nodded his head in admiration. Then he asked; "Why in the world, would you… why did you, accept a position in the South, tutoring two rich, probably spoiled-rotten… rich kids?"

"I spent my teen years, growing-up helping raise my two brothers, in the Nebraska Territory. My father's national political views, which he routinely shared with all who would listen... was for the "Abolishment of Slavery".

"My father, Sean Leary was…and is, an outspoken, staunch opponent of Slavery."

"While I at first, believed that father's political views were in large part, due to the Anti-Irish discrimination, that our family had experienced as Irish- Immigrants in New York City, however, in retrospect, I suspect that father's Anti-slavery position, is heavily influenced by economics."

"My father… whom I love and adore—as did most Northern-farmers—resented the fact, that is…the practice of Slavery.

"More precisely, our little farming community, resented that their competitors, Southern farmers, had ready, legal-access, to free labor… access to, four million black-slaves, which gave Southern farmers, a monumentally huge, unfair, advantage, in the pricing, of their cash-crops."

"As for my personal opposition to slavery, my anti-slavery position, before I spent time teaching in the South, was almost entirely based upon my conviction, my belief, that Human-Bondage is not only cruel, but is in fact, inhumane."

"After my having spent time living in the South... living among the oppressed, as well as living with the oppressors… my seeing first-hand, the white's amoral, sanctimonious-attempts, to excuse, and to justify, that which is inexcusable; to defend a society… a slavocracy, that is morally- indefensible, solidified my opposition to slavery."

'Professor Winslow, I stand before you...well right now... at this moment, I'm actually seated ... before you. I am an unabashed, 100%, inveterate, Abolitionist."

"My commitment and my belief, my advocacy and support, for the Abolishment of Slavery, is and will always be, unshakeable."

"I chose to teach in Virginia, because I wanted to... to see for myself, to observe up-close and personal, if you will... to witness and to objectively study, the South's Peculiar Institution... that of legalized, Human-Bondage."

"Those Paul, are the primary factors; And of course, the fact that I was teaching two "brilliant students", who I had come to love and respect… those are the reasons why, I remained …teaching in the South.

"I found Jesse Billings, the son and heir of the plantation, to be an intelligent, above average, student."

"On the other hand, the adjective intelligent, is grossly inadequate, when attempting to describe Jesse's sister Rebecca, and Rebecca's black-sister, Mandy".

"If I had to articulate the intellectual potential, of those two, pre-teenage girls... let's see" ... for a moment, Eleanor appeared to be lost in thought, she then abruptly, looked at Paul and said, the single word, would be *"Infinite"*.

"Paul, you hardly know me. However, over time… I am confident, that you will come to recognize, and I hope appreciate, that I make it a point, to avoid the use of hyperbolic, language.

"But as to those two, young women... the word, infinite, is to me, ideally and appropriately, suited."

"Infinite is the one word, that best describes my honest assessment, of the potential of those two young ladies, my former students, Rebecca and Mandy Billings."

A confused, inquisitive look had replaced Paul's previous attentive, demeanor.

Paul spoke, interrupting Eleanor's enthusiastic, obviously, heartfelt, narration;

"Excuse me Eleanor... I'm becoming a bit confused. Did I misunderstand?"

"I thought that you said, that you were hired to teach, two children, the son and daughter, of the plantation owner. If I heard you correctly, I believe your pupils names were Jesse and Rebecca."

"If you don't mind my asking...who exactly, is Mandy?"
Instead of her giving a direct response to the professor's question; "Who's Mandy?" Eleanor —in a quiet, almost reverent voice— answered Paul's question... with a question.

"You know that feeling that we as educators... if we're, ever fortunate enough to experience it, that moment, when you realize that you are teaching...in addition, to your teaching, you are being taught... in my case, being taught, simultaneously by not one... but by, two brilliant students?"

Paul nodded. "Indeed, I do. Fortunately for me, in my career... I have on several occasions, experienced, that exhilarating feeling".

While Paul had—by a few of his, few, non-faculty friends—been referred to as; *"The Forgetful Professor"*, professionally in the world of academia, Dr. Paul Winslow was universally admired, and respected for his intellect, for his demonstrable, accumulated knowledge, and for his ability to retain, and to analyze, both pertinent, monumental, as well as seemingly trivial, factual data.

If a fellow faculty member, was fortunate enough to ——, after having had Dr. Winslow review his paper——be given the "Go Ahead", for publication, Paul Winslow's *"Stamp of Approval"*, was considered by his colleagues, a strong indicator that your work, your paper, would with almost certainty, be welcomed by the Academic Community.

A frequently apt, and accurate phrase, that his colleagues used when describing Professor Winslow was that; Paul Winslow, has the talent, the knowledge, and the ability to;

"Separate the Wheat, From the Chaff"

Paul's brow was furrowed, as he concentrated, reading for the second time, the essay that he held in his right-hand, while with his left-hand, he unconsciously stroked his neatly trimmed "Salt & Pepper", goatee.

The student author of the essay that he had randomly picked-up from the large stack of papers, had been written by Matthew Crockett, a nineteen- year-old student, from Monte-Clare Pennsylvania, had submitted the below critique of Shakespeare's Othello:

"I thought that in the play 'Othello', Shakespeare managed to successfully entertain, while more importantly, communicating to the reader the truth, as well as to the consequences, of that old adage;

"Oh What A Tangled Web We Weave; When First We Practice, to Deceive!"

Paul placed the student's essay onto the table. He looked up, and with a mischievous smile radiating from his face, stated; "I really like this guy…he glanced at the student's name…Mr. Crockett's style. He seems to have managed to state briefly, succinctly, and in my opinion accurately, Shakespeare's intended, message.

Eleanor, who initially had been intimidated and nervous, at being seated in the presence of this renowned social scientist, after having been encouraged to share her thoughts with him, was now relaxed.

Paul's obviously genuine interest, and his enthusiastic responses, to her reasoned comments, his unexpected…though greatly appreciated, barrage of questions, served to bolster her self-confidence.

Eleanor reached for the small stack of papers that she had separated from the stack. These three student submissions were the essays that she thought expressed, racially motivated themes, in their analysis of the play.
She pulled out the paper that had been authored by her *"prize"* student, Loretta Watkins.

Eleanor picked up from the desk, the essay authored by, Miss Loretta Watkins. She carefully, with meticulous deliberation, folded the paper, in such a manner, that the student's name, as well as the content in the body of the essay, was not visible.

Without prelude… without uttering a word, Eleanor handed the folded essay, to Professor Winslow.

Paul at first, glanced at the essay, then with a quizzical look in his eyes, he questioned Eleanor; "What's this…why did you give me this particular essay?"

Before I answer…I ask that you, please not be offended. Your previous comment, after reading Mr. Crockett's essay, leads me to believe that my next question is superfluous. However, it's important that I ask, have you read <u>*"Othello"*</u> ?

Paul smiled, and then answered, "Absolutely no offense taken. Yes, I have read Othello, as a matter of fact, over the years; I've read _"Othello"_ several times.

"Othello" and **_"Macbeth",_** are my two, favorite works that were penned by;

"The Bard".

A huge smile spread across Eleanor's face; "I asked that question of you, because, I would greatly appreciate your thoughts, your opinion— she pointed to the folded essay that he held in his hand ——, of that particular, Essay".

"If you'll bear with me…I'll explain".

"Paul, I'm not asking you if you agree or disagree, with the opinions expressed by this student. I would however, very much like to hear your opinion… your assessment, as to the credibility… the validity, of her foot- noted references, that the student used, in support of this review, of Shakespeare's _"Othello"_ .

Paul did not immediately respond. Instead, he sat silently for a few seconds, his eyes, locked on Eleanor's face.

Finally, he spoke; "Why did you fold the paper, concealing its' contents and just leaving visible, the footnotes?

Eleanor, instead of responding… again, requested that he, focus his attention on the footnotes that the student, had referenced.

References:

1. *Agassiz, L.: Principles of Zoology For Use of Schools and Colleges (Boston, 1848)*

2. *Gobineau, A.: An Esssay on the Inequality of the Human Races (1853-1855)*

Almost immediately, following his reading of the footnotes, Paul looked-up.

He cleared his throat and begin to speak; "I am familiar with the work of both, of these gentlemen."

"Jean Luis Agassiz, is a world renowned, respected, scientist. Dr. Agassiz's, fields of expertise are those of, Biology, and Geology."

"As to your question why, your student referenced Luis Agassiz's Textbook, "***Principles of Zoology***"; because I have not been made privy, to the contents of the essay, I honestly, cannot answer."

"As to the Frenchman... I believe his full name is *Joseph Arthur Gobineau*".

"Monsieur Gobineau is a writer who in a series of well-read publications, argues that there are intellectual differences, between the different races... and that civilizations decline and fall, if and when, the races are mixed.

"It is Gobineau's belief, that the white race, is superior, to all other races"... is not only misguided, Gobineau's beliefs are not supported... they are in fact, totally devoid of any scientific—be it the physical sciences, or the social sciences—, data that supports the racist misinformation, that Gobineau, and/or Agassiz, are espousing.

"By the way Eleanor, my chosen area of expertise is that of the Social Sciences... which as you're aware, is the study of the development, structure, and functioning of human society."

Precious In His Sight

Because she was not familiar with either the names, or the work of the those referenced by Miss Watkins, she had hoped to hear from Professor Paul Winslow, words to the affect that; Agassiz and Gobineau were… to the world of academia, either unknown, or at best…lightly regarded.

Eleanor could not hide her disappointment.

Eleanor attempted to keep the disappointment that she was feeling, from showing. Although she had tried... tried her best to remain objectively unbiased, she could not conceal her disappointment, at Paul's comments.

Paul looked at Eleanor. It was apparent to him that Eleanor was far from satisfied, with his assessment of the two references, which had been cited by the student.

His gaze shifted from Eleanor, to the folded sheet of paper that he held in his hand.

Paul asked; "May I read this essay?" Eleanor nodded her head, giving her consent.

Paul unfolded and read Miss Loretta Watkins' essay, her critique of Shakespeare's, ***"Othello"***.

After having read the student's essay, Paul refolded the paper and placed it on the table in front of Eleanor.

Eleanor had instantly, become aware of a change in Paul's demeanor, in his tone-of-voice. That of a businesslike, professorial-orator had replaced his friendly jocular tone.

With the index finger of his right hand, Professor Paul Winslow pointed to the first listed reference.

"If I were to be asked… as you are apparently doing, … for my professional, scholarly, opinion, as to why your student referenced Agassiz's, Textbook; _"Principles of Zoology"_, I would hazard a guess, that your student, ahh— Paul glanced down at the essay… I would suspect, that Miss Watkins has read or heard, Agassiz's public declarations…his arguments, espousing what he proclaims is; '_The Innate-Inferiority of the Negro_'.

"Thus, Agassiz attempts to camouflage, his white supremacist, agenda, by attempting to lend credence to his non-scientific rhetoric…alluding to…even outright expressing, his racist's theories, in an accepted scientific, textbook".

"Agassiz's buttresses his … his racist beliefs, on what I, as do most of my Social Science colleagues, consider to be _"pseudo-science"_, employed by those attempting to cloak and to justify, white-supremist mantra, their dogma, under a veil of unproven, multisyllabic, scientific-sounding, gibberish."

"Though they utilize polysyllabic words, to put forth their believes, these pseudo-scientists have yet to…have not produced any scientific…and I might also add, any theological, evidence, in support, of _"Polygenism"_.

Eleanor sat quietly, attentive, respectfully, listening. She was mesmerized— not only by Paul's words—she was literally captivated by his insight, his intensity… captivated by the conviction that resonated in his voice, as he spoke.

Eleanor relaxed. The disappointment that, just a few moments ago, she had been experiencing… had dissipated, had vanished.

Paul had seen her "mood-swing". Before he could comment, Eleanor breathlessly, explained.

"Paul, your blunt, matter-of-fact, dispassionate, comments, after you read the names that Miss Watkins gave as references, in support of her essay… your words were…were…

Seeing that Eleanor was struggling for the appropriate words, Paul spoke;

"I am familiar with the work of both of these gentlemen, which led me to conclude… well not conclude, I guess a better way to express my thoughts would be … to concede…, to at least, acknowledge, that Miss Watkins' views are shared, by a few…a very few, respected scholars."

Paul raised an eyebrow. With a wry smile, he looked at Eleanor. And in a voice, which Eleanor could only interpret as being "Professorial", he elaborated.

"Dr. Agassiz—in his field, which is Biology and/or Geology—Professor Luis Agassiz, is recognized as a well-respected, scholarly, brilliant… in his field, scientist."

"However, as for the Social Scientists—those of us who study the development, structure, and functioning of human societies—of which I am a member, I regard the polygenists-opinions and theories being put forth by Luis Agassiz, as being that of "pseudo-scientific-gibberish."

Inexplicably, a wry smile… a smirk, had formed at the corners of Paul's lips. Seeing the confused look on Eleanor's face, at what she probably considered "inappropriate", instead of contrition, the smile… the smirk, on his face, morphed into a broad grin.

Forgive me Eleanor. When I was lauding the credentials and scholarship of Agassiz and Gobineau, a thought popped into my head.

Eleanor's involuntarily, raised an inquisitive eyebrow. Suppressing a smile; Paul, obviously attempting an impersonation, said; my mother would have summed-up, what I was trying to convey, in but one, sentence;

"Thou shoud-est Render therefore, the things that are Caesar's to Caesar; and to God the things that are God's."

Eleanor, as did Paul, smiled. Despite their mutual, tacit, unspoken, acknowledgement, that Paul was at times, *"Ah-bit-Windy"*, nonetheless, Professor Paul Winslow continued.

"The foundation of both *Agassiz and Gobineau*… of these men's assertions, is that of… what they regard… they believe, is the innate racial-superiority of whites; and thus, conversely their assigning the Negro, to the status of innate racial- inferiority, is anchored in their purported theological-belief, that the human-species, originated, not from a single origin, but instead they believe that the origin of the human species, is the result of multiple pairs, of progenitors."

"That fringe group of scientists, the polygenists—who incidentally, I feel and regard as being pseudo-scientists; those pseudo-scientists that espouse and promote polygenism—are basically, racists, who under the cloak of science, are promoting their belief, in "White-Supremacy" …the dominion of the white race, over all others… dominion over all non-whites."

"Those supposedly intellectual, accomplished men of letters support their dogma…that since God grants dominion by humans over all non-human animals; these men have extrapolated this to; *"God grants the white race, dominion, over all non-white, races of man."*

That is to say… that whites, Negroes, Indians, Polynesians, and Orientals, arise from totally different origins. And due to these men's polygenetic, White-Supremist beliefs… that of the distinct, *separate,* origin, of each race; that therefore, the different races, have developed… and are endowed, with differing degrees of intelligence."

"Polygenists theorize that God, at the creation, for each of the races… that God created separate pairs of progenitors. It's been said by a few outright racists… unabashed *"Pseudo Scientists"*, that God… for the white race, created Adam and Eve; and for the blacks… the pair of progenitors that he created was, *"Sambo* and *Beulah."*

Eleanor smiled…not at the racist slur; her smile was because of Paul's obvious denunciation, and repudiation, of racist *"Pseudo Scientists"*.

"Paul, my turn…a few moments ago, you pointed-out to me that your field of expertise, is that of the Social Sciences. I'm sure you would agree that, turn-about is fair play."

"My area of expertise… no, more accurately, my area of post- graduate, advanced-study, is that of Western Civilization – Western Literature."

"I say that, to say this. I understand, and I appreciate your assistance… your alerting me to the possibility, that her racial bias, may have influenced Miss Watkins', choice of references. However, now I am forced to confess… I am not familiar with the term "polygenist"."

Dr. Paul Winslow returned Eleanor's smile. Once again, when he spoke, his demeanor and his voice, was that of the educator, the scholar: "In the field of Anthropology, there exists two theories as to the origin of man.”

“Monogenism is the belief that all humans, all races, descended (originated), from a single ancestral pair. Monogenism is consistent with the biblical account of the origin of man.”

“Polygenism is the belief that… that each race, descended (originated), from that particular race’s unique, ancestral pair. Remember…Adam and Eve the ancestral pair for whites; Sambo and Beulah for the blacks, etc, etc.”

“Southern politicians and many of the so called, southern educational-elite, use polygenism—which I believe to be pseudo-scientific arguments—to characterize Negros, as being an inferior sub-species. Thereby justifying, the practice of Legalized Human Bondage… moral justification for the Southern Society’s *“peculiar institution”*… Slavery.

****

Paul Winslow was born April 13, 1826, in Philadelphia Pennsylvania. He was the only child, of Willem and Sana Winslow.

The Winslow family were devout god-fearing Christian believers; members of Pennsylvania’s, Religious Society of Friends (Quakers).

When Paul was five-years-old, he had innocently asked his father, why they were called Quakers. His father had placed his hands on his son’s shoulders, looked into his eyes, and in his deep baritone voice answered, “We *Friends* are called Quakers because thou art said, “to tremble in the way of the Lord.”

Both Willem and Sana Winslow, Paul’s parents, were the grandchildren of hard-working Dutch Quakers’, who in the 18th century, seeking a life free from religious persecution, had immigrated from the Netherlands, to the English-New World colony of Pennsylvania.

                                    Precious In His Sight

Along with their bedrock solid, unshakeable religious faith, Willem and Sana inherited from their fore-bearers, the Quakers communal-commitment to respect civil authority, and the need to adhere to, societal rules and laws.

In addition to their faith, these secular civic responsibilities were by, Willem and Sana Winslow instilled, into their six offspring.

However, Quakers also believed that those laws of man, that were contrary to their faith, those secular edicts, should not...would not by them, be obeyed. In fact, *many* adherents to the doctrines of the Religious Society of Friends (Quakers) felt that as true Christians, it was their duty to help, to lend a hand... a non-violent hand, to victims of persecution.

Two glaring existing societal, federal laws, that the Winslow family rejected, laws that had been legally passed...implemented, by their adopted, revolutionary-democratic, country, the United States of America, were:

That section of the U.S. Constitution, that acknowledged Slavery, and allowed human-chattel-bondage, to be condoned and legally practiced, in the United States, and;

> *"The Fugitive Slave Act (1850)", that compelled citizens of all of the individual states that comprise, the United States of America, to notify the authorities of escaped slaves... and to return runaway slaves to their owners... their Slave Masters.*

For the entirety of his life, Paul Winslow had respected, embraced, and actively practiced, his family's faith... faith whose tenets influenced and enhanced, his humanity.

During his formative years, Paul and his five siblings attended and received a solid education in the School District of Philadelphia, Philadelphia's Public-School System.

Because Paul was the oldest, it fell upon his shoulders, the responsibility of setting a good scholastic-example for his siblings...his five younger brothers.

Paul was an above average student. Through grammar school (1835-1841), Paul maintained a solid, boring "A" scholastic average, thus sitting a stellar example for his five brothers.

It was at the age of fourteen, that Paul's teachers began to notice, and to appreciate that one of their star pupils, Paul Winslow—a normally alert, inquisitive, attentive, student— was becoming increasingly bored, disinterested, in the level of the material, that they were teaching.

Although his grades were never an issue, Paul's enthusiasm, his thirst for knowledge, was clearly not being quenched, not being stimulated, challenged, by Philadelphia's school system.

It was during his second year in middle school, that he was introduced to the relatively new discipline, the *"Social Sciences"*.

It was at the urging to Paul's father, by the school's Guidance Counselor and by the School's Principal, that his son, the young prodigy Paul Winslow, seek admission to Indiana's Earlham College.

Almost immediately, following his graduation from Earlham College— in large-part, due to Paul's having received straight "A's", for each and every course he studied, during his three years as an undergraduate— that the University of Pennsylvania, recruited and offered, seventeen-year-old, Paul Winslow, a full scholarship for post-graduate studies, which led to his earning a Doctor of Philosophy Degree, awarded by the University of Pennsylvania's Department of Sociology.

****

March - 1863

Professor Paul Winslow, now Chairman of the Pennsylvania College's, Department of Social Sciences, along with the Department of Western Literature's junior, Assistant Professor, Dr. Eleanor Leary, had become regular fixtures, at the college's faculty lounge. And that during off-hours, Paul and Eleanor could be found together, usually until closing time, at the campus library.

The two educators could be found regularly, spending hours on end, discussing literature, politics, and the latest news of the tragic, ongoing civil war, that threatened to permanently fracture…to split the United States, into the Dis-United States; The Free Non-Slavery United (Union) States, and The Slave Holding, Confederate States of America.

A strong common bond that existed, between Eleanor and Paul, was their mutually held abhorrence, of the South's state sanctioned practice and support, of legalized, Human-Chattel-Bondage.

Eleanor and Paul, oddly enough, were both, in total agreement, that the South's professed, official reason for their seceding from the Union, that being, the frequently stated, ad nauseam, trite, officious sounding, bromide to protect "States Rights", was patently false, and deliberately, misleadingly, was actually… if only partially, true.

Both Eleanor and Paul, believed that if *those* States' Rights… if they were to be enumerated, and quantified, the number one States' Right, at the very top of the list, would be:

1. The right to own, and to enslave four million black human beings.

And that the Confederacy wanted to protect—primarily for economic reasons (Free-Labor), cloaked in *"cherry-picked"*, selected-misrepresentations of the bible, and pseudo scientific theories —, was the right of the Southern states to enslave, in perpetuity, four million black human beings.

After having spent many enjoyable hours with Paul, primarily in the college's faculty-lounge, or in the college's library, and time spent taking long walks, exploring the campus, exploring the town of Gettysburg, Eleanor could not deny, that their friendship had gradually morphed from being that of collegial-professionals, to *"Something Else"*.

Exactly what that *"Something Else"*, was, remained a mystery to Eleanor.

Quite honestly, although the use of, and the creative application of words—to communicate, to educate, to enlighten while inspiring—was as Paul would say, was Eleanor's area of expertise, in this instance… her relationship with Paul Winslow, that (*"Something Else"),* Eleanor simply, could not define.

****

During Eleanor's time in the South, her time teaching, while concomitantly studying and observing the life-style of the black slaves, and that of their white owners, Eleanor had come to rely on the nightly notations, that she made in her journal.

That habit…the documenting of events, observations, and the interpretation of those events during her time spent at the plantation,

---

were, essential tools that Eleanor used, in support of her recent, successful Doctoral Thesis:

*"The Observation of/and The Rendering of Negro Literacy
– Debunking Pseudo Scientific - Support of Polygenism"*

Now in the confines of her small apartment, here at Gettysburg… each night in her bedroom, before falling asleep, Eleanor would write in her personal "Diary".

She would sit in bed, her back propped-up with multiple pillows, recalling the day's events, and her reaction to those events. Eleanor would meticulously, enter the highlights of her day's activities, in her little green book, her Personal Diary.

Eleanor had gotten into the habit of closing that day's diary entries, with the same three, simple interrogative sentences.

1) *"Something else"*, what does that mean to me?
2) What's happening…is Paul experiencing *"Something else"*?
3) And if so…what does *"Something else"*, mean to him?

****

Thirty-eight-year-old Paul Winslow lay in his bed, tossing and turning.

Lately he had been experiencing numerous, fragmented, dreams. Though he could not remember the details of the dreams, he did remember one…no he remembered two constants. Eleanor was in the dreams. And each morning, after one of those dreams, his underwear and his bed linen was saturated with his pent-up, spermatic, bodily fluids.

For most of his life Paul Winslow—because of his relatively, small physical- stature, coupled with his "huge intellect"—had led, what could best be described as a monastic-academic, life.

For the first time—at less as far as he could remember …for the first time, Paul Winslow was wrestling with thoughts, and feelings similar—unbeknownst to Paul—to those that were being felt by Eleanor.

Never before, in his entire life, had Paul experienced, felt these intense emotions, these feelings… this unrelenting need…desire to be constantly in the presence of another…one particular, female, human being, Professor Eleanor Leary.

Paul was an enlightened, well-educated man of science. As such he was… intellectually, fully aware of the intense, physiological, events that his body was experiencing.

However, despite the fact that he was an acknowledged and acclaimed, Social Scientist, a sociologist, an authoritative, academic, expert on the theories, and principles of the social-intercourse, that governed societies,

Paul Winslow, Ph.D., Doctor of Social Sciences, Chairman of the Department of Social Sciences, at one of Pennsylvania's most prestigious institutions of higher learning, was totally lacking in personal knowledge and experience, as to the activities, expressions of love, that engendered a different kind of intercourse… to be precise, sexual-intercourse, between two colleagues…in their case, two people in love.

After having weighed all of the evidence accumulated over the past two years, … the thoughts, principles, interests, and feelings, that was shared between himself and Eleanor, Professor Paul Winslow, Chairman of Social Sciences, after careful thought and analysis, intellectually…

but more importantly, emotionally, had arrived at the conclusion that he loved, Associate Professor of Philosophy, Eleanor Leary.

No, Paul admonished himself…I love my mother, I love my father, I love my siblings.

Paul gave voice to his feelings. "This is different. I more than love her … I am *"In Love… In Love"*, with Eleanor Leary."

****

Eleanor and Paul were seated in the rear of the historical-fiction section, of the campus library. For the past half hour, neither Paul nor Eleanor had spoke. They were both fully absorbed in their respective reading materials.

Eleanor was reading the current edition of "The Adams Sentinel, the town's twice/week, Monday and Friday, newspaper.

Paul had been reading a small, gray, book that he had removed from the row of books, stacked, on the shelve.

Eleanor proceeded to turn the page of the newspaper.

Paul had been patiently…nervously, biding his time, waiting for a break in Eleanor's concentration. Before she could continue reading, Paul seized the opportunity… he began to speak.

"Ellie do you remember… two years ago… when I asked you for permission to be seated at your table in the Faculty Lounge? You were grading essays… oblivious to your surroundings, pondering the motives of your students', critiques of Shakespeare's *'Othello'?"*

Eleanor placed the newspaper that she had been reading on the table. She smiled at Paul; "Two years ago… has it been that long? Time really flies, doesn't it? Yes Paul, I remember. In fact, I think that I will always remember that day. That encounter marked the beginning, of our friendship."

"Ellie, how did…what was his name, the name of your recalcitrant student, the son of the plantation owner, who was upset, after having read the play, _'Othello'_?"

"Eleanor responded, "Jesse…Jesse Billings. Jesse was my sole white, male, student."

Paul nodded his head. "What part of the play upset young Jesse Billings? Did he have specific objections? Did he confront you with his objections?

Eleanor hesitated…concentrating, attempting to recall. When she spoke, her voice was strong, yet tinged with melancholy.

"Jesse's sister Rebecca told me that her brother was offended by _"Othello"._ She said that Jesse thought that the play was malicious fiction. Yankee Abolitionist propaganda. Jesse insisted that the premise of the play, a black military general, commanding white troops, was unbelievably absurd.

Jesse asked Rebecca if she had read the entire play. When she said that she had not, Jesse had shouted; "that black nigger bastard Othello, kills his white wife".

Rebecca assured me that her brother's attitude and beliefs, as they pertained to Negroes, were those of the vast majority, of the South's white-male population. Rebecca quoted to me verbatim, a few cherry-picked passages from the bible, used by the clergy, to justify slavery."

Paul, who as a devout, practicing Christian, and an outspoken advocate for the abolition of slavery, asked; "Ellie, which passages in the bible, did the slave preachers and slave owners, use to promote and/or, to condone slavery?"

Eleanor reached into her bag. She removed a small, green book. Eleanor opened the book and turned to the back cover, and read:

(Genesis 1:27), "God created man in his own image…

(Genesis 9:25), "Cursed be Canaan. Let him become the lowest slave to his brothers."

(Romans 13:1), "Let everyone be subject to the governing authorities…that have been established by God."

Eleanor's interest was peaked. She gently placed her hand onto Paul's forearm, and asked:

"Why do you ask…Paul, what are you reading?"

Paul closed the book that he had been reading. He extended his hand… the hand holding the book, toward Eleanor.

Eleanor took the book from his hand and read the cover:

UNCLE TOM'S CABIN; LIFE AMONG THE LOWLY BY HARRIET BEECHER STOWE
With a raised eyebrow, Eleanor, without commenting, returned the book to Paul.

Paul accepted the book… he looked down at the cover and began to speak, "Uncle Tom's Cabin, by Harriet Beecher Stowe."

Paul looked up. His eyes met those of Eleanor. Paul gleaned from her eyes and her facial expression…curiosity.

Eleanor remained silent. Paul, *in response* to the attentive way that she continued to look at him was clearly waiting for an explanation. In a measured tone, he began to speak.

"Harriet Beecher Stowe is an educator. She taught in Connecticut, at the Hartford Female Seminary."

"As are we…Harriet Beecher Stowe, is an Educator, as are we… she is a devout abolitionist, vehemently, opposed to slavery. Again, as are we."

"Mrs. Stowe, as have you and I, have chosen to educate… to attempt to dispute and to discredit, those vast, ubiquitous, Southern propaganda campaigns, that are cloaked in pseudo-science, and are continuously being used by the Confederacy, to justify slavery."

"Harriet Beecher Stowe, used the genre of fiction, as her vehicle... attempting to educate—via entertainment—the masses, to the horrors of slavery."

"With all of the carnage occurring on the battlefields, loss of life on both sides, because of slavery…the rebels fighting to keep slavery, and the Union fighting to end Slavery, Mrs. Stowe, without firing a single shot, managed to—by writing of this little book—strike a mighty blow, in the pursuit of her, and our shared goal, the abolishment of slavery."

"Ellie, you chose to go to the South…to teach in the South…and to see, and document, by obtaining first-hand knowledge, the facts. Facts that refute and dispels, the pseudo- scientific theories, that portray the Negro as a sub- human…a sub-species."

Eleanor, due to Paul's serious, professorial, and tone-of-voice, had immediately leaned forward, concentrating, intently, listening, to his every word.

She sensed that Paul was about to share with her, something weighty…
something that he considered serious, something of vital importance,
not only to him...but important to the Union, important to the survival
of the United States of America.

"Ellie, in just two years, hundreds of thousands of Americans, from
both North and South…yes I include the misguided rebels under that
umbrella…Americans, hundreds of thousands of Americans, have been
killed and/or maimed, because of the issue of slavery."

Paul reached for Eleanor's hand; "Ellie, I know that you were raised,
in the Roman Catholic faith. I've mentioned to you before, that I was
raised a member of the Religious Society of Friends… that I am a
Quaker."

"While neither you, nor am I, a religious zealot I…as I know you too,
subscribe to and adhere to, many of the same, universally important,
Christian tenets of our, respective faiths."

Eleanor was becoming increasingly anxious. Over the past two years,
she and Paul had had innumerable conversations. Usually the topics
were either work-related, or issues of national interest—war news—
such as, the outcome of Union and/or Confederate, military-campaigns.

Judging by Paul's demeanor, and the solemnity resonating from his
voice, Eleanor silently mused, that this conversation appears to be
moving in the direction, of possibly becoming the most substantive,
personal issues- conversation yet, between herself and Paul.

Suddenly, an exciting momentary thought, flashed across Eleanor's
mind.

Could it be…was Paul about to, unbeknownst to him, answer her
frequently thought, but never spoken, question… the question that

she could neither answer, nor ignore; *"Something else"*, what does *"Something else"*, mean to him?"

Eleanor shrugged, and refocused on the tone and the sincerity, of Paul's words… words which like torrents of water, cascading down, rushing through, and over, a broken, collapsing dam, were now pouring forth, from his mouth.

Abruptly, Paul stopped talking. He tentatively took Eleanor's hand in his and
…looking deeply—Eleanor thought, lovingly—into her eyes, Paul took a deep breath, exhaled and exclaimed in a firm whisper; "Ellie while the fact that I am a Quaker, is not news to you..." Paul took, yet another deep breath; again, he exhaled and exclaimed in a conspiratorial stage whisper; "As Miss Harriet Beecher Stowe has done, without firing a single shot, I too am, and have been for years, making a non-violent, I believe substantive contribution, toward the abolishment of slavery."

"Eleanor, I and my mother and father are, conductors on the Underground Rail-Road."

Paul, who had been intently staring at Eleanor; looking deeply, into her eyes, attempting to read, to interpret, her facial-expression.

Eleanor was speechless. Instead of speaking, she smiled and squeezed Paul's hand.

At first Paul, by looking into her eyes—*The mirrors of the soul"*— could not decipher Eleanor's reaction to the enormity, of his confession.

He had confessed to being a felon, literally…an outlaw, by his admitted breaking of, Federal Law, namely, the 1850, Fugitive Slave Act.

Eleanor had become aware of the Fugitive Slave Act, during her freshman year, at Oberlin College.

It was during an Anthropology class, that Eleanor Leary, an Irish-Catholic girl, from O'Fallon Nebraska—born in Downy-Court Ireland—met her classmate, Dorothy Diggs, a Southern-Baptist black-girl, from Chicago Illinois—originally born a slave, on a tobacco plantation in Raleigh, North Carolina.

With the help of the Underground Railroad, Dorothy's father and mother— carrying their infant daughter—had managed to escape slavery, by making their way North, to freedom.

Eleanor had long been an admirer, of the proactive activities of those people, whites and free-blacks, the famous, or as the Slave Holding Southerners called it—that *"Infamous Horde of "Yankee Scum"*, that caused…and continues to cost them, the loss of hundreds of thousands…millions of dollars worth of their property… runaway, escaping, black slaves.

Paul was relieved. Not only by Ellie's warm smile, he was relieved by what he saw…or thought that he saw, in her eyes. Was it merely the fact that she approved …or was it *"Something else"* and, Paul mused, if it was the latter,
…what does *"Something else"*, mean to her?"

"Ellie, are you busy next Saturday?" Eleanor's heart began to race. Still holding his hand…she replied; "No Paul…I don't have any thing in particular planned for Saturday".

"I would very much like to take you to dinner. I would very much like, you to meet my mother and father."

****

GETTYSBURG, PA. April 18, 1862

Paul gently applied slight pressure, on the rein that he held in his left hand. The mare pulling the small buggy trotted toward the small, neat, single story, two-bedroom, whitewashed farmhouse.

Paul jumped down from the buggy. He walked over to the passenger side of the vehicle, extended his arms and assisted Eleanor, as she planted her feet firmly on the ground.

Standing on the porch…a broad smile radiating across her face, was a neatly attired, elderly, woman, wearing a plain black smock, overlaid with a startling white apron. On her head, she wore a white cap, tied in a neat bow beneath her chin.

"Willem, he is here. Thine son Paul has arrived." Paul bolted up the two steps leading to the porch.

He wrapped his arms around his mother, gleefully-hugging her while lifting and twirling, her around.

"Paul, thou art making thy mother dizzy. Thou shouldst put thy mother down." Paul gently lowered his mother to the porch. He held her at arm's length.

"Mother thou art as beautiful as ever. Thy smile makest the Sun, dim by comparison."

Eleanor was surprised by Paul's manner of speaking. Months ago, he had told her that he was a Quaker, a member of the 'Religious Society of Friends.

The initial conversation between mother and son, had not prepared her for Paul's seamless, transition…his ability to revert, to the dialect of his up bringing.

Paul kissed his mother on her cheek. He then turned, hurried down, the steps, and took Eleanor's hand.

"Mother… father, this is Eleanor." Unable to contain himself…before his parents could speak, Paul blurted out: *"As do I… I am sure, that thou too, shall love her."*

Sanna Winslow smiled and opened her arms: *"Eleanor, thou art welcome to our home; Paul's father and I welcome thee to our home… to our family."*

Paul was momentarily pleasantly, shocked at his mother's words; *"Paul's father and I welcome thee to our home…to our family."*

Not knowing how she would react to that unexpected, very personal greeting… with mounting trepidation, Paul furtively, glanced at Eleanor.

Eleanor—who was now enfolded…being embraced—in the arms of Paul's mother, was beaming… smiling.

Paul was angry with himself, for his not having told his parents, that he had not made known to Eleanor his intentions... his intent to propose… to ask her to be his wife.

Willem Winslow, Paul's father opened the screen-door and stepped onto the porch. Without uttering a word, he walked over to the two women, who where standing, swaying to and fro, hugging each other.

With his strong, calloused, farmer's hands, ignoring his son's presence, Willem separated the women. Before either woman could react, Paul's father put his right arm around his wife's waist, and his left arm around Eleanor's waist.

Paul stood dumbfounded…as he bore witness for the first time, to what he hoped… that he had been praying, would be, his new, extended, family.

****

April 18, 1862 - Home of Willem and Sanna Winslow Paul's Bedroom (8:PM)

Eleanor sat in bed, Paul's childhood bed—propped-up by three goose-down pillows, writing in her diary.

Today, was a wondrous, gloriously, beautiful, day. Today I met Paul's parents. Today they… not Paul, told me of their son's intentions, his marital intentions.

Although since our arrival, we haven't… literally spent a moment alone. "Is that Quaker custom? Are unmarried adults, not allowed to spend time together, alone? That's certainly a question that I'll ask Paul just as soon as we're alone."

Paul's mother Sanna, and his father Willem (I think that Willem, is the Dutch equivalent of the [English], William), but I digress… I think that Paul's parents are two of the warmest, most down to earth, pleasant, people that I have ever met.

When she greeted me, I was not surprised by her speech pattern, her fluency in the use of Archaic English is impressive. Paul had told me of the Quaker's use of Archaic English. On that topic, I recall that Paul stated that retention and the use of 'Old English Grammar', is primarily that of pronouns and verbs.

When I asked Paul as to why were the pronouns "thee" and "thou", so prevalent in the Quaker's speech pattern, his response had been, that today, even in 19th century "Modern" English, "thee" and "thou" are used in most formal Christian religious context. In addition to formality and solemnity, Friends feel that the use of "thee" and "thou", is egalitarian, "plain speaking", a principle which is fundamental to the tenets of The Religious Society of Friends.

What really surprised and amazed me, was Paul's ability to seamlessly, adapt his speech patterns, i.e., that of Professor Paul Winslow, and that of Paul Winslow, the loving Quaker, the son of Willem and Sanna Winslow.

Paul's effortless transition from modern day English, to the Archaic English that his parents spoke, reminded me of my time spent teaching in the south on the Virginia, slave-holding, Cotton Plantation.

When my white student, asked her best friend, who happened to be black (who to this day... I believe is her sister); Why, when they were together alone, did she with blacks, speak "nigger talk?" I never forget what Mandy, the black girl told Rebecca, her white sister.

Mandy explained her chameleon linguistic proclivity, thusly; she said that her black mother constantly reminded her that she is a slave, that her speaking like white-folks, would get her into trouble, would hurt, make her look stand-offish.
If black folks were to hear her speak, grammatically correct English, black folks would think that she was putting on airs—they would think, that she thought, that she was better than them.

White folk, Mandy said, if they heard her speaking "white", they would think that she was a trouble maker."

This evening as we sat down to dinner, I felt privileged and awed, to actually witness, and be truly inspired, by the faith and the courage of this family.

The four of us, myself, Paul and his mother and father, were seated at the kitchen table, eating. I found Paul's parents to be extremely affable, both religiously and socially, tolerant people.

Sanna, Paul's mother—I believe in an attempt to put me at ease—in her sweet gentle voice, flawlessly inserted religion, into the conversation.

I now know longer have to speculate, as to what may have in his past, influenced Paul... what had led him to become such a superb educator. The answer to that unasked question was seated, across from me at the kitchen table, Sanna Winslow, Paul's mother.

I had asked that the platter of steaming-mashed potatoes, be passed to me.

While handing me the platter, Paul's mother—in her beautiful, Shakespearean-English, dialect... commented; "Paul has told us that thine, faith is that of the Irish -Catholics".

Paul squeezed my hand...and gave his mother a scathing, reproachful look.

I, in turn, squeezed Paul's hand. Then I asked... "How does Quakerism differ from Catholicism?"

I remember the enchanting, sincerely, delightful smile that spread across Paul's mother's face, prior to her continuing: "We, The Religious Society of Friends, as are Roman Catholics... we are Christians. Friends believe that God can speak to everyone directly, through his son Jesus, without the need of human intermediaries, clergymen... Priests. Friends, or as you say, Quakers, believe in the equality of all mankind".

As I was about to, as is my nature... to ask for more information, to encourage her to continue, I heard the tinkling sound, of a bell.

Abruptly, Paul's father Willem stood, and asked to be excused. Without waiting for a response, he left the room.

I believe that Sanna saw, the confused look on my face. She explained. Sanna said that the bell that I had heard was attached to a string... tied to the door of their root cellar.

Paul realized that his mother's explanation had resulted in only heightening my confusion.

Paul looked... pleadingly, at his mother—giving her consent to her son's silent question—Paul's mother nodded her head.

Still holding my hand, Paul and I stood, as did his mother.

Paul and I followed, his mother, to the door leading to the six steps, that lead to the dirt floor of the cellar.

As we descended the stairs, I heard Willem's voice, he was talking to a small, thin, barely five feet tall, black woman. The woman wore a dark skirt. Her head was covered with a dark scarf. Standing in the corner, huddled together, was a black man; a black woman; and two black children, who appeared to be pre-teen boys.

Paul's mother, who was leading our little procession, stopped half way down the stairs.

She, in a subdued voice, whispered; "Minty... has thou returned... is that you?"
When the black woman turned, I was shocked. Her right hand was around the handle of a pistol that was held in place, tucked under a scarf, tied around her waist.

When his mother hurried down the steps…Paul turned to me and silently motioned, that we stop, that we go no further…that we should sit on the cellar steps.

As I literally strained my eyes… attempting to see and to hear, I realized that from our vantage point that neither I, nor could Paul, see or hear clearly, what was happening in the cellar.

Paul looked up at me and motioned that we should return to the kitchen.

For no more than a minute—to me it seemed much longer—before he again, spoke; He said; "You're probably wondering—what's happening…, what's going on in the cellar."

"I remember—I think it's verbatim— my exact response. I believe my voice had gone up an octave. I said; "Probably… Paul, that is the biggest understatement that I have ever….ever heard. Who were those people…were they…runaway slaves? Who was the black woman with the pistol? What were they doing in your parent's cellar?"

Paul answered my questions. He stated that the four-black people in the cellar, huddled together, were probably a runaway slave family.

I then asked…I'm sure in a voice dripping with incredulity who was the black woman with the pistol? I believed I heard your mother call her "Minty".

Then Paul, did what I thought at the time, was melodramatic. He slid his chair right up next to mine, and in a hushed, conspiratorial voice whispered; "The lady with the pistol, is Harriet Tubman."

I remember my idiotic response; "<u>Thee</u>… Harriet Tubman?"

It's only now, as I am writing this, that I realize, that I, inadvertently....as do the Quakers, by using 'Thee', had without thinking, slipped into the usage, of what I usually refer to as, Elizabethan-Shakespearean English.

****

CHAPTER 3

Gettysburg PA., Home of
Paul and Eleanor Winslow
July 1, 1863 (2:15 PM)

Eleanor was seated at her kitchen table. The table was strewn, with cooking and baking paraphernalia. She was adroitly preparing, for her husband— meticulously following Sanna's recipe—one of Paul's favorite dishes, his mother's Shepherd's Pie.

Eleanor, because of her having been raised, brought-up in Ireland, where the potato was for her family, their primary staple, was especially adapt at preparing a dish…any "dish", that consisted of the 75% potato component, of her mother-in-law's recipe for Shepherd's Pie.

Eleanor ran her forearm across her brow, leaving a smudge of flour on her forehead. Absent-mindedly she dropped her hand to her swollen abdomen, as her and Paul's unborn infant, had just delivered a gentle kick.

In October, she and Paul would be celebrating their second wedding anniversary and hopefully, they would be welcoming into their family, their first child.

Any moment now, Eleanor expected Paul to return from his meeting, at the Gettysburg chapter of the Pennsylvania Anti-Slavery Society.

The keynote speaker at this week's meeting of the Anti-Slavery Society, was, one of Society's founders, Robert Purvis.

In early February, Eleanor had been introduced to Mr. Purvis. When she at first met Robert Purvis, she had assumed from his appearance, that he was an abolitionist... a wealthy, altruistic, white man.

The fallacy of that assumption became clear to Eleanor, when the tall, handsome philanthropist, had proudly identified himself, as being a Negro.

Eleanor remembered immediately thinking; "I wonder how my former student Mandy, the black-slave girl, would have translated my assumption, into what she and her white sister Rebecca, referred to as "Nigger-talk"?

To Eleanor's surprise, the answer to her imagined question, had instantaneously, literally, popped into her head.

Her former student Mandy, the black-slave girl at Virginia's Rosewood Plantation would have been, employing the language of the plantation's slave community—when referring to Mr. Robert Purvis, would have been; *"Dat, dare... bees, ah dam ne-ah "white", nigger".*

Seventy-five percent of Robert Purvis's immediate ancestry, his father, and both of his father's parents, were white-Europeans. His mother was a freewoman-of-color, of Moroccan and Jewish descent.

Though he could have readily and easily, lived a life of privilege as a wealthy white man; Robert Purvis chose to instead, identify himself as

Negro, and to dedicate his life and fortune, towards the abolishment of Slavery.

At any moment, Eleanor expected to hear Paul, opening the door, and invariably, as usual, greet her with his one-word, two syllable question… *"Ellie?"*

It had been her intent to surprise her husband, by instead of verbally answering to … when he opened the door … to flood his senses, his olfactory, and salivatory senses, with the delicious aroma, of freshly baked, Shepherd's Pie.

For three hours, now… she had been attempting to judiciously, follow Paul's mother's recipe for Shepherd's Pie.

Eleanor recalled how, at their recent dinner with her in-laws, Paul had wolfed-down, three servings—of what he had, with his mouth full—claimed was his favorite dish.

After dinner, when she and her mother-in-law Sanna, were washing the dishes, Eleanor had asked Sanna: "Doest thy son…my husband Paul, always react like this to thou's Shepherd Pie?"

When Sanna had not immediately answered, it was apparent to Eleanor that Sanna had heard…but did not actually hear, what Eleanor had said.

Sanna had been thinking of that time, a little more than a year ago, when she and Paul's, then friend Eleanor, had come to dinner. She and Eleanor had been washing the after-dinner dishes, when she had boldly proclaimed to Eleanor; "Paul has told us that thine, faith is that of the Irish Catholics".

Initially, Eleanor had been wary, hesitant… to discuss religion. Now that Paul's mother had introduced religion, as a topic of discussion,

Eleanor had, without rancor, answered; "Yes, I was born to the Roman Catholic faith. My religious faith and belief, is in God's goodness, his grace, and that of his grand creation, the egalitarian, human race.

Sanna, despite her reservations, despite the centuries of cultural and religious feuds, between the Irish Catholics and the Anglican Church of England… the Christian-Protestants, from which The Religious Society of Friends, had separated, had come to truly love, her Irish-Catholic "daughter".

Sanna, when Eleanor's question penetrated, shook her head. She then warmly smiled, and nodded her affirmation. "I wouldest often say to Paul… thou dost love my Shepherd's Pie, more than thine love, of my breast milk".

Sanna's love for Eleanor was not merely because Eleanor, loved her son… she loved Eleanor because, Eleanor was to her, a special person… a person worthy of and deserving to be loved.

When Paul had first confided in her his feeling… his love for this girl… this girl who was not one of them…not a follower of the teaching of George Fox, the founder of the Society of Friends, this Catholic girl, Sanna had been disappointed.

Both Sanna and Willem had been devastated when their son, after his first year, at the University of Pennsylvania, had made the life altering decision to abandon the practice the customs…the speech, the simplistic dress, of the "Religious Society of Friends".

Paul had explained that while he cherished and respected, the principles and beliefs, thru the study of the Social Sciences. He had haltingly breathlessly, said that he wanted to buttress…to strengthen his faith, with proven scientific-fact.

Yet following the beliefs and the teaching of the "Friends", and having met Eleanor and after many hours, of prayer sitting alone, in solitary silence, communing with God, experiencing the joy of having the *"Inner-Light"*, flow through her body, Sanna had accepted, and enthusiastically welcomed Eleanor, as a member of the Winslow family.

Sanna had come to regard Eleanor as, not only being morally equal, she thought of Eleanor, her new daughter, as being someone, quite special.

Though Eleanor had not converted to the faith—the faith that was commonly called by those who were not "Friends"—Quakerism, Sanna's inner-light, their communion, showed her that Eleanor respected, the sincerity and the piety, of the Religious Society of Friends.

Instead of mocking and ridiculing, the Friend's, as many did, for speaking plain, simplistic English, Eleanor instead, attempts to learn and to… when in the presence of Friends, to speak their language.

Although she had at Paul's urging, occasionally, accompanied him, to meetings of the Pennsylvania Anti-Slavery Society, Eleanor had felt uncomfortable at being the only woman, in attendance.
It was at one of the Pennsylvania Anti-Slavery Society meetings, that Eleanor was introduced to Robert Purvis' wife, Harriet and her friend Margaretta Forten.

Both of these women-of-color, Harriet Purvis and her friend Margaretta Forten, in 1833, had been founding members, of the Philadelphia Female Anti-Slavery Society.
Eleanor had been instantly, drawn to these two, highly educated, activist, Negro women-abolitionists, and women's rights, advocates.

When she had first met Harriet Purvis, Eleanor had been momentarily stunned. She was astonished… flustered to be standing there, looking into the beautiful-brown, intelligent, eyes of what she imagined, could have been an adult "Mandy".

Mandy was the brilliant black pre-teen slave-girl, that she had taught, along with her equally brilliant, white sister—what now seemed to Eleanor, to have been ages ago —, at Virginia's Rosewood Cotton Plantation, before the war.

While she was shaking Harriet Purvis' hand, Eleanor remembered thinking, that in twenty years, if she manages to survive this war, Mandy Billings, a former slave, who defied Southern Law by seeking and obtaining knowledge, might very well become, a formidable advocate, and leader of the fight for civil-rights.

Last year, in mid-1862 Eleanor, began attending meetings and joined, the local chapter and of the Philadelphia Female Anti-Slavery Society, the nation's first interracial, female, activist, anti-slavery organization.

****

July 1, 1863 – Ten Miles Northwest of Gettysburg Pennsylvania (14:35 hrs)

The Union cavalry division, bivouacked northwest of town, was under attack and overrun, by a large contingent of Confederate soldiers. The union lines collapsed.

The Union soldiers were ordered to "Fall-back…to retreat". The path of retreat for the Union soldiers was through the streets, of the little town of Gettysburg, Pennsylvania.

July 1, 1863 – Gettysburg, PA- Home of Paul and Eleanor Winslow (3:10 PM)

The weather for this time of year was typically hot and humid. The grandfather clock in the pallor, chimed three times.

In the distance Eleanor heard what she initially thought, was the distant rumbling of thunder.

Her first thought was that the approaching thunderstorm, would break the stifling oppressive heat. She hoped that Paul would not be caught in the storm.

Eleanor groaned as she struggled to rise from her chair. She shuffled over to close the kitchen windows. As she approached the window, she heard a commotion… the sound of men running.

Eleanor looked out the window; first five…no ten, twenty Union Soldiers… in apparent panic, were running down the street.

The booming, crashing sound of cannons firing…what she had thought was an approaching thunderstorm, was growing louder.

Eleanor began to panic. The route that the panicked, fleeing Union soldiers were running, indicated that their flight had been directly consistent with their passing the meeting place, of the Pennsylvania Anti-Slavery Society.

As she ran toward the door, Eleanor's hip smashed into the table… cutlery and dishes crashed upon contact, with the floor.

Eleanor ignored the noise or the mess of broken china and glasses. She opened the screen-door and ran toward the meeting place… ran toward Paul.

****

Eleanor gasping for breath, gulping air…her heart pounding, rushed forward toward what had been…a neat-whitewashed house that had been serving as the meeting place for the Pennsylvania Anti-Slavery Society.

The formerly pristine building was in shambles. The roof of the structure had crumbled inward, after having sustained several direct hits, by Confederate artillery-fire.

Eleanor, with her left hand supporting her "with-child", swollen-belly, ran up the four steps leading to the hole…a gap, where the door had been. With her right hand she lifted two planks…shards of splintered wood that had once been the door.

Frantically, Eleanor's eyes darted from side to side, across the room that was strewn with broken glass and furniture.

Eleanor thought she heard the sound of someone moaning. She strained her eyes. In the farthest corner of the room, she saw two men, slumped on the floor.

While continuing to support her belly with one hand, frantically, as fast as she could, with her free hand, Eleanor began clearing a path, stumbling, making her way across the room.

She emitted an involuntary, anguished whimper; "Paul…Paul", as fast as she could, Eleanor scurried over to the two men.

She quickly discerned that the man moaning, was underneath the body of a dead man…a body impaled on a shaft of debris… his chest skewered on an iron rod.

When she attempted to free the man trapped, under the weight of the obviously dead man, Eleanor, recognized and realized that the dead man was Paul.

Eleanor fainted.

****

July 1, 1863 – Gettysburg PA. (Ruins of the Pennsylvania Anti-Slavery Society Meeting House) (8:35 PM)

Eleanor slowly opened her eyes. She was disoriented… she had a splitting headache. She was lying, uncomfortably, on a hard, uneven surface.

Eleanor's right arm was weightless…dangling in space. As she reflexively lifted her arm toward her head, the back of her hand struck a hard, metal object...a doorknob. Momentarily confused, Eleanor quickly realized, that she was lying on a door.

A cacophony of mournful, agonizing sounds, pervaded the room. As she attempted to rise, she was restrained by the strong hands of man in short sleeves…a Union soldier, who wore a blood- stained apron, over his uniform-shirt.

"Hold on there Ma'am. You best lay yourself, back down. You had a nasty fall… hit your head.

Confused, Eleanor surveyed the room. Cots—on which lay wounded soldiers—covered the floor.

As she was reclining…complying, with who she assumed was the doctor's directive, Eleanor as she had unconsciously done, hundreds of times during her pregnancy, placed her hand on her stomach.

Instead of her hand caressing the familiar bulge—her baby, her stomach was flat; her hand was "sticky".

Horrified, overcome with grief, Eleanor lifted her hand…and gazed at her fingers. Her hand was covered with blood.

Silently… forlorn, Eleanor cried. However, her red-rimmed dry eyes, were incapable producing, a single tear.

****

For three weeks, following the death of her husband and the loss of her unborn child, Eleanor spent sitting alone… secluded, attempting to cope with her grief.

Paul's parents, themselves grieving the loss of their son and unborn-grandchild, took comfort and solace, in their faith.

Respecting the fact that Eleanor—their Irish Catholic daughter-in-law—was not a Quaker, Willem and Sana, urged Eleanor, to seek religious guidance by turning to her faith… by seeking the help of a priest, to help her cope with her grief.

During countless hours alone with her thoughts, Eleanor would reminisce about her [thus-far], life's experiences. The time spent, as a young girl, teaching her younger brothers. Her time as an undergraduate at Oberlin College, living amongst and interacting with classmates and teachers, who had seen, had experienced, communal life in multi-racial, multi-cultural, pluralistic-religious societies.

Inevitably, Eleanor would smile, when she thought of her time—before the onset of the war—time spent in the South, at Virginia's Rosewood Cotton Plantation.

Her time spent getting to know, and to teach… to enlighten, by introducing the brilliant Billings sisters (Rebecca the white girl; and her sister, Mandy, the black girl, born a slave…legally by Southern-Law, the property of her white-sister), to a world other than that of the Slaveocracy, of the Antebellum South.

Inexorably, as one's tongue, would alight on an aching tooth… Eleanor's thoughts would return to her time with Professor Paul Winslow, her beloved husband, the love of her life… Paul.

Of the numerous, countless, discussions that she and Paul had had during their all so very, very, brief time together, the one that resonated with her most, was when they, as educators—each having authored numerous papers that appeared in scholarly journals, in reverent awe—discussed the influence throughout history, of teachers… Plato, Sophocles, Euclid, and certainly of more relevance, during these war-torn-times, that little book, written by that diminutive, New England school teacher, Harriet Beecher Stowe.

Eleanor remembered Paul's closing phrase that had ended that lengthy discussion; "I guess it's true honey. To paraphrase the words of the English author, Edward Bulwer-Lytton; *'The Pen Can Indeed, Be Mightier, Than the Sword'*."

Ultimately, it was the sum of these… his and her life-experiences, those beliefs and principles, that Willem and Sana Winslow, had lived by, solidified and ingrained in their son; those beliefs and the principles, that his parents had instilled in Paul; the need and the courage, to be proactive and to, when necessary, … to take action, to redress man's inhumanity towards his fellow-man.

These were the primary reasons that led to Eleanor's decision, to resign her faculty position at Gettysburg College, and to offer her services as a teacher, an educator, to the American Missionary Association.

****

Early on in their marriage, when Paul had first casually mentioned to, his wife Eleanor —his fellow Gettysburg College, Faculty Colleague—his admiration and respect of and for, the American Missionary Association, Eleanor had half-ashamedly, admitted to her husband that, while she had heard of the AMA, she was not that well-versed in the history, or the activities, of that organization.

Paul had cleared his throat, and knowing his wife's unquenchable appetite for knowledge, without hesitation, immediately assumed his professorial demeanor, and in that crisp, authoritative voice, that she had grown to love, he began to speak; "The American Missionary Association, was founded in 1846, nearly twenty-years-ago— well before the start of the WAR—by a biracial-group of both white and black, Protestant abolitionists."

"The primary intent and purpose, …the goal and the mission, of the organization, was then, and remains, to end slavery; to educate America's black peoples, and to encourage and promote, racial equality."

Eleanor remembered—as Paul had continued his impassioned speech—how her husband's obvious respect and admiration, for the American Missionary Association, had shone through, with each word he spoke.

She recalled seeing the gleam in her husband's eyes, his passion, his belief and his admiration for the societal contributions, being made by that organization… by the AMA.

Eleanor knew what she wanted to do…what she in her mind and heart, felt that Paul would want, her to do…what she knew, she had to do.

Eleanor wrote to the American Missionary Association…volunteering her services to assist in the AMA's efforts to teach, many of the multitude of escaped-slaves—individuals that the Union Army now classified as being (*Contraband*) basically as being the "*Spoils-of War*"—, to read and write.

August 3, 1863, at 10:00 AM, at the Gettysburg, Pennsylvania Rail Road Depot, Professor Eleanor Leary Winslow, Ph.D., accompanied by her mother and Father-In-Law, Willem and Sanna Winslow, purchased a one-way rail-road ticket; final destination, Fort Monroe-Hampton, Virginia.

****

Chapter 4

Roanoke Island Freedmen's Colony Roanoke Island, North Carolina (1863)

While she was but one of the several-dozen AMA teachers, in the "Roanoke Colony", Eleanor was the sole educator, who had earned an advanced- degree… *let alone a doctorate*…a Ph.D., from Pennsylvania's, Gettysburg College.

The first assignment given to Eleanor Winslow, Ph.D., by the American Missionary Association, was to teach "Contraband", escaped black-slaves, on the Freedmen's Colony of Roanoke Island, North Carolina.

The Union Army classified runaway-slaves, seeking their protection, as being "Contraband. Contraband, which has been historically defined by armies as; Captured, *"Enemy Property"*, that can be utilized, by the victorious-army.

Eleanor was one, of several *"white-teachers"*, who had been dispatched by the AMA, to teach fundamental, basic, courses of reading, writing and arithmetic, to the inhabitants of the Roanoke Island Freedmen's Colony.

Eleanor, along with her new friend and colleague, Elizabeth Jones, the first female who had volunteered to teach at the Roanoke Island Freedmen's Colony—Elizabeth Jones, who would eventually, become Eleanor's best friend, *"Lizzie"*—who, happened to be a cousin of Chaplain Horace Jones.

Horace Jones was the man, selected by the Union Army, to serve as

"Superintendent for Negro Affairs in the North Carolina District."

Eleanor Winslow and Elizabeth Jones, were among the first white-*Yankee- Teachers"*, sent by the AMA, to educate the *"contraband"*, the escaped— yearning to be free—black-slaves.

It was the goal… the mission of the AMA—to assist in transforming this massive group of illiterate *"Contraband"*, this community which was, increasingly being referred to as, the Roanoke Island Colony… through education—, into becoming a self-sustained, viable-community.

****

The Administration, as well as the faculty-members of the Roanoke Island school system, had assumed that, because of Eleanor's having earned multiple, postgraduate degrees… that Dr. Eleanor Winslow, would find it frustrating, difficult, and boring, in her attempt to teach students, at this academically-extremely, elementary level.

The teaching the three *R*ˢ reading; '*r*iting; and '*r*ithmatic to a student-body, comprised of a multitude of downtrodden, illiterate, deprived refugees… "Contraband"… Ranging in age, from six to sixty— some seated, many standing, in the same classroom.

Teaching the letters of the alphabet; Word structure, the sounds made by the various combinations of the twenty-six letters of the alphabet; Teaching simple arithmetic, an essential prerequisite-skill, needed by people, who had never received wages, for their labor. This was deemed by most, as being a truly challenging… daunting, task.

In addition to the "Contraband-students", ignorance—attributable to, the fact that in their life-time, they had not been exposed to the concept of learning the three R[s], twenty-six of the twenty-seven "Yankee-Teachers", were having serious-difficulties, understanding the "language" of the former slaves.

Nonetheless, to the surprise of the vast majority of the faculty— twenty-six, of the twenty-seven AMA volunteer-teachers—Eleanor Winslow, Ph.D., former Assistant Professor of Western Literature, at the prestigious Gettysburg College, had immediately… seamlessly adjusted… Eleanor had exceled, at teaching, the thought of as essential, and absolutely necessary, elementary-level, curriculum, to the former slaves.

Eleanor remembered one particular night—five weeks following the commencement of their first semester; when she and her roommate Elizabeth *("Lizzie")*, Jones, were in the room they shared.

They were both seated, at their respective "desks", preparing their lesson- plans, for the next day's classes.

"Lizzie" had looked up from her writing… without uttering a sound, while staring at Eleanor… in wonder, *"Lizzie"*, silently, nodded her head.

As Eleanor continued reading… she abruptly stopped; Scribble a few notes into her lesson-plan… then she resumed reading.

Eleanor noticed that when she stopped writing, that there was no other sound in the room.

She squinted her eyebrows together, then she glanced at Lizzie …who instead of busily, preparing her lesson-plan, Elizabeth was staring at her… shaking her head from side to side.

Eleanor continued to look quizzically at her friend; She placed her pen on the desk, and asked; "Lizzie…what's wrong? Why are you grinning… why do you have that mischievous-smirk on your face?"

Lizzie sighed; "Ellie, people are talking…they're puzzled. Eleanor now completely bewildered and confused, asked; "Lizzie, what are you talking about…what people… and why are they… these people, puzzled?"

Annoyed, when "Lizzie" didn't immediately answer, Eleanor repeated her question. She again asked; "People are talking… they're puzzled? Who and what, are these people, talking about?"

"Again Lizzie, I am asking you who are these people that are puzzled, and why are they… those "persons", confused?"

Without uttering a word… Lizzie… a bit overly dramatic, in what she imagined was an accusatory gesture pointed her finger at Eleanor.

Now, Eleanor was really confused. "Lizzie, why are you pointing your finger at me? Why are you still… staring at me?"

Elizabeth shrugged. "Ellie… perhaps it is due to the fact that we are room- mates; however, I honestly believe, that it is because we both… you and I, genuinely like, and respect each other; And, that I think of you as my best— she paused and gestured with her hand, out-lining the dimensions of the small room that they shared— that I think of you as most definitely, my very closest-friend, on this island."

"I say that Ellie, in an attempt to cushion what I am about to confess."

"I too… have wondered why… and how, you, an acclaimed scholar… the only one… of us; I am of course, referring to, *"us"*… we, the female educators— you're the sole member of our little *"hen-house"*, the female- educators, who has earned a "Doctoral-degree".

"Ellie…*Dr. Eleanor Winslow*, you are a person considered by many… myself included—considered to be a scholar, at the pinnacle of her, academic career."

"That being said, we all…all of us are curious. How is it that you… hands- down, just also happen to be, the absolute best among us; at teaching these State-Mandated, illiterate-former slaves—Elizabeth picked-up from her desk, a shift of lesson-plans and waved them in the air—these…these utterly boring, simplistic-basic, yet admittedly, foundationally necessary, elementary, concepts."

Eleanor smiled as she closed the *very*-elementary-English-Grammar textbook that she had been, leafing through.

"Lizzie, do you recall my telling you, that shortly after I graduated from Oberlin College in 1858, that I… on a whim, answered an advertisement in my home-town's local newspaper."

"What caught my eye was that the ad had been placed, by a Mr. and Mrs. Henry A. Billings, Master and Mistress of a large cotton plantation, in Richmond Virginia."

"The Billings were seeking; *"A Young Female-College Graduate"*, to tutor their 'two children. A pre-teen girl Rebecca, and her seventeen-year-old- brother, Jesse."

"Because my post-graduate research was; *"An In-Depth Analysis of the Southern Slave-Society", I recognized that this was not only an opportunity for me to teach, but also a chance for me to see first-hand, life…black and white life, on a slave-holding, Southern Cotton Plantation."*

"I applied for, and was accepted, for the position."

"We don't have time, for me to tell you in detail, of all of the eye-opening experiences, that I encountered during my time at the plantation."

"However, relevant to my answering your implied question… that experience… my time at the Rosewood Plantation… is I think, why I am successful at teaching, illiterate former-slaves."

"To that I will speak."

"I daresay without equivocation… the answer to that question can best be summed-up, by my stating two names: *Rebecca* and *Mandy Billings*, the daughters of Henry Billings, the Master of the Rosewood Plantation."

Lizzie interrupted; "Ellie, who is Mandy…correct me if I misheard you. I thought you said that Mr. and Mrs. Billings had two children. A daughter Rebecca, and a son… I believe you said that the boy's name is Jesse."

Eleanor, with a slight mischievous smile forming at the corner of her lips, nodded her head.

"You're correct Lizzie, I was indeed, hired to tutor Rebecca and Jesse Billings... the children of Henry and Margaret Billings, the owners... of the Rosewood Plantation, who incidentally were the owners of more than one- hundred black-slaves."

"Mandy is a slave, the *"Property"*, of the Billing's family. Mandy is the daughter of Ruth... Margaret Billings, the Mistress of the Rosewood-Plantation's, enslaved, black, seamstress."

"Mandy's—as is Rebecca's... father—is Henry Billings, the Master of the Rosewood Plantation."

"Biologically—although sanctioned... but not recognized by the laws of the state of Virginia—in every humanistic-meaning and interpretation of the word sister... Rebecca (white), and Mandy (black), are most-definitely, sisters."

"While it was illegal for me...or for that matter, illegal for anyone, to teach slaves, at the request of both girls, I taught Rebecca and Mandy, the classics; but most importantly, Rebecca and Mandy taught me, of life...white and black, life; Master and slave, relations, in the Southern-Slavocracy."

Lizzie's eyes were riveted, glued... fixed upon Eleanor's face. Eleanor gazed out of their solitary window. The sun was setting in the western sky. The sky was a twilight-bluish-orange.

"Oh dear...I've been rambling. Excuse me Lizzie; it's just that when I think of, as I often do... when I think of those two brilliant girls... Mandy and

Rebecca Billings... who those far, I regard as my absolutely, two brightest- ever, students, I tend to get carried away."

In answer to your question…I belief it was… please excuse me for paraphrasing…the gist of your question was how do I do it? How have I managed to so easily… get through… to communicate and teach, my former, illiterate slaves the so called, "Contraband".

"Actually, the answer to that question is quite simple. I get through to them because, I understand and speak their language."

Lizzie was intrigued. "Ellie, what do you mean… "I speak their language". What language? Sometimes it takes me a considerable amount of time; just try to try to understand what they're saying.

Again, Eleanor smiled. When I was in the South, living on the Rosewood Plantation, Mandy, who's English was fluent, pristine, and always grammatically correct, was bilingual.

Mandy taught me a second language, her first… her primary, language. Consequently, I too, as is Mandy… I too, am bilingual."

"The reason that I am not having difficulty teaching our illiterate, former slave-pupils is because I speak their language. I am fluent speaking… well not so much *"fluent-speaking"*, but definitely fluent-understanding, the words… the idioms, *spewing forth from the mouths* of our former slave- pupils. Their language… the language that Mandy and her white-sister, Rebecca called; *"Nigger-Talk"*.

Elizabeth was surprised, shocked… somewhat offended, hearing that vile racial epithet "Nigger", coming from the mouth of her friend and colleague.

Eleanor… on the other hand, was not at all shocked, by Lizzie's reaction. In fact, she had anticipated her friend's reaction.

"Lizzie, is it…is it, that word *"Nigger?"* That precipitated, that intense-disapproving, frown on your face?

Before Elizabeth could respond, Eleanor continued. "It's not the word *"Nigger"*, per-say, that's offensive, it's the history behind... the intent behind, the use of the word, that imparts to the word *"Nigger"*, either a malignant or a benign, connotation"

"For centuries, the white slavers and the slave-masters... and for that matter, many whites in general... they have used that word to denigrate... to control and to dehumanize, blacks."

"When my then, employer Mr. Henry Billings, the Master of Virginia's Rosewood Plantation, gave me permission to *"tour"*, the plantation... when I was shown the cotton-fields... I was shocked... offended."

"When I saw and heard, the plantation's white-overseer, "lashing" with a whip, the slaves picking the cotton... while he simultaneously, continuously, shouted... *"You bess be movin' your lazy-black ass nigger!"*; I was ashamed and appalled that man's use of that word, *"Nigger"*.

"Believe me...to those slaves... black-men, black-women, and children, laboring under the sweltering, hot, Virginia-Sun—that word, relentlessly shouted at them by the white-overseer—that word *"Nigger"*, to those folks... under those circumstances, found that word *"Nigger"*, to be absolutely... highly demeaning and offensive."

"However, one Sunday—Sunday is the slaves' day of rest—, at my request, Mandy gave me a tour of the slave community. At first, I was completely shocked and surprised, at the frequency that I heard that word, "Niggah", being banded around, between friends and families. The word... they pronounced it as "Niggah", was being jocularly, exchanged and applied to and by, just about every member, of the slave-community.

I remember… in fact I don't think I will ever forget, what I heard, watching an obviously loving father, playfully arm-wrestling, with his pre-teenage son.

Despite the boy's repeated attempts to best, his dad at hand wrestling, his father would invariably, prevail. I remember the boy…I guess that he was about nine or ten, saying to his dad…

"One ah dez daz Pa,…I'se gunna beats ya."

"I remember watching the look of love and joy on the boy's father's face. And this I will never ever forget… that loving dad's words, to his son."

"Boy wen youse bees jus ah baby" "You bees my tiny Niggah!"
"Youse small now… and now youse bees, my Little-Niggah!" "Wen's youse dun growed-up, youse bees ah man" Den boy, youse gunna be, my Biggah-Niggah!
Dun't mata nun, how bigs, or how ole, you bees. "Boy always, youse gunna be, my Niggah!"
"Lizzie" when I said "I Speak their Language", what I was trying to convey was that I understand… I am not put-off… by their grammatically incorrect use of the English Language. That I, as we all do, …want our students to learn the skills that will help them to survive… to succeed, and prosper as free-people, in this… our Eurocentric-White-Society.

"Lizzie" smiled. Not only was she impressed by Eleanor's words… Elizabeth was dumbfounded by the "the accuracy, and the ease", of Eleanor's ability to so-closely, alter her speech-pattern… so as to sound like an illiterate, slave.

"Lizzie" picked up and extinguished, from Eleanor's desk, the oil-lamp that Eleanor had lit, midway through her lengthy, unplanned… very informative, dissertation".

"Lizzie" walked over to the bed of her friend and colleague. Eleanor was still seated, on her bed. Lizzie bent over and gently placed her lips to her friend's forehead.

"Thank you...my very, very, best friend. I needed to hear that. Good night Ellie... Good night, *Professor Winslow*."

****

Fortunately for the Roanoke Island community, the need to teach the, *"Contraband"* how to farm, how to raise crops for food, and how to domesticate animals for both food, and for labor...how to tan leather, how to play the "fiddle".

These were requisite-skills... skills mandated by the Slave-Master... that had for generations, been taught to slaves by generation, upon generations, of their enslaved- forebearers.

After having, taught for two years—one-year post, the end of the Civil War—*the AMA-faculty continued to teach* to the *"Contraband"*, the basic, elementary curriculum.

Unlike most of her fellow AMA teachers, Eleanor was not, an Evangelical Protestant.

Although, possibly... more likely probably, because of her marriage to a member of the Religious Society of Friends (Quakers)... her marriage to Professor Paul Winslow, and the genuine admiration and respect, that she felt for the beliefs and the "real-life", practices, and morality of that faith... but more likely, *because* she was born and raised an Irish-Catholic, Eleanor did not share her fellow AMA teachers' zeal for evangelical-political- missionary.

For a little more than a year…Eleanor continued teaching fundamental-rudimentary, literacy skills, to the continuing, constant influx of "Contraband(s)", the inhabitants of the Roanoke Island community.

Then as Eleanor had hoped for, and had anticipated, gradually the emergence of a cadre of the Island's "brightest" students, those with an unquenchable, "Thirst-for Knowledge", emerged.

Eleanor requested and was granted, permission to develop and to teach, these *"the brightest"*, more advanced, academically challenging, courses, to those qualified students.

Despite her satisfaction at now being able to teach *"the brightest"*, it was becoming increasingly apparent to both Eleanor—, but far more obvious to Eleanor's best-friend Elizabeth Jones—that her very best friend, Dr. Eleanor Winslow, was becoming bored.

Through no fault of their own—other than the corps of AMA-teachers—, there were no potential students academically advanced, to the point of being taught, the subjects that were near and dear, to Dr. Eleanor Winslow's, heart.

Eleanor and her room-mate, Elizabeth Jones—who incidentally, in addition to being Eleanor's room-mate and best friend—was the cousin of The United States Army's "Superintendent for Negro Affairs in the North Carolina District"—Elizabeth had on several occasions… when she met with her cousin, gone on and on, lauding, extolling, the character and the intelligence of her room-mate, Eleanor Winslow.

It was during one of her lunches with her cousin, the "Superintendent for Negro Affairs in the North Carolina District", that the topic of the government's plans to support the opening of an institution of higher learning, a college for Negroes. And, that the government was looking for Academically qualified Educators, willing to teach at a Negro College.

Elizabeth's cousin Horace, informed her that the site of the college, is to be in nearby Hampton Virginia, and the Negro College is to be named; The Hampton Normal and Agricultural, Institute.

****

Following the assassination of President Abraham Lincoln… In 1865, Andrew Johnson, Lincoln's successor… Andrew Johnson, *the 17th president of the United States,* under his "Amnesty Proclamation", returned to the *insurrectionist,* Slave Master's, "their-property" (*With the notable exception, of their former-slaves*), all of —their "Pre-Civil War" property.

That is to say that; Andrew Johnson, 17th President of the United States of America… by law, took from the "Freed Slaves", Roanoke Island… and gave it to the Island's former, seditious, Confederate-Insurrectionists.

It was Eleanor's best friend, Elizabeth Jones, who unbeknownst, to Eleanor, urged her brother, Horace Jones, the Superintendent of Negro Affairs in the North Carolina District, to recommend Eleanor Winslow, Ph.D., for a faculty appointment at the newly chartered and accredited, Negro College; the Hampton Normal and Agricultural Institute, in nearby, Hampton, Virginia.

In Mid-September, 1868, Eleanor Winslow, Ph.D., joined the faculty of the Hampton Normal and Agricultural Institute.

****

BOOK II THE COMANCHE

At the conclusion of the Civil War, during the post-war era of so-called *"Reconstruction" — the* revamping of Southern Society—the United States Congress, turned its' attention towards the *"Indian Problem"*, by actively implementing, the provisions of the 1851- Indian Appropriation Act.

This legislation—which was but one of several, related, congressional-bills—was signed into law, by the 13th president of the United States, Millard Fillmore.

The 1851law in effect, ended the individual, autonomy of the various indigenous, tribal, sovereign-nations, of America's Native Peoples.

Proud independent nation-states—societies that had existed on the North American Continent for thousands of years, nations with different cultures, different languages, different religions—were often, herded together, forced to live together, on government assigned, Indian Reservations, that were scattered throughout the United States.

****

Chapter 5

Fort Sill - Indian Reservation - (Comanche; Kiowa; Apache) August 1877 -

The Fort Sill Indian Reservation was situated in the southwestern section, of what the United States Government had officially designated as, *"Indian Territory"*.

The assignment of a contiguous single acreage of land—sub-divided by the government—resulted in the cohabitation by three formerly autonomous, Native-American, nation-states; the Comanche, and the Kiowa—who were allies, and the Comanche-Kiowa's ancient tribal enemies, the Apache.

The Fort Sill Indian Reservation, was but one of many, often desolate and barren plots of land, designated by the government for the resettlement, of three of the U.S. Army's fiercest, most lethal-skilled…, in horseback mounted-combat tactics, the proud, nomadic-warrior tribes; the Comanche; the Kiowa; and the Comanche and Kiowa's ancient enemy, the Apache.

Dull Knife, the bands oldest warrior, and a veteran survivor of countless battles, flanked the Kutsueka Comanche Political Chief-Headman, He Who Speaks To Ghosts. Thunder Cloud, the former War Chief, who had for a decade led raiding and war-parties against the enemies of the People, stood stoic, tall and proud, on the Headman's left.

The three Comanche warriors, watched as the remnants of their band—the three families who had choose to remain on the plains, and to continue their fight against the white invaders—escorted by blue-coated, cavalry men, members of the Black-tribe, known to the People as the Buffalo Soldiers— approached the open gates, of the "Fort-Sill Indian Reservation".

Walking at the head of the procession, his head held high, was Gray Wolf, life-long friend of, He Who Speaks To Ghosts', the Headsman of the "Kutsueka band of the Comanche Nation.

Gray Wolf was holding the hand of his wife, Little Flower; who squeezed her husband's hand, while with her free hand, she firmly gripped the reins of the mare that was pulling the travois, laden with the couple's possessions.

Standing directly in front of He Who Speaks To Ghosts, was a short, stout— hat in hand—balding white man, the Fort Sill Indian Reservation's Indian Agent, Terrence Lawrence.

Despite the 102° degree, oppressive summer heat, the Indian Agent wore black, long woolen pants, and a long-sleeved cotton shirt-buttoned at the neck.

Following Gray Wolf and Little Flower, were the widows and children of War Chief Stone Fist, and the widows and children of the warriors, Silent Stalker, Bear Claw, and Crooked Eye, all courageous Comanche warriors, who had been killed during their failed raid, in Kansas, at the New- Rosewood Cattle Ranch.

Terrence Lawrence, the Indian agent stepped forward and extended his hand in greeting, to Gray Wolf, who the agent assumed, was the leader of the procession.

As if he had not seen the white man… Gray Wolf, disengaged his hand from the hand of his wife Little Flower, and walked directly to his old-friend the Headman, Chief He Who Speaks To Ghosts. The two old friends greeted each other…their hands grasping each other's elbow.

Gray Wolf spoke; "My chief, I return to you the families of Chief Stone Fist, Silent Stalker, Bear Claw, and Crooked Eye. Our Comanche warriors slain in battle, who will forever be with us, through the songs of the People.

With his back to the Indian Agent, Gray Wolf asked his life-long friend; "Who is this white man?"

He Who Speaks to Ghosts smiled and responded; "This man, who is by the People, called *Pot-ta-wat Pervo*…he is the white-man, the Indian Agent, sent to us by our Great White Father, the Headman, of all of the white-eyes, their Chief, President Grant.

Gray Wolf turned to face the white man. Gray Wolf, in the language of the Comanche, began to speak. As he spoke, he slowly, with an exaggerated, emphatic motion, placed his right forearm, diagonally across his chest;

"I am Gray Wolf. As asked of me by the Great White Father, and by my chief, He Who Speaks To Ghosts… I bring to you…to the white-man's fort, the last of the Kutsueka Comanche."

Indian Agent Lawrence, as Gray Wolf had done, placed his right forearm, diagonally across his chest, and in a solemn, raspy voice…

                                                    Precious In His Sight

in the tongue of the Comanche, not that of the white man, spoke; "You Gray Wolf, as are all Comanche, are welcome here at your new home… the Fort Sill Indian Reservation".

The five bands; *Kutsueka, Quahadi, Penateka, Yanparika, Tanima* collectively, were the *"People", the Lords of the South Western Plains*…the Comanche Nation.

A proud people…a *"Hunter-Gatherer Society"*, that had for centuries, lived free on the vast western plains.

A proud people; Living their lives, raising their children, religiously communing with the spirit world, while for centuries coexisting in a symbiotic, existence, with their animal-brothers, the millions upon millions, of buffalo; who too, like the Comanche, had roamed freely on the North- American continent; their way-of-life, had ended.

CHAPTER 6

New-Rosewood - Cattle Ranch [August] 1877

William (Billy) McCloskey—who along with his wife Rebecca, were the owners of the New-Rosewood, Cattle Ranch—while his horse was still in motion… with his right foot still supporting his weight in the stirrup of his McClellan saddle, nimbly jumped to the ground.

Billy sprinted over to the calf, removed his lasso from the animal's neck, and gave… with his right hand…, gave the calf a resounding smack on its' rump.

Billy's thirteen-year-old son Hank, ran over to his father, and mimicked what he had just witnessed. Hank unceremoniously, soundly, swatted his father on his behind. "Way to go Dad. That calf didn't stand a chance".

Billy, grimaced…in mock-pain, he grabbed the seat-of-his pants, and shouted "Ouch". "You best be easing-up on those slaps son".

Billy playfully cupped his son's face in his hand; Billy intently, leaned forward examining the cheeks of his thirteen-year-old son."

He rubbed his hands over Hank's cheek; "Ouch…just as I thought, you're sprouting chin whiskers, you're becoming a man".

Both of Hank's hands, immediately flew to his face. "Really dad…am I really growing a beard?"

Billy chuckled and gently placed his hands, on his son's wrist… "Patience son…I was just funning. Don't be in such a hurry. You'll be a full-grown man, soon enough."

****

The McCloskey family; William (Billy) McCloskey, his wife, Rebecca Billings McCloskey, and their two children; thirteen-year-old son Henry (Hank), and their two-year-old daughter, Mandy-Margaret, were all together, enjoying an occasional evening-breeze—a more than welcome respite— following another day of enduring, the relentless, oppressive heat, of the Kansas mid-summer sun.

Mandy-Margaret—the two-year-old… the youngest member of the McCloskey Clan—, was cuddling her favorite rag-doll. When Mandy-Margaret had been given the doll by her mother, the little girl had squealed with pleasure; "mommy, mommy, what's her name?"

"What's my dolly's name?"

Rebecca, with a broad smile on her face… had instantly replied… "Patty", sweetheart. Let's name her, Patty".

As a little girl, growing-up on Virginia's Rosewood-Cotton Plantation; Rebecca hd been exposed to, and lived in, two very different…polarly opposite societies; the opulent-world of the wealthy, aristocratic, slave-owner; and the world of the retched, oppressed, black-slaves.

During her formative years, from infancy to age thirteen, "Becky's" two closest friends had been her black-sister Mandy—who her father insisted was not her friend, but was instead, her property—and for a very brief period of time, her tutor, Miss Eleanor Leary.

Between the ages of two and seven, before the arrival of Miss Leary, "Patty", Rebecca's rag-doll—although inanimate—had been the third member of the two-girl's, Rebecca and Mandy's, little- isolated, play-group.

Rebecca and her husband, Billy often-times, playfully referred to baby-Mandy as, *"3-M^s"* and/or *"M Cubed"*.

The three 'M's, were the first letters of the baby's baptismal name, Mandy Margaret McCloskey.

The first *"M"; "Mandy"* was the name of Rebecca's beloved, *black-Comanche*, sister-Mandy; the second *"M",* for her mother, Margaret, and the third *"M",* was for Billy's..., now their family's, Scottish surname, McCloskey.

Baby-Mandy's big brother Hank, instead of "3-M's, had *recently* bestowed upon his baby-sister, *what he considered his* own favorite, *clever,* nickname, *"M-Cubed"*, which Hank had ultimately shortened, to *"Cube"*.

The inspiration for the nickname M-Cubed, had come to Hank, following one of his math-tutor's lessons, explaining the power of mathematical- exponents.

Thirteen-year-old Hank had decided to instead of "Three 'M's'", he would confer upon his precocious little sister, the sobriquet, M-Cubed (M^3).

When Hank was asked by his tutor; "Why do you refer to your sister as M- Cubed?", Hank had explained that his sister Mandy had been named after their aunt *M*andy, their grandmother *M*argaret, and their family surname, *M*cCloskey.

Hence in mathematical terms—by far, Hank's newest... most favorite subject—when he thought of his bright, precocious, baby-sister Mandy, Hank mentally equated her, as being the product of three generations of $\underline{\textbf{\textit{M}}}^{s}$.

With an impish, mischievous, conspiratorial, smile, at the corners of his mouth, Hank had explained to his math-tutor...;

"First, generationally, there was our grandmother (*M*argaret), a White-Aristocratic, Antebellum Southern-Belle, and the owner of a multitude of black-slaves; followed by *our* aunt, he and his sister's namesake—their mother's black/slave-Comanche, sister, (their aunt *M*andy); and finally, the third $\underline{\textbf{\textit{M}}}$ in my equation, *is for* my family's surname, McCloskey;

($\underline{\textbf{\textit{M}}}$ x $\underline{\textbf{\textit{M}}}$ x $\underline{\textbf{\textit{M}}}$) = ($M^3$); *the product of three generations that culminated in* my kid-sister's nick-name; Ergo;

M^3andy = ($\underline{\textbf{\textit{M}}}$-*C*ubed).

******

Rebecca McCloskey—with a relaxed, contented, smile on her face—sat rocking to-and- fro, on the comfortable, meticulously hand-crafted lounge- swing, made by her husband, William (Billy) McCloskey. Billy had proudly, in celebration of their third-year wedding anniversary, unveiled for his wife, her handcrafted, lounge-swing.

This time of day…the evening as the sunset… relaxing, surrounded by her family, this spot…this activity, these precious moments spent gently rocking, while with adoring-eyes, watching her growing family, were among the happiest, blissful, moments of Rebecca's, still young, but extremely thus far, …very, eventful life.

****

Rebecca and her sister Mandy had both been born in 1848, three days apart, to two different women… one woman… her mother, a white aristocrat; the other woman, Mandy's mother, a black-slave.

Rebecca and her sister…her black-slave Mandy, were fathered by the same man, Henry Billings, the "Master" of Virginia's Rosewood Cotton- Plantation.

Rebecca, was born into the rich-white, Plantation Owner society, while her black-sister Mandy, was born into a life of perpetual-slavery.

As 29-year-old Rebecca Billings McCloskey, watched the frolicking antics, and the activities of her family; her Scottish-Immigrant husband Billy; her mixed-blood-Anglo/Comanche, 14-year-old son Hank; and her 2-year-old Scottish/American, toddler-daughter Mandy, Rebecca closed her eyes, and allowed her mind to wander.

Rebecca began to reminisce…recalling her memories of her, and her sister Mandy's formative years, of living and growing-up, on the slave-plantation. The period that her mother Margaret, referred to as the girls;

"Reign of terror; the Terrible-Two's…Three's…Four's. and Five's.

Rebecca smiled as she recalled the expression that the house-slaves would seemingly… spontaneously, in exasperation, mutter as she and

---

Precious In His Sight

Mandy would disrupt, break, or destroy each and practically, everything they touched.

"Dem two gals… ebb-knee an iv-ree; dem two's lik two peas inna pod; lik grits 'n' gravy"

"Iffin ya sees jus one; da udda ain't fur behin."

Rebecca fondly recalled the countless hours… those wonderful times that she and her black-sister, through the years—despite her parents repeated admonitions—spent growing-up together exploring their world-the plantation.

The countless, joyous, hours spent "playing school". Hours that she—in her role as *"the teacher"*, had spent defying Southern Law, the law that was essential for the preservation and the perpetuation, of slavery. The law that forbade… prohibited, the teaching of slaves, to read and write.

She remembered the day…that life-altering day, that her mother and father introduced her and her brother Jesse, to their new teacher— a recent graduate from Ohio's Oberlin College—a northerner, Miss Eleanor Leary.

Abruptly, Rebecca's reverie was interrupted. Her husband Billy—his hand lightly squeezing her shoulder— was speaking; "Becky… sweetheart, are you all right…are you okay"?

Momentarily startled, a puzzled-quizzical look in her eyes, Rebecca refocused her attention. Before she could respond, Billy continued speaking:

"Jeez Honey, if you could have seen the grin on your face. It stretched across your face, from ear-to-ear. Just now, when I looked at you, I thought of that drawing of that grinning cat, in that book that you've been reading to Mandy."

Two lines… furrows, creased Billy's forehead; "For the life-of-me hon, I can't remember the name of that book".

Rebecca took both of Billy's hands into hers, she looked lovingly into her husband's eyes…, and smiled. *"Alice's Adventures in Wonderland"* dear…that's the book's title."

"That wonderfully, imaginative, book was written a little more than a decade ago by an Englishman. His name is Lewis Carroll."

"The illustration that you're referring to, is that of the oft-times invisible, mischievous, overweight, feline-character… the grinning, Cheshire Cat."

"My thoughts just now, were of mine, and my sister Mandy's time, —time before the war… before our being taken prisoners of the Comanche. I was thinking of our time…Mandy and I, our childhood, growing-up in the then, slave-holding state, of Virginia".

"I was thinking of how, since we were babies, I… Rebecca Elizabeth Billings—born the white daughter, of a *"White-Supremist"* father.

A man, who was the owner and Master of more than a hundred black-slaves; my father, the father…or as he insisted upon saying…the *sire*, of my black- sister Mandy, who was born a black-slave, who by Southern Law and custom, was NOT my sister; but was legally, instead, my property… my black-slave.

I was reminiscing; remembering how Mandy and I, together, the two of us…Rebecca and Mandy Billings, while living at the Rosewood Plantation, how we forged a color-blind bond, of unshakable, sibling-love".

Rebecca sighed. Then in a soft whispery voice, she continued speaking: "Oddly…, though I suppose that it's human nature…oddly, my thoughts were only those, of the good times that Mandy and I experienced…, not of the brutal, hideous, things that we witnessed together, …the whippings… the deplorable-mistreatment, of the slaves."

"Mandy and I… probably because, other than the black-slave children of Rosewood's field-hands…, Mandy and I, were the only children of our age group, on the plantation."

"Mandy, the daughter of my mother's personal slave, and I—ostensibly the Rosewood Plantation's *"White-Princess"*—spent practically every waking moment of our childhood together."

"For the first twelve years of our lives, instead of the "Master and slave" relationship that my father insisted, and constantly encouraged that I have with my *"black-slave"* Mandy, Mandy and I… the two of us… together, had become in our eyes, one-unit. We were inseparable, the two of us… a duo… Becky and Mandy…, Mandy and Becky.

Then Miss Eleanor Leary, the Yankee School Teacher that my mother and father hired to broaden mine, and my brother Jesse's education, entered our lives."

"I was fondly remembering the time that my sister and I, welcomed into our private, little, world… for an all too short… but fabulously glorious time, Miss Eleanor Leary".

"It was for that brief period in our lives at the plantation when our… the Becky and Mandy duo, shared our thoughts and secrets, with an outsider."

"My thoughts just now were of those happy-times. When Mandy and I, … where no longer alone. Our duo, had become a trio."

"At last, the two of us… two children… two adolescent girls, life-long friends, one white, the other black—defying the bigoted, racist rules and laws, of the *"Grown-Ups"*, the White Supremist-Slavocracy "Adult- Society"— we now had Miss Leary. Mandy and I…, we were no longer alone."

Billy had stood, shaking his head in awe. Once again, he was mesmerized by Rebecca's articulation, and the passion, behind her words.

Billy smiled at his wife; "There it is again honey." With a puzzled expression on her face, Rebecca asked: "There it… is again. Billy exactly, what do you mean by <u>it</u>…, is there again? What is *"<u>IT</u>"*?

Billy's smile broadened. Gently, affectionately, he squeezed Rebecca's shoulder; "It, is that ear-to-ear grin, that lights-up your face. Remember, that cat…the Cheshire cat, in that children's book… *"Alice's Adventures in Wonderland"*, that you read, night after night, to M-Cubed?"

"The drawing…the illustration, of that cat's grin…, my dear; That is what I think of…, when I see your face light-up. That ear-to-ear smile on your face, reminds me of that silly cat's, grin."

Rebecca reached across her body, and placed her hand onto Billy's hand, which was resting on her, left-shoulder.

"I vividly recall the discussion… following Miss Leary's promise to the two of us. Miss Leary promised not to reveal our deepest, sacred-secret, to my father, that Mandy…, that his slave Mandy, was literate…, that Mandy could read and write…she could read and write as well as I"

"Instead of divulging that information to her employer…, my father…, Miss Leary offered to join our, Mandy and mine…our week-end reading and tutorial sessions…, Miss Leary volunteered…she actually asked to join us…to teach the two of us…, to teach us together."

"Still… to this day, I remember that day, that miraculous day, when the "Becky/Mandy *"Duo"*, became…the Becky/Mandy/Miss Eleanor Leary- Academic, *"Trio"*.

Once again, Billy McCloskey marveled at the sophistication…the wisdom, and the intelligence, of one Rebecca Billings McCloskey…, his wife.

****

For as long as he could remember, for most of his young life, Henry (Hank) Billings-McCloskey, had struggled, grappled with his feelings of isolationism…of not belonging.

At an early age—before he could walk…before he could talk— "Little Hank" had gradually become aware of the fact that he was somehow for some reason, *"Different"*.

Hank had first experienced those feelings when as a toddler, playing with his aunt Delilah's sisters' children… his "white" cousins, Clayton and Seymour, had repeatedly, referred to him, as "that dirty-redskin".

Hank still had vague, disturbing, memories of his "cousins… rebuffing his attempts, to join-in their games.

He remembered at the age of four, having asked his mother—after seeing Aunt Delilah's sisters… his cousins, with their fathers—asking his mother "Becky"; *"Mommie, where is my father?"*

When he told his *"Uncle Looyee", that his cousins called him a* "dirty-redskin", *he remembered his uncle mumbling that "Becky", his mother had been a captive of the Comanche-Indians.*

He remembered that eventful day when he was seven-years-old, …the day when his classmate, his best friend, Timmy Jones had suddenly, inexplicably, become distant.

When he had asked Timmy why he no longer wanted to play with him…Hank vividly remembered, and knew that he would never forget, his former best-friend…seven-year-old Timmy Jones' reply;

"My Mom and Dad said that your mother is a "whore". That when she was taken by the Indians, instead of killing herself; she "*slept*" with them. My Mom and Dad said that you are a mongrel, redskin bastard. And that I should not play with you…, that I could not be your friend."

Seven-year-old, Hank remembered being confused…, perplexed. He knew from his *"Uncle Looyee"*, that his mother had been for a year, a captive of the Indians.

Seven-year-old, Hank, did not understand…, he reasoned that, since he slept in the house with his mother, his uncle and aunt…, Timmy slept in the house with his parents, why did Timmy's parents say that they couldn't be friends, because his mother *"slept"*, with Indians.

Seven-year-old Hank, did not understand…, to him, it did not make sense.

> *Mommie was with the Indians for almost a year. Mommie could not, go a whole year, without sleep… stay awake…, for a year. Mommie, as did he, as did everyone, had to sleep… sometime.*

Hank remembered having been jeered at… of being tormented by his classmates; of his *being* almost daily, subjected to a barrage of hurtful, nasty, insults. "Dirty redskin; heathen-savage; the bastard son of a white-whore, who shamelessly, slept with godless, wild-Indians".

Hank remembered the early years…growing-up in Richmond, …those exclusive private schools that his wealthy, politically connected uncle, Luis Frazier, Esq., had arranged for him to attend.

Hank also vividly recalled at having been called a *"red-mongrel"*, the bastard-son-of that *"white-squaw"*—by students at several of those elite, private prep-schools.

It was only after eight-year-old, Henry Billings II, —sporting a black-eye and a swollen split lip— was confronted by his horrified-mother and was forced, to explain his injuries, that he had opened-up, and told Rebecca of his almost daily abuse, by his classmates.

He told his mother of the taunts, and of the name-calling. His mother had insisted that he tell her in detail…as much as he could recall, the actual slurs that had been said.

Hank remembered his mother's reaction. He remembered the hurt and the despair that shown in her red-rimmed, blue eyes.

Although he then, hadn't understood the meaning of many of the words, that had been spewed-forth about his mother… because of her reaction, he knew that she had been deeply, hurt.

Six,-seven,-eight year,-old Henry too, had been hurt more so—by the obvious vindictive manner, that the taunts had been shouted—than by the words themselves.

Quite frankly, Little-Hank did not know, the meaning behind, many of the taunts, nor why he and his mother, were the targets for the abuse.

Little Hank, as were most of his classmates, was familiar with the terms; dirty-redskin; red-savages; and the like. These were "words", routinely shouted in the play-yard, when the little boys were playing, cowboys and Indians.

However, because of his paucity of information, as to the identity, and the life, of his father, his lack of knowledge…, that his father was an Indian…a Comanche warrior, Little Hank had failed to associate in his mind, those "school-yard", pejorative, vindictive, racial slurs, with either Rebecca, or her son… himself, Henry Billings II.

Fourteen-year-old Hank, remembered the conversation between himself and his mother, when he—six-year-old Henry—returned, home, battered and bruised; after his fight with his best friend Timmy, and two of the other boys, in his class.

Hank chuckled, as he recalled his mother's reaction, after her first time seeing, him with a puffy-swollen face.

When Rebecca first saw her *"baby's"* face—his right eye puffy, his lips swollen—, she had involuntarily emitted a moan-of-anguish. Rebecca ran to her son, and embraced him.

"Henry…baby, are you all right… What happened?" "Have you been fighting?"

Little Hank, gasping for air, pleaded; "Mom…please Ma, stop hugging me. I can't breathe."

Realizing that she was squeezing her son, too tightly, Rebecca instantly, stopped. She stepped back, held Little Hank at arms-length, and asked.

"What happened…who did this to you?"

Little Hank told his mother of the taunts and names that his friend Timmy and two other boys, had been calling him, and with a sheepish-look in his non-swollen eye… "I hit them, for what they were saying about you Mom, I belted Timmy, and kicked George and Wilbur."

Henry remembered his mother's frantic voice, as she called-out to her guardian, Luis Frazier's housekeeper; "Hattie…Little Hank's been hurt. I need a cold towel."

More than anything else that occurred that day, eight years ago, Henry vividly remembered, and would always remember, his mother's carefully thought-out response, when he… six-year-old Henry Billings II, had asked;

"Why did Timmy's mother call you a red-nigger loving, "whore" momma, what's a whore? Why did Timmy's mom say that you "slept" with the Indians?"

Henry remembered the forlorn look in his mother's eyes, as she had gently wiped his face with the now blood stained, luke-warm towel.

When she looked at Henry, Rebecca saw bewilderment…confusion. Rebecca took her sons hands into hers; "Honey, I think that right now, you're too young to know…to fully understand the meaning of those evil words."

"Honey, I don't know why she said those horrible, hateful words. I have never met, Timmy's mother."

"Although I have never met her, I have met many, many, like her."

"The so called "Respectable, God-Fearing" people. Those supposed "God- Fearing" people, who pretend to live their lives in accordance with the words in the Bible, yet ignore; Matthew. 7:12; "Do unto others, as you would have them, do unto you."

Henry…baby, Timmy's mother said those things about me…because she is an ignorant, bigoted, relic…still living in the past."

Rebecca had lovingly smiled at her little boy's, look of confusion. She gently caressed his bruised cheek.

She then held his hands in hers; she looked into his eyes, and softly, resolutely, spoke; Henry I promise…when you are old enough to understand, I will tell you… I will share with you everything…including my life, as a captive… living among, and with the Comanche.

****

It was two-years-ago, after she; her husband Billy, and her son Hank, had met, Hank's paternal, Comanche-Grandmother, Little Flower; and Rebecca's black-sister, Mandy's brother; Sgt. Justin Gulliver, (formerly…Jason Billings); that Rebecca and her husband Billy, decided that it was time.

The time had come for them… for Rebecca and Billy, his parents—to tell their son… their then, thirteen-year-old son Hank, the history… the life- changing events, experienced by his mother, that contributed to…, that led to his birth.

It was time to tell Hank, the identity…the name… of his biological father.

****

Rebecca and Billy McCloskey… the parents of *thirteen*… soon to be *fourteen*-year-old, Henry Billings McCloskey, were seated... holding hands, on the lounge-chair, awaiting the arrival of their son.

Abruptly, the screen-door—that separated the veranda from the house, swung-open.

Their *thirteen*-year-old son Hank—who constantly reminded his parents that he was practically fourteen—burst onto the porch.

Hank was wearing his chaps. Unceremoniously, he removed his wide-brimmed, cowboy hat revealing his head of uncombed, straight-black hair. Hank slammed his hat against his leather-chaps, causing a small cloud of Trail-Dust, to be released into the air.

"Mom; dad…you sent for me?"

Billy gave his wife's hand, a gentle, reassuring squeeze. Rebecca smiled. She then removed her hands, from those of her husband.

Rebecca pointed to the closest, of the four wicker-chairs, that surrounded an oval-wicker, end table.

"Please Hen… Rebecca caught herself…please Hank, be seated. Your father and I, feel that now… now that you're practically…as you keep reminding us…now that you are practically grown, we feel that the time has come to tell…, for me to share with you, some of my family's history…some of the circumstances, and life altering events and that I, and my sister Mandy, experienced, growing-up in Virginia, and after what happened after we… my father and I, … my sister Mandy, and Mandy's mother, left Virginia."

Hank placed his hat on the table; he pulled the chair out, from beneath the table; he then turned the chair, so that the chair's back, faced his parents. Hank, straddling the chair, leaned forward resting his face, on his folded arms…and gave his parents, his full, undivided, attention.

Again…Billy took Rebecca's hand, and gently squeezed. Rebecca swallowed… she took a deep breath… she looked lovingly at her son, extracted her hands, from those of her husband, and inhaling the warm summer-air, began to speak.

"Hank, do you remember when you asked…and I told you why your father and I, had decided to name your sister Mandy? That your sister is named after your aunt…my sister, Mandy?"

Hank nodded his head. Rebecca… gathering her thoughts, reached for the glass of water on the end table…she took a sip, and then returned the glass to the table.

"Twelve years ago, just a few months, before you were born Hank, right here…here in the United States of America; despite the end of the war—the Union's Victory over the Confederacy—, Slavery…human bondage, the legal right of one human being, to own…to buy, and to sell, other humans…, Slavery, the institution, that my parents…your grandparents, and their parents, had advocated and defended—Slavery, was still, strictly speaking… was still Constitutional-Law."

Conspiratorially, Billy glanced…looked at his son. Hank quickly, and accurately interpreted, "the look".

That look, when that they shared… when they suspected his wife… Hank's mother was slipping into her, what she called, her "Professorial" mode. A demeanor she had in the past confessed to them… that she had "acquired", from her former tutor and mentor, Miss Eleanor Leary.

Not noticing the furtive, look…that *"Ah-Oh", here we go"* glance, between father and son, Rebecca continued; "Sweetheart, you remember having been taught how, less than a hundred years ago, in 1776, the thirteen former English Colonies—during my great-grandparents-time, —rejected being ruled by a monarch; by a King; a Queen; an Emperor, or a Dictator."

How our ancestors fought and won the Revolutionary War. How they, instead of forming an American Monarchy, whereby the rulers are determined by family lineage, they chose to establish, and to be governed, as a constitutional-republic.

They chose to form a nation where the people democratically, by-majority- rule), elected the chief executive (the President), who enforced the laws passed by our duly elected representatives in Congress, laws that are in compliance with our then, new country's governing-document, the United States-Constitution.

"The thirteenth amendment to our Constitution, abolishing slavery, was finally ratified, in early December, 1865."

Rebecca stopped. For a brief moment… she thought; "I'm beginning to sound, like Miss Leary. Then instead of stopping…she remembered that she and her sister Mandy, were about Hank's age… with young impressionable minds…eager to learn, when Eleanor Leary, opened their minds and their hearts, …to a "World of Knowledge".

A conspiratorial smile, heightened the cleft in her "dimpled", cheeks, as Miss Leary's favorite saying, flashed across her mind; "Always remember young-ladies";

"Knowledge Is Power"!

Rebecca's eyes, searched the faces; first of her son; then, that of her husband. Rebecca's interpretation of the expression, on both of their faces was that of puzzlement… that look that said; *"where is she going with this?"*

Rebecca lowered her head. With her handkerchief, she blotted a tear that had trickled-down her cheek. She raised her head, her normally bright blue eyes, were now, red-rimmed.

Billy—seeing that Rebecca was becoming upset—reached for her hand. Instead of taking his hand… Rebecca shuddered.

Hank…who no longer thought of himself as "Little-Hank"—he too, when he saw his mother fighting back tears— became upset; "Mom… why are you crying?"

Rebecca raised her hand. "I'm sorry; I'm sorry. For a moment there, I lost control".

"I was thinking of my sister Mandy, who I miss; whom I both loved and respected. I was thinking of the years and years, and years, that she was subjected to ignorant, callous bigotry. How she was forced to hide from the world…the white and black world, her brilliant, mind."

"I was thinking of the time…the elapsed time…ten months after Robert Lee's surrender at Appomattox, before my sister Mandy, was constitutionally—no longer a slave".

"Eight months after the South's defeat—she was at last, as were four million freed-slaves"—now, with the ratification of the 13th Amendment to our Constitution, legally free".

"And as if to add insult to *more than two hundred-fifty years of* injury, it wasn't until recently; in 1868, three years after Lee's surrender; two-hundred-sixty years, after blacks were brought here in chains… that the former slaves were recognized by the government, as "Citizens", of the United States."

"Guys…, I apologize for going on and on, and on. That impromptu historical-civics lecture, was my attempt to emphasize that; despite having fought a civil-war to abolish slavery; despite having loss more than a half million men; despite the loss of a whole generation of American-youth…, it took more than eight months, before ratification of the 13th Amendment, changed Constitutional-Law; out-lawing slavery in the United States."

"But above all else, I am truly, truly, sorry for all of the white-families; including my own three generations of Billings; that moralized and justified…the enslavement of my sister Mandy; the enslavement of millions of our black… fellow, human-beings.

I am so very sorry, for my having unknowingly, unwittingly fostering … encouraged—by not speaking-out in opposition to—the *BIG* **_"GEST"_** *LIE;* the concept, and the gulling belief that, the white race, is inherently superior to all others."

"I am sorry that when I… as a child—not knowing any better… sorry for my acceptance, of that…, the *BIG* **_"GEST"_** *LIE*.

I am so very, very, sorry, for my complicity, as an adult citizen, by my silence…, my unwitting-tacit, aiding and abetting the spreading of the *BIG* **_"GEST"_** *LIE;* that of universal, global, racial, "White-Supremacy".

"I am sorry for, the gulling-egotistical, self-serving belief that the "White- Race", is inherently, Superior to… and should therefore, have dominion over… all, non-whites.

"I am sorry for, the underlying doctrine… that some of us… before and during the war, consciencely…and for some whites—mostly, those whites that could not afford to own slaves—; unconsciously, shamelessly used, to moralize and to justify, Slavery."

Both Billy and Hank were speechless. Although they both knew and appreciated Rebecca's erudite-intelligence, neither father nor son, had ever heard Rebecca Elizabeth, Billings, McCloskey, speak…lecture, with such conviction…, such passion.

Rebecca seeing on their faces, the effect of her unplanned oration, extended her hands, palms forward… "I'm sorry…I'm sorry. I am ever, so very sorry… sorry for having to keep saying… that, I am sorry!"

****

After an uncomfortable moment of silence, Rebecca in a subdued calm voice, continued; "My sister… my best friend Mandy and I, were born— three days apart—on Virginia's Rosewood-Cotton Plantation."

"As fate or chance, would have it, I was born the white-daughter, of the owners of that plantation. Born into that "White Supremist Society… the world of my parents; your grandparents… Henry and Margaret Billings, two staid-paragons, of the Wealthy-Southern Ruling Class."

My birth was recorded in the 'Billings' Family Bible, as:

Rebecca Elizabeth Billings
- July 19, 1848;

Daughter of
Henry and Margaret Billings

Fourteen years later...that is, after mine and Mandy's birth, in preparation for our leaving Rosewood—my father, myself, Mandy's mother, and my sister Mandy—my father delegated to me, the task of packing mine, and his belongings.

During the course of clearing out my father's office..., I came upon an old Rosewood-Plantation, business ledger-journal. In the section of the ledger labeled; Slave-Property, I discovered this notation.

Rebecca read, verbatim..., to Billy and Hank, those words..., which had been indelibly etched, into her mind.

July 22, 1848 – Born, one nigger
wench; Name: Mandy
Mother-Ruth
Father-Unknown.

Although... I had, of course, always known that Mandy was a slave, it was that entry, those words callously written, by my father's hand, that I experienced... that I fully understood, the dehumanizing meaning, and the resultant impact of those words, on my sister Mandy's life.

"My sister...my best friend, your Aunt Mandy... was born—and therefore, in accordance with the intent of the laws of Virginia—would forever be, a "Black-Slave".

Rebecca's eyes were focused on the pronounced, inquisitive, expression, on her son's face. Rebecca had anticipated, and now appreciated, the turmoil...the questions, that, her heart-felt, intentionally provocative, pronouncements, would invoke in Henry.

For years, Little Hank... now *please call me "Hank"*, had wondered— never quite having the courage... nor had the opportune-moment or occasion occurred..., to ask his mother these nagging questions; *"Who is my father? How can Mandy, a black-slave, be your sister?"*

After he had experienced—what the ranch-hands had teasingly, called—his first "wet-dream", and his dad, Billy—when they were having their *"Birds and the Bees"* talk— had referred to as his first "nocturnal-emission", it was then that Hank asked his dad…those two repressed… salient, questions.

"Dad…how can Mandy, the black-slave girl… that Mom grew-up with… how can she be Mom's sister?

Hank's question, surprised his father. While he and Rebecca had in the past, discussed the possibility…, the probability, that at some point, their children would ask those questions…, still those perfectly innocent questions, asked by his son…took Billy by surprise.

Billy hesitated…he did not immediately answer his son's question. He and Rebecca had tacitly agreed that, when and if…, the question was asked, that they would…together, answer. They would…, as their children's parents, provide the answers…, as well as, tell them of the extraordinary circumstances, that led to those life-altering, events.

Instead of putting his son off—by waiting for Rebecca to be present—Billy instinctively realized, that this opportunity…, the *"Wet-Dreams"*, the *"Birds and the Bees"* talk, was the "Right-Time and the Right-Place", to answer his son' question.

Billy gathered his thoughts. While he knew that Rebecca…, the boy's mother's, *"book-learning"*, was far superior to his, and that she had the knack…that Rebecca was a *"natural-born"* teacher, never-the-less, Billy truly believed…was convinced, that the answer to these, particular questions…from a boy…a young man, should be done…, Man-to-Man.

In his mind, Billy thought of…, he felt that the discussion—the answers to Hank's questions—, as being *"Man's-Talk"*.

As Billy looked at his son's earnest, inquisitive, face, a myriad of thoughts…questions were coursing through his mind. The question that bothered him most was… should he, here and now—without Rebecca being present, answer their teenage-son, Hank's…, the obviously, no longer *"Little Hank's"*, questions"

Or…, as he and Rebecca had discussed…, should he wait. And the two of them… together, answer Hank's questions?

Billy decided not to wait. Now was the right time…he would answer Hank's questions…and would later explain to Rebecca, why he had made that decision.

Before speaking, Billy took a deep steading-breath, and nervously swallowed. "Hank growing-up here on the ranch, I'm sure you've seen plenty of cute baby-horses, cute little calves…, those precious little baby chicks, that your sister loves to stroke."

"You've watched, horses…stallions and mares; cows and bulls, ah, ah…, hump…I mean, mating."

Hank, suppressing a smug-smile…nodded. Billy pushed-on. "Well son…what they're doing is…what they're doing is…its natural. Those animals can't help it, they're responding to the call of nature. They have to mate, in order to reproduce…to make babies. They're bodies are telling them to mate".

Billy pressed-on; "Well son, on many…most, of those plantations in the South…the white men…the owners and the overseers, in addition to coupling…mating with their wives, would frequently, force…coerce, their female black-slaves, to couple with them.

Usually the white-men, coupled with their female black-slaves, to gratify, their lust, if their coupling resulted in a "baby", by law that

baby— regardless of the baby's color or his/her white parentage—
the "*sucka*", that's what they called new-born black-babies—, was
considered a black- slave…the property of the plantation-owner.

Although the Plantation Master's wives were aware of their white-
male family members…, their husband's, their son's, their nephews,
"dalliances" with the female black-slaves, they … the Plantation
Master's wives—for the sake of propriety—would not acknowledge
their husbands, their sons, and nephews, activities…nor did they
acknowledge the '*Light-Skin*" children, the "*suckas*", that resulted
from these "dalliances".

Hank, having had never lived in the South…much-less on a slave-
holding- Plantation, was intently, listening …giving his dad, his full
and undivided, attention.

"Your grandfather…, your mother's father, Henry Billings, the Master
of Rosewood Plantation, in addition to having church-sanctioned,
"sexual- relations", with his wife…, your grandmother Margaret…,
Henry Billings, the Master of Rosewood Plantation, for more then
twenty-years, had had continuous "sexual-relations", so-called
"dalliances", with one of his female-black slaves…, Ruth, your aunt
Mandy's mother."

Billy paused…hesitated to collect his thoughts…to choose the right
words. He took a deep breath, let it out slowly… then, he continued.

"Hank, you were born before I met and married your mother. Your sister,
baby-Mandy, was born as a result of our…, the church-sanctioned,
"sexual- relations", between your mother and me…her husband.

Because you and your sister share a parent your mother Rebecca, the
two of you, Hank and baby-Mandy, are brother and sister."

"Because your mother Rebecca, and her sister Mandy, share a parent, your grandfather Henry Billings, Rebecca and the then, black-slave Mandy, are sisters."

Billy, seeing a momentary look of confusion in Hank's eyes, repeated.

"Your mother Rebecca and your aunt Mandy, share the same father; your grandfather, Henry Billings."

Billy was intently, studying Hank's face…looking for his son's reaction thus far, to the partial-answer to his questions.

It was obvious to Billy, that his "almost-Fifteen-Year-Old", son was struggling…attempting, to connect the events…the relationships, that had resulted in his white-mother, being the sister of a black-slave.

In an attempt to assist Hank, in his effort to… connect the familial-dots, Billy decided to reinforce his answers to Hank's questions, by using as an example…, the McCloskey Family…Hank's…, their immediate family.

"Hank, just as you and…what's that nickname you gave your sister… oh yes, "M-Cubed" …, just as you two, are brother and sister; so too, are Rebecca, and the former black-slave, Mandy…, they are sisters.

Unbeknown to father and son, Rebecca…, her hand on the knob of the screen-door—had hesitated, —not wanting to interrupt. She had been quietly, standing behind the screen-door, listening to the father/ son, exchange.

****

Rebecca opened the screen-door, and stepped down, onto the stone-floor of the patio. Billy stood…walked over to his wife, and kissed her cheek.

Hank, who had remained seated, smiled and greeted his mother; "Hi mom. Me and dad…" Rebecca raised a reproachful eyebrow. Hank immediately corrected his grammar.

"Sorry…, Dad and I, were just having a *"Man-to-Man"* talk".

Rebecca smiling asked; "So I heard. Apparently, I came in on the tail-end of your "Man-to-Man". I hope I'm not interrupting you guys."

Billy, a little flustered, spoke; "Hank asked me a personal male-hygiene, question, that I at first… thought to defer…then I decided, to at least… partially, attempt to answer".

Rebecca smiled. "I walked in on the tail-end of your conversation. She sat down beside her husband. "Hank, I believe your father… in explaining mine, and my sister Mandy's kinship, with you. I think that his comparing you and your baby-sister Mandy, … *"M-Cubed"*, with me and my sister…Mandy, a black-slave, was both appropriate, and is accurate.

She turned to her husband. "Billy that kinship-analogy that you used, was certainly apropos…, simply brilliant".

Billy blushed…although he was not familiar with the word "*apropos*" or for that matter, *many of the* words, that haphazardly, randomly, spewed-forth from Rebecca's mouth…, over the course of their marriage, Billy had grown to appreciate and marvel, at the extent of his wife's intelligence…of her literacy.

Usually when Rebecca, seamlessly injected a word or concept into their conversation, that he was not familiar with…did not understand, Billy would hold-up his hand…signaling, to her, stop…; What's the meaning of that word.

This time—not wanting to interrupt this mother/son, moment— Billy remained silent.

Rebecca squeezed her husband's hand. She turned her head toward her son; "Hank…, Rebecca paused; Unless you have questions?" Hank shook his head …indicating that he appreciated, understood, and was satisfied with his father's kinship, explanation.

"Hank, while your father's comparison of the sibling-bond, between you and your sister M-Cubed…, and the bond between, myself and my sister Mandy, is biologically accurate, in several very important aspects—because of the times and the circumstances, that I am about to detail… and attempt to explain—the comparison of these two pair of sibling-relationships; Me and my sister Mandy; and you, and your baby-sister Mandy…, sorry, between you and your sister *"M-Cubed"*, are biologically, accurate".

Hank sat…leaning forward; mesmerized, intrigued by the intensity and solemnity of his mother's voice… of her words.

Both her husband Billy, and her son Hank, were somewhat confused, when Rebecca made a fist of her left hand, and then, she continued;

"What I am about to say, I say… not as a comparative critique, but as indisputable fact(s); "Hank, there are several differential factors… differences, between you and your sister *"M-Cube's"* sibling-relationship; and that of me and my sister Mandy's, best-friend-sibling-bond."

From her clinched left hand, Rebecca extended her index finger; "One…, Hank, you're a male…your sister is female. Believe me, in our world…in our society, believe me, that really matters."

Rebecca extended the middle finger of her left hand; "Two…, there is a 12- year difference in age, between you and your sister. The amount of time that you spend with your sister *"M-Cubed"*…, and rightfully so, at this point in your lives, as compared to my time spent with my sister Mandy, is miniscule."

"My sister and I were born during the same week…three days apart. From infancy to when we were about your age Hank, my sister Mandy and I spent, practically, every waking-moment together."

Rebecca as Billy had previously done, paused and gathered her thoughts. She took a deep breath, then in a steady, reverent, whispery, tone…she once again, began to speak;

"This is no exaggeration, I honestly don't…, I do not remember a single-day; not one day of my …of our lives on the Rosewood Plantation, that *"Becky and Mandy"*; *"Mandy and Becky"*… from birth, to age 14, were not together."

"When and where, we grew-up in the slave-holding South, neither Southern Law…nor would my father, acknowledge that we were sisters."

"However, neither Southern-Law, nor could my father, prevent my sister Mandy and I, from developing and sharing, a profound sibling-love for each other, nor could they…, though lord knows they tried…, prevent our becoming best-friends."

In fact, guys…, now that I think about it, the first time that I spent a day without seeing…, without being, with my sister Mandy was…, the second day of our lives as captives of the Comanche. But I digress. I promise you Hank..., I'll speak at length..., detail, about Mandy's and my life with the Comanche, in a little-bit.

Billy...seeing Rebecca moisten her lips with the tip of her tongue, handed to her, his glass of water. Rebecca accepted, and gratefully, sipped the water.

Hank was silent, mesmerized..., staring in wonder, amazement, and admiration, as his mother for the first time, continued to share with him details of her life, back in...what he thought of as, the *"olden"* days.

The bygone days of slavery... and especially, the days when Indians—his biologic-father and now, his Aunt Mandy's people—were free, formidable, adversaries, of the white-man's aggression...their attempts to "steal", the Comanches' Homeland.

Rebecca had noticed a discernable change in both her son's, as well as her husband's demeanor, when she had mentioned, Mandy's and her time, living with the Comanche.

Intuitively, Rebecca decided that "The Time" was right. While she had told her husband of her captivity by the Comanche, she knew that out of his love for her, and his desire to protect her; to not upset her, many of the questions that he undoubtedly had, about her life amongst the Comanche, had not, by Billy...been asked.

Rebecca, naturally...without thinking about it, had adopted her teacher..., Miss Eleanor Leary's, teaching style..., *she would led them, guide them, to ask and through discussion, listen and learn.*

Instead of lecturing her two *"students"*, she would teach them, by stimulating, provoking their questions, and answering; and encouraging discussion, between Hank and Billy; as well as between Billy, Hank, and herself.

However, rather than lecturing the two…the two most important *"men"* in her life—, she would as Miss Leary had done when teaching her and her sister Mandy, she, would teach them, by employing the *"Socratic Method"*.

She recalled how Miss Leary, instead of lecturing her and Mandy, would instead let, "her students", glean their answers, through their questions and the resulting discussions. She would guide the discussion, and when necessary, she would "fill-in" the gaps.

"Hank, I think…I think, I know the question that is uppermost in your mind…the question that you most, want answered."

Hank with an eager, anticipatory look on his face, gave his mother his full, undivided attention.

An awkward period of silence ensued. Instead of responding…instead of her stating the question that, the three of them knew, hung like a dark rain-cloud, in the hot, oppressive, night-air; Rebecca remained silent.

In an attempt to "cut-through" the mounting tension, Billy began to speak; "I believe that…".

Rebecca, her eyes fixed on her son, raised her hand; palm forward, facing her husband…, the universal signal to "Stop".

In mid-sentence, Billy stopped.

Hank felt the blood rushing to his face. He took a deep, relaxing, cleansing breath:

"Mom, remember…when we took, those wagons to the Comanche Village? When we offered those wagons, to help the Comanches transport their belongings, to their government assigned, Indian Reservation?"

Knowing that the question was rhetorical; Rebecca remained silent.

Hank, not expecting an answer, continued. "Remember when, you introduced me to my Comanche relatives. My grandmother, Quiet One; to Gray Wolf and Little Flower, the Comanche's who adopted your sister…my aunt, Mandy; to my aunt Spring Blossom; and to your sister…, my aunt Mandy's son…, my cousin, Dark Eagle?"

Still not expecting an answer, Hank pushed on.

"I will never…ever, forget that day. How on that day, when in addition to my Comanche relatives, you also introduced me to my aunt Mandy's brother… my black Uncle, a U.S. Army Calvary Sgt., Justin Gulliver."

"Mom…do you remember?" Rebecca slowly nodded her head.

"Mom, that day, was probably, one of the happiest days of my life. But mom, still when I think back to that very special day…as wonderful… as enlightening and special that it was, what I remember most is…, not the meeting of all of my new relatives…, what I remember most, is that no one…not you…not my new found Comanche relatives…no one, spoke of or mentioned, my Comanche father."

"Mom, who was…, or who is…, my Comanche father? Was my Comanche father, a ruthless animal…a savage beast?

Billy, whose attention had been focused on his son, quickly shifted his gaze, to Rebecca.

He was surprised. For the first time today…, Rebecca appeared to be flustered.

****

Though for years—actually since baby-Hank had uttered his first words— Rebecca had been expecting, …anticipating, her son's asking that inevitable, dreaded, question. "Mom, who is my father?"

Over the years, in her mind, she had mulled over, …, rehearsed…time and time again, the words…that she would say to her now…practically, adult, son.

Over the years her planned, measured-response had run the gamut. Her initial thoughts had been, that when the time came, when he asked, she would tell him the unvarnished truth.

She would tell him—what she had, fifteen years earlier…, when they were captives of the Comanche—had told her sister Mandy.

She would tell her son of how she, with hysterical tears cascading down from her eyes, fell into her sister's arms lamenting, "Oh Mandy, he hurt me. Again, and again, and again, he hurt me…Stone Fist raped me."

She would tell her son that his biologic father, the "*animal*" who had raped her, was a heathen savage, incapable having human emotions.

She would convey to her son, the hate, the loathing, that she had felt then, and had carried over the years, for *"Stone Fist"*, the Comanche Warrior that was his biological father.

Now, *"That the Time Had Come"*, now that her son had met, his biological father's people, his Comanche relatives… now that he was truly, no longer *"Little Hank"*, a boy grappling, with issues of self-esteem…with questions of *"Who am I…Where did I Come From?"*

Wrestling with the same, identity crisis, that had for years, plagued her black sister Mandy, now despite her, hate…, her loathing of those acts of rape…, for her son's sake, she would not vilify, "Stone Fist", nor his…, her son's, Comanche-Heritage.

****

"Baby…I'm so sorry, *Henry*…wow…goodness, I did it again, Hank. It's just that when I feel that something might hurt you…, I still, think of you as my beautiful, innocent, baby-boy."

Fourteen…almost fifteen-year-old, Hank squirmed in his seat. He was embarrassed. Here he was…after having had a *"Man to Man"* conversation with his dad, while his mom, still… thought of him as a baby".

"Mom, I'm not a baby, I'm practically full-grown…, almost a man."

Hank looked to Billy…, hoping that his dad, would bolster his entreating assertion.

That instantaneous, wordless, fleeting, visual, communication between father and son, was successful.

Billy chimed-in. "He's right honey. Ole Hank here…can ride, rope, shoot and brand cattle, practically as well as I can."

Rebecca, welcomed the light-hearted banter. A broad grin lite-up her face; before her expression morphed into that of-a-stern, no-nonsense, look.

She forced a smile…, looked into her son's eyes and said; "Well scouse me, cow-poke".

And then, in a serious tone-of-voice, Rebecca said; "Hank, I stand corrected. Hank…, not, baby or Henry. I will try to remember…, Hank is your, ere…, is your moniker.

The two…, almost three, adult members of the McCloskey-Clan, relaxed.

After having taken a final sip—of her now empty—glass of water. Rebecca placed the glass on the table, and continued.

"Hank, please bear-with me…be patient. I will answer all of your questions. However, I feel…, I know, that for you, to fully understand your origin…, to know what led to your birth…, the birth of Henry Luis Billings, McCloskey, my son…Hank, you need to know…, you should know, some of my…, your mother's—thus far— life's-journey."

"Billy…please ask Juanita, to feed baby-Mandy, and to put her to bed. I think that my verbal-dissertation…, my historical-recounting of my past…, my life on the Rosewood-Slave Plantation…, my time living amongst the Comanche…, my meeting and marrying the man of my dreams…, you, William McCloskey; might…, will take a considerable amount of time.

Don't worry…we'll wait for you. Hank, while we're waiting for your father, why don't you take a break…, stretch your legs. I don't know about you… cowboy, but I could use…, would you mind getting your old-tired mom, another glass of water."

When Hank returned with his mother's glass of water, he saw that his mother and father…, Rebecca and Billy, were engrossed in a subdued, animated, conversation.

In an attempt to announce his return…, Hank noisily, cleared his throat. Rebecca reached for and took from her son, the proffered glass of water.

Accepting the water, Rebecca smiled. "Hank I appreciate your extending to us…, your father and I, the courtesy of not eavesdropping. However, son I assure you that it was not necessary."

"In fact, son, what your father and I were discussing was the time that you actually met your Comanche father."

Now Hank was totally confused. He looked first at his mother, then at his father.

Billy responded by providing an answer to his son obvious…, but unstated, question…, with a question.

"Hank do you remember two years ago, when we were being attack by those Indians?" Before Hank could answer, Billy continued…of course you remember…we… all of us, will never forget that day."

Hank's eyes, which had been focused on his father, switched to the face of his mother. Rebecca attempted…but failed to smile. Instead, she looked at Billy…and nodded her head, indicating that he should continue.

Billy continued, I was at the top of the landing… the fiercest, most menacing, frightening man, that I had ever seen, came charging up the stairs. Before I could raise my rifle, the warrior's swung his war-club and knocked me senseless.

In my dazed state—limp as a rag-doll—I remember being lifted by my hair, then as if from heaven, an angel, a voice …, you my son… was shouting "don't hurt my dad…leave my father alone".

It was after the attack…, that your mother told me that the Comanche Warrior, that was about to scalp me, was Stone Fist, your biological-father.

It wasn't until we visited the Comanche village, and I saw your cousin…, your mother's sister Mandy's son, "Dark Eagle" that I finally understood why we, you and I..., why we are still alive...why Stone Fist hadn't killed the both of us.

Now, Hank was really confused. Billy..., seeing the confused-look on his son's face, explained. "When we visited that Comanche Village, and I first laid eyes on your Mom's sister Mandy's son Dark Eagle, I remember thinking..., "if you were to cut his hair, that young Indian... your cousin Dark Eagle, would be the "spitting-image" of you."

"Son both your mother and I think..., we agree, that at that moment, at the ranch, when Stone Fist, saw you...he saw what I saw..., when I first saw Dark Eagle."

Rebecca walked over to her bewildered son. Hank stood. Rebecca held her son's hands, and in a calm, reverent voice stated: "Hank you actually met, your father. Your father spared you and your dad Billy's lives."

Stone Fist, the Comanche War Chief, is...was, your biological-father."

****

"Your father and I agree, that I should tell you everything. However, Hank, despite the fact that we all...you, me, your father...have established that you are *"almost-grown"*, while I will recount for you the gist, of what I have seen and experienced, I however..., your mother, do not, and will not... speak-graphically, of what I have seen... nor of what I, have personally, endured."

"We..., your father and I, have agreed, that if and when you ask for specific- details about those despicable, events...he will decide if and when, the two of you, will have, yet additional future..., *"Man to Man"* talks."

 Precious In His Sight

Though he did not understand…, could not imagine the need for them, to withhold from him details of what he was about to be told…, Hank decided not to…at this time, verbalize his feelings.

Hank chuckled to himself. He was thinking of one of Hattie's—his aunt and uncle's former black-slave…now their salaried-maid's, —favorite saying…, *"Honey-chile, youse needs ta membah…haf-a loaf; sho nuff bees betta…, din nun-atoll."*

Absent from hearing an objection…, a comment from her son, Rebecca resumed, providing him with a brief-synopsis, of what she called;

"The life—thus far, of Rebecca Elizabeth Billings McCloskey".

****

"As I previously mentioned, my sister Mandy—who by Southern-law, was my slave, my property—, Mandy and I, were born, three days apart, in the state of Virginia, on my family's Rosewood Plantation…, one of that state's most successful…wealthiest, cotton plantations.

Growing up…, from infancy to age…she smiled, from infancy to… using your *"lingo"* Hank, to age fourteen…almost fifteen, I can't remember a single day…, not one day, that I was not with my sister Mandy."

"I was told that…when we were infants Mandy and I, would both…, together at the same time, nurse at Mandy's mother Ruth's, breast. Your Aunt Mandy and I, were inseparable."

"My mother, your grandmother Margaret, insisted…ordered that— other than at night when I was put to bed—ordered, that Ruth's little *"Pick-a- ninny"* Mandy, be my constant companion; That Mandy be, in essence, my *"Real-life…black, doll-baby"*.

"I actually remember when we…, Mandy and I, were your sister's age; going through those terrible two's, three's', and four's. I remember hearing our house-slaves—after the two of us Mandy and I, had knocked-over something…, more often than not…, we had knocked-over many-things— hearing the house-slaves, exasperated, moans;

"Dem two's bees lik two peas inna pod; lik grits n gravy." "Iffin ya sees one, da otta ain't fer behin."

Hank was pleasantly surprised. This was the first time, that he had ever heard his mother, speak in that dialect. The dialect that he had constantly heard, being spoken, by Hattie and Willie, their *Colored* house-servants, when he and his mother, were living in Richmond, Virginia, with his Uncle Luis, and his Aunt Delilah.

Hank had always associated that bizarre *"English"*, with the former black- slaves, the *"Freedmen and Women"*, that were a large segment, of Richmond's population.

Rebecca noticing the perplexed look…the frown, on her son's face, stopped. She too was Puzzled.

"Hank, you look confused…do you have a question?" Hank, not realizing that his facial expression had changed, answered his mother.

"No Mom, I'm not confused…I guess I'm just a little-bit surprised. I don't remember ever hearing you speak colored…, *"nigger-talk"*.

Without any sort of advance warning, Rebecca, now visibly upset, trembling, stood…, "Henry Luis McCloskey, don't you ever, in my presence, use that filthy, demeaning, derogatory, word, nigger!"

Billy, surprised by the sudden change in his wife's tone-of-voice…, in her demeanor, stood and gently, firmly, wrapped his arms around Rebecca.

"Becky…honey, relax…, take it easy. Hank didn't mean anything by saying that word, nig…"

Before he could finish his sentence, Rebecca tore herself from his grasp, and in an exasperated, yet calm, steady, steely voice…, exclaimed; "That's exactly what sickens and infuriates me."

"Don't you both understand, that I know…, that he didn't… that he didn't mean anything… anything offensive, by saying that, loathsome, dehumanizing, word?"

"That's…that's the problem. We've grown so accustomed to nonchalantly, bandying that despicable word *"nigger"* around, that we…, those of us that literally *"Don't mean anything offensive"*, either don't know…, or have conveniently forgotten, the origin…, the intent, and the meaning of the word, nigger."

Both Billy and Hank, stared in awed silence…, aghast at the emotion…, the vehemence, of Rebecca's words.

Billy sat. Rebecca, who had remained standing…, wearily…, deflated, sat down next to her husband.

Billy, once again poured and handed his wife, a glass of water. Rebecca gulped down the, now tepid liquid. Rebecca reached over, and took both of her son's hands.

"Hank…I am truly sorry that I raised…, snapped…, raised my voice. Please son…please, accept my apology."

Hank's face relaxed. He gently, reassuringly, squeezed his mother's hands. "Gee mom…, I think that I should be the one, who apologizes. I had no idea that my saying that word, would upset you."

Rebecca managed a forlorn, wistful-smile. She removed her hands, from those of her son.

She first, glanced at her husband, then at Hank. "Believe me guys… I had neither planned…nor had I intended, that outburst."

"What I had intended to do…, and I promise you…, I will do", she looked into her son's obsidian-colored, eyes, "was to answer Hank's question. The question that I knew at some point son, you would ask…, and that I will now, candidly, answer."

"However, I think that before answering that inevitable, *simple*-question, I feel that I should make you aware of the events…our family, the Billings' family's events, that led to my meeting, and my—her voice became tremulous—my interaction, with *"Stone Fist"*, your Comanche father."

"I have given much thought, as to what and how, I should go about answering your question."

Rebecca raised, then dropped her hands. "Believe me guys, I had neither expected to hear…, nor had I imagined that I would react as I did, to that loathsome, vile, word.

Again, I ask that you…, both of you…please accept my sincere apology, for my uncalled-for, outburst."

First her husband Billy, then her son Hank, assured Rebecca, that while they still, did not understand why she had reacted as she had…, they both, none- the-less, accepted her apology.

****

Rebecca sighed. "Okay…, change of plans... instead of starting my "Billings-Family" narrative, with the history of Rebecca and my sister

Mandy, that vile word that triggered my not so elegant outburst, gave me pause."

"Therefore, instead of starting my narrative with the history of myself and my sister Mandy, I feel the need to take you back-further, a few generations …, to share with you…the Billings-Family's history…, of three generations, of Billings. My father-Henry; his father-Artimas; and his grandfather…, my Great grandfather…, Hank…, your Great, Great, grand father, William Billings".

At this point…, in this setting, and honestly, because I don't know a lot about my Great grandfather, William's life, …I will share with you a salient- detail, that I do know…that was boastfully…, with pride, told to me, by my father."

Before continuing…, once again, Rebecca took a sip of water.

"I remember sitting on my father's lap—at that time, I was seven-years-old, my teen-age brother Jesse, was standing behind us—when daddy beaming with pride, opened our family bible.

Father proudly pointed to the top entry, on the Billings-Family page, of that Sacred-Tome:"

THE BILLINGS FAMILY

William Billings_______________________________**Dorothy Jenkins Billings**
(1771 – 1818)   **(1780 – 1833)**

"This man, your Great grandfather, William, was the founder…the creator of the Billings Family fortune. "Our ancestor, William Billings, was a ship's- Captain".

"He was the captain of a merchant ship… a *"Slaver"*. A slave-ship, that transported—under the most horrific, deplorable, inhumane, conditions

captured Africans. Black men, women, and children snatched, from their African homeland, shipped across the Atlantic Ocean, to the "New World; to the sea-ports of the "fledgling", newly established, southern states,
of the United States of America."

"I will never forget, the reverence..., that resonated in my father's voice, as he spoke, of the courage, the industriousness, the acuity and business- brilliance, of his grandfather.

My father Henry Billings told us..., me and my brother Jesse, of how his grandfather..., our great grandfather, your great, great, grandfather, was one of the men who were instrumental, in providing the Agrarian-South, with the key to the South's prosperity. That being a the least-expensive..., practically free labor force..., a limitless supply, of black-slaves."

"And that our ancestor, William Billings, by promoting and profiting from slavery, was hugely responsible, for helping to create the economic "back- bone", of Southern-Wealth and prosperity, "Slavery".

"I cringe in shame, when I think of how your great grandfather, by transporting—under the most horrific conditions— and selling as if they were human-chattel..., millions of human-beings into slavery, became enormously wealthy.

It is certainly not too far-fetched, to speculate..., to believe, that my sister..., your aunt Mandy's grandparents... may have been victims of our—yours and mine—"Billings" forebearer's, avarice..., his greed, his insatiable desire for wealth and power."

Before continuing..., purposefully, for a full minute, Rebecca remained silent. It was her intent, to provide enough time..., for her words to register with Hank..., as well as with her husband, Billy.

"When I read, in one of Miss Leary's text-books— *"The Unabridged History of the United States"*; When I read of how the captive-slaves, before being put aboard the "Slave-ships" had been torn from their inland homes— forced to walk…trot, run, hundreds of miles, shackled-in-chains; Of the captives being constantly lashed…, being berated, being cursed, being taunted…, by that phrase, that phrase that I…, as a child heard our Overseer…, heard my brother Jesse, while lashing them with their whips…,continuously shouting at our slaves, *"Lazy-nigger…, Lazy,*
shiftless-niggers", as the slaves worked the fields, of our plantation.

In Miss Leary's text-book, that vile word *"Nigger"*, was the primary… the most often used malignant, epithet, spewed forth by the slave-traders, and by the subsequent, generations of Masters, of my sister's… of the millions of enslaved human-beings, of African descent".

Rebecca let out a long, cleansing breath. "Again, I apologize; Hank when you my son…, when you, your aunt Mandy's nephew; So cavalierly, nonchalantly, used that vile word *"nigger"* it…, to put it mildly…it upset, it got to me."

"I sincerely thank you both for listening… for indulging me. Okay, if you will allow me to …I will continue."

Hank was speechless. Although his mother had not yet…, answered his question, *"Who is my Comanche father?"*, the Billings family-history that she had just shared with them, was…, as Rebecca, had hoped it would be…, enlightening, and profoundly, affecting him.

Slavery, which to him, had always been thought of as, a rather mundane…, albeit, historically-recent, abstract issue. Now slavery, to him… was no longer… considered mundane, nor was it abstract.

Thanks to his mother's impassioned-recitation, Hank was on the verge of…, if not quite yet understanding, the evils of slavery…, he was beginning to empathize with those…and the families and descendants of those, who had been enslaved.

His mother had for Hank, personalized Slavery. And some of the evils that it entailed, that had been fostered and practiced, by his family's… by his ancestors…, by both his white and red, ancestors.

His mother had raised the question…, the possibility that his aunt Mandy's, his mother's sister's great, great, grandparents, may very well have been, abducted; transported under horrific conditions; been packed like sardines into the ship's-hold of his great, great, grandfather, William Billings' slave- ship; and that of his mother's sister Mandy's… his aunt's ancestors…, being sold, by his great, great, grandfather, William Billings.
A mischievous grin, had formed at the corners of Rebecca's mouth. Rebecca attempted…, but failed to suppress that smile...that smirk.
Billy, was surprised. His immediate thought was; "Why is she smiling…, grinning, after confessing…, telling us that her great, great, grandfather, William Billings, was the captain of a slave-ship?"

After regaining her composure, Rebecca explained; "Please forgive my inappropriate lapse. It just struck me…, that if my seafaring ancestor, Captain William Billings, had been a gallant-privateer…a pirate, capturing and transporting stolen treasure, that they probably would have called him, *"Captain Billy-Billings"*.

William (Billy) McCloskey, laughed. Hank joined in the laughter and chimed in; "If I had been around during his time, I would have called him, *"Captain Billy-Squared"*.

****

Billy had sat silently in wonder… a smile of appreciation, on his face. Billy was quietly, admiring and marveling, at the depth of knowledge, and the intellect of his wife…, the mother of his children…, the love of his life, Rebecca Elizabeth McCloskey.

As in the past, he had often said, "That teacher…, that teacher that she constantly raves about…the one who back on the plantation, taught her and her sister Mandy…, that Miss Eleanor Leary…, must have been one *"Hell- of-Ah-Teacher"*.

Rebecca resumed speaking; "Hank I apologize. I know you must be thinking…when is she going to answer my question… why is it taking so long? I say to you…have patience my son. All of the things… the events, that I am telling you, are important…I believe them to be necessary factors, to the answering of your question. Please bear with me… I promise you son…, I'll get there"

Before Hank could respond… once again, Rebecca continued.

"This narrative is taking a lot longer than I had anticipated. So…, in the interest of time, and in an attempt to…, not bore you, I am going to be less detailed…considerably less detailed, about our lives…, mine and Mandy's, on the Rosewood Plantation."

As eager as he was to hear the answer to his question; *"Who is my father?"*, Hank was surprised to hear these words…, words which would invariably delay his mom's response, to his question; coming from his mouth; "Mom, this is fascinating. I want to hear it all."

Billy chimed in. "Yeah honey…take as much time as you want… as much time as you need."

Rebecca smiled. "You two are being very gracious and generous. However, still…, I think that I'll summarize with the caveat, that if you like…, at some other time of your choosing …, I will fill-in the blanks… provide details of mine and my sister Mandy's life, on the slave-holding, Rosewood Cotton- Plantation."

"Oh, however…, this particular fact is extremely important. When we were kids…six or seven-years-old, until we were fourteen, Mandy and I, were felons. We two together, constantly and consistently, knowingly broke one of Virginia's…, one of the South's, most sacred Laws."

"I taught… Mandy, and Mandy learned…, how to read and write."

"When my father found-out, that Mandy could read and write, he threatened to sell Mandy; her mother Ruth; and Ruth's son…, Mandy's older-brother Jason."

Rebecca saw a surprised quizzical look in Hank's eyes. Before he could ask the question, she volunteered; "Yes, Mandy's older-brother Jason… is the same Sergeant Justin Gulliver, that you met, when we visited your Indian- relatives, at the Comanche Encampment."

Hank, fascinated by his mother's sharing, of these here-to-fore unknown, facts of her life, with him, blurted-out; "What happened Mom? Did your…, did my grandfather, sell Mandy?

Rebecca sighed. "He was determined—despite my hysterical-pleadings—to sell Mandy."

Hank…now sitting on the edge of his chair, persisted; "Did he mom…, did grandfather, sell Mandy?"

Rebecca answered. "No son, your grandfather—despite his absolute belief in… and his determination to uphold Southern Laws… to protect the institution of Slavery— he did not sell Mandy."

Rebecca, sensing that Hank was about to ask, what her teacher, Miss Eleanor Leary insisted was the shortest… but probably the most important question, uttered by man, *"Why"*, quickly added; "As to the what, when…, and/or the

who, persuaded your grandfather not to sell Mandy, requires a detailed, lengthy, answer, which I will gladly provide, at a future family meeting."

Both her son and husband looked disappointed, but refrained… reluctantly, from asking…, repeating that simple one-word question; *"Why"*.

Rebecca picked-up, her now practically empty, glass. Billy—water pitcher in hand— half-filled, her empty-glass.

****

Again…, Rebecca took a sip of water. She then cleared her throat…, and continued.

"It should not come as a surprise to you— after hearing what I just told you— or for that matter, come as a surprise to anyone, who knew my father, that when the Civil-War began; that my father…Henry Artimas Billings…, the grandson of the slave-ship captain, William Billings…, that when the war began, that my father, would go "All-In". That he would whole- heartedly, support the rebellion…support the Confederates' attempt to preserve human chattel-slavery, thus dissolving the Union.

"I tell you this as preamble."

For a full thirty-second, the room was quiet…, no one spoke.

Hank…, with a frown on his face, turned his head, and looked quizzically, at Billy.

Billy shrugged his shoulders. He then gently touched his wife's arm.

"Honey, we the two of us, …our son Hank, and your immigrant-husband Billy, unlike you have, … Hank and I, have not been taught by your Hero…, Miss Eleanor Leary."

"Me and Hank…, your son and I…well we honestly, don't know, what you meant." Rebecca raised an inquisitive, eyebrow.

Hank continued: "When you said that this… is "preamble", what does that mean?"

Rebecca, with a smile, accepted her husband's mild chastisement. "Guys…I apologize. Sometimes without even being aware of it…, I slip into my "Eleanor Leary", mode of speaking.

"Preamble" means; "in preparation of or for; it's an introduction to and for, the weighty-discussion, that usually follows, the word "*Preamble*"."

****

"In his patriotic-zeal, and his fervent belief in the necessity of…, and the ultimate success of the insurrection…, the rebellion, my father instructed his best friend and business manager—Rebecca paused and looked directly at Hank—your "Uncle Luis", to withdraw from the North, all of his financial- holdings. To convert everything into gold…, and to then reinvest in numerous Southern munition factories, thereby assisting and supporting, the Confederate war-effort.

To raise money for the war…, the rebellion, Papa, your grandfather, mortgaged our home, Rosewood, the Billings family's plantation.

Rebecca paused. She waited a moment…to give time, for her words to "sink-in". Then she continued; "When it became evident that the South was losing the war, the banks called-in…, demanded immediate payment, of the Rosewood-mortgage."

"Not only did the war cost the Billings family the loss of Rosewood, it cost us the life of my brother Jesse and ultimately…, the life of my mother…your grandmother, Margaret."

"Had it not been for the wisdom of your "Uncle Luis", who wisely…, despite Papa's explicit-directive, did not invest all, of our assets in the Confederacy…we would have lost everything."

"After your grandmother Margaret's death…, to this day I believe that she literally, died of grief—following Jesse's death, at the first battle of "Bull- Run"—the banks foreclosed on the Rosewood-mortgage.

My father, your namesake, Henry Billing, decided that we…, my father and I…, Mandy's mother Ruth, and Mandy, should go west…to relocate in "Lost Springs, Kansas".

When our little party arrived in the little town of New Franklyn Missouri, my father signed onto a large wagon train, led by the famous western- pathfinder, Captain Samuel Smith.

It was when our wagon, was separated from our 27-wagon, wagon-train, that we were attacked by five-crazed …, wild, Indians.

My father and Mandy's mother, were killed. Mandy and I, were taken-prisoner, …captive slaves, of the Comanche."

Billy, as too, was Hank…, sat mesmerized. Hank's mouth was agape.

Rebecca, seeing their reactions, suggested that they take a break, Billy and Hank. Both, almost in unison implored her …, that she should continue.

Rebecca made a swift mental decision. She would continue; however, she would not describe, in graphic-detail, the attack…, nor would she describe in detail, the multiple times that she as a captive…a female slave, was repeatedly, raped.

She would…, as well as she could manage…, tell only that which was needed, to explain why she had reacted as she did, to her son's use of the word, *"nigger"*. She would tell how Mandy had decided to remain with the Comanche…, to become, Comanche.

She would tell of her sister Mandy's—who had been given the Comanche name, *"Pretty Buffalo Hair's"*— persuaded her Comanche-Husband,

Running Eagle, to return *"Bee-Kee"* to her…, how had Mandy put it…, to return her to her *"white-world"*. And most importantly, she would answer her son's question; His most fervent… salient, question;

"Who is my father?".

"I was a "slave"! I was forced, by my Indian Slave-Master, "Stone Fist"—a fierce Comanche warrior—, to obey and to work, and work, and work, as payment for my food and shelter."

I was prodded…quirted, struck repeatedly, with a buffalo-tail-whip, …, with sticks, by an old hag whose name was Hen's Tooth, my master Stone Fist's, grandmother.

Hen's Tooth constantly berated me; called me despicable, demeaning, names…, *"Lazy Dog; Pale Wolf-Eyed Dog;"*, and other vile, names.

Those words, vile-words…as is that word *"nigger"* …, which my *baby-sister*—Mandy who was three days, younger than I, —endured being called…, every day of her life, on the Rosewood Plantation. Those vile- words are intentionally used by the slave-master, to dehumanize the slave".

A fleeting look of contrition, passed between Hank and Billy. Rebecca sighed, gathering her thoughts. Finally in a soft, steady, firm, voice…, she resumed speaking.

"I, a female-slave owned by Stone Fist…; I, as were my sister Mandy's mother Ruth…, and my sister Mandy's eleven-year-old, aunt Sadie…, owned by our family, the Billings…, and me your white-mother, owned by Stone Fist…, we were all victims of rape, by our Slave-Masters".

"The man who raped me, *"Stone Fist"*, my Comanche-Master, is…, that man … was, your *father"*.

****

Two days following the "Talk", between Himself and his parents, Hank asked for a subsequent meeting.

Billy and Rebecca, thinking that Hank wanted clarification…to obtain additional information, acceded to his request.

When the three of them assembled on the veranda, Before, either Rebecca or Billy could speak; Hank blurted out; "I want to…, I think that as a family I…we, should visit my Comanche relatives, at the reservation.

Both…; Hank's mother Rebecca, and his father Billy…, without hesitation, agreed.

In two weeks, the McCloskey family, would visit Stone Fist's mother… Hank's grandmother, Quiet One; his cousin, aunt Mandy's son, Dark -Eagle; as well as his Aunt Mandy's Comanche relatives; Gray Wolf and Little Flower, his Aunt Mandy's, adoptive parents; and Spring Blossom, Aunt Mandy's Comanche-adoptive-sister…, all of whom, was Rebecca's son Hank's, Comanche-family.

****

Chapter 5

Fort Sill, Indian Reservation
- North West Texas 1877

Gray Wolf sat waiting patiently in the outer office of Terrence Lawrence, the Reservation's resident, Indian Agent.

Earlier that morning, Swift Feet, the young Comanche brave, who worked for the agent, had informed Gray Wolf that...; "This day at noon—the time when father sun was highest in the sky—Gray Wolf, was to come to the office of *Pot-ta-wat Pervo*, the Indian Agent.

The agent opened, the door to his office and motioned, that Gray Wolf should enter.

Immediately, following Swift Feet's, departure from their lodge, Little Flower, Gray Wolf's wife, who had been seated on an old-frayed, buffalo robe, quietly, attentively listening by the cooking-pit, rose and asked;

"My husband, do you know why you have been sent for, by the "Bald-One". Is there reason, for the fear, that I now feel, in my heart..., and in my mind?"

Gray Wolf went to his wife…, his *"Bride"*, of more than thirty-five winters. "Little Flower…, he gently lifted her chin…my still fragrant…, yet not quite as slender "Little Flower", I do not know why I have been sent for, by Pot- ta-wat Pervo".

"Although I do not know the reason for the counsel…, if it was to discuss a serious matter, our Headsman, He Who Speaks To Ghosts…, would too, have been sent for.

As soon as the reason is made known to me…, after I make it known to, He Who Speaks To Ghosts…, I will then, My "Little Flower", then I will make it known to you."

****

Terrence Lawrence, the Fort Sill-Indian Agent, opened the door to his inner- office.

"Gray Wolf", thank you for meeting with me…, especially on such short- notice. Please come in…, have a seat."

Seated in the corner of the room, was the Agent's interpreter, the New Mexican Comanchero, Jorge Menendez.

Gray Wolf as he had been told to do…entered the Indian Agent's office.

When the Indian Agent had seated himself behind his desk, Gray Wolf — uncomfortably, directly in front of the Agent's desk—remained standing.

With a distinctive edge to his voice, the Indian Agent asked, once again, requested… ordered…, that Gray Wolf be seated.

Resigned…Gray Wolf complied…, Gray Wolf, sat.

Terrence picked-up a sheet of paper from his desk. Silently, for the third time, he reread the document. Then he read aloud, the document to Gray Wolf.

From: Bureau of Indian Affairs

The prominent, Kansas-Politically-Active McCloskey family, avid supporters of President Grant's "Peace Policy", have requested permission for their family, to visit, the Fort Sill Indian Reservation.

Specifically, the family is requesting, permission to "Spend the Day", with ostensibly, their "Comanche relatives", the family of Gray Wolf and his wife, Little Flower".

The Commissioner of Indian Affairs, would greatly appreciate, your
cooperation, in your granting, and facilitating, the McCloskey's request.

Sincerely,

Oliver P. Simpson
(Secretary to: Ezra A. Hayt,
Commissioner of Indian Affairs)

Indian Agent Terrence Lawrence, removed his "pince-nez-spectacles", and deliberately—still holding the document in his hand—gently, deliberately, placed his spectacles, onto his desk. He then looked, quizzically, at Gray Wolf.

Neither man spoke. After an awkward silence, the agent spoke; "Gray Wolf…my friend…, Gray Wolf, do you know—he glanced down at the document on his desk—do you know these people…this ah, ah, McCloskey family. Do you know them? If so…, what are they…, to you?"

For what to the Indian agent, was an interminable period of silence…, Gray Wolf, apparently deep in thought…, finally spoke.

Just as Terrence was about to insist…insist, that Gray Wolf respond…, it was then, that the veteran Comanche warrior, Gray Wolf—his voice strong and steady—, began to speak…to answer, his questions.

"This many summers past—he held-up his right hand, his thumb folded across his palm, five fingers extended. Gray Wolf then opened and closed his fist, three times—my son Running Eagle and his friend Stone Fist, brought to our village, two captive-girls; one black, one white."

"My son, Running Eagle, was the leader of the small group—he held up four fingers—of young warriors, gave the captive-black girl, to my woman, his mother…, Little Flower. My son's friend Stone Fist, gave the captive-white girl, to his widowed mother, Quiet One".

"The captive-black girl, "*Mahn-dee*", who was at first our slave—because of her tireless-work, and her acceptance of the ways of the Comanche, our ways—became our adopted-daughter".

"Our daughter…, the black-one, "*Mahn-dee*", was given by me—because her hair reminded me of the woolly-hair of the buffalo—the Comanche name *"Nananisuyake Ta?Si?Woo? Tso?Yaa"*, which in the talk of the People, means, "Pretty Buffalo Hair".

"The captive-white girl, that Pretty Buffalo Hair ..., my black-daughter, said was her white-sister, *"Bee-kee"* ..., the white girl was given by Stone fist, to his mother, Quiet One."

"It is my thought that Stone Fist's grandmother, Hen's Tooth, gave the sniffling white girl *"Bee-kee"*, the name *"Eebi Tseena Puis"*, which in the talk of the People, means, "Blue Wolf Eyes".

Gray Wolf was surprised. When *"Pot-ta-wat Pervo"*, had initially demanded of him, an explanation..., an explanation as to why, "The Great White Father", had ordered that he, Gray Wolf, greet and host, this white-family.

Gray Wolf had thought they he had heard in the agent's voice, anger..., annoyance. Yet, not once, Gray Wolf thought—not once, had *"Pot-ta-wat Pervo"*, the Indian Agent, interrupted his "long-talk". In fact, the bald- white-man, seemed to him..., to be totally engrossed, with his words.

Terrence Lawrence was indeed, "engrossed", fascinated by Gray Wolf's lengthy-narration.

Growing-up, a white-man..., more importantly, growing up, a member of the Religious Society of Friends (*Quakers*), Terrence had heard myriad stories..., from white-men, many supposedly-factual, accounts, of the fate..., the atrocities, inflicted upon any white-woman, taken captive by the *"Godless"*, savage, heathen, Indians.

This was the very first time that Terrence had heard, a first-hand— nonchalantly, dispassionately given—what he believed to be, an actually truthful account, of such an event.

Terrence did not have any reason not to believe..., but indeed, every reason to believe, that what was being told to him by Gray Wolf, an Indian..., a man, who he knew to be, both honorable and truthful about his tribe's, …, his family's, treatment, of their, female-captive, to be accurate, to be…, to be the truth.

Terrence stood. He walked over to Gray Wolf; "My friend, I know that you are a man of honor."

"As a man of honor, you may feel it your duty to inform your friend, the Headsman of the Kutsueka-Comanche, He Who Speaks To Ghosts, of the impending visit of the *"White-Family"*.

"This, that I ask of you, is to protect you and your family, from being thought of as being in-league… of colluding, with the white-man."

Gray Wolf looked confused. For the first at this meeting, Gray Wolf looked to the New Mexican interpreter… Jorge Menendez, the third man in the room, the interpreter, who had remained silent, during the meeting.

Gray Wolf asked; "What is the meaning these words; "being *in-league-colluding?*"

Mendez responded; "What them words…, what they mean, is that you ain't friends…, that you ain't being work'n with the whites…, you know…like the Comanche and Kiowa, be's."

Gray Wolf grunted, acknowledging that he understood. He turned to the Indian Agent, who was now once again, seated behind his desk.

"Pot-ta-wat Pervo", I cannot keep from my Chief…, my friend, He Who Speaks To Ghosts, news of the visit to our village, of this "White-Family".

"I cannot keep from my Chief…, my friend, He Who Speaks To Ghosts, that this visit came to be…because of the wishes of our Great White Father."

Terrence grimaced. He looked directly, intently, at Gray Wolf. Gray Wolf's expression was that of determined, stoicism. Gray Wolf did not..., flinch.

Terrence broke eye-contact; he sighed, picked-up the letter-opener from his desk and deep in thought, holding the "tail-end" of instrument, he began to rapidly tap his desk.

The Indian agent laid the letter-opener on the desk. His eyes returned to those of Gray Wolf; "Very well then. Gray Wolf, I respect your integrity and your honesty."

"I therefore, I propose a compromise; I will send for your chief. I will tell Chief He Who Speaks To Ghosts..., in your presence, the impending visit to your home..., by the McCloskey Family."

****

Turtle's Pace—whose name and gait, was the total antithesis of that of his lifelong friend Swift Feet—teasingly, chimed in; "It is an honor Swift Feet, to spend time, with one as busy as you. One who helps... labors for, and is so close, to our jailor, Pot-ta-wat Pervo".

Swift Feet either ignored...or was oblivious, to the sarcasm...the resentment in Turtle's Pace's voice.

Leaning over...panting, attempting to catch his breath, Swift Feet, with one hand on his knee...the other raised, began to speak; "Chief He Who Speaks To Ghosts and...pointing the index finger of his raised hand at Dark Eagle, your grandfather, Gray Wolf, have been summoned to the lodge of Pot-ta- wat Pervo".

Neither Dark Eagle, nor did Turtles Pace, appear to be alarmed or concerned by their friends' pronouncement.

However, the impish, mirthful, smile that had been on the face of Owl Face, had vanished. It had been replaced by a sudden look of panic… of fear.

Dark Eagle and Turtles Feet—at the same instant—had both seen the sudden change in the demeanor, of Owl Face.

Dark Eagle—who at the prepubescent age of 12, was the youngest member of their group—despite his young age, and because of his not having obtained his personal medicine, from a benevolent member of the spirit world…the personal medicine needed, before one was eligible for "Warrior" status in the band—because of his frequently exhibited youthful… yet insightful, exuberant-maturity, "born-leadership" abilities, was the unofficial leader, of this small enclave of friends.

Dark Eagle placed his hand on the suddenly, tremulous, shoulder of Owl Face—the slightly less bellicose—newest member of the band's Warrior- Society.

Owl Face quickly regained his composure.

Dark Eagle asked; "Swift Feet, do you know for what purpose, the Great White Father's agent, "Pot-ta-wat Pervo", summoned Chief He Who Speaks To Ghosts, and Gray Wolf, to his lodge?

Swift Feet, with a worried, puzzled, expression on his face, shrugged; "I do not know of what they spoke".

Swift Feet too, had seen the unexpected, sudden change in their friend, Owl Face.

Dark Eagle was the first to speak; "Owl Face…why do you show alarm at the news that Pot-ta-wat Pervo, sent for and now sits, in council with Chief He Who Speaks To Ghosts, and my grandfather, Gray Wolf?"

Owl Face told of the previous night's raid…his first foray, as a novice-warrior…an actual member, of a raiding-party.

He told of the cattle and the chickens that they had taken from the white settler's ranch.

Owl Face told of Crooked Eye, the leader of the raiding party's rapid orders to return to the reservation, after he had been told by Spotted Horse, the warrior who had been detailed as the raiding party's rear-guard… that many white soldiers… following the soldier's Tonkawa scout, were in pursuit.

Dark Eagle asked; "Were the war whoops that we heard last night… were they being made by your returning raiding-party?"

Owl Face nodded his head.

Dark Eagle, a youth who had seen but twelve summers, without uttering another word, turned and ran to the lodge of Gray Wolf…to the lodge of his grandfather.

****

Office of the Fort Sill Reservation – Indian Agent July ?, 1877 (12:55 PM)

When the two leaders of the Kutsueka-Comanches entered his office, the Indian Agent saw in their faces, both wonder and awe. As Terrence had anticipated, the size, the furnishings…, the trappings of his office, appeared to being having the effect, that he had hoped.

Both Chief He Who Speaks To Ghosts, and Gray Wolf—the elderly warrior that Terrence known to be a respected advisor to the chief, he thought, were impressed at the size— if not by the opulence and intended, authoritative, majesty—of the room.

The impressive trapping of the office of Indian Agent—the large oakwood desk; the flag of the Bureau of Indian Affairs; and the flag of the United

States of America—that stood erect in on the floor, framing a large painting of Ulysses S. Grant, President of the United States of America.

This was the very first time, since their arrival at the reservation, that these two Comanche leaders had actually been in the Indian Agent's inner-office.

In the past—out of conscience design—Terrence had deliberately met with He Who Speaks To Ghosts and with Gray Wolf, either at the Chief's 's lodge, or in the small anteroom that led to his office.

Terrence's reasoning for avoiding his office for the holding of *"Pow Wows"*, to discuss what he considered at most…to be minor, mostly trivial, issues, in his office, and to instead, hold *"Pow Wows"*, in the lodges of the Indians, was Terrence's attempt to show respect, and to acknowledge the Comanche-Culture.

It was because of the gravity of this meeting…the gravity of what he had to impart to these honorable, men these leaders, of an honorable "People", that Terrence had chosen his office…this room, this bastion…, this blatant, overt display of the White-Man's power, and authority, to deliver this life-altering message, to the Comanche leaders.

After many hours of thought and contemplation, Terrence had decided that this office…the office of the Resident, Indian Agent—empowered by president Grant's "Indian Peace-Policy", bestowing upon him the authority to act as the Governor, the Legislature, the Judiciary, and the Sheriff, for the Comanche Agency, at the Fort Sill Indian Reservation, his office—was the correct…the only appropriate venue, for this meeting.

****

The Indian Agent sat in his solid-oak, swivel-chair, behind his desk. He was fidgeting, uncomfortably, studying the faces of his guests, Chief He Who Speaks To Ghosts and Gray Wolf.

Although Terrence had become simi-literate…just marginally conversant, in his ability to speak, and in his understanding of the Comanche language—because of the importance of this meeting, the Indian Agent had asked Jorge, Benito Menendez, a fifty-year-old, New Mexican Comanchero, one of the few, non-Indian, men at Fort Sill, who for more than two decades, had traded with the Comanche and was fluent in the language of the Comanche—to sit-in, and if needed… to serve as an interpreter.

Two wicker-chairs had been placed approximately three feet, in front of the Indian Agent's desk.

Jorge Menendez was seated in a straight-back chair, which had been strategically placed at the end of Terrence's desk. The interpreter's chair was at an angle, which allowed the ageing Comanchero, to see and to speak if needed, to both the Indian Agent, and as well, to the two Comanches.

The Fort Sill Indian Agent looked up and gestured, indicating that—the two, still standing Comanches, be seated.

He Who Speaks To Ghosts sat. Gray Wolf remained standing. Gray Wolf…with an expressionless face, looked to his friend…his chief. He Who Speaks To Ghosts, nodded his head. Gray Wolf sat.

Prior to their coming to this meeting…, before the rising of Father-Sun, Gray Wolf and He Who Speaks To Ghosts, had met to prepare for this sudden, unexpected summons, to meet with *"Pot-ta-wat Pervo"*.

While both Comanche-Leaders were grateful for the Indian Agent's actions—his preventing the soldiers, who were in hot pursuit of last night's raiding-party, from entering the reservation—the two Comanche leaders, both believed that there would be some sort of retribution…a price to pay for *"Pot-ta-wat Pervo"* intervention.

The two Comanche Leaders, had concluded that the events of last night…the raid on the white-settler's ranch, was the reason for their being summoned to meet with the Indian Agent.

After several hours of discussion, He Who Speaks To Ghosts and Gray Wolf, had decided to explain to "Pot-ta-wat Pervo", the circumstances which had led to some of their young men's raid on the white-settler's ranches.

He Who Speaks to Ghosts stood; *"Pot-ta-wat Pervo… I would speak"*.

At the sound of the chief's voice, the eyes of the Indian Agent, shifted from the document that he had been reading, to those of stately…now standing, leader of the Comanches.

Terrence cleared his throat; "Chief He Who Speaks To Ghosts…I welcome your words…please, speak"

The leader of the Kutsueka Comanches, stood and began to speak;

"The food…, the blankets, the horses, and guns promised to us by the Great White Father, have not been delivered as promised. When food is given…it is spoiled. If blankets are given, they are thin, worn-out. Our hungry women and children wrapped in the worn-out blankets, shiver and shake in the cold."

"These are the reasons that some of our young men…our warriors raid the ranches of the Tejanos."

"It is the duty…the purpose, of the warrior to provide food, shelter, clothing…animal-skins, for their women and children. Our warriors feel shame. If they cannot do this…, if they cannot feed and protect their families, they feel that they are not warriors…they are not men… they are not Comanche.

Instead of responding to the words of He Who Speaks To Ghosts, The Indian Agent picked-up from his desk and silently, reread, the embossed paper.

Then…as if he had not heard the words of the chief, Terrence…his head bowed, began to speak;

"Chief He Who Speaks To Ghosts…Gray Wolf, I asked that you…, two of the most respected of the Comanche, meet with me, so that I could tell you this…he raised the paper that he had read and read, and reread, above his head. The thoughts, the words…the commands, of the Great White Father, President Grant".

Instead of reading the dry legalistic text of the document, Terrence opted to—in his own words —state the essence of the Bureau of Indian Affairs directive.

Terrence took a deep-breath, and began to speak; "Many of the Great White Fathers' people are angry with the Comanche."

"The white settlers have asked…they have petitioned and pleaded, that our Warrior-Chief, President Grant, unleash the blue-coat soldiers—with their awesome firesticks that spit-out hundreds of bullets, before the need to reload, and their thunder-cannon, that hurls huge iron-balls, capable of collapsing your lodges—against the Comanche."
"They…the white settlers, want the Great White Father, to destroy…to annihilate the Comanche."

With looks of confusion on their faces…both He Who Speaks To Ghosts, and Gray Wolf turned to each other.

Gray Wolf was the first to speak; *"Pot-ta-wat Pervo"*, *AH- KNEEL-AH- LATE*? what means this word? Do you speak of our defeat in battle?"

He Who Speaks To Ghosts spoke; "I too do not know this word white-man word, *AH-KNEEL-AH-LATE*. What does it mean?

Before Terrence could respond, the New Mexican-Comanchero, interpreter Jorge Menendez joined the discussion.

"What that word ANNIHILATE means, is that ifin you don't do like they says…the white folks wants ta kill each and every Comanche. Every last one of you".

"Kill all the men, all the women, and each and every Comanche child. They wants to do to the Comanche, just like what they dun dun ta da Buffla."

Terrence's remained silent…close-mouthed. His immediate thought, had been to object to Jorge's harsh words. However, when he saw that the bewilderment, in the eyes of He Who Speaks To Ghosts, had been replaced by looks of shock and horror, the Indian Agent decided not to rebut, the words of his interpreter.

                                    Precious In His Sight

After an awkward moment of silence, Terrence stood and began to speak; "The great Warrior-Chief, President Grant, wishes nothing but peace and happiness for the Comanche. He wants you, the Comanche… his children, to thrive and to prosper".

"President Grant, our Great White-Father, believes that in order for the Comanche…for his children to thrive and prosper…to survive as a People, in the White-Man's world, the Comanche must learn the white-man's talk.

"The Comanche must abandon his superstitious customs and rituals. The Comanche must learn and speak, the white man's-talk"
"You must…but of far more importance, your children and your children's children, must learn and acquire, the white-man's skill at planting and harvesting crops. Your children and your children's children, must learn and become proficient, in the many trades needed to survive and prosper, in the white-man's world".

"These things can be best achieved, by having your children and your children's children, learn these skills and learn to understand, and to speak, the white-man's language."

Once again Terrence read from the document; "Therefore, by order of the Commissioner of Indian Affairs, all Reservation-Children, between the ages of five and fifteen, are to be transported to, and be boarded at, one of the numerous, recently created, Indian Residential Technical-Vocational Schools, established by the United States Bureau of Indian Affairs."

Terrence folded the paper, lowered his head and slowly, returned to his chair.

"Pot-ta-wat Pervo", was intently looking for clues; attempting to read the facial expressions of these two prominent, stoic, Comanche Leaders.

Terrence was looking for clues as to these men's reaction to his having "*Lain Down the Law*…the Federal-Law that mandated, the removal… the separation…, of their children from their families, their homes…, from their heritage".

In the eyes of the Holy Man…, the Shaman, Chief He Who Speaks To Ghosts, Terrence saw sorrow, defeat, and resignation.

In contrast, in the smoldering-eyes of Gray Wolf, the veteran warrior, the Chief's confidant and advisor, "*Pot-ta-wat Pervo*" saw anger, resentment, and defiance.

<u>Fort Sill Indian Reservation-Lodge of Gray Wolf-July ?, 1877 (12:55 PM)</u>

Gray Wolf was seated on the floor of the teepee, near one of the few remaining, buffalo-hide couches left, in the village.

The bowl of rabbit-stew, that Little Flower had placed before him upon his return from his and Chief He Who Speaks To Ghosts' meeting with "Pot-ta- wat Pervo", was untouched.

While stew, flavored with the meat of a scrawny-rabbit, did not stir in her husband, the digestive juices that a bowl of buffalo-stew would have, Little Flower could not help being concerned with her husband's uncharacteristic, loss of appetite, and with Gray Wolf's moody silence.

"My husband, what is it that has caused your prolonged silence…your loss of interest in the food …she pointed to the untouched bowl of stew, that I have placed before you?

My husband, does something trouble you?

With his left hand, Gray Wolf pushed the now cold meal…, the rabbit-stew, to the extreme edge of the thin, faded, government-issued blanket.

Gray Wolf rose, walked over to the *buffalo-hide couche, and sat. He patted a spot next to him; "Little Flower, I would speak with you"*.

Little Flower, slowly…concern, worry-lines etched into her forehead, sat beside her husband.

****

Gray Wolf told to his wife— the matriarch of the expanded family of Gray Wolf— of his and He Who Speaks To Ghosts' meeting, with the Reservation's Indian Agent.

Gray Wolf told of last night, his and He Who Speaks To Ghosts', having heard the faint sound of the *"Battle-Cry"* of the horse-soldiers.

He shared with Little Flower, the dread that both he and their Chief, He Who Speaks To Ghosts, associated with that sound.

Gray Wolf explained that that strident sound…, the musical *"Battle-Cry"* of the horse-soldiers, was heard at Sand-Creek, by Chief Black Kettle and by Chief Niwot, just before their Cheyenne and Arapaho village, was attacked and destroyed, by the horse-soldiers.

Little Flower, as her husband of more than twenty-winters, was speaking— despite the anguish and sorrow, that she heard in his voice—, Little Flower remained silent.

While the words that Gray Wolf was saying were alarming, those words…, or similar words, had been spoken many times in the past.

Little Flower, as had all Comanches, over the years—for centuries, had heard shouted the "Battle Cry" of their enemies; the Pawnee, the Apache, the Tonkawa, the Ute—prior to and/or, during attacks by these and other enemies, of the "People".

For centuries, the "People" had been subjected to; won, lost, and survived, attacks by their enemies.

Other than the inevitable loss of Comanche-lives, why had this council with "Pot-ta-wat Pervo", caused in Gray Wolf, such apparent anguish, dread, and concern?

Little Flower placed her hand on Gray Wolf's shoulder and gave her husband, what she intended to be, a reassuring squeeze.

Infrequently, throughout the long-history of the Comanche Nation, the enemies of the "People", had surprised and defeated the "People's" warriors, resulting in the loss of many Comanche lives.

Despite these rare, occasional defeats…these losses of many Comanche lives, the Comanche Nation… the *"People"*, always survived.

"My husband is it because our warriors no longer have sufficient weapons to defend the "People"; sufficient weapons to protect Comanche women and children…is this the cause of your despair?"

Gray Wolf placed his hand over Little Flower's, he stood, and looked into her eyes; "My wife, it is not defeat by an enemy that frightens me. It is the ANNILATION of the Comanche, by the White-Man, that I fear."

When I asked *"Pot-ta-wat Pervo"* the meaning of this word ANNILATION, before the Bald-One could answer; the Tejano-Comanchero Jorge, told me the meaning of ANNILATION. It means the killing of not a few…not of many…, but the killing of all Comanches; Men; Women; and Children.

The word ANNILATION means the destruction…the end of the Comanche!

ANNILATION; Little Flower remembered hearing that word. It was a word once used by their adopted daughter, the captive black girl, Mahn-Dee…, to whom Gray Wolf had given the meaningful Comanche name, *Nananisuyake Ta? Si? Woo? Tso? Yaa"*, ("Pretty Buffalo Hair").

ANNILATION, spoken to by her, and Gray Wolf's adopted daughter, that

Pretty Buffalo Hair, when explaining her reasons for teaching her husband— their son Running Eagle—, to talk and to understand the words of the white-man, was *so that he might help to* prevent, the *"ANNILATION…the GENOCIDE" …, of the* People… the end of the Comanche.

Gray Wolf told of his, and He Who Speaks To Ghosts meeting, in the chief's lodge, immediately following their earlier meeting with *"Pot-ta-wat Pervo"*.

Gray Wolf's impassioned response, to the demands of the Indian Agent, was that the band of Kitsueka-Comanche, should leave the Reservation…should return to the plains and resume, their centuries-old-lifestyle as Nomadic Hunters…, as proud Warriors.

Chief He Who Speaks To Ghosts, did not interrupt his friend and trusted advisor's, lengthy, heated, cathartic moment.

Instead, after Gray Wolf's resentment and frustration, at the Indian Agent's instructions, had been voiced, He Who Speaks To Ghosts, passed to Gray Wolf, the Comanche Ceremonial Pipe.

Both men sat, silently smoking the pipe. Without speaking, Chief He Who Speaks To Ghosts stood; He blew smoke first to the East; then to the South, the West, then the North.

"We will do as the Great White-Father orders; We will learn and speak, the talk-of-the white-man. We will no longer seek or heed talk from the spirit world; we will no longer smoke the pipe-of-peace; we will send our children to the white-man's Indian schools."

These things we must do; If…, the *"People"*, are to survive.

****

Immediately following the council-meeting between "Pot-ta-wat Pervo"; Chief He Who Speaks To Ghosts; and Gray Wolf…, Gray Wolf returned to his lodge.

Little Flower had been patiently awaiting her husband…, Gray Wolf's return.

As the hours passed…as the anticipated "short-counsel", that had started when Father-Sun was highest in the sky— and had lasted well into the evening…, Father-Sun, was now beginning to slip into the darkness, of the night sky, —Little Flower's disquietude…, her anxiety had heightened.

For the third time, she heated the rabbit-stew that had gone cold, as she anxiously, awaited, the return of her husband.

When Gray Wolf entered their lodge, an audible sigh of relief sprang forth from Little Flower's lips.

She managed to put-forth a wry-smile; "My husband, your short-counsel meeting with "Pot-ta-wat Pervo", has consumed more time than expected.

What do you bring back from the counsel, good..., or is it bad, news?

Gray Wolf walked over to the tripod, from which was suspended, the pot from which emanated the mouth-watering aroma, of what he thought to have been, his dinner.

Gray Wolf, nonchalantly, stuck his index finger into the surprisingly still warm, concoction.

Little Flower, relief now spreading across her lips, playfully, with the ladle that she held in her hand, lightly rapped Gray Wolf's hand.

Gray Wolf exclaimed; "Ouch woman…is that how—he held up his rabbit- stew, covered finger—is that how my forever fragrant "Little Flower", greets her ravishingly hungry old, Gray Wolf?

****

CHAPTER 7

Fort Sill Indian Reservation ["When Ponies Shed Their Hair"], 1877]

William, Rebecca, *"Hank"* and Mandy *("M-Cubed")*, the McCloskey Family, were all seated in the two rows, of the fort's multi-passenger, *"Dignitaries"*, carriages.

Indian Agent-Terrence Lawrence, and six black troopers, "Buffalo-Soldiers, three on either side of the carriage, led by the fort's military Commanding Officer, Colonel Reynold McKenzie, flanked the carriage.

Both Hank and his little-sister, *"M-Cubed",* were fascinated by the sight and sounds of the Comanche-Village.

For some inexplicable reason…, Rebecca, holding her husband Billy's hand—was puzzled.

To Rebecca, who had spent almost a year livening among the Comanche, the sounds of dogs yapping at the arrival of strangers, was familiar… yet in still, something…something was missing.

Then it struck her…, the children…, where are the children?

****

Fifteen minutes prior to the "McCloskey's" leaving Pot-ta-wat Pervo, the Indian Agent's office; Swift Feet the Agent's teenage "porter-runner", who was incidentally, Dark Eagle's (Gray Wolf's Grandson's friend), had sprinted ahead of the "caravan", to alert Gray Wolf of their arrival.

Gray Wolf thanked the youth. Then he requested that he… Swift Feet; "Go to the lodge of Quiet One, the white-boy's grandmother. Tell Quiet One that her grandson…, the son of Stone Fist…, is here, among the Comanche."

"Tell Quiet One, to come to the lodge of Gray Wolf".

Gray Wolf, his wife Little Flower, and their daughter Spring Blossom, stood rigidly in front of their teepee.

The McCloskey Family, accompanied by Terrence Lawrence, the Indian- Agent, escorted by the small detachment of soldiers…, reigned in their mounts, approximately, twenty feet, in front of the Lodge, of Gray Wolf.

The Indian Agent, followed by the McCloskeys, walked toward Gray Wolf.

Rebecca removed her hand from that of her husband's…, and rushed forward, and in the tongue of the Comanche, spoke;

"Little Flower…, Quiet One, it is I, *"Eebi Tseena Puis"*, *"Pale Blue Wolf Eyes"*. I…, we have come with my son…she then looked directly at Quiet One…, with your grandson…, *huutisi*…, the son of Stone Fist."

<hr>

We have come to visit my sister *Ta?Si?Woo? Tso?Yaa, Nananisuyake Ta?Si?Woo? Tso?Yaa, Pretty Buffalo Hair's*, my black sister…*Mahn-dee, Mahn-dee's* …, we have come to visit, our Comanche family".

Hank, understanding but a few of the words spewing forth from his mother's lips, did in fact, immediately recognized the word *"huutisi"*, which his mother had previously told him, in Comanche, meant grandmother.

Impulsively, Hank walked over to Quite One; Stood in front of her, and in a halting voice, repeated the sentence that his mother, Rebecca, had taught him; *"Aho…, huutisi…,* I am Hank. (Hello grandmother, I am Hank.")

Quiet One, who had been standing…, as her name implied; stood, silent- rigid, not speaking. Then a smile began to spread across her face. Quiet One, opened her arms; Hank and his one and only, living *"huutisi"*, embraced.

Simultaneously, Rebecca, as did Billy, let out their breath…, they both, smiled.

****

Gray Wolf pulled-back, the flap that allowed entrance to his lodge. Rebecca turned to the Indian Agent; "Mr. Lawrence, if you don't mind…, my family and I, would like to visit with our "Comanche relatives, alone."

Terrence, eyes shifted to look at Colonel McKenzie, who was vigorously— from side to side —shaking his head.

The Indian Agent spoke: "One moment…, please excuse me Mrs. McCloskey."

Terrence walked over to the Colonel. The two men…, two senior officials, representing the United States Government, held a brief, intense, whispered conversation.

The Indian Agent walked back to Rebecca. "I'm sorry Mam. The colonel says that he is responsible for your…, your family's safety. In essence what he insists…is that, while we are in this Indian-village, he cannot allow you and your family, to be out of his sight".

Rebecca clinched her jaw, and in a calm…, steely, voice said; "Very well…, thank you, agent Terrence".

Then, raising the volume of her voice, so that it could be clearly heard by the Colonel, she added. "I shall notify, General Sherman, and my Uncle Luis Frazier, who I am sure will tell his friend, President Grant, that the military, denied us…, prevented, our spending a few moments alone, visiting our Comanche relatives."

Rebecca turned and rejoined, the McCloskey-Comanche, family reunion.

While listening to Quiet One, her former Slave-Master, Rebecca—out of the corner of her eye—saw the Indian Agent and Colonel McKenzie, in an animated conversation.

As it became obvious to her that the Indian Agent and the Colonel, had concluded their heated-discussion, Rebecca quickly, returned her full attention to Quiet One…, her son, Henry Billings II, Luis McCloskey's, paternal grandmother.

Terrence walked over to the group, and lightly tapped Rebecca' shoulder.

"Mrs. McCloskey, the Colonel has reconsidered. He will permit…, he will give your family twenty-minutes alone, in the lodge of Gray Wolf, provided that I, the Fort Sill - Indian Agent…, the government's representative…, the colonel insists, that I be present…, at this family-reunion.

****

The McCloskey family…, Rebecca, with "M-Cubed" cradled in her right arm, while holding the hand of, her husband Billy and her son Hank, who was holding the hand of Quiet One his *huutisi*, and the Indian Agent, Terrence Lawrence, entered the lodge of Gray Wolf.

Gray Wolf was seated on a worn buffalo-robe-couch. His wife, Little Flower and Hank's paternal grandmother, Quiet One, stood behind the stately, Comanche Brave.

Rebecca was attempting to extricate her three-year-old daughter—who had shyly sought the protection of her mother, by engulfing herself in the folds of Rebecca's dress.

Little Flower stepped around, from behind Gray Wolf, bent down…, and in a gentle, soothing voice, spoke; "Who do we have here? Who is this cute, shy one…with the delightful dimples of her mother …, and the dimples of her mother's black sister, Pretty Buffalo Hair?

Rebecca extricated her daughter from the folds of her dress. She picked her up. "Mandy, this lady…, this lady is the Comanche-mother of my sister…, your Aunt Mandy.

Little Flower, although she did not understand much of the talk of the white- man—from her time, with her adopted daughter *Mahn-dee*, who her husband Gray Wolf, gave the name Pretty Buffalo Hair—Little

Flower understood the meaning of those words, spoke by *"Bee-Kee"*; the white sister of her beloved, adopted black-daughter, *Mahn-dee*.

"Baby-Mandy" …, *"M-Cubed"*…, *"Mahn-dee"*, shyly extended her arms…toward Little Flower. Little Flower with open arms, welcomed the niece of her black-daughter, Pretty Buffalo Hair.

Little Flower…, rocking the little girl in her arms…repeatedly spoke the one white man's word, that she loved and truly cherished …, *"Mahn-dee"*…, *"Mahn-dee"*.

Rebecca turned, and spoke to Gray Wolf; "When we entered the village, I found it odd… strange, the absence of the children. I had anticipated hearing their excited-voices, announcing…, acknowledging our arrival."

An awkward silence, fell upon those in the lodge of Gray Wolf. No one spoke.

Finally, realizing that "the clock" was ticking…that they were losing valuable time , allotted to them by the colonel…, time alone with the Comanches, Rebecca shifted her attention. She went directly to Little Flower and asked:

"Little Flower where are the children?"

As if she was seeking permission to speak…, Little Flower looked to her husband, Gray Wolf.

Then not waiting for his permission, in a tremulous, subdued, voice and unable to prevent tears from forming in her eyes, Little Flower spoke;

"All of the children…, *except* those — she made a fist of her right-hand; opened her fist, and extended four fingers— those who had not yet reached"

— she made a fist…then opened her hand, extending all five fingers, including her thumb, she slowly…, methodically, opened and closed her fist, three times— "these many winters, were taken by the reservation-police, put on the Iron-horse, and sent toward the rising Sun …, sent to school."

At the request of Chief, He Who-Speaks-To Ghosts, and as a courtesy to the chief's advisor Gray Wolf, Terrence Lawrence, the Fort Sill Reservation's Indian Agent, had agreed to **Not**, separate from each other…, the grand- children of Gray Wolf and Little Flower.

The sounds of children that usually emanated from the lodges of the Kutsueka-Comanches, had been reduced from the raucous sounds of healthy, happy children…, to the all too frequent plaintive plea of the little-ones— the three- and four-year-olds, that where not subjected to mandatory removal to, Indian Residential Industrial-Vocational Schools— *Where are my brothers and sisters…; Where are my brothers and sisters?*

Billy and Hank, stood silently behind Rebecca…, awaiting her translation of Little Flower's, sorrowful…, gut-wrenching, words.

Rebecca's initial reaction was that of shock…, of disbelieve. She turned to Billy.

"Little Flower says that the reservation-police, took all of the children; ages four through fifteen, and sent them by train, to schools in the East."

Without waiting to hear a response from either her husband or from her fourteen-year-old son, Rebecca bolted from the lodge.

Colonel McKenzie, immediately, upon seeing the enraged white-woman running from the lodge, fumbled for, and hastily removed his watch from his pocket. The colonel noted that…, but twelve of the allotted twenty-minutes, had passed.

His initial thought was; *"Something's gone wrong! I knew it...I should have never left those people alone with these savages."*

The colonel unholstered his revolver, he turned...raised the pistol over his head, and signaled that the troopers, should advance.

The Indian Agent—a man of *"Peace"*, Terrence Lawrence, quickly responded. He threw his hands into the air, shouting and giving the universal signal to; **STOP..., STOP! STOP!!**

The Indian Agent stepped between the Colonel, and the obviously upset..., Mrs. Rebecca McCloskey.

"Mrs. McCloskey, what's wrong..., is everyone okay?" Colonel McKenzie, with four troopers..., their rifles cocked, had followed their Commanding Officer.

Rebecca, not wanting to precipitate a "massacre", raised her hands, as the Indian Agent had done..., into the air, and shouted; "Stop, everyone is fine..., we're all fine".

Rebecca and Colonel McKenzie, were both rapidly advancing—from opposite directions— upon, the Indian Agent. When they reached Terrence, they both stopped.

The realization that in her haste, to confront the Indian Agent, and the Fort Sill Commandant—the terrifying thought that she had nearly caused a riot— served to mollify..., to calm the incensed, *"Eebi Tseena Puis"* (Rebecca McCloskey).

By waving his hand..., the hand that seconds ago, held his fully-loaded, cocked service-revolver, Colonel McKenzie signaled to his soldiers, that they should halt.

The black-sergeant, leading his squad of "Buffalo Soldiers", turned and raised his hand. His troopers, relief showing on their faces, lowered the hammers of their carbines, and *"stood-down"*.

****

Following the "near-riot", to the relief of all; The Comanches; The Indian Agent; Colonel McKenzie; and the McCloskey family…, their visit to the Comanche village was concluded.

When the McCloskeys were walking back toward the "Dignitaries Carriage" Rebecca abruptly stopped. She motioned to Billy that the family should proceed…, that she would be, but a moment. Rebecca turned and hurriedly, walked back to Little Flower, Spring Blossom, Quiet One, and Gray Wolf.

When she reached the Comanches, she took Little Flower's hands, into her own…, "I will find-out where your children have been taken. I promise you, *mother* this…, I promise."

Tears welled-up in both Little Flower's and Rebecca's eyes. *"Eebi Tseena Puis"*, *(Pale Blue Wolf Eyes)* Rebecca, joined her McCloskey, family, in the Fort Sill-Dignitaries Carriage.

****

Rebecca and her husband Billy, were seated in the Indian Agent's office.

Little Mandy *(M-Cubed)*, was seated…, squirming, on her mother' s lap.

Henry (Hank) McCloskey, had asked, and had been given permission by the colonel, to for fifteen minutes, "roam-around" …, to explore non-restricted areas of the fort.

Rebecca, with a pleading look in her eyes, looked to Billy; lifted *"M-Cubed"*, and extending her arms... proffered their fidgeting..., squirming toddler, towards her husband.

Billy accepted his wife's offering. "Come on squirt, let's give Mommy a little alone-time, with Mr. Lawrence."

With Billy, holding "Little-Mandy's hand..., father and daughter left the office.

While he had not, been overly enthused about the McCloskey's visiting the reservation, the resident Indian Agent, having no other choice... had reluctantly, acquiesced.

Frankly, after having read the Commissioner of Indian Affairs', directive..., although he most certainly, was not a politician, Terrence Lawrence, had astutely realized..., accepted the fact, that the *"Politically-Connected"* family's visit, would be an inevitable, occurrence.

The near-riot, that Mrs. McCloskey had precipitated, caused this "man-of- peace", to question his decision to; not *"rock-the boat"*.

Terrence's reason...his motivation, for joining the Bureau of Indian Affairs...for accepting the position of Fort Sill -Indian Agent, was to protect the lives of his charges..., the Indian-inhabitants, of the Fort Sill-Indian Reservation.

After she and the Indian Agent were alone, Rebecca, attempting to control her temper..., in a calm incredulous-voice, laced with derision, spoke; "Agent Lawrence, is it true..., did the agency-policemen..., men who report directly to you, did they..., at your direction, remove and relocate the village's children?"

Despite his life-long adherence to the teachings of the Religious Society of Friends (*Quakers*) …, and a life of adherence to the pacifist practices and beliefs of his faith, Terrence Lawrence—sitting across from this, nearly hysterical, impassioned, indignant, woman…, Terrence Lawrence was "tempted", really tempted, to…, raise his voice.

Afraid that he might not be able to control the volume of his voice, Terrence instead, silently, reached into the middle-draw of his desk, and extracted an official-looking document.

Terrence slid the paper across his desk. Rebecca picked-up the paper, and began to read the document;

From: Bureau of Indian Affairs

In fulfillment of the United States' Governments' goal to eradicate poverty and, ignorance of the Indian Population, through the process of assimilation of the Indian(s) into mainstream American culture, by act of Congress;

Hereby authorize and mandate, the removal of Indian children, between the ages of four through fifteen from reservations, and the subsequent transport of said children, to the numerous "Indian Residential Vocational- Industrial Schools", situated within the United States of America.

Indian Agents are directed to assist in the implementation, and the success of this initiative. The Indian Agent(s) shall:

1. *Instruct and direct; The Reservation Police in the collection and the transporting, of the children.*

a. *Parents of, and/or guardians, who fail to cooperate with this Federal Initiative, are to be informed; That until such time as families, are in compliance; Government rations, clothing, and annuities, will be withheld.*

After having read…and then reread the document, Rebecca raised her eyes, and looked into those of the Indian Agent. Though she did not ask…, Terrence Lawrence answered her unspoken question.

"Chief He Who Speaks To Ghosts…, in a meeting with his tribal Council, told them of"—the Indian Agent pointed his finger, at the document that Rebecca still held, in her now trembling hand—of that."

"Chief He Who Speaks To Ghosts, made it clear, that the survival of the Comanche…, now, and in the future, was for their children, and their children's, children…, to learn the ways of the white-man."

Rebecca folded the document, placed it on the Indian Agents desk, and rose from her chair. Without uttering a word…, her head held high, she turned and walked towards the office-door

When she reached the door…, she turned and before opening the door, in a deflated…, defeated, tone-of- voice… Rebecca Billings McCloskey (*Eebi Tseena Puis"*) said; "Good-day, sir."

****

BOOK III

Residential Vocational-Industrial School(s)

Chapter 8

Indian Residential-Vocational School - (Carlyn, Pennsylvania) October - 1877

In total, sixty-two of the Kutsueka-Comanche children, had been sent to various "Indian Residential Schools", scattered across the United States. Fifty-two, of the total of sixty-two, were sent to the Carlyn Indian Residential-Vocational School, more than 2,000 miles from their home; At the Fort Sill Indian Reservation.

****

The Carlyn, Indian Residential-Industrial-Vocational School occupied the grounds, and the facilities, of a decommissioned, abandoned, Union Army- base.

The architectural-lay-out of the school was that of typical, military-garrison; the barracks (dormitories); the communal "mess-hall"; (cafeteria); the
"Drill-Hall" (student-orientation); the parade grounds; (Campus Quad).

This…, the physical "military" lay-out, was considered to be ideally suited, for the *"Pratt- Method"*; For the educating, and the subsequent

"Americanization" ..., the assimilation, of America's *Indiginous peoples,* as equal-citizens, into what Pratt considered to be; the "Ideal Euro-American- Society."

****

Chapter 9

Carlyn, Indian Residential-Industrial-Vocational School - Freshmen Student-Orientation (October 1877)

Franklyn Schmidt, the recently retired army officer, was noticeably uncomfortable, in his unaccustomed-to, civilian clothing.

Prior to his resignation from the army, Lieutenant Franklyn Schmidt— had assisted Captain Richard Henry Pratt, at the *Plains Indian Prisoner of War Camp* located at Fort Marion, Florida, to successfully accomplish, what the army referred to as; *"The "breaking"* of the most hostile, and recalcitrant, of the Indian-Warriors *(Prisoners-of-War),* captured by the Army, during the Indian-Wars.

With the enthusiastic endorsement of Captain Pratt; the United States Government's Bureau of Indian Affairs, appointed Franklyn Schmidt, as the Superintendent of the Carlyn, Indian Residential-Industrial-Vocational School.

Schmidt was determined, committed to; by any means necessary, to transform…, to mold, through their total assimilation into the white-civilization—what he thought of as the still pliable— "Youth, *"The*

Young- Savages" to assimilate…, to become productive, "self-reliant" members of the American-White-Society."

Franklyn Schmidt, the Superintendent of the Carlyn, Indian Residential-Industrial-Vocational School, was a true believer, a disciple of his mentor, Captain Richard Henry Pratt's philosophy; *"Kill the Indian; While Saving the Man"*.

The ex-army officer, a twenty-five-year veteran—who during the Civil War had attained the rank of brevet-major—was exerting every bit of his will- power…, to not unbutton his stiff, high-necked, shirt-collar.

Standing next to the Superintendent, Mr. Schmidt—Franklyn hated being addressed…, by what he considered the demeaning title of Mister—was a rather stern-looking, middle-aged white woman, Miss Agnes Wallace.

For the past fifteen years, prior to her accepting the position of; Student Female-Principal-Matron, at the Carlyn, Indian-Residential Vocational School, Agnes…, Miss Wallace had been "Head Mistress" at the exclusive, "Harrisburg Finishing School-For the Refined Young Lady".

When initially, Agnes had been offered this position, at that Government school for *"Savages"*, Agnes had haughtily… but she thought, politely, declined.

However, when Agnes was told that the position would pay fifty dollars per month, with free room and board— almost twice her salary (not to mention – the free room and board) — that was her current compensation at the finishing school, Agnes Wallace, had sat aside her fixed-social and racial prejudices, and had hastily accepted the Bureau of Indian Affairs' offer; As *"Matron of Female-Students"*; and, had agreed to teach the little *"Savages"*.

The Superintendent and his female assistant—in military precision-lockstep, strode toward the center of the cavernous hall. The sounds of their hard- soled leather shoes, striking the highly polished floor, echoed throughout the building.

Dark Eagle stood—in the center of the "Drill-Hall". In each of his hands, Dark Eagle was holding, the trembling hand(s) of two of his three sisters.

"Golden-One", Dark Eagles youngest sister—who had recently entered her fifth summer and was therefore, not allowed to remain at the reservation, under the care of their grandparents, Gray Wolf and Little Flower—stood on trembling legs…, silently weeping.

"Golden-One", until last week, had been one of the children…, in the exempt group of; *"New-born–to age five"*, who were excluded from the government's mandate that;

"All Indian children, ages 5 through 15, must be removed from their families and their homes, on the Reservation(s); And must attend a government- sanctioned, *"Indian Residential-Vocational School"*.

At the age of fourteen, Dark Eagle was the oldest of the "children", from the Kutsueka-Band, of the Comanche-Nation…, and because he was the son of the mighty war chief, Stone Fist…, Dark Eagle had become the titular-leader of this contingent of the student-body.

Among this contingent of boys, in addition to the fact that Dark Eagle, was the oldest student, Dark Eagle was also the student, most comfortable speaking…, listening to and understanding the *"white mans"* talk.

When the white man and woman entered the hall, Dark Eagle reassuringly, squeezed the right hand of his sister, "Moon-Glow'", who had lived through nine- winters…, free on the plains; and the left hand of his youngest sister *"Golden-One"*, who had thus far, lived but five-summers.

Dark Eagles caught the eye of his of brother of six winters, "Under-Foot", who too, was holding the right-hand, of *"Golden-One"*, his and Dark Eagles' sister of barely, five-winters.

Dark Eagle, attempting to assess the number of "students in the Hall, slightly turned his head.

Afraid that her Big Brother was about to abandon her, with all of the strength in her small-body…, little Golden-One, pulled her hand from that of her brother "Under-Foot, and with both hands, grabbed the hand of Dark Eagle.

A piteously mournful moan, escaped from the little-girls' lips. She looked- up into the eyes of her big-brother. Dark Eagle withdrew his left hand, from that of his sister Moon-Glow. He then bent over, and scooped-up into his arms, his trembling, frightened, little-sister.

Dark Eagle bent down, and in a clear voice, that resonated in the hushed hall; these reassuring words, to his little-sister;

"Nut ʉ soyuni, nʉ?niikwiitʉmui kʉhyaarʉ tua taa Ta?ahpu, taaParukaa; hanʉ nanakuya?arʉsumu. Nʉ? naabia, Tupisibip Iʉ Kwihnai yuyuksrʉ".

Yuyukaru tue?tu nasutamʉ katʉ tamaiʉ bia samohpʉ ; su?urarʉnʉ nu; ture hpʉ; taa; Tʉ mak ʉ ma? Na?arutʉ.

("My sister, I speak to you in the tongue of the "People", of our ancestors, of the Comanche; "Do not be afraid "Golden-One". "I am here…, your brother…, Dark Eagle. I am here.)

("Be proud little-one, and remember my sister; Remember that we are the sons and daughters of our father ..., the mighty Comanche-Warrior-Chief, Stone Fist.")

Suddenly, an angry voice split the relative quiet, of the hall.

Franklyn Schmidt, the Superintendent, of the Carlyn, Indian Residential Vocational School shouted; "Who Said That?! Who is speaking that ? **"HEATHAN GIBBERISH?!"**

Dark Eagle, faced-forward. He was looking directly, into the fiery-eyes of the Superintendent, of the Carlyn, Indian Residential Vocational School.

"Young- man..., what is your name? Do you speak English?"

Golden-One buried her head—away from this strange white-man—deeper..., into the comforting-shelter of her brother's chest.

Dark Eagle nodded his head. The Superintendent, repeated his question. If you understand me..., answer my question; Do you speak English..., do you understand what I am saying to you, and if so, I want you to..., verbally, answer my question.

It was when he had used the word "verbally", that he saw, what he thought was confusion, appear in the boy's eyes.

Franklyn thought that perhaps, the boy's confused look was because, while the boy may have indeed, understood rudimentary English, perhaps he was not familiar with, the not so-commonly used word..., "verbally".

Franklyn repeated his question..., this time, he eliminated the word, "verbally".

The thirty-nine-year-old Superintendent, in halting, fractured…, yet understandable-Comanche, that he had—during his time as "Assistant Warden", at the Fort Marion Prison for Recalcitrant Indians"— picked-up, asked;

"Young- man, do you speak…, do you understand, English?

With his strong arms, cradling…, comforting his little-sister, Dark Eagle spoke. "Yes, I hear and know the meaning, of your words".

"I am Dark Eagle…, son of Sone Fist. I was taught English by my grandmother Little Flower…, who learned the white-man-talk, from her adopted black-daughter…, my mother *"Mahn-dee";* Who my grandfather Gray Wolf, gave the Comanche name; *"Pretty Buffalo Hair".*

Mentally, Franklyn Schmidt, Superintendent, of the Carlyn, Indian Residential Vocational School, relaxed.

Franklyn Schmidt, who was committed to ensuring the success, of what he believed to be his mentor…, Captain Richard Henry Pratt's vision—

"The Assimilation of America's Indiginous Native-Peoples", the Indians, into this Euro-American, Society; which in Schmidt's mind, translated to…, the turning of the *"Noble Redman",* into the *"Docile, Red/White-men".*

Franklyn felt that his efforts to successfully achieve his goal, could be assisted by… could be enhanced, with the help of this semi-literate Comanche.

Franklyn Schmidt's, immediate thought was that he may have just found his "Judas Goat". A potential Indian-student-leader, who would help lead this *"flock" of heathens",* into civilized, white-society.

Franklyn, intending to ingratiate himself with his *"Chosen-One"*—his perceived, potential *"Judas Goat"* —extended his hand…, his index-finger pointing towards the little girl.

Golden-One turned her head away from, the Superintendent's finger.

Franklyn withdrew his hand, and once again, this time in a loud, authoritarian-tone-of voice, spoke to Dark Eagle.

"Dark Eagle, you say? Did you say that your name is "Dark Eagle"? Before Dark Eagle could respond, instead of speaking directly to Dark Eagle, the Superintendent took two steps back, and waving his arm to encompass the entire assemblage, and loudly proclaimed;

"As of now, none of you are allowed to keep your Indian names". He pointed his finger at Dark Eagle. His name is no longer "Dark Eagle".

"When you are shown to your dormitories—your living spaces, you will find four-lists of acceptable, proper, names. One list of first and last names for girls; And the other, a list of first and last names, for the boys.

"You are each …boys and girls, allowed to choose a name, from the lists. You are to present, to your instructor, for his or her approval or rejection, of your chosen, new-name."

You boys, dressed as you are…, are to immediately proceed to the Male- Students Dormitory, where you will be given a proper Christion Hair-Cut. You will then, be marched back to this hall, where you will be issued Carlyn-School-Uniforms".

"My assistant, Miss Wallace, will supervise the issuance of new-uniforms, to each and every one of you."

As the Superintendent, of the Carlyn, Indian Residential Vocational School, turned to leave, the shrill, clarion, voice of Miss Wallace, could be heard to shout; "*ATTENTION*".

Ninety-six Native-American children, Comanche; Kiowa; Apache; Sioux; All with puzzled expressions on their faces, looked around, not moving, exchanged questioning-glances.

****

Chapter 10

Carlyn, Indian Residential-Industrial-Vocational School – Home of the Superintendent- (October 1877)

When Superintendent Schmidt, opened the door his two-story, cottage— which consisted of; a spacious parlor; what his wife Ingrid, referred to as a "Neat little kitchen"; and on the second floor; a "Master-bedroom"; a smaller bedroom, occupied by the Schmidt's 16-year-old daughter Sarah; Additionally, the *Superintendent's quarters*, had a room on the first floor; equipped with, "indoor-plumbing"—his wife Ingrid, with a broad, mischievous, smile on her face, was waiting to greet him.

Ingrid Schmidt, formerly, Ingrid Johansson, a broad smile, enhancing her bright blue eyes, which lite-up her face, in her lilting-Swedish accent… which Franklyn found to be absolutely enchanting, asked: "Sveet-heart… And how vuz your day… what vuz your impression of the new students?"

Franklyn offered his cheek to receive Ingrid's, still welcomed—after twenty years of marriage—soft lips on his cheek.

Ingrid assisted Franklyn in the removing of his coat. She ushered him into the parlor... opened for him, the lid of his box of cigars.

Ingrid, with her husband's coat drabbed around her arm, stepped back. "Sveet-heart, I am afraid that dinner will be delayed".

Franklyn twirled his cigar between his thumb and forefinger, he then placed the cigar under his nose, sniffed the fragrant tobacco... sighed and declared in a teasing voice, mimicking his wife's Swedish Accent; *"Sveet-heart shy is dinner de-laid?"*

Ingrid was neither offended, nor was she annoyed at Franklyn's, horrible attempt to impersonate her lingering Swedish-Accent. Ingrid knew... that he knew, that while she still had a little difficulty pronouncing a few English words... because Franklyn enjoyed... he invariably smiled, whenever she spoke, in what he called; *"her lyrical-accent"*.

"Delores'—Delores was their housekeeper-cook—*Delores 'son was not feelin' so goot. She did not come to verk today. Sarah, our almost grown-up daughter; Begged me to let her cook dinner for her pappa. Unfortunately, our "almost-grown" daughter... who refused her Mama's help, has not quite yet finished, making our dinner."*

Ingrid, walked over to the sidebar, half-filled a glass with equal quantities of water and bourbon-whiskey. With her Franklyn's drink in one hand... and a seashell-ashtray in the other, Ingrid turned and walked over to her husband.

"Sveet-heart, dinner will be de-laid." She then walked to the kitchen... to at least offer, to their teenage daughter, her help.

After accepting the drink, and the ashtray from his wife. Franklyn placed his cigar in the ashtray… kicked off his shoes, and leaned-back, into the soft cushions of his chair.

He smiled, chuckled, as he thought of his "almost-grown", daughter's efforts to please
her father; her "Old-Man" …, her "Dad".

Franklyn nodded-off, succumbing to fatigue that induced…memories of his past.

****

Chapter 10 *(cont.)*

Southeastern Colorado Territory (Sand-Creek) November 29, 1864

Lieutenant Franklyn Schmidt, the officer leading the 2nd-platoon of Company "A", an integral component of the approximately 700-man force, of the 3rd Colorado Cavalry—under the command of Colonel John Chivington—rode at the head of his platoon of mounted cavalry.

As a young, relatively inexperienced-junior, cavalry officer, the Lieutenant had eagerly anticipated participating in his first combat action against, the Cheyenne *"Dog-Soldiers"*, the military arm of the Cheyenne, the Arapahos, and the Lakota's.

While the young cavalry officer, was eager to prove himself in combat, against the vaunted, *"Dog-Soldiers"*—a society of warriors lauded for their bravery and their and lethal combat skills—, instead of the anticipated adrenalin "rush," that usually coursed through his veins before a daunting- challenge, Lieutenant Schmidt was instead, confused and troubled.

The previous night, after the conclusion of Colonel Chivington's pre-battle, discussion with his officers… in which the Colonel outlined his battle-plans, his strategy for defeating the Cheyenne warriors… the *"Dog-Soldiers"*, that the Colonel's Tonkawa Indian scouts, reported as being in the village… the *"Dog-Soldiers"* who were known to have been responsible, for most of the recent attacks and raids, on the white settlers and ranchers.

In response to the colonel's concluding, single word, interrogative-sentence;

"Questions?"

A battle-hardened captain, standing in the rear of the command-tent, had asked; "Sir, when we attack the village…, if we encounter unarmed, non- combatant squaws and children, what are the *"Terms of Engagement"*?

What should we do… what are we authorized to do?"

Between clinched teeth, Colonel John Chivington, had shouted; "Damn any man who sympathizes with Indians! … I have come to kill Indians, and believe it is right and honorable to use any means under God's heaven to kill Indians Kill and scalp all, big and little; *"Nits make Lice"*.

Without uttering another word, Colonel John Chivington, the "Evangelical- Christian, Colonel, had turned, and exited the tent.

****

Lieutenant Schmidt's uneasiness, was growing … intensifying, as his company drew closer and closer to the sleeping Indian Village.
The young nineteen-year-old officer… a recent graduate from the United States Military Academy (West Point) was eager to prove his recently learned…acquired, military prowess and leadership.

Lieutenant Schmidt was both excited and eager to implement in-the-field, the military tactics, drummed into his head, during thousands of hours of lectures and simulated war-games at the academy; However, last night's briefing… particularly, the colonel's implied and his specific, instructions concerning the "Terms of Engagement", with non-combatants, troubled the young, *shavetail-officer*.

One particular, isolated lecture at West Point, was giving Lieutenant Franklyn Schmidt, the recently commissioned—very Junior-Combat-Officer—pause.

The subject of that troublesome lecture was; *Military Ethics and Military Law"*.

The troubling sentence of that oath that he and his classmates had sworn to; That oath… to him, that very long and, very important sentence—that now was, constantly, and continuously, resonating in his mind; "I will obey the "***Lawful***" orders of the President of the United States and the "***Lawful***" orders of the officers appointed over me. So Help Me God."

Lieutenant Franklyn Schmidt, did not consider, nor did he believe… when the Colonel was asked; *"Colonel, if we encounter unarmed squaws and children, what should we do?"*

Lieutenant Schmidt, did not believe that Colonel Chivington's response, directing them… ordering them to; ***"Kill and scalp all, big and little;*** ***"Nits*** *make Lice"*.
Franklyn Schmidt, did not believe that Colonel Chivington's order, was either ***moral***…***ethical,*** *nor*, was it *"**Legal**"*.

****

Born and raised in McKeesport, Pennsylvania, a small city just outside of Pittsburg, Franklyn Schmidt… the fifth of seven children, born to

German Immigrant parents, attended school… and grew-up amongst a potpourri of Central-European-Immigrant, families.

The McKeesport's communities were comprised mostly of Italian, German, Polish, Austrian-Hungarian, Emigrants.
For young Franklyn, although there where an abundance of ethnic, neighborhood squabbles, rivalries, and disputes, the one thing that they… the kids of these European Immigrants… the thing that they all had in common, was the color of their skin.
They were all, white… white-descendants, of predominantly, Central-European ancestors.
For the most part, aside from multicultural-whites, and religious (Catholic v. Protestant) differences, in young Franklyn's life, "diversity… in terms of the color of one's skin was never a defining issue.
In the world that Franklyn Schmidt was raised; societies populated by, intelligent, caring, *"Black-skin and Red-skin"* people, were merely, abstract, hypothetical, concepts.

****

Chapter 11

November 29, 1864 Sand-Creek, Village of Cheyenne-Chief Black Kettle (Dawn)

The insistent, agitated, barking and growling of four skinny, mongrel-dogs, were the only sounds that disturbed, the quiet serenity of the sleeping village.

As the Sun was beginning to slowly creep over the horizon, Lieutenant Franklyn Schmidt, seated-astride his cavalry mount, gazed through his binocular "Field-glasses", at the still sleeping Indian-village. As he swept his binoculars over the inner circle of teepees, he abruptly stopped.

With his left hand, Lieutenant Schmidt lowered his binoculars; with his freed-righthand, he removed a kerchief from his uniform-blouse, and wiped his eyes. Then still holding his handkerchief in his hand, he once again, looked through his "Field-glasses", at the village's largest teepee, that of Chief Black Kettle.

Through the glasses, the young Lieutenant saw…a pole, on which was hanging a U.S. Flag. The flag was rippling in the early-morning breeze; and tied directly below the U.S. flag, was a white flag.

Lieutenant Schmidt, as had the entire officer corps… had been told the significance of the Indians' displaying… waving —in a peaceful-setting— the United. States Flag.

The officers of the United States 3rd Colorado Cavalry knew that, the displaying, in a peaceful-setting, of the U.S. Flag. by Indians, was to be interpreted as: *These Indians are "Friendlies"; non-hostiles,* and the sighting of the raised "Stars and Stripes", should forestall any authorized, sanctioned-attack, by the soldiers.

As Lieutenant Franklyn Schmidt was about to hand his glasses to his 1ST sergeant; he heard the thundering voice of Colonel Chivington; "***ATTACK! ATTACK! ATTACK!***"
Lieutenant Schmidt, immediately, *turned in his saddle, thereby facing his men; he* threw up both of his hands, signaling, to his platoon, to "***stand- down***", to remain in place.

****

Chapter 12

Encampment of Cheyenne-Chief Black Kettle November 29, 1864 (Pre-dawn)

Limping Woman, the wife of Strong Man, one of the villages' most prolific hunters, was awakened by the plaintiff-hungry cries of her suckling-daughter of six moons, "Cries A Lot".

In addition to her infant daughter, Limping Woman was the mother of three other young children. Her twin boys, who had seen but six summers, and her eldest boy, Hawk Eye, a strapping young brave of eight winters.

While her husband—as were most of the Cheyenne warriors—was away hunting, fulfilling their responsibility as providers… in order to feed, clothe and provide shelter for their families, by bringing-down enough buffalo, to see them through the harsh plains-winter.

At this moment in time, Limping Woman was the sole adult, left in the lodge of Strong Man.

Hastily in response to her baby's strident cries, which Limping Woman was afraid would awaken her sons, Limping Woman freed he left arm from her loosely fitting deer-skin dress, thereby exposing and presenting, the nipple of her left breast, to her hungry baby.

Limping woman smiled as she fondly looked down, at her nursing,

"perfectly-formed", baby girl".

****

During each of her previous three pregnancies, Limping Woman had worried…worried that the babies that she was carrying would be born as she had been… born deformed.

Limping woman had been born with a "minor", birth defect. Although both of her little chubby legs, when first seen by her mother, appeared to be symmetrical, her left leg was an inch and a half, shorter than was her right leg.

While the asymmetry of her otherwise, perfectly formed legs, had not hindered her ability to perform the duties of a Cheyenne-wife, Limping Woman had—thankfully needlessly, feared—that had her boys been born with one leg shorter than the other, that defect might have prevented their attaining "Warrior-Status".

As her baby… "Cries A Lot" contentedly, continued to suckle at her mother's breast, unconscientiously, Limping Woman's right-hand, strayed to caress both of her baby's symmetrically perfect, chubby, little legs.

****

Chapter 12 (cont.)

Limping Woman's Teepee
November 29, 1864 (Pre-dawn)

With her baby contently, nursing, Limping Woman heard the sound of, what she at first thought were rolling thunderclaps. Then she heard for the second time in her life, the blaring sound of the white soldiers trumpeted; "battle- cry".
She instantly knew that the village was being attacked by the white-soldiers.

Limping Woman, held her breath when she heard the *"whoose-whoose"* of cannon balls, flying overhead. She shuddered at the sound of the subsequent explosions.

A cannon ball struck the top of the teepee; splintering the poles surrounding the lodges smoke-hole.
Limping Woman screamed as the family's teepee collapsed around her.

Because of the frigid late November night-air, Limping Woman's sons, had slept, fully clothed, in their sleeping robes.

When the boys heard the shrill sound of the soldiers' trumpets; as they had been taught, and instructed to do, by their father; *"In the event of an attack, run to... and secure, the village's pony-herd"*, the three young boys together, ran from the lodge.

With her baby cradled in the crock of her left arm; With her right-hand, Limping Woman grabbed the baby's red-blanket, and ran limping, from the ruins of the collapsed lodge.

****

Fifty of the sixty-five Cheyenne adult males, who because of age and/ or physical-infirmity—had not joined in the hunt, but had instead remained in camp… with their tomahawks and lances in-hand, had run, shuffled, to meet the onslaught of Chivington's crazed-soldiers.
Scarface, a thirty-year-old Cheyenne Warrior, who because of a severely bruised and sprained thigh muscle, had not joined the recently departed hunting-party; Upon hearing the shrill-trumpeted battle-cry of the white- soldiers, Scarface grabbed his lance and ignoring the sharp-excruciating pain, radiating from his throbbing-thigh, limped towards the enemy.
Scarface led what he knew to be a futile defense… at best, a delaying action—that would allow, at least some of the women and children of Chief Black Kettle's, Sand Creek village, to escape.

****

Chapter 13

Sand Creek; Encampment of Chief Black Kettle *(Under Attack by Col. Chivington's 3rd Colorado Cavalry)* - November 29, 1864

Limping Woman looking to her left saw Scarface, a crippled- warrior— a Cheyenne *"Dog Soldier"*, his war-lance in hand—hobbling to meet the attacking white-soldiers.

Limping Woman, turned and ran in the opposite direction, with but one… overriding, urgent-thought, coursing through her mind; *"My baby…I must save my baby"*.

All around her, running in every direction, were panic-stricken, screaming and crying, women and children.
Limping Woman joined a gaggle of disoriented, panicked, and frightened, women and children, who were fleeing towards the creek-bed.

As fast as her uneven legs would permit… Limping Woman, hobbling… ran away from the one-sided battle, between the well-armed white-soldiers, and the "old and crippled", Cheyenne warriors.

****

Lieutenant Schmidt's immediate thought was, that the colonel had not seen the flags flying in front of Chief Black Kettles' teepee.

The young Lieutenant, reached for, and snatched his binoculars, from the hands of his startled sergeant.

Lieutenant Schmidt pivoted his head, training his binoculars on the commanding officer.

Colonel Chivington—his field glasses raised to his eyes; in his left-hand; — was pointing his Sabre, held in his right hand, directly at the flag, now gently waving in the morning breeze, in front of Chief Black Kettles' lodge.

Colonel Chivington sat astride his horse, a satisfied smirk on his lips, surveying the slaughter, as the soldiers, shot, clubbed and bayoneted; The frantic Indians… a few old-men, but mostly women and children, running, while being shot, stabbed, bludgeoned, butchered, by his soldiers.

****

Lieutenant Schmidt, scanning with his binoculars, took in what could only be described as "A Massacre", the mass killing of scores of unarmed women and children, being defended… as best they could, by a few practically defenseless, crippled and/or old-men.

Conscientious of the fact that his men…the men he had held back from participating in the massacre, were watching him; Looking to their

"shavetail" platoon-officer, for orders…for guidance, Lieutenant Schmidt, stood-fast…he did not countermand his order to the platoon, to hold their position.

Through his binoculars Lieutenant Schmidt, witnessed heinous, barbaric, atrocities being, meted-out upon the multitude of innocent, helpless, women and children, fleeing for-their-lives.

Despite his repulsion… his urgent need to throw-up, Lieutenant Schmidt, clamped his jaw shut, and said nothing.
Feeling tears welling-up in his eyes; the young officer again, raised his field glasses to his eyes.

He saw three soldiers laughing while they were casually—as if they were at a carnival—taking turns shooting at a young boy running, "zig-zagging", trying to avoid being hit by their bullets… until a bullet from the gun of one of the laughing-troopers, found its' target.

The five… maybe six-year-old child, fell to the ground; as bone-fragments and gray-matter, spewed-forth, from what had seconds ago, been a human-skull.

Disgusted and horrified, Lieutenant Schmidt redirected his binoculars. In the midst of the mass hysteria and confusion, the Lieutenant noticed a young squaw— with a pronounced limp— carrying a bundle wrapped in a red- blanket, running…hobbling, in her attempt to escape the carnage. The woman because of her limp was being jostled, pushed… and passed by the fleeing horde of panic-stricken, women and children.

As she was knocked to the ground by the "Human-Stampede", he watched as the woman, clutching her red blanket, to her chest, crawled over to the ridge of the creek-bed, and on her knees, while maintaining her tight-grip on the blanket, with her free hand, the squaw began frantically digging, clawing with her free-hand, at the mud at the edge of the creek-bed. The squaw hastily stuffed the blanket into the excavated, shallow depression.

As the "lame" woman turned her head, attempting to rise, she was bayoneted… skewed in her abdomen, by a grizzled soldier. eviscerated the soldier placed his boot on the young Indian woman's stomach and pulled upward, his blood-streaked bayonet, free from the eviscerated woman's body.

Then, as if it were an after-thought, the soldier removed a long "Bowie-Knife" from his belt, and scalped the young-woman; the soldier then with the toe of his boot, rolled her over, and sliced her right-breast, from her chest.

The soldier placed the women's severed-breast still dripping blood, into his tunic; he then, casually, moved on.

Lieutenant Franklyn Schmidt struggled to suppress the sudden wave of nausea that he was experiencing. He hastily dismounted and unashamedly… stepped into the weeds, and vomited.

In the immediate aftermath, following the order to cease-firing… the butchering escalated.

Colonel Chivington and his officers watched as the men under their command, the United States 3rd Colorado Cavalry, set-about the grislily-task; the collecting of souvenirs, body-parts, "battle-trophies"; Fingers, ears, scalps, both male and female genitalia, were hacked or sliced, from the bodies of the massacred, victims... the defenseless, Cheyenne and Arapaho, women and children.

While the troopers were gleefully-basking in… celebrating, their victory, Lieutenant Schmidt… on a whim, slowly, avoiding the rollicking soldiers, rode his horse to the spot in the creek-bed, where he had seen the "lame" squaw, stash the red blanket.
Lieutenant Schmidt slowly dismounted. With the reigns of his horse in his left-hand, he slowly walked toward the spot that he thought, that he had seen the lame-squaw, frantically digging.

As he approached the bank of the creek-bed, he saw the edge of the red blanket; then he saw movement… he thought he heard a whimper.

Lieutenant Schmidt unholstered his side arm, he withdrew his service-revolver, and cautiously… he approached the red blanket.

Again… he saw movement in the blanket. Lieutenant Schmidt, with the thumb of his hand that was holding his weapon… cocked the pistol.

This time instead of a whimper, Lieutenant Schmidt heard the unmistakable sound of a baby crying.

The lieutenant, gently lowered the hammer, and holstered his pistol. Still holding the reigns of his horse, he walked over and with his free hand, unfolded the red blanket.

Gazing up at him, and reaching out to him—as he later proclaimed to his wife Ingrid —was; "The cutest little creature, that I had ever seen."

As he later told his wife Ingrid; "Honey, I don't know why… but instead of immediately going to the baby, I turned to see if anyone was watching. No one was."

"Apparently the officers had all left the field, and the men were busy… collecting their trophies and celebrating their *"victory"*.

"Then…I hastily tied the reigns of my horse to my belt, bent over and picked-up the baby. I don't know why… but instinctively, I covered the baby's head with the blanket, and with one arm holding the baby, and my free-hand holding my saddle-horn, I remounted, and rode directly… straight home, …to you."

****

Chapter 14

1864

Married Officer's Quarters - of Lieutenant and Mrs. Franklyn Schmidt

Franklyn and Ingrid sat on the edge of their bed, in the cramped Junior Officer's quarters. Ingrid was gently rocking, the now hungry… crying baby.

Franklyn stood and began nervously pacing. Ingrid was rocking and cooing…the baby. "There…there, *lilla… pappa och mamma, we are here.*"

While Franklyn was by no means fluent in Swedish, he instantly… looking at the expression on his wife's face, and the sound of her lilting-voice… he knew that this beautiful motherless child, wrapped in the red-blanket, was… no longer motherless.

Franklyn watched, as Ingrid gently separated the baby from the blanket. She then, with one of the two towels hanging on the bedframe, gently wiped the baby's bottom, and between her legs.

Ingrid, while holding the naked infant pressed to her left-shoulder, with her free hand, gingerly, spread the second towel, onto the bed. The baby, lying naked and vulnerable, her little fists flailing in the air, continued squiggling, on the towel.

It was then that Franklyn—first looking at the smile on the face of his glowing wife…then at the tiny cooper-toned, squiggly infant… it was at that moment that he knew that these two beautiful females… that he was not just looking at his wife…, he was now looking at his wife, and…his daughter.

****

Franklyn Schmidt, was a true believer, a staunch disciple of his mentor, Captain Richard Henry Pratt.

Captain Pratt was the *"Warden"* of the Army's prison for recalcitrant, captured Indian-warriors.

The Prisoner of War Camp, was located at Fort Marion, Saint Augustine, Florida.

Subsequent to his action…or rather as the Army initially viewed it… the lieutenant's inaction at Sand Creek, and the subsequent bandying around of the word, *"Massacre"*; That *"For the Good of the Service"*, Lieutenant Franklyn Schmidt, was transferred to Fort Marion, Saint Augustine, Florida, as Captain Pratt's, Assistant Warden of the Government's Indian-Prisoner of War Camp.

****

Chapter 15

Superintendent of the Carlyn Indian Vocational Industrial School Home of Mr. Mrs. Franklyn Schmidt (October 1877)

Franklyn Schmidt was determined, totally committed to Captain Pratt's philosophy; to "Kill the Indian: But Save the Man".

To by any means necessary, transform…, to mold, through their total assimilation into the white-civilization, these still pliable, *"young-savages"*.

Franklyn was convinced that, through their total assimilation into the white- civilization, these students, who came to him as *"young-savages"*, could through total assimilation, become productive, "self-reliant", members of the American-White-Society."

****

Superintendent Schmidt, felt a soft feminine hand gently squeezing his shoulder. "Dad… Daddy, are you awake?" Franklyn opened his eyes.

Staring down at him was the beautiful, dark…obsidian, black, eyes of his daughter, Sarah.

As usual, Franklyn was captivated by the radiant, enchanting smile, of his…as she so constantly reminded him…, "Daddy, I am your and mom's, fourteen…nearly fifteen, year-old, daughter.

"Hi sweety…I must have dozed-off." Standing in front of Franklyn… were to him, the two most beautiful… the loveliest females, on the planet; his tall statuesque, blonde, wife-Ingrid; and their beautiful dark-complexioned, petite, raven-haired, daughter, Sarah.

Franklyn stood… and with the thumb of his outstretched-hand… he gently, lovingly, rubbed a smudge of the white-flour, from his daughter's coppertone-colored, nose.

The two adult members of the Schmidt family were seated, at their dining table. Sarah, her back to her parents…was proudly removing from the brick- oven, the rolls that she had — meticulously, following their cook Delores' recipe — created.

Franklyn scooped onto his fork, a hefty portion of mashed potatoes. As he raised his fork to his lips, a milky substance fell through the tines of his fork, soiling his shirt.

Franklyn hastily picked-up his from his lap, his napkin and dabbed at the warm liquid. He opened his mouth to comment; however, before he could speak, Ingrid caught his attention. She was shaking her head, while silently mouthing the word, "No".

Franklyn replaced his napkin, onto his knees. Sarah gingerly, holding in her hands, a tray of smoldering, charred, rolls, pursed her lips, turned toward her parents; and blew at a lock of her raven-black hair, that was obscuring her vision.

Sarah joined her parents at the table; Beaming with the "pride of accomplishment", as she…and as had both, her parents" dug-in", and together…the Schmidt family, thoroughly enjoying Sarah's first…all-by- herself, *"Culinary-Masterpiece"*.

After having swallowed, her last spoonful of mashed-potatoes—which later that night in the privacy of their bedroom, Franklyn had jokingly referred to as his baby girl's "potato-soup"—Ingrid had asked; *"Franklyn…Sveet Heart, how was your day?"*

Before he could answer, Sarah joined the conversation. "Yes dad, what did the new class look like? Are any of the new students my age? Are any Cheyenne?

Franklyn and Ingrid looked at each other…and smiled. Without verbally communicating, they both knew that they were both…together, remembering, that day…that day when their daughter…, eight-year-old Sarah had innocently asked; "Mommy… daddy, why am I…, so much darker than you?"

****

Prior to that day…actually two years, prior to that day; after having read to his then four-year-old daughter, the Fairy-Tale, the story of *"Goldie Locks and the Three Bears"*; How after kissing Sarah goodnight; In his and Ingrid's bedroom, Franklyn had shared with his wife, but one… of the many questions, that their extremely "bright" little girl, had asked, and would almost assuredly, in the future, ask; "Daddy… *"Goldie Locks"*, that's a funny name, why was the girl named Goldie Locks?

Franklyn without giving it too much thought, had immediately answered; "Well sweetheart, she was called Goldie Locks, because of the color of her hair."

Sarah with a confused look on her face had asked… "Daddy, what color…, what color is the color; *"Goldie Locks*?"

Franklyn had explained that while gold is not a color… that gold is a yellow- metal, that often instead of referring to something as yellow…, in this story, someone decided instead of calling the girl "Yellow Locks", because the girl's hair is yellow, chose for the girl, the name "Goldie Locks".

Sarah appeared to have been pondering her father's explanation. Franklyn tucked his daughter in, blew out the lamp…and walked over to the door. As he was about to turn the doorknob, Sarah asked…Daddy why is Goldie Locks hair, yellow?

Without answering her question, Franklyn mumbled…go to sleep Sarah. Then quietly, he closed the door.

****

Franklyn and Ingrid looked at each other…and smiled. Without verbally communicating, they both knew that they were, both… together, remembering, that day…that day when their six-year-old daughter, Sarah had innocently asked; "Mommy… daddy, why am I so much darker than either of you?"

Ingrid and Franklyn had exchanged between them, a silent glance. Although their glance was silent, to them it conveyed a loud and clear message; "The time had come."

It was time for them…together, to tell their beloved daughter, how the three of them, how they became a family.

Ingrid had put aside, her yarn, and the knitting needles, that she had been expertly wielding.

She sighed... and motioned for her six-year-old daughter; that she should come to her... that Sarah should sit on her mother's lap.

Ingrid in her pronounced Swedish-accent, told Sarah of how her father... then an Army officer, six years earlier, had been at...but, and she emphasized... did not participate, ...in fact your father... *förhindras*... prevented, his men, from participating in the "Sand Creek Massacre".

Six-year-old Sarah, with a perplexed, confused expression, had looked-up, and seen the hurt, the anguish in her mother's bright blue-eyes.

Franklyn too, had seen and heard in Ingrid's voice, the emotional turmoil, that she was experiencing.

In an attempt to give Ingrid time...to give her time to collect herself, Franklyn spoke to their inquisitive daughter; "Sweetheart when you're older, at an appropriate age, I will tell you details...of what I saw, when the soldiers...the white-soldiers killed...I'll use the appropriate word when you're old enough to understand...when the white soldiers *"Massacred"*, scores of helpless women and children...Cheyenne and Arapaho, women and children.

Sarah, obviously still confused had looked from her father, to her mother. Sarah saw tears, from Ingrid's now reddened, bright blue eyes, streaming down her mother's cheeks.

Ingrid, while clutching her daughter's hands...in the most sorrowful voice that Franklyn had ever heard..., he heard Ingrid say..., "My darling Sarah, your birth-mother, a woman of the Cheyenne Nation, was one of those defenseless women, killed by Colonel Chivington's soldiers, at the Sand Creek Massacre."

Franklyn Schmidt, the Superintendent of the Carlyn Indian Vocational Industrial School..., also Franklyn Schmidt, father of a thirteen... nearly fourteen-year-old, Indian teenage daughter; that daughter, who was now…for the first time, surrounded by Indian children…, a population of Indian children, who by law, would not have reached the age of fifteen Franklyn answered his daughter's question, by first repeating her question; "Are any of the new students my age? Are any Cheyenne?" By asking Sarah a rhetorical question;

"Sarah, do you not remember my…, sitting here, at this very table, with you and your mother, explaining that by law, the school's enrollment is restricted to "Indian children, who are between the ages of five and fifteen?"

Ingrid interrupted; And in a voice, that could only be perceived as… that of a mother defending her child; *"Ja"* Franklyn, of course our daughter *"minns"*
…, she remembers."

"But *Sveet* Heart…Do you not remember, how excited Sarah was, when you told us, that this… this Carlyn school that you will be running, is to educate "Indian Children"?

Reservation Children", children who have…, children *"med kopparfärgad ton hy"*.

Seeing the confused look on Sarah's face, Franklyn quickly translated Ingrid's Swedish phrase; *"Children with a Golden-tone complexion"*
—

Ingrid continued; *"Children yust like you.* Franklyn chimed in…; "But unlike you…, these Indian children have not been taught, the lessons and the skills, needed to be successful, in our society?"

Franklyn had been momentarily flummoxed… by his wife's impassioned multi-lingual diatribe.

Franklyn Schmidt, the Superintendent of the Carlyn Indian Vocational-Industrial Boarding School..., also Franklyn Schmidt, the father of a thirteen...nearly fourteen-year-old, teenage-Indian-daughter—a daughter raised from infancy, by Franklyn and Ingrid Schmidt, her white parents; Raised in a White Euro-Centric Society— Franklyn Schmidt, had found himself at a complete and total, loss for words.

Now it was Sarah's turn to protect her father; "Mother...daddy; My asking that silly question...a question that in my excitement..., at having hundreds of Indian kids, here...here with us, I forgot that daddy had told us weeks ago, that the children would be between the ages of five and fifteen."

Franklyn looked appreciatively, at his daughter; "There's no need to apologize honey. In answer to your question...he paused in thought;

"Excuse me for just a moment ladies."

Franklyn stood and walked to the hall closet. He reached for his coat... stuck his hand in the breast pocket, and retrieved a sheet of paper and walked back into the dining area.

"I believe you asked about the size and the composition, of the new class. What does the new class look like? Are any of the students your age?" Franklyn, once again sat.

He unfolded the paper and began to read; The total class size is 96. Fifty- eight boys; and 38 girls. The boys ranged in age from 15 (1); to 5 (5); girls range from 15 (2); to 5 (2).

Franklyn folded the paper. He then, looked directly at Sarah...; "There are no Cheyenne or Arapaho, in this class."

Sarah's anticipatory smile had disappeared. Though she did not speak, her slumping shoulders, silently spoke for her. Spoke of her disappointment.

For a month now…ever since her parents had told her that she would soon be living among scores of "Indians", Sarah had imagined what it would be like to get to know…, to have as a friend, an Indian girl; preferably, a Cheyenne teenage-girlfriend.

Attempting to not show her disappointment, Sarah smiled and focused her attention, on the ongoing conversation between her parents.

She heard her mother ask; "Comanche, Kiowa, Apache, Sioux, heavens Franklyn, aren't those the most war-like…, the most dangerous of the tribes?"

Franklyn's eyes swiftly met those of his daughter. Because of his time in the Army, serving in the west, during the "Indian Wars", Franklyn knew, and was grateful that either Ingrid did not know; or that she had purposefully omitted, that the Cheyenne, and Arapaho, were members…, members of the formidable, Indian-Alliance, fighting to halt the westward incursion of white-settlers, and miners, into their homelands.

Judging by their body-posture, their attentive gaze—that Franklyn interpreted as genuine interest in the discussion—in his authoritative voice… the voice of the Superintendent of the Carlyn Industrial-Technical, Indian School, Franklyn continued.

"While, it's true ladies, that the children…, let me repeat that…this time with emphasis on the word _**children**_." "While, that is true…, its' also true, that these children…, this class, our student-body, are from tribes that militaristically, fought, brilliantly…valiantly, to maintain and to protect their land, their way of life. It's also true, that our students' parents, have all willingly, left the plains, and moved onto government reservations."

For an awkward moment, no one spoke. With her fork, Sarah was nonchalantly, pushing a now cold, lump of potato on her plate. Ingrid appeared to be mulling-over her husband's words.

Franklyn decided to change the subject. He picked-up his glass of water, took a sip, sat his glass on the table, and spoke; "At today's student- orientation, I met a very interesting young man. A Comanche …I believe.

This young man, was one of but a few, of the students that understood, and spoke English.

Apparently, the young Comanche, was attempting to calm a very, … young girl—who to me looked to be about 5 or 6 years old—possibly, the young Comanche's sister. I did not understand what he was saying, …the young man was speaking to her in their native language.

"Although I surmised, from the soothing tone of his voice, and his interaction with the little-one, that he was comforting the child, I seized upon the moment…that opportune moment, to drive home to the assembled students, an absolutely fundamental rule…, a rule that would be vigorously enforced here, by the Carlyn staff."

Intrigued… Ingrid, spoke; *"My gootness Franklyn, vhat is this important rule?"*

Franklyn took a deep breath before responding; "Students are not to speak their tribal-language."

"All students…at all times, even among themselves, are not allowed to speak their tribal-languages. All students…at all times, are to speak only, English."

Seeing the puzzlement…and disapproval, on the faces of both his wife and daughter, Franklyn quickly added. "Of course, we don't expect immediate compliance with this edict."

Franklyn reached across the table and took Ingrid's hand and lovingly, looked into her eyes; "*You… my dear, of all people…*I don't have to tell you, how difficult it is to learn, and to become comfortable speaking a new language, it takes time."

However, … and you my Swedish Angel, …you can attest to the fact that, learning a new language is a whole lot easier, if all of the people around you speak only, the language that you are attempting to learn

Sarah asked; "Daddy if that boy was speaking a language that you did not understand, what made you think that he, would understand what you were saying to him? That he understand's our language, … that he understands English?"

Franklyn, gave his daughter an admiring look; "That's very astute of you sweetheart. In fact, I did not know if the young man would understand what I was saying. In fact, I knew that in all probability, that he would not know, what I was saying."

"What I did know was that, these 96 individuals…our new students, had all come from government reservations. And therefore, had been at least exposed, to English."

"In any event, at this point in their education, it was not so much, the "message", it was the manner that the message was delivered, that was important."

"Luck-alee for me, when I asked the young Comanche his name, he answered in perfect English; "*My name is Dark Eagle*".

Ingrid had enthusiastically, welcomed this turn…, this change in the tone, of the conversation.

With a furtive glance at her daughter, Ingrid winked and smiled; A universally feminine-coquettish silent-smile, that roughly translated; meant *"For females only — that boys… men, just wouldn't understand."*

Sarah…, lost in thought absentmindedly, placed the fork that she been using to propel the cold lump of potato, onto her napkin, onto the table.

Ingrid, in a female- conspiratorial tone-of voice, spoke to her husband: *"Svet heart, this interesting boy that you met, what did you say vas his name?*

"And Vhat about this boy impressed you? And, she winked at Sarah… how old is he?"

Franklyn, not noticing the wink; welcomed his wife's ebullient entry into the conversation. He was relieved that Ingrid had so adroitly, and smoothly, changed the topic.

Franklyn stood; "I'm thirsty. He walked over to the side-bar, picked-up the pitcher of water and asked; "Can I refill your glasses?" Both mother and daughter declined.

When Franklyn turned his back, Sarah caught the attention of her mother, and silently mouthed…, "Thank you mom."

****

Water-glass in hand, Franklyn returned to the table. "Sorry about that, ladies. My throat's a little dry. It seems to me, that most of my day, has been spent talking."

He saw the "disappointed-looks", that in unison, had suddenly appeared on his wife and daughter's faces.

Hurriedly he resumed. "Ingrid, would you please repeat that for me… what was it, that you were asking?

Ingrid, smiling…beaming, responded; "This boy that you mentioned; "*Vhat*" did you say vas his name? How vas it that this boy impressed you? How old is he?"

Concentrating on his wife's questions…Franklyn did not notice the barely audible sigh of relief, that escaped from his daughter's lips.

Franklyn, pleased that Ingrid was showing interest, in his work, responded; "Dark Eagle", … the boy said that his name is Dark Eagle. "However, as I immediately explained to the entire assemblage; none of the students, would be allowed to keep their Indian Names.

That a vital, necessary step in their assimilating…their entering "civilized- society", is that they replace their Tribal names, with proper, civilized, American names."

Franklyn, concentrating on Ingrid's questions, failed to notice the frown that had gradually began to appear, on his daughter's face.

Sarah's unspoken thoughts were; "Dark Eagle", what an interesting name…I wonder if there is any significance to that name…, what, if anything, is the meaning of "Dark Eagle?"

Sarah's thoughts were interrupted by her father's voice; "What was your second question … Oh yes; "Dark Eagle's age"; According to the Comanche roster, submitted to us by the Fort Sill-Indian Agent, the boy who will…very shortly be…the boy formerly known as "Dark Eagle", is fourteen.
Franklyn picked-up his glass; he took a long thirsty drink of water, and again, placed the now empty glass, onto the table.

Franklyn sighed. "And finally, your last but most definitely, not the least important question; What's special about this particular boy. Why was I, so impressed?"

"Actually, there are several answers to that question. The first is; the young man's bearings."

"There is something about his demeanor…how he carries himself; Second, although the students are from four different tribes, I got the sense that this young man, either had the respect…, or was capable of gaining the respect of most, if not all of the individuals, from the four, disparate, tribes."

"And lastly, I think that this young fellow, because of his age, and because he is multilingual; he just might be the *"insider"* that…that I need, *"My Judas Goat"*, if you will."

"That Indian-student… that special-someone, to help me in the transitioning of these students, into our modern day-society."

****

Chapter 16

Carlyn Indian Vocational-Residential School (Community-Room) October - 1877 (2 PM)

Dark Eagle, and Underfoot were sullen…, depressed. They were both, silently lamenting, what they had-not, done…, the fact that they, had done nothing.

That they had not been able to keep the promises, that they had made to their grandparents; To Gray Wolf, their venerable-grandfather, and to their beloved-grandmother, Little Flower.

That they …more so the elder grandson Dark Eagle, had promised to "Protect and to Care for their sisters".

Dark Eagle, and Underfoot …the sons of the Mighty Comanche War-Chief, Stone Fist, had…, instead of protecting their sisters, they had stood by silent, mute…, helplessly watching, as their sisters; 12-year-old, "Never Weeps";
9-year-old, "Moon Glow"; and "Golden One", the 5-year-old, were taken away from them, by the white-woman-chief, called Miss Wallace.

Dark Eagle, and his younger brother Underfoot, stood together, in one of the three lines, of the school's fifty-two, male-Indian students.

At the front of the room, three white men, dressed in the work-clothes of the local sheep-ranchers, were standing behind, three chairs. Each of the white men was holding in his hand, a pair of scissors.

Within minutes of sitting, the long, black, glistening, shoulder-length hair of the Indian-boys, covered the floor.

Underfoot, who stood in front of his brother exclaimed; "Dark Eagle… my brother, the white men, without shedding our blood…, we are being scalped!"

After having been "bloodlessly-scalped", the boys were instructed, to remove, and throw their "Heathen-Clothes", including their moccasins, into a large basket". They were then issued by an elderly Indian—a "White- Redman", 2-gray-shirts; 2-pairs of trousers; 2-pairs of gray-wool socks; and 1pair of leather shoes.

The fifty-two, Indian boys, each wearing a set of their government issued "uniform" clothing; while holding the remainder in their arms, were told to form three lines.

Dark Eagle, and his brother Underfoot, joined a line…line "A", consisting of eighteen boys. One of three adult Indians, school-employees, dressed in the white-men's clothing, walked over to Dark Eagle and began to speak. "Are you the one who speaks the white talk?"

Dark Eagle nodding his head, replied; "Yes, I am Dark Eagle." The adult Indian—clearly a "White-Redman", in league with the school—

looked quizzically…, suspiciously at the youth who was standing in line…, literally looking-up to Dark Eagle.

Dark Eagle proudly…, protectively put his arm around his brother; "This is Underfoot; he is my brother."

Inexplicably the adult Indian, grabbed Underfoot by the arm, yanking him out of line "A". He pointed his finger toward the line of students, two rolls removed…Line "C".

The *"White-Redman"*, shoved Underfoot, propelling him toward Line "C". Underfoot did not resist. Instead, his eyes locked, with those of Dark Eagle.

Dark Eagle spoke ; *"Miarʉ, wʉm? arʉ smohpʉ? Nʉnu sauna tʉsu? atsipʉ tʉi" ("Go my brother. We will talk later)."*

Three *"White-Redmen"*, all menial Indian-employees, of the school, led the three lines of boys, to their assigned dormitories.

From that brief encounter… his innocently, voluntarily, providing information to the white man, Running Eagle had learned an invaluable lesson.

In this *"new"* world; This white-man's world; If not asked…, Never voluntarily provide information, to the white-man…, or to his Indian, *"White-Redmen"*, lackies.

****

Dark Eagle was assigned to, Boys-Dormitory (A); his younger brother, Underfoot, to Boys-Dormitory (C)

The tribal distribution, of the roster, of the eighteen student occupants, assigned to: Boys-Dormitory (A), was as follows:

Comanche – Eight (8); Kiowa - Eight (8); Apache - Two (1) and Sioux - Two (1)

Dormitory assignments were not random. It was the policy of the school(s), to the extent possible; i.e., the number of available, accommodations; to separate, family, friends, and tribal members.

This policy of separation, was instituted, in an attempt to separate... to remove the student, from any and all things, including family and friends, that would remind him/her, of their "uncivilized" existence, on the plains.

****

Chapter 17

Carlyn Indian Vocational-
Residential School -
Boys-Dormitory (A)

The physical dimensions of the long-narrow room were; (12') x (18'). Eighteen Iron- cots were lined-up; (1½') equidistance apart.

Nine Iron-cots, were situated against the two opposite walls of the room. At the foot of each cot, was an open wooden box. The opened-hinged lid of each box—relative to the body of the box—formed a perfect, (90°), right angle.

Dark Eagle and his seventeen, fellow "room-mates", were crowded together in the center of the room. Not knowing what to do…, not knowing what was expected of them, resulted in a cacophony of sound…, as a flurry of questions; put forth in three distinctly different, tribal languages, filled the air.

A surly white-man, whose pock-marked face, resembled that of a survivor of "*The Pox*", stood with his hands on his hips, near the solitary door, of the dormitory.

The white-man lifted an empty, metal-barrel over his head, and slammed it down onto the hard-wood floor.

At the sound of the barrel striking the floor, in unison. The thirty-six eyes of the eighteen Indian boys, focused on the white-man.

"All right boys…, I'm gunna give you that one. "I want yall to know, that that there…, you speaking that heathen talk, will be the one and only time that, you won't be punished, for using that filthy, Injun-talk. Yall all, gotta learn proper English, licky-dee-split"

Seventeen of the eighteen Indian-students, looked at each other, bewildered…, confused.

Seeing their reaction…the white-man shouted; "Does anyone hear speak English? Does anyone know…, understand what I just said?"

Dark Eagle stepped forward. "I know the white-man talk." The middle-aged white man with the pock-marked face, grinned. "Okay then…, you boy, come stand next to me. You gunna be my interpretor."

Dark Eagle did as he was instructed. As he stood next to the white man, he wrinkled his nose. As the foul odor of cheap fire-water, assailed the young Comanche's, sensitive nose.

"The white man, with the pock-marked face, placed his arm around Dark Eagles' shoulders; "What's your name boy?

Dark Eagle gritted his teeth. In his mind…, and in every fiber of his being, he wanted to knock this white-man's arm, off of his shoulder.

Realizing that, while giving vent to his emotions would be satisfying…, self- satisfying, he remembered his promise to his grandfather, Gray Wolf. He replied; "My name is Dark Eagle".

                                              Precious In His Sight

"Well now boy, that there ain't exactly true. In just a few minutes you…, as will all of you, will be shed of those Injun names. You will take…, or be given proper, Christian names.

By the way fellows, my name is Andrew Jones, I'm the Dormitory Manager, of this here Dorm (A)

Andrew Jones, the Dorm manager walked over to a rectangular table. He pulled out, and sat down, on one of the two wooden chairs at the table. He motioned to Dark Eagle to join him at the table.

The sounds of the chair being pulled-out from under the table, and that made by Dark Eagle's uncomfortable shoes on the hardwood floors, was the only sound heard in the dormitory.

Dark Eagle joined the Dorm Manager at the table. Andrew… "call me Andy, in his high-pitched voice spoke; I know that you understand the white-man talk but…, and this is an important but…, he held up one of the sheets of paper…, can you read, this…, the written words of the white-man?

Dark Eagle, shook his head; "I can speak…and I know the meaning of the words of the white-talk". He pointed to the paper that Andy was holding. "I cannot follow the trail…, the "sign", left on this paper."

Andy sighed…; Okay boy. I didn't think you could actually read. But it would have made my job a hell-of-a lot easier, if you could read."

"Okay…, we'll have to do this the hard way. For the life of me, I don't know why Mr. Schmidt, insists that we give you Indians the chance to pick your own …, new civilized names. If it was up to me…, which it isn't, we would just give each and every one of you, a proper Christen name.

"Okay boy, since you're going to be my helper, my main-man…, it's only right that you get first pick. I'll read the names, when you hear one you like, stop me. That will be your new civilize-Christen name…, understand?"

Dark Eagle nodded…then said; "Yes I understand."

Andy looked at the Two sheets of paper; One, a list of common Anglo-Saxon, Male-First-Names; The other, a list of common Anglo-Saxon, surnames.

<u>List #1 (Male - Names)</u>

1	Adam	11	Edgar	21	Leonard
2	Aaron	12	Edward	22	Matthew
3	Benjamin	13	Frank	23	Marvin
4	Bruce	14	Franklyn	24	Oliver
5	Bryan	15	Gary	25	Patrick
6	Charles	16	Gregory	26	Raymond
7	Clifford	17	Harry	27	Robert
8	Daniel	18	Henry	28	Ronald
9	David	19	Jerome	29	Thomas
10	Douglas	20	Joseph	30	William

<u>List #2 (Surnames)</u>

1	Adams	11	Grant	21	Mitchell
2	Allen	12	Green	22	Morris
3	Ambrose	13	Hill	23	Nelson
4	Blake	14	Henderson	24	Parker
5	Bryant	15	Hernandez	25	Robertson
6	Carter	16	Jackson	26	Rogers
7	Daniels	17	Jones	27	Scott
8	Davis	18	Kelley	28	Smith
9	Bird	19	King	29	Taylor
10	Edwards	20	Miller	30	Williams

The Dormitory Manager—In turn—pointed to each name, on the two lists of names. He read and pronounced twice, for Dark Eagle's benefit, the name under his finger.

"Okay *"Dark-Bird"* …, or whatever you said, your name was; I saw that you were paying close-attention as I pointed to…, and I read those civilized names. Well, *"Dark-Buzzard"*, have you picked out a name for yourself? Or should I just do it for you?"

As the Dorm-Manager had observed, Dark Eagle had been listening …, concentrating when the white man "Andy", was reading, the individual names.

When the Dorm Manager read the 17th name on the list of boys' names; and the 9th name on list of surnames, Dark Eagle knew that he wanted that name… "Harry Bird", to be his mandatory, *"civilized"*, name.

****

Chapter 18

Carlyn Indian-Vocational-Residential School (*Dining Hall*) October - 1877 (5:30 AM)

Dark Eagle' s *("Harry Bird's",)*, assigned living-space in the dormitory, was the area best described as; *"The first Iron-cot & storage box"*, on the right- hand side of the wall, opposite the door, of Dormitory "A".

The bed assignment of Harry Bird *("Dark Eagle")*, had been, at the *"suggestion"* of the school's superintendent, Lieutenant *(Ret.)*, Mr. Franklyn Ludwig Schmidt, to Andrew Jones, the Manager of Dormitory "A".

The Manager of Dormitory "A", did not know why…, but he most definitely, with absolute certainty, knew that, for whatever reason…, student Harry Bird, was "the Boss's" favorite, student.

****

The students at the Carlyn Indian-Vocational-Residential School, were mandated to adhere to, a strict-regimented, daily schedule of activities.

5:30 AM - 5:45 AM — Make-up bed; 5:46 - 6:00 AM — Time allotted: (AM toiletries);

6:00 AM - 6:10 AM — Marched to School Yard (Student-Body, Roll- Call);

6:25 AM - 6:30 AM — Student-Body, Marched to Dining Hall (Breakfast);

7:15 AM - 7:20 AM — Student-Body, Marched to classes

12:00 PM- 1:00 PM — Student-Body, Marched to Dining Hall (Lunch) & Recess);

1:45 PM- 1:50 PM — Student-Body, Marched to classes

4:05 PM - 4:15 PM — Marched to School Yard (Student-Body, Roll- Call);

4:20 PM - 4:30 PM — Marched to Christian-Religion-Studies

6:00 PM - 6:45 PM — Student-Body, Marched to Dining Hall (Dinner);

6:50 PM — Student-Body, Marched to Dormitories; (For prayers)

****

Chapter 19

5th^d Day (Student-Body, Roll-Call); 4:25 PM

At roll-call, as in the classrooms, the male students and the female students were separated.

When he heard the name…, "Harry Bird" being called by a white man—a staff member responsible for roll-calls, Dark Eagle, in a clear, loud voice, responded; "Here-Sir". The white man checked off the name Harry Bird, on his roster.

A white man, at the female section, called out the name; "Brenda Johnson", a young female voice responded; "Here-Sir".

Dark Eagle was startled; That voice…that soft, sweet…, familiar voice, was the voice of his sister, "Never Weeps".

Dark Eagle elevated himself, by standing on the balls of his feet, trying to get a glimpse of his sister. Then, he felt a firm hand on his arm.

Thinking that he was about to be disciplined for "breaking-ranks", Dark Eagle immediately "braced-himself", and assumed what they had taught him, was the position of attention.

Standing before him was the now familiar face of the white-man…, his Dorm Manager Andrew Jones.

The white-man…, his Dorm Manager pulled Dark Eagle from the ranks while muttering under his breathe, "Come with me".

Dark Eagle, did as he had been told.

****

When they were out of earshot, of everyone, Andrew in his clipped nasal voice began to speak; "Harry, I just left the Superintendent's office. Don't ask me why, cause as God is my witness…I don't know why…, anyhow, Mr. Schmidt wants you to have dinner with him…, tonight…, at his house.

"You scoot back to the dormitory, wash-up, put on your clean uniform, and be at his house at 5:30 sharp.

Before Dark Eagle could respond…Andrew— *"Call me Andy"*, shoved him away from the school yard; towards Dormitory "A".

****

Franklyn was a determined, and a totally committed zealot, of his mentor…, his former commanding officer, Captain Richard Henry Pratt's philosophy; that of the need for; *"The Total Assimilation"*, of the Indian into, American- White-Social-Oder".

Superintendent Franklyn Schmidt was convinced…steadfast, in his belief that, in order to save the Indian from total annihilation…from

becoming an extinct footnote in the history-books; was through their—
"the youth's", total assimilation, into the white-society.

Franklyn believed that, in order to accomplish *"Total Assimilation"*, his students, in addition to acquiring literacy…, had to reject, to abandon…, all vestiges of his/her, former lives… their language, their customs… their spiritual beliefs, *and the unspoken, but definitely encouraged by the school(s), family-ties.*

Franklyn Schmidt, the Superintendent of the Carlyn Indian-Vocational-Residential School, did not agree with…nor, did he support the belief that they…, the "educated Indian-youth", who had—through education and training, acquired the requisite skills needed to survive in white-society—, that they should return to the reservations; to their elders, the "savage- people".

Franklyn believed that instead of improving the lives of the elders… the *"savages"*; Franklyn felt that the return of the *"educated Indian-youth"* to the reservation, would result in the *"educated Indian-youth"*, reverting to the *"barbaric, savage practices and rituals"*, of their elders.

Franklyn Schmidt was an adherent to that old cliché; That while you might be able to train…to teach a puppy; *"You can't Teach an Old Dog…New Tricks"*.

After all, Franklyn rationalized; His and Ingrid's, being the loving, nurturing white-parents of an exceptionally beautiful, well-adjusted, Indian Daughter…a daughter, who had not been exposed…, subjected to *"pagan- rituals"*, gave credence to…and validated his beliefs.

****

Chapter 20

Home of the Superintendent - Carlyn, Indian-Residential-School

Dark Eagle stood on a "crunchy" carpet of yellow and red leaves, at the base of a large Elm tree. The thirty-foot high tree, was approximately fifty feet from the white-picket fence, that surrounded the neat, two-story home of the Carlyn Indian School's, Superintendent.

Although in the past, he had once met and "socialized" a brief encounter, with a white family—his cousin Henry (Hank), Billings family—that had been at his home, at the Fort Sill Indian Reservation.

Dark Eagle, reflexively, without thinking, nervously placed his right-hand, on his head, intending to disentangle, any knots…., clusters of follicles, in the strains of his long, straight-black hair.

For a second…a very brief second, he was surprised, when instead of his silky tresses, his hand encountered "stubble".

At what he thought to be 5:30 PM, Dark Eagle…tentatively, knocked on the door of Superintendent, Schmidt's home.

Almost immediately as if he had been waiting at the door; the Superintendent, opened the door, and extended his hand. "Harry… come in, come in. Welcome to my home."

Dark Eagle placed his hand into that of the former Army Officer, and winched at the pressure that Franklyn was exerting…gripping his hand.

Franklyn disengaged his hand from the hand of his student, and asked; "How was your day…did you have trouble finding the house? Without waiting for an answer, he continued; "here son…hand me your jacket.

The Superintendent draped his guest's jacket, onto one of three hooks, mounted on an oak-wood that was attached to the wall.

Franklyn placed his left hand, on the boy's shoulder and gently propelled him from the foyer, toward the living room.

"I want you to meet the rest of the family." Seated on the sofa, with her long shapely legs crossed at the ankles, was a strikingly handsome, white woman.

Dark Eagle's immediate unspoken thought, was that; the woman's blonde hair reminded him of the kernels of a stalk, of ripe, golden-maze, once it had been removed from its' protective, green-husk.

The woman, with a radiant smile on her lips, stood and extended her hand. "So nice to meet you Dark" …before she could complete her greeting, Franklyn abruptly interrupted.

"Ingrid, this is Harry Bird, the young man that I have been raving about. Harry, this is my wife…, Mrs. Ingrid Schmidt."

Ingrid, realizing that she had inadvertently, almost violated one of her husband's principal *"assimilation"* tools; the changing of the Indian students' names, to a more acceptable "*American name*", attempted to quickly, change the subject.

As it frequently did when she was flustered, Ingrid's Swedish-Accent, became pronounced.

"*Din, välkommen...*, *velcome* to our home Harry. I'm sorry *middag*... dinner *vell* be delayed. Sarah...our *dotter*, *vell* join us shortly."

Though he at first, he didn't understand what she was saying, Dark Eagle quickly and accurately concluded that, English, was not the native-tongue, of this strikingly, beautiful..., tall, woman.

Again, Franklyn spoke; "The ladies...my wife and daughter, will be joining us shortly, for dinner."

"While, most of the time..., I am annoyed...when the women-folk keep us men, waiting; I must confess, that today, I asked that before *we all together, sit down to dinner*; that the ladies give us a little alone-time, to talk."

Turning his head, Franklyn spoke directly to Ingrid; "Please excuse us dear; I want to discuss with Harry, a few school matters. We'll be in the den."

****

Franklyn opened a glass-paneled-door, and indicating that Dark Eagle should precede him... they walked into his den.

The room was small. However, a relatively large desk, was situated in the center of the room. There was a chair behind..., and two chairs, facing the desk.

Franklyn closed the door, and instead of seating himself behind his desk, he instead sat in one of the small chairs facing the desk…and motioned to Dark Eagle, that he should be seated in the adjacent chair.

While seated, with his feet planted firmly on the floor, Franklyn, with both hands on the arms of his chair, lifted and turned his chair; So *that he was facing* Dark Eagle; "Harry, when we first met…a week or so ago, at student orientation, you impressed me."

"I was at first impressed, by your ability to both understand, and to speak English; and just as, …if not more, importantly, I was impressed by the respect that you engendered…from your fellow classmates, for lack of a better phrase…, I was impressed by how they all, appeared to defer to…to respect you as a leader."

"This class…your class, is Carlyn's…the school's first class. This school, as the name implies… no, as the name states, the "Carlyn Indian-Vocational- Residential School", is different."

Here at Carlyn, not only do we intend to teach you to read and write; we intend to teach you the skills needed, for your **assimilation**, into the white- man's, civilized society.

"Your class has students who range in age from 5 to 15. Our Carlyn students will be with us… year-round, until they reach the age 18."

"Best case scenario, you Harry age 15…, you will graduate three years from now, in the year 1880, while our youngest student age 5, will graduate in 1890, thirteen years from now."

"It is imperative that this…the initial class, be successful. To help us achieve that success, I am asking that you, for these next three years…, that you Harry Bird, that you work with me…be my student-advocate, help me to ensure, that we successfully, achieve the true mission of Carlyn; To educate and to train; Indian youth, so that they…you, and your children, and their children, can successfully **assimilate**, into civilized society."

Dark Eagle had not moved…he sat silently staring at the floor…he was confused. He was not familiar with all of the words that had just gushed- forth, from the superintendent's mouth.

Although, Thanks to his grandmother, he possessed rudimentary knowledge of the English language; His ability to speak and understand English, had not progressed to the level needed…required, to allow him to understand all of the Superintendent's words.

There was one particular word; the word; assimilate that the superintendent continuously spoke, and each time that he spoke that word assimilate, he would pause and stare at Dark Eagle.

Sensing Harry's uneasiness…and his confusion, Franklyn stood and walked behind his desk. Instead of sitting he leaned over and said; "What I am asking, is that you Harry, that you be a leader. That you work with me…that you be my student-liaison, be my "Judas Goat".

There was a soft knock on the door. Franklyn walked over, and opened the door. Ingrid whispered to her husband; "Franklyn, dinner is ready. Sarah will join us in the dining room."

****

Dark Eagle sat, in the center of the dining-room table. His back was to the dining room door. The Superintendent and his wife, sat at opposite ends of the dinning-room table. and his wife. Directly across from him was an unoccupied chair, he presumed for the couple's daughter.

Delores, the family's black cook, brought in a platter steeped with hot rolls, and placed them in the center of the table, directly in front and between, Dark Eagle, and the still, unoccupied chair, directly across from him.

Delores, walked over to a cart, picked-up a large Chaffin dish, placed it next to the dinner-rolls, and removed the lid. Instantly, the mouth-watering aroma of sizzling beef, filled the air.

To his chagrin, Dark Eagles' stomach emitted a barely audible, "growl". From the corners of his eyes, he surreptitiously, peeked at his hosts

Neither the superintendent, nor did his wife, give the slightest indication, that they had heard the sound of their guest's involuntary…, anticipatory, *"plea"* for food.

Dark Eagle heard behind him, the faint sound of footsteps, echoing on the hardwood floor.

Stone Fist, Dark Eagle's father, had trained his son…, to while hunting… to listen intently to his surroundings, for the sounds made by small animals, scurrying in the underbrush.

In the corner of his eye, he saw his host, the superintendent, rising from his seat. Then Dark Eagle, heard a sweet, subdued, melodic-voice.

"Sorry mom and dad. I had to go back to my room, for my handkerchief."

Because he thought it impolite…, Dark Eagle did not turn his head. He thought it impolite, to swivel his head…, which would require his turning his back, to the Superintendent and his wife.

Sarah Schmidt, holding her skirt and crinoline-petticoat, in her gloved hands…, hurried over to…, and kissed her mother's cheek.

Dark Eagle not wanting to stare, kept his eyes fixed, on the white linen tablecloth.

Franklyn spoke; "Harry let me introduce you to our tardy daughter, Sarah. Sarah, this is the young student, Harry Bird…, the young man… actually comparatively speaking; of the ages of our student population, Harry, is actually one of our "senior-citizens".

"But I digress…, our guest is the young man, whose talents I have been…, to you and your mother, extolling, all week."

Dark Eagle was dumbfounded. He stared in disbelief, at the beautiful daughter of Mr. and Mrs. Franklyn Schmidt.

Although Dark Eagle did not give voice to his thoughts; a simple, exclamatory sentence, exploded in his head. "She…Sarah, the Superintendent's daughter, is an Indian!"

****

Chapter 21

October - 1877

Dark Eagle lay in his bed… unable to sleep, staring at the dormitory's white- washed, ceiling.

His thoughts were a jumble of fragmented remembrances, of this evening's dinner, at the home of the superintendent.

Dark Eagle was attempting to understand…to analyze—should he reject, or should he accept, the superintendent's request; That he assist, in helping the Superintendent, to achieve the school's mission, of achieving its' goals; that of teaching…preparing, us… the Indian students, to acquire the skills needed to successfully exist, in white-society.

Harry Bird… *"Dark Eagle"*—despite his reasons… reasons that he had shared with Sarah… as to why and what, had led him to choose… to choose for himself, those two names, *"Harry and Bird"* —Dark Eagle was not by any means as yet comfortable, with the name, his new name, Harry Bird.

As to the Superintendent's request, that "Harry Bird", aide in the education of his classmates; it at first to Dark Eagle, seemed a reasonable and honorable, thing to do.

However, after his pleasant conversation with the Superintendent's daughter… when he had asked Sarah, the meaning of the term "*Judas Goat*", the term that her father had used, in their earlier conversation, and Sarah had innocently answered, Dark Eagle… not quite yet, "*Harry Bird*"; Dark Eagle became apprehensive, concerned, as to what exactly, was the Superintendent, asking of him.

As he lay on his cot, staring at the ceiling… concentrating… his brow furrowed in thought; in his mind, Dark Eagle recreated the tail-end of this evening's dinner at the home of the Superintendent.

****

Delores, the family's housekeeper, was clearing the table. As she leaned over the table, preparing to remove the empty plates; Ingrid gently placed her hand on the arm of the housekeeper; "Delores…you go home now, tend to your boy. Ve… Sarah and me…*ve vill* clean-up."

As Delores attempted to protest…Ingrid gently squeezed the housekeeper's arm; You go home now…and tend to your boy.

Delores turned towards the door. As she was removing her apron Delores, in a subdued voice mumbled; "*I wonts ta thanks you mame.*"

As she placed her neatly folded napkin on the table, Sarah, with a mischievous grin, at the corners of her mouth, spoke to her mother; "Mom, why don't you and dad…you old folks, go…relax in the parlor."

"Harry and I, will clear the table, and wash the dishes."

****

Wordlessly, Sarah and Dark Eagle, cleared the table…placing the soiled- dishes onto the serving-cart, that Delores the housekeeper, had abandoned… in her haste to attend to her, *"Ma I don't feel so good"* … *five-year-old child.*

With Sarah in the lead…and Dark Eagle followed… pushing the ladened- cart, the two teenagers made their way to the kitchen.

Sarah removed a large basin from beneath the sink. She placed the basin into the sink, under the hand-pump. She then, began the strenuous up and down strokes, the pumping, needed to fill the basin with water.

Dark Eagle, not really knowing what she was doing…none-the-less— seeing that her exertions were physically taxing—hurried over to Sarah... and removed her hand from the pump-handle…replaced it with his... and vigorously, continued the up and down "squeaky" activity.

Sarah stepped aside. She smiled when she saw the startled look of wonder and surprise in Harry's eyes, when at first… a trickle of water… then a gushing-torrent of water, flowed from the nozzle of the pump.

Sarah began to place the "dirty-dishes" into the basin. She picked-up a plate, and with a cloth, began "washing the dishes". After she finished washing the plate, Sarah picked up a clean towel, and wiped the plate, thus by absorbing the moisture…drying the plate.

Sarah handed a dry, clean, towel to Harry. At first "Dark Eagle" was confused. Why had she given him the towel?

Seeing Harry just standing there…the towel in his hand, a confused look on his face…Sarah asked; "Harry, aren't you going to help?"

Dark Eagle was confounded…perplexed, this… this was the work of women. It was not seemly, for a Comanche Warrior, to do "women's-work".

The role of a "Man" of the "People" was to provide food, shelter, and protection for his women and children.

Not to do the work of women.

Then Dark Eagle remembered the stated goal of Sarah's father, the school's Superintendent the; *"Total Assimilation of the Indian; into the white- society"*.

Dark Eagle experienced a momentary feeling of loss, as he, *"Harry Bird"* picked up a clean, wet, plate, and dried it with the towel.

After they, working together, had put away the dishes, Sarah and Harry set down at the kitchen-table, for a cup of tea

Sarah opened the conversation; "Harry, I'm curious. I know that its' mandatory school-policy, that the students "drop" their Indian names, and adopt "American" names."

"What was your Indian name…and what did you choose, for your American-name? Did you choose…, or were you assigned…, the name, Harry Bird?"

Dark Eagle hesitated. Before speaking…silently he thought… does she know that she is an Indian? Dark Eagle made a decision; I will answer her question, then I will ask of Sarah Schmidt—the daughter of Franklyn and Ingrid Schmidt—does she know that she is Indian?

"Sarah, Comanche names, are names that…, to and for the People, have meaning.
The name that I was given by my grandmother, is "Dark Eagle".

"I am the son of the Comanche-Warrior, Running Eagle; and of his wife, a captive black-slave, that my grandparents adopted. My grandfather gave my black-mother *"Mahn-dee"*, the name, *"Pretty Buffalo Hair"*, because her hair to him, was like that of our animal-brother…, the buffalo.

I chose from the lists of names, the name Harry and the name Bird, to honor and to always keep with me, the memory of both, my mother and father.

Sarah looked puzzled; "I don't understand. You said that your mother's name is *"Pretty Buffalo Hair"*, and that your father's name is *"Running Eagle"*. How does your chosen name, Harry Bird, remind you of… and honor the names of your parents; *"Running Eagle"*, and *"Pretty Buffalo Hair"*?

Harry took a deep breath, exhaled, and explained; "From the lists of names that we were given by the Dormitory Manager; the names on the lists that had meaning to me were, **Harry**; to honor my mother; and **Bird**, to honor my father."

"The name *"Harry"*, reminds me of my mother's name "Pretty Buffalo **Hair**", that is the name that my grandfather, gave to the black-slave girl, *"Mahndee"*, my mother."

"The name *"Bird"*, reminds me of the name of my father, "Running **Eagle**". My father chose for himself, the name "Running **Eagle**", because of a **bird**, that he had seen, in a *"vision"*.

"Now Sarah, it is my turn to ask of you, the answer to two questions that formed in my mind, the moment that I first saw you.

Sarah was curious… intrigued. "My goodness, I will certainly answer…provided; one, that I know the answers; two, if your question or questions, are not too personal."

From the expression on the young man's face; It was to Sarah, obvious that Harry…that *Dark Eagle*, was puzzled by her response.

Before she could clarify… Dark Eagle spoke; "Though my English is passable, sometimes I speak the wrong words, Sarah, if I have angered you… if my words have angered you; that is…was not, my purpose."

Sarah immediately responded; "No, no Harry, please, please, ask your questions. If I think a question is inappropriate…that is if I think the question is too personal, I won't take offence, I will just choose not to answer.

"With that being said; Please Harry, ask your questions."

Dark Eagle was hesitant, the change in the tenure of Sarah's voice, lead him to believe that she was either angry…, or that she was on the verge, of becoming angry.

Despite his apprehensions, Dark Eagle decided to continue; to seek the answers, to his questions.

"Earlier tonight…before dinner, your father was talking to me in his office. He asked for my help with the students. He said that he wanted me to be his; "*Judas Goat*". I do not know what this means, what is a "*Judas Goat*".

Sarah hesitated. Before attempting to answer Harry's question, she needed a moment to think. Sarah stood; and walked over to the sink. She picked up a water glass and began pumping water into the glass.

When the glass was half filled, Sarah placed a second glass under the spicket, and looking over her shoulder asked; "Harry, would you like a glass of water?" Dark Eagle declined.

Thirteen-year-old, Sarah Schmidt, returned and sat across from Dark Eagle.

Sarah took a sip of water, placed the water-tumbler on the tabletop, and responded to Dark Eagles first question. "I do not know what the term "*Judas Goat*" means." However, in Sunday school class… Dark Eagle interrupted; "What is Sunday School?"

Sarah explained… "Sunday school classes are classes held in church… on Sunday, where we kids…Christian-kids, learn about the bible."

Anticipating Harry's next question, which Sarah assumed would be; What is the bible?

Sarah explained that, knowledge of the contents of the Holy Bible, was fundamental, for all, *"True-Christians"*.

That adherence to the words in the bible, was essential for the survival of civilized societies; that disobedience, to the teachings in the Bible, leads ultimately, to disaster.

Sarah assured Harry, that his class would receive frequent…daily, Bible lessons.

"Harry, the reason that I mentioned the bible, is because, in Sunday school…, that is where I first heard… the word… the name, Judas. As you will learn when you read the bible, Judas was one of Jesus's, twelve disciples."

Of those twelve disciples, Judas was the one who betrayed Jesus.

Again, Sarah saw on Harry's face, that now, familiar to her… look of confusion. As Harry (*Dark Eagle*) was literally opening his mouth to speak… Sarah held up her hand.

"Believe me Harry, you will learn all of this during your classes. I assume…, in fact, I am pretty sure, that you were about to ask me, who is Jesus. Am I right?"

Dark Eagle shook his head, affirming the accuracy, of Sarah's assumption.

Sarah's answer was simple and concise. "Jesus" is the Son of God". "Whether or not daddy was referring to that Judas… *Judas Iscariot*, Jesus's disciple, I don't know.

In fact, Harry, I do know of another use for the word *"Judas"*.

"Sheep ranchers, when they want the flock to leave the fields…to return to the ranch, or to be sheared, the flock of sheep, follow *their leader;* a sheep or goat, that has been trained to lead the flock, is a non-biblical, use of the word…the term, *"Judas"*

With his curiosity, overriding his need for caution, Dark Eagle decided to ask the second…, what he considered, the more "sensitive" question.

"Sarah I am having trouble thinking of the right English-words to say this. He took a deep breath and said; "Sarah, you do know…he gulped and swallowed air… then blurted out his question-statement; "Sarah you do know… that you are an Indian?"

Before she could answer, Dark Eagle continued; "And Sarah, I say this…, with respect and possibly…envy in my heart, Sarah I believe that, by blood…you are more Indian, than am I."

There was an awkward silence in the Kitchen. Neither Sarah, nor did Dark Eagle, speak.

Dark Eagle thinking that Sarah was either offended by his words; Or perhaps, by his giving voice to his thoughts, was about to apologize, when in her angelic, sweet, melodic-voice, Sarah said;

"Harry, of course I am aware that by blood, I am Indian. In fact, not only do I know that I am Indian, I know that I was born, a member of the Cheyenne Nation."

"I remember when I was a child… seven or eight-years old, coming home from school and asking my mother and father, Franklyn and Ingrid Schmidt, the only parents that I have ever known; "Mommy… daddy, why am I so much darker than you?"

"That's when my father—than an Army Officer—with me seated on my mother's lap, told me how, in 1864, he had found me, …rescued me, an infant, -buried… swaddled in a blanket, in the clay, along the banks of Sand Creek, in the then Colorado Territory."

"I know that thanks to my father, Franklyn Schmidt, that I am one of the few Indian-children, that survived Colonel John Chivington's unprovoked, massacre of my people…mostly women and children, at the Sand Creek."

"While, as you correctly said, my blood is Indian, my mother and father, my parents… the only parents that I have ever known…, the parents that I love and cherish, are white.

****

Chapter 22

Carlyn Indian Vocational-Residential-School – October – 1877 Girls-Dormitory (D)

Dark Eagle's eldest sister, "*Never-Weeps*", who had recently seen the passing of her thirteenth-summer, was seated on the edge of her cot.

The physical lay-out of the girl's dormitory — (12') x (18'). Eighteen (2') x (6') Iron-cots, were lined-up; (18") equidistance apart; nine cots against opposite walls, was identical to that of the boys.

Never-Weeps—as had all of the 36 female students had been ordered by three of Miss Agnes Wallace's — the "Chief-Matron of Female-Students"— underlings, to remove all of their clothing.

The female-students, were then subjected to a rigorous scrubbing—literally from head to toe—by Miss Wallace's subservient-minions. The female- students, were then issued sets, which for many of them for many of them, were ill-fitting, drab-gray, school uniforms.

The girls were then split into two groups that corresponded to their dormitory assignments; (D), and (E).

Groups (D) and (E) each, consisted of nine girls. Each group of girls—ranging in ages, from 4 to 14; had been assigned, to one of the dormitories. School-Policy, which stated that; At least one Indian-female-student, who was in her teen-years, be assigned, to each dormitory.

Ostensibly, the policy to assign at least one, of the teenagers to each dormitory, was intended to assuage the anxiety, of the younger girls; The policy was based on the presumption that a teenaged student, could provide some semblance of adult "maternal-comfort", to the younger girls.

****

"Never-Weeps", who had randomly by Miss Wallace been assigned, the name, "Brenda Johnson", sat on the edge of her cot forlorn, despondent; reflecting upon, the day's whirlwind, of life-changing, events.

Her sole consolation was that, both she and her sister of five summers, "Golden-One", had been both assigned to "Dormitory" *"D"*.

Abruptly, her moment of self-pity was interrupted when, two of the students who had been quietly talking…, conversing in a corner of the room, were unceremoniously grabbed by the arms, and yanked to their feet by a "burly- husky," female-matron…, one of Miss Wallace's subordinate-underlings.

The matron shouted; "That's it. You've all been warned…, told that speaking that savage-heathen talk, is prohibited.

The enraged-matron dragged one of the students…the smaller of the two…, off into an adjacent room.

An eerie period of total silence, fell over the jam-packed—with eleven students and two matrons—dormitory room. The terrified little girl pleaded…pleaded in the only language that she knew, the language of the *"People"…the language of the Comanche;*

Keta?… keta?…tsaa manʉsurʉrʉ …keta? tsaa manusʉrʉ" ("Don't… don't, please…someone please don't…, someone please, don't*).

Then from the small room…, came only muffled sounds…unintelligible garbled sounds, that neither the Indian students, nor could the white Matrons, decipher.

The burly matron opened the door…, and shoved the crying, gagging, little Indian girl into the dormitory. The little girl, with her free hand, was attempting to dislodge chunks, of black-abrasive, lye-soap from her mouth.

The girl…, gagging, threw her hands over her mouth, and vomited. The matron reacted by walking over to a bucket filled with sand.

With her right foot, she kicked the "fire-bucket" toward the still, violently- retching, child; And shouted "Clean-up" that mess!

While in the process of re-stuffing her blouse into her skirt, the matron proclaimed in a husky, authoritarian voice; "There is to be no more, of that heathen talk. It is forbidden …, even between friends!"

The two matrons, who had not participated in this *"disciplinary action";* Both, had satisfied smiles on their faces. However, the faces of the eleven Indian children, reflected only fear, and confusion.

None…not a single Indian-child, understood, what had happened. Nor had they understood a word of the *"white-talk"*. Words shouted at them by the burly, white-matron, which to the Indian-children, sounded like; loud, nonsensical, *"gibberish"*.

Precious In His Sight

****

In addition to the universal, teaching of all of the students—both male and female, the 3 **_R's_**; **_R_**eading, w**_R_**iting and a**_R_**ithematic; And the obligatory two hours, devoted to the proselytization of Christianity—the teaching…the training, of vocational "skills "aspect of the children's education, was based strictly on…, and in accordance to, the student's gender.

Boys were trained as: "Carpenters"; "Smithy(s); "Farm-hands"; "Leatherworkers-Harness & Saddle Makers";

Girls were trained as: "Domestic-servants"; "Laundresses"; Seamtresses.

****

Carlyn Indian Vocational-Residential-School – September 8th, – 1883 Girls-Dormitory (D)

The sounds of the "morning-bugle", announcing the beginning of another, day, awakened "Never-Weeps". Never-Weeps, made up her bed, and as she did each morning, sat on her bed, awaiting the radiant smile of her sister, "Golden-One".

After having waited five full minutes, her annoyance at her little-sister's tardiness, was beginning to turn into alarm.

Because of the school policy to separate friends and family; Attempting to keep both herself and her little sister, together in the same dormitory, "Never-Weeps", who had been given the new "American name", Eighteen year-old Brenda Johnson…Brenda Johnson *("Never-Weeps")*, the "Dorm- Captain", of Dormitory (D), had assigned the last cot, in the row of cots, on the opposite side of the room, to her little sister, nine-year-old *"Golden- One"*, whose name, five years earlier, had been changed to; Rose Grant.

"Brenda Johnson *("Never-Weeps")* was surprised to see that her sister, was still in bed, wrapped tightly, in her blanket.

Brenda Johnson *("Never-Weeps")* called out her sister's *"new"* name; "Rose…Rose, did you not hear, the sound of the bugle?"

Brenda bent down and pulled the blanket, which was being tightly held by her sister.

Rose was shivering. She moaned; and began spasmodically coughing, "Brenda…Brenda, I don't feel so good".

"Rose'… *("Golden-One's")* face was flushed. Brenda bent-down and put her hand on her sister's forehead. Rose' forehead was hot and wet.

Brenda yanked the blanket off of the bed adjacent to her sister's, and spread the dry blanket over Rose', shivering body.

Frantic with fear, Brenda stood; turned, and as fast as she could, ran towards the infirmary, screaming at the top of her lungs…, "help", "help".

****

Book IV

Hampton Normal and Agricultural Institute

Chapter 23

Hampton Normal and Agricultural Institute; Hampton, Virginia September, 1868

The Office of the "Principal" of the Hampton Normal and Agricultural

"Dr. Winslow, please take a seat. It is a pleasure to finally meet you. I've read and been, an admirer of your scholarship, at Gettysburg College…; And your willingness to leave…, a tenured position, at that prestigious temple, of liberal-academia, to join the AMA, and help impart to the black- freedmen and Native American's, the fundamentals needed, for their success."

Eleanor sat quietly, her hands folded in her lap, in awe, listening to this bona fide "Civil-War-Hero", General Samuel C. Armstrong.

For a brief moment, while he was speaking, Eleanor loss focus… she did not hear the words being spoken, by the principal, as she in her mind, was reminded of exactly why, she so admired Samuel Armstrong.

This thirty-nine-year-old still, relatively *"young"* man seated behind his desk, across from her, had during the war—after having been a prisoner-of- war, in rat and vermin, infested, Confederate Army Prison—had, after being released in a prisoner exchange—returned to active-duty, in the front lines.

In addition to his laudable commitment—his continued fight for the abolition of slavery—Eleanor had strong, personal reasons, for her admiration and her gratitude, for this man…, her new employer, Samuel Armstrong.

It was during that tragic, fateful, lifechanging year in her life; in 1863— when Confederate General Robert E. Lee's Army of Northern Virginia, invaded Eleanor's hometown; Gettysburg, Pennsylvania, —, that had ultimately resulted, in the deaths of her husband, and of her unborn child.

Captain Armstrong, fighting alongside his men, helped to protect her community… protect her and her neighbors, by leading Union troops… and defeating Lee's invading forces.

Eleanor's mind snapped out of its' stupor…, and returned her to the present, she refocused on the principal's words; "Dr. Winslow… Eleanor interrupted, "Eleanor" …, please sir…, General Armstrong…, please call me Eleanor.

Samuel Armstrong, the Principal of the Hampton Institute, smiled. "Very well, unless we are in a formal sitting… I will address you, as Eleanor."

"And conversely Eleanor, here at Hampton, even though I am no longer a serving General Officer, in the United States Army, General Armstrong…or just General, is how I wish to be addressed."

"As I was saying Doc…, pardon…as I was saying Eleanor, Hampton's primary…, its 'initial goal, was the teaching of reading writing and arithmetic, to illiterate, former slave."

"However, ultimately once this has been accomplished…, as an institution, we intend to pivot, instead of just teaching the fundamentals, we intend for Hampton to become an institution of "higher-learning", to be a place where blacks and Native Americans— after their successful completion their- fundamental education—can take the necessary courses needed to become teachers. Additionally, we will be teaching our students job-skills, needed to succeed in our modern-society."

"Eleanor…, now… I will use your academically earned title, now Doctor Winslow you;" Inexplicably he chuckled…; "Because you have excelled, at teaching, at all levels…, you Eleanor Winslow, Ph.D., are what we need…, you are just…, what… pardon the pun; You Doctor Winslow…, you are just what the *"Doctor"*, ordered."

****

The first decade of Eleanor's time as a faculty member at the Hampton Normal and Agricultural Institute, saw her advance from: Instructor (1868- 1870); to Assistant Professor (1871-1873); to Associate Professor (1874- 1875);; to Full Professor (Tenured), and the Chair of the Department of English and American Literature;(1876-).

****

In addition to her classroom teaching, Professor Eleanor Winslow had—as a consequence of her assistance in the development of the Hampton curricula, that served as the template, for curricula employed by the numerous predominantly "Black-Normal, and Agricultural Colleges", that were founded, after the Civil War— gained national recognition as an innovative educator.

Initially, Eleanor had whole-heartedly embraced, General Armstrong's methods for the advancement and the assimilation of the former black-slaves, into white society.

However, over time, it became evident to Eleanor, that while the General stressed... as did she, the importance of educating the "*Negroes*", and that of educating "*Native-Americans*", Eleanor had gradually, come to believe that General Armstrong's, and her views on the education, and the incorporation into society, of the emancipated slaves, and of the Native- Americans, in many substantive... important ways, differed.

Despite these differences, Eleanor's respect and admiration for the General, the man..., never wavered. She respected his ..., service as a Union Army officer, fighting to abolish slavery. She respected his work as an educator, in his creating..., founding, the Hampton Normal and Industrial Institute.

However now, that in addition to her teaching..., now, as a senior faculty member at Hampton..., Eleanor had more and more, become involved in the setting of the school's mission; Its' goals, its' curriculum, and objectives.

At no point did Eleanor doubt the man's sincerity, his conviction...his desire to prepare through education, the assimilation of freed slaves and Native Americans, into main-stream, white-society.

However, with the passage of time…, Eleanor had reluctantly come to view *"the general"*, as she now thought of "Hampton's Principal… Eleanor had no doubt that had her beloved husband Paul had met the man, Paul would have undoubtedly categorized him as; *"The General"*.

As she usually did when she thought of Paul; Eleanor felt both happy as well as sad.

Eleanor, when thinking of how to categorize the General she thought of using Paul's catch-phrase, when he described those, he considered to be well meaning *("Do-Gooders")*. His faculty colleagues who sympathized with the downtrodden, while they retained their unspoken belief in their *"God-*
Given" racial-superiority.

Paul, she thought… and agreed with, would have referred to General Samuel Armstrong, as being a *"Benevolent-Benign, White-Supremacist"*.

The term *"Benevolent-Benign, White Supremacist"*, was one that she remembered, having heard her husband, Professor Paul Winslow, frequently use.

Paul had used that descriptor, to describe that segment of the "white population", that adamantly, insisted that they were not racist. That they were strong-supporters of the *"Advancement of the Coloreds."*

Those very same people that adhered to…, believed and trumpeted, their belief—buttressed by unsubstantiated…unproven theories, that blacks…for that matter, that all non-whites, are inherently, inferior to whites—that was being bandied around amongst… by those, *"White Supremacist"*, that Paul had believed to be proponents and purveyors, of what he called *"Pseudo- Science"*.
Eleanor had reluctantly— after having read a quote, attributed to General Armstrong—come to believe that the General was, as were

                                        Precious In His Sight

many unknowing well-intentioned whites; a *"Benevolent-Benign, White Supremacist"*.

The General had publicly-proclaimed that;

"It is the duty of the Superior White Race to rule over the weaker dark- skinned races until they were appropriately civilized. That this civilization process would require several generations of moral and religious development."

While the General believed—as did she, that vocational-training and fundamental-education, were tools needed to erase the cultural and psychic damage inflected on Blacks, by centuries of enslavement, he also believed, that the passage of time, *Lots and Lots of Time,* of multiple-generations of educated Blacks, was essential, before Blacks would be ready, to participate in society, as full-fledged citizens.

While the general's motives were intended to improve the lives of non-whites, he also believed, that centuries of black slavery, and Native American *"savagery"*, precluded educated *"Negroes"* and *"educated American-Indians"*, at this time, from achieving professional status, in white society.

General Armstrong therefore, contrary to what Eleanor believed, the general did not believe, that at this time, in the year 1877 that blacks, … that all non- whites were not ready, to participate in government.

General Armstrong believed that the Hampton Institute curriculum, should be tailored to educate and train *"smart-coloreds"*, to be teachers, who would in-turn, teach less intelligent *"coloreds"*, the value of learning trade(s), that would lead to their obtaining gainful employment; which would allow them to support, their *"colored-families"*.

Thus, General Armstrong's adamant belief that; "The primary means through which "White Civilization" could be instilled in African

---

Americans, and Native Americans, was by the moral-power of labor and manual industry."

Eleanor believed…was convinced, that the bedrock… the core of the general's beliefs; was his *"Benevolent-Benign, White Supremist"* belief, supposedly supported by a plethora, of *"pseudo-scientific"* literature, *"Junk-Science"*, extolling the *"The Innate-Inferiority of Non-Whites"*.

The Principal… (*The President*), of the Hampton Institute, believed that blacks should refrain from voting and politics.

Eleanor was convinced that the primary motivation, that kept and sustained the General's emphasis that;" *Technical-Vocational Studies"*, as opposed to giving an at least equal emphasis, to Eleanor's particular area of expertise; that being, Liberal Arts and Sciences - *"The Humanities"*, be emphasized at, the Hampton Institute Normal and Industrial Institute, could be attributed to what she thought were; the General's *"Benevolent-Benign, White Supremist"* beliefs.

The General was of the belief that, vocational-training…, *supplemented*, with basic academic courses, were the tools needed to erase, the cultural and psychic damage inflected on the Negro, by centuries of enslavement.

He believed that time, measured in terms of generations, of educated Negroes, was essential, before blacks would be ready, to participate in white-society, as full-fledged citizens.

The General did not believe, that at this time in the United States, in the year of our Lord, 1878; that blacks, were ready to be participants in either local, city, state, or the National government.

****

Over the past decade, despite her ambitious and frantic schedule, burying herself in her work, Eleanor had…, as would most single, healthy, 36-year- old, adults—especially those who had enjoyed the intimacy and the companionship of a blissfully, happy marriage—was lonely.

While Eleanor missed her *"intimate"* time with her slain-husband Paul…; the *"intercourse"*, that she most missed, was that of their *"social- intercourse"*.

The time that they had spent just talking, laughing…, she even missed those times when they had argued over silly little things; things that now; no matter how hard she tried, she just could not, remember.

When one of Eleanor's colleagues, Professor, Oliver Jenkins, in the school's "Department of Mathematics", asked her to go out…, to have dinner with him, Eleanor— although she was both lonely…, and flattered—had declined the mathematician's, invitation.

Fifteen years, had elapsed, since the death of her beloved husband Paul, and even after 15 long, lonely years, Eleanor could not shake… what she knew to be…the irrational feeling, that being with another man, meant that she would somehow, be cheating on…despoiling, her cherished memories of, Paul.

Eleanor realized, that lying alone night after night, thinking of Paul, and replaying in her mind…if not all, definitely most, of their *"Good-times'*…, paradoxically, she could not recall…, at least in detail…, not a single memory of one of their occasional, marital-squabbles.

Intellectually, Eleanor knew that "living in the *"dead"* past, and not moving on with her life, was a major cause of her increasing, episodic, bouts of depression.

Eleanor's lonely-nights, lying in her bed…, remembering, and silently crying into her pillow, until exhausted… before finally falling asleep, was beginning to have an adverse effect on her mental-health.

It was only after confiding in correspondence, with her friend, Elizabeth Jones…, and Elizabeth's vehement, almost pleadings…, encouragement, that she, Professor Eleanor Winslow, abandon her monastic existence, and *"Get-out There"*, that Eleanor accepted Oliver Jenkins latest, dinner invitation.

The combination of her best friend's constant, pleadings, *"Lizzie's"* well intentioned *nagging*, coupled with the persistence of Dr. Oliver Jenkins, her *"suitor"*, that Eleanor, had reluctantly agreed to accept the latest request for a *"date"*, from her twice-widowed, colleague, Dr. Oliver Jenkins.

****

It was after six "delightful" but boring dinners, with Oliver Jenkins—the details of which, were shared, via the U.S. mail with her best friend "Lizzie"
— that Professor Eleanor Winslow finally, did not stop, Oliver's wandering hands from massaging her thighs, and when they kissed, she reluctantly, did not prevent Oliver's probing eager-tongue, from entering into her mouth.

When Oliver left her apartment, following their third *"Time-In-Bed"*, immediately following his leaving the apartment…after changing the bed linen; instead of attempting to sleep; Eleanor sat up in bed…, and increased the flow of oil, to the bed-side lamp; thereby illuminating the room.

Eleanor took pen and paper from the drawer of her bedside-table, and in a letter to her best-friend Elizabeth Jones; she began to put her thoughts to paper:

Dear Lizzie,

I write this note to you almost immediately after having "slept"; twice now, with Oliver.

Both times (the sex) has been... I don't wish to be cruel, both times the sex has been "uninterestingly", boring. However, that is not my major complaint, after all, even boring, can be satisfying.

Lizzie, its' not the sex..., what I do find to be intolerable, is the "after-sex", conversation(s). Oliver's, during dinner..., after sex..., casual favorite, topic of conversation is the "Goldbach's Conjecture, which he has explained to me ad nauseum, is some, as of yet unsolved, mathematical problem.

I know I'm being "shallow", but honestly, "there's a time and place for everything. I submit to you; lying in bed, in the arms of your lover, immediately after having sex, is not the time to discuss the "Goldberg Theory".

Seriously though, I feel... I know, that I am not being fair... that I am being dishonest with Oliver. He thinks..., he implied... as much as said, that he intends to propose marriage. I have decided to end whatever this is... to break-up with Oliver.

I don't want to spend the rest of my life, with someone I like..., instead of with,
someone I both like... and LOVE". As always...,
Ellie

****

Chapter 24

Fort Concho, 10th Cavalry
- Angelo Texas (1883)

Sergeant Justin Gulliver (*Alias; Jason Billings; Jason Ruth*), had been soldiering, on and off, in the United States Army, since1863.

First, he had served during the Civil War, as a member of the Massachusetts 54th Infantry Regiment. Fighting rebels, the white-men that were fighting to keep him a slave.

Then as a member of the10th Cavalry, the *"Buffalo Soldiers"*, Justin *(Jason)* had fought Indians…, to protect white-settlers, from Indians… the Indian- Warriors…, who were fighting to retain their freedom…, to defend and maintain, their way of life.

After his having visited…, seen the people of the "Comanche Village" … his sister Mandy's people, the people that she had chosen to live with— Justin…though he rationalized that as a "Buffalo-Soldier, he was actually fighting Indians, to protect the lives of his fellow black soldiers—Justin Gulliver, could not help the nagging, gnawing at his conscience…, the insidious, feeling of guilt, at his fighting his sister's adopted-people...people who, as he had been doing, when he joined the Union Army...people, fighting for their freedom.

During this time, his second stint in the army, Justin had managed to amass..., savings and poker winnings, that amounted to the respectable sum of; $7,089.[55]

Justin decided that it was time..., that he had done... had achieved what, back in '62, he had set-out to accomplish. He had joined the Union Army to fight to free his people, the more than four million, enslaved blacks. Justin allowed himself a satisfied smile as he thought; *"Mission Accomplished"*.

After the completion of his current enlistment, forty-two-year-old Justin Gulliver (Formerly Jason Billings; Jason Ruth), declined the army's offer, that he re-enlist. Justin Gulliver quit, the United States Army.

At the age of forty-two —Justin thought himself to be at the cross-roads, of life.

He rationalized that at his age 42, he could be considered, either, an *"Old- young man"* or, a *"Young-old man"*. Justin opted for the latter.

To honor his kid-sister Mandy, who when they were slaves on the Rosewood Cotton Plantation, in defiance of the law, taught her big-brother Jason, to read and write, would constantly remind him that; "Knowledge is Power".

And although at the age of forty-two... gaining admission as a freshman, entering college would be difficult; Justin hoped that his status as a combat- veteran, and that since technically, he was a *"Freedman"*, a former slave, eligible for enrollment in one of the *"Colored Colleges"*, he just might gain admission.

When he thought about it, he chuckled; "*Free Black* and well over the age of 21", Justin Gulliver applied for and was admitted, as a freshman student, at the Hampton Normal and Agricultural, Institute.

On the morning of September 6th, 1883, Justin Gulliver, A.K.A; Jason Billings; A.K.A; Jason Ruth, purchased a one-way train ticket:

"Angelo, Texas to Hampton, Virginia"

****

Chapter 25

Carlyn Indian Vocational-Residential-School – July 8th, – 1883 Superintendent's Home

Harry Bird (formerly Dark Eagle), and Sarah Schmidt, the Superintendent's daughter, sat across from each other, at the dining-room table of Mr. and Mrs. Franklyn Schmidt, the first family of the Carlyn Indian Vocational- School's administration.

Sarah was the first to speak, "Yesterday I, we…the letter was addressed to my father, received this letter from the office of Admissions, at Ohio's Oberlin College."

"Although the letter was addressed to my dad, it was all about me. Do you remember last month, when I mentioned that I had applied for admission to Oberlin College?"

Dark Eagle reached across the table, and took Sarah's hands into his. A broad grin lite up his face. "See Sarah, I told you that you'd get in."

Sarah, with a stern look on her face…withdrew her hand from his.

Dark Eagle, who had earned the reputation—among his peers when hunting—of being the best at reading sign…, was mortified.

A broad grin flashed across Sarah's face. She laughed…, Harry, I was teasing you. Then she squealed…shouted; "I got in…, I got in."

Dark Eagle was relieved. Although he would miss Sarah, he knew how much she wanted to continue her education…to attend college at the prestigious, Co-Ed, Oberlin College.

Sarah saw the look on Harry's face… abruptly change from that of joy, to sorrow. She correctly interpreted her friend's feeling. She could not contain herself.

Laughing, she mischievously asked, Harry do you think me so shallow that I would be laughing at my good-fortune, while knowing that your time her at Carlyn is over…that you will be soon… returning to the reservation?

Dark Eagle failed at his attempt to smile. Sarah stood, reached into the pocket in her smock, and pulled out an envelope. The envelope was addressed to The Honorable Franklyn Schmidt, Superintendent of the Carlyn Indian Vocational-Residential School.

Sarah removed the letter from its' envelope, and began to read its' contents, aloud:

> "FROM THE OFFICE OF ADMISSIONS; The Hampton Normal and Agricultural, Institute
>
> To: The Honorable, Franklyn Schmidt, Superintendent of the Carlyn Indian Vocational-Residential School
>
> Sir,

It is with great pleasure that I write to inform you, of the acceptance of Mr. Harry Bird, as a freshman at the Hampton Normal and Agricultural Institute.

Mr. Bird is to report to Hampton's Dean of Admissions:

Wednesday, September 10th, 1883, at 9:00 A.M.

Sincerely,

Johnathan T. Bennett, Dean of Admissions"

With a flourish, Sarah gleefully, tossed the letter into the air. She and Dark Eagle ran around the table, towards each other.

Laughing, she leaped into Dark Eagle's outstretched arms. Dark Eagle, hugging Sarah, lifted her off the floor, and spun her around and around.

Still laughing, Sarah breathlessly exclaimed; "Harry, put my down… I'm getting dizzy".

Dark Eagle gently lowered Sarah to the floor. They silently, stared into each other's eyes, as they both, at the same instant, shared the same sobering thought; that they would soon be separated… Harry would be leaving to attend college, in Hampton, Virginia… Sarah would be leaving to attend Oberlin College, in the state of Ohio.

Realizing that in just a few days, that they would be separated… that they would no longer be able to talk… to share with their *"Best Friend"*.

Two resilient, culturally deprived persons, who had found each other. Sarah, born an "Indian", raised by loving white parents; yet knowing practically, nothing, of her heritage.

Harry Bird (Dark Eagle), born and raised, "Comanche", who was now being told that he must abandon his heritage, become "civilized", and live his life, as a white man… a red-white man.

Both Harry and Sarah, with sad forlorn expressions on their faces, sat on the floor, in silence… holding hands; both dreading… not wanting to speak…to say… to hear, that dreaded word, "Goodbye".

****

Chapter 26

Hampton Institute – (Student-Cafeteria) – Wednesday, September 8th 1883 (8:30 AM)

Eleanor was seated at one of six, twelve feet-long dining tables, which were covered by white-linen clothes, interspaced in the center of the student- cafeteria.

Seated behind five of the six tables—which were stacked high with literature, describing the various on-campus, buildings and activities—was a "Junior" member of the faculty.

The last table, in the row of tables, differed from the others, in but one respect.

Seated behind that table, was the very senior in academic-rank, Professor Eleanor Winslow, the Chair, of the college's Department of English and American Literature.

As the new, wide-eyed, freshmen of the diverse-heterogeneous, "Class of 1887", milled around, Eleanor once again…, wondered how and why, she, a department head…, the only female to Chair a department, had been "saddled", with this "mundane" task.

As she shifted her position, in the less than comfortable, cafeteria chairs, her thoughts were wondering…, loss in the reverie, of the pleasant time, that she had spent this last summer, in the nearby town of Gettysburg, visiting with her in-laws, Sanna, and Willem Winslow, her slain husband Paul's, parents.

Eleanor chided herself, for not having thought to bring a pillow, to place between her posterior, and the hard surface, of the uncomfortable chair.

Professor Winslow's bout of nostalgia, morphed from being those of pleasant memories, to that of frank curiosity… as to why and how, she had been stuck with this particular assignment.

Eleanor's thoughts returned to the events of this last Monday, her second day back, on campus, after having spent her summer vacation, in Gettysburg, Pennsylvania, visiting her …, her deceased husband Paul's, parents.

When she opened the door to her office, her nostrils had been assailed by the "musty" stale odor, that accumulates in an unoccupied; for a two and a half month- door locked, windows closed, 14' x 10' space.

As she was enjoying the feel and smell, of the cool, salty-air, wafting off of the Chesapeake Bay, her blissful moment was interrupted by the voice of a young man. "Excuse me ma'am…ah… Professor Winslow?"

Eleanor withdrew her head from the window and turned to face the young man. "Yes, I am Professor Winslow."

The young-man, still standing outside the open door, extended his right-hand in which, he was holding an envelope.

Eleanor walked over to the messenger. The young-man gave Eleanor the envelope.

Professor Winslow sat at her desk and examined the envelope. In the upper left-hand corner of the envelope, was the name and title; Samuel C. Armstrong, Principal/Hampton Institute.

She opened and read the single sheet of paper, which requested that at her earliest convenience, she come to his office. The brief note was signed: Samuel C. Armstrong.

When she arrived at "The General's" office, The Chief Administrative officer of the college, greeted her with a series of salutary, pleasantries.

"Come in Eleanor, have a seat. How was your vacation…, are you glad to be back…as we say in the cavalry…glad to be; "back-in-the-saddle-again"?

Before she could respond, General. Armstrong, continued. "Eleanor, I'm in sort of a pickle, here…, I need to ask, a favor of you."

Eleanor leaned forward; "Certainly sir…how may I be of assistance?"

The "Principal", cleared his throat; "I was just notified, that one of our instructor's…, he picked up…and read from a sheet of paper, from his desk; that a Mr. Joseph Cartwright…, I believe that he is one of your people, is ill, and will not be able, to fulfill his assignment… Wednesday, to meet and greet, our incoming "freshmen".

"I hate to ask this of you…, but would you mind substituting…, replacing…; Once again he looked at the paper, in his hand…would you replace Mr.
Cartwright?"

As the cafeteria continued to fill with incoming students, and the volume of their chatter increased, Eleanor refocused her attention on the influx of young faces…predominantly the faces of young…, she presumed, eager to learn, "Negroes".

She once again was amazed by the vast array of skin-complexions of the "Black" students.

The skin tones of the "Black" students, reminded Eleanor of an artist's palette; the ran the gamut; from ebony; to dark-brown; to light-brown; to as her former "Black", student Mandy had succinctly described as; *"Damn near white"*.

Eleanor, as she had been 23 years earlier—, in her first position as a salaried-teacher, a position teaching in the antebellum South—, the two teenage children, of one of Virginia's wealthiest, Aristocratic-Planters Society families, the Billings Family.

Eleanor's employers, Mr. and Mrs. Henry Billings, the owners of the Rosewood Cotton Plantation and subsequently, the owners of more than one-hundred black slaves, had hired the then recent college graduate, to supplement… to augment, their children's home-school, education.

In addition to her teaching, Eleanor had in her spare time, spent many hours observing and documenting, "The South's Peculiar Institution, human- bondage; Black-Slavery".

Eleanor had observed and written about, the many variations in the actual color or colors, among the "Black" plantation's, slave population.

As her "off-the-books-clandestine student", a brilliant teenage "black-slave girl"—though in reality, the color of "Mandy's skin…, Mandy was the student's name, —, was what Eleanor would describe as "Mahogany".

When Eleanor had mentioned her observation to Mandy, Mandy had replied, using the dialect, that she called *"Nigger-Talk"; "Mis-see Lee-ree, it bees cuz of dem white men's, ah pester'n, us nigger-gals, dats why, us "black- folks" color bees frum pitch-black, ta dam nears white"*.

Eleanor smiled, at how, she had many years later…, when she submitted to the faculty of the University of Pennsylvania, her *Doctoral Thesis*;

"The Observation of/and The Rendering of Negro Literacy—Debunking Pseudo Scientific - Support of Polygenism"

How she had inserted verbatim, *"Nigger-Talk"*, Mandy's exact quote. And how in the foot-notes, she had listed amongst her 106 references;

References:
44) Billings, Mandy; Personal Conversations

****

Sprinkled among the many shades of *"Colored-faces"*, Eleanor silently counted the coppery-toned faces of six young, Native Americans, two of whom, were female.

Eleanor's initial impression of the incoming freshman-class, made her think of an expression her father would invariably say, as he and her two brothers were about to harvest their semi-ripened vegetables; "Well boys, looks like what we got our- selves here…, is a "bumper-crop"!

The "bumper-crop" of incoming students, consisted of predominantly "colored", young men.

Just as she was about to turn her head, she noticed a tall, well-built, "Mahogany-brown complexioned, student, standing alone, leaning against the wall.

                                              Precious In His Sight

That in itself, was not what caught her eye…what caused her to stare, was the fact that the freshman, had *"Salt & Pepper"* hair.

Eleanor's scrutiny, was interrupted, when a man…, a faculty member whose name she could not recall; stood in the center of the room, and speaking through a cardboard megaphone, that he held covering his mouth, shouted; Attention… attention, students."

Out of the corner of her eye, she noticed that the tall, *"Salt & Pepper"* haired-young, or was he an old man— for a split-second, the man's…, his posture stiffened.

The din in the room, abruptly subsided. The man with the megaphone spoke; "Alright gentlemen, you see those tables; well, the people seated behind those tables, for the next four years…, will be your teachers."

"I want you to form lines behind those six tables. "Your teachers will give you literature about the school and will answer what they consider, your relevant questions."

"Okay then…, as the students were about to form lines, the speaker raised the megaphone to his mouth; Oh, lest I forget… on behalf of General Samuel C. Armstrong; Welcome to Hampton."

Eleanor checked the three piles of "Hand-Outs", that she had been instructed, to give and discuss, with each incoming student.

The "Welcome to Hampton"; The "Student Rules of Conduct"; and the list of obligatory classes i.e., Agriculture (Farming); Trade (Tanning; Blacksmiths; Ironworkers; Culinary, etc.).

Eleanor, looked-up at the long line of students that had formed at her table.

At first glance, she noticed and appreciated the "diversity" of students in "her" line.

She estimated that a dozen or so students were waiting to; as they had been mandated; to "pick-up" their orientation "Literature", and leave.

And that those who might actually have legitimate, questions about what the Hampton Agriculture and Industrial College, could and would, do for them would, as she was determined to do; *"stick-it-out"*.

After she had—with a humorless smile on her face—handed the first five- students, the three obligatory-pamphlets, and murmured; "Welcome to Hampton, the sixth student, a rather tall Native American, instead of simply taking the proffered material and moving on, spoke…; "Pardon me Ma'am— he pointed to the triangular cardboard "name-plate" in front of Eleanor, which identified her as *"Professor, E. Winslow, Dept. of American and English Literature"* —"Professor Winslow, I am interested in …I would like, to take a class in your department".

Eleanor was surprised…caught off-guard. Although the teaching of Native Americans at Hampton— which commenced, just three years-ago— as far as she knew, this was the first Native American student, who had shown an interest, in studying; *"The Humanities"*.

Eleanor…, *Professor* Winslow, the chair of the *"Dept. of American and English Literature"*, was intrigued.

Eleanor asked; "What is your name young man? Your command of English is impressive. Where did you learn…where did you attend, school?"

Harry as three of the students in line behind him, moved to the adjacent, rapidly moving line to his left, now realizing, that he was holding-up the line; quickly answered; "I am a graduate of "The Carlyn Indian Industrial-Vocational, Residential, School".

In his haste, to get the line moving again, he answered; *"My name is Dark...,* ah, my name is Harry Bird.

Another impatient student, moved to the rapidly moving, adjacent line.

Eleanor, sensing the young man's anxiety, and realizing that she was the cause of his discomfort, swiveled in her chair, and reached into her hand-bag, that was hanging...suspended by its' straps on the back of the chair, and pulled out her business card, and handed it to the now flustered young man.

"If you would like to enroll in one of my classes, I would very much, like to participate in the furtherance of your education."

Harry sheepishly nodded, and left the line. Eleanor was delighted to see that her line which had been reduced to six students, had now been "miraculously" decreased, to three.

The next two freshmen, did not ask questions. They instead, eagerly took their orientation packets from Eleanor, and left. A sheet of paper, dropped by the last student, slipped from his packet and fluttered to the floor, beside Eleanor's chair.

Simultaneously she, as did...., the last freshman-student in her dwindling queue, bent over, to pick-up the paper.

The student's hand was the first, to encounter the paper. He picked it up and extending his hand..., proffered the "errant" sheet-of-paper, towards the out- stretched hand, of Professor Winslow.

Eleanor accepted the paper. She raised her head...preparing to thank the student, and did a double-take.

This tall "mahogany" complexioned young man..., was not—in comparison to the other students—he was literally..., not, a "young", man.

In addition to the predominantly black curly hair, with the attractive, admixture of…a sub-population of gray curly hair, that caused Eleanor to realized, that this was the student that she had, from across the room, earlier noticed. Crow's-feet, thin lines…wrinkles, …, extending from the outer corners of his eyes, accentuated, the man's alert but wary, light-brown eyes.

A faint, but noticeable, jagged-scar on the chin, of his still handsome face…, led her to believe, that this "not-so-young man…, was a man, who had lived, endured…, and survived, a hard-life, during these recently, turbulent, times.

****

Chapter 27

Hampton Normal and Agricultural, Institute – October 1883

(Two weeks following the start of classes;
(Professor E. Winslow's Office 4 P.M.)

Eleanor seated at her desk, was preparing her lesson plan for tomorrow's lecture. The lecture was entitled:

Ralph Waldo Emerson; The man; his views, his essays; And, their impact on American and World Society.

Professor Winslow was keenly aware that *"The General"*; that is that General Samuel C. Armstrong, the founder and "Principal-Officer" of the Hampton Normal and Agricultural, Institute, was not…, and had never been, an enthusiastic proponent, of her teaching *"his"* student's, American and European Literature.

In fact, *"The General"* had not minced-words, in explaining to Dr. Winslow, that, contrary to his better judgement; why he had acquiesced to the creation of the *"Department of American and European Literature"*, and its' insertion into the curriculum, at the Hampton Normal and Agricultural, Institute.

Eleanor 's thoughts were of the General's tersely delivered explanation to her, as to why and how, the teaching of the *"Humanities"* …, the teaching of American and European Literature, found its' way into the Hampton curriculum.

"Eleanor, the reason that I allowed your inclusion of the "Department of American and European Literature", as an optional course of study here at Hampton, was to appease supporters…; "Liberal" political and financial, contributors, to the school."

"When it became obvious to me; that their continued support, was contingent upon appeasing those donors; those who were adamant, that the teaching of the "Humanities-Liberal Arts", was a necessary component of a well-rounded education…, that I—with the caveat, that it be optional and not a core-required, course of study—that I approved the creation, here at Hampton, of "The Department of American and European Literature".

Eleanor vividly remembered, the General's personal; *"Welcome to Hampton"*; greeting, addressed to her, in the privacy of his office.

In essence, the General's closing remarks to her were; *"Dr. Winslow, it is our duty to teach our students…, to give our Negro and Native American students the requisite-skills needed to support themselves, and their families."*

"We are here, to give them an education, not only of the head…, but more importantly, here at the Hampton Normal and Agricultural Institute, and might I add at all of the "Colored-Industrial Schools", we are here to train the students; to teach…, the practical-subjects and the lessons that they have learned here, to their Negro and Indian neighbors…, those who have unfortunately, not had the privilege, of attending Hampton."

"In fact, he had made it crystal clear that the goal… his mission for the school, was to; To provide his Negro and Native American students,

Precious In His Sight

with the essential skills (Industrial-Vocational skills), needed for them *to make a living*…to survive in the "White-man's World".

It was with those thoughts in mind, that Eleanor, was preparing tomorrow's lecture;

Ralph Waldo Emerson; "Self-Reliance"

As she was deep in thought, pondering if this was the right time to "expose" her students, to the transcendentalist thoughts of who, she considered to be, America's pre-eminent abolitionist-philosopher, when her thoughts were abruptly interrupted, by someone knocking on her office-door.

Eleanor returned her pen, to the ink-well, on her desk. Although she did not have a "scheduled" student's-office-hours appointment, it was not out of the ordinary, for a student to unannounced, drop-by.

The young man who opened the door, a Native American, was not one of her students. However, Eleanor thought that his face looked vaguely, familiar.

Then it came to her…this was the *"Indian"*— school policy was to refer to Indigenous Americans as: "Native Americans" — this was the *"Indian"*, that two weeks earlier, during new-student, orientation, had been in her queue.

Eleanor Immediately chided herself for mentally…, in her mind, referring to the young man as the *"Indian"*.

As an adult, who had actually researched and studied the history of the *"American Expansionist Movement…, of "White America's"* quest to achieve president Andrew Jackson's ambitious goal…his dream of; *"Manifest Destiny"*, the continental expansion, of the United States; From the Atlantic Ocean to the Pacific Ocean;

"From-Sea-to-Shining-Sea".

Eleanor was aware of, and well-versed, in the history of the "taking of the land, by white-settler-colonization, of the Americas', from the continent's *"Indigenous Peoples; the Native Americans"*.

However, after having spent her teen-years before the war, growing-up, in a small settlement, on the then, western frontier, in the town of O'Fallon, in the Territory of Nebraska; Eleanor had routinely, regularly, participated in both "family and communal drills"; drills practicing what to do…, in the event of *"Indian"* attacks.

Eleanor, as had all of the kids, in the little farming community of "O'Fallon Nebraska, where taught that in the event that they *"saw a bunch of those- murdering, heathen-redskins"*, that they were to run as fast as they could…, yelling; shouting, *"Indians…, Indians, the Indians* are coming!"

She smiled when she thought of that time, when her brother Patrick, after seeing what he mistakenly thought was an *"Injun war-party"*; Came running across the creek, to the house yelling; *"Injuns…, Injuns", the Injuns are coming!*

She chuckled when she reimagined, in her mind that same incident. This time instead of her brother yelling; *"Injuns…, Injuns", the Injuns are coming!*

In her mind she saw…she envisioned her brother Patrick, running as fast as he could run…, running and stumbling, while hysterically, at the top of his lungs yelling; *Native Americans…, Native Americans…, the Indigenous Peoples; the Native Americans are coming!*

Eleanor believed that she, sub conscientiously, …, in her mind… because of her having spent her teen-years, growing-up on the American frontier… the word *"Indian(s)"*, instead of Native Americans, and/or Indigenous Peoples, was the first descriptive word to have leapt, into her mind.

The young man took a tentative step forward. Eleanor waved her arm, and stated; "Come in…come … she concentrated…, "Harry…Harry, isn't it?

Surprised and flattered, that she remembered his name, Harry stepped into the room.

Professor Winslow—by pointing to one of the two chairs facing her desk— indicated that Harry, be seated.

In a pleasant, inquisitive voice, Dr. Winslow asked; "Harry…how can I help you?"

"Professor Winslow…, I took a chance, I didn't think you would remember me. I'm going to push my luck. I'm hoping that you remember my telling you, that I am interested in learning more about American and European Literature."

Eleanor acknowledged that she indeed remembered their; "orientation" conversation.

Seeing that her visitor was nervous…fidgety, Eleanor attempted to put the young man, at ease.

She asked; "How are you, Harry? Are you satisfied with your classes?" I hope your expectations, are being realized."

An awkward silence, filled the air. Eleanor was the first to speak. Harry…., are you alright…, are you okay?

Harry shook his head. "No professor. I am not okay. The courses that I have been given …, well I'm just not interested, in what I am being forced to study."

Eleanor did not respond…, she remained silent. She had decided to give this obviously upset…, anguished young man, the opportunity to unburden himself.

However, when Harry slumped in his chair, and not speaking…, staring at the floor, Professor Winslow asked; Harry what are the courses that you have been given…, the courses that you object to?"

Harry looked up, his eyes met those of Professor Winslow, he took a deep breathe; "My first class…, 2 hours daily, is: "Fundamental Agricultural Technics" …; My Second class…2 hours is: "Working with Iron".

"Then, we have a break…, 1 hour for Lunch.

"After lunch…; "My first class…, 2 hours is: "Masonry and Brick-Laying

Harry, seeing the confusion—that he thought, was akin to disappointment— in Professor Winslow's eyes, quickly added; "I think that farming and being a brick-layer, are honorable…, are worthwhile professions. *I want to*
teach…, but I don't want to be…, or to teach, farming and brick-laying".

"I do want to…, as did my mother…, I want to teach English…, I want to teach American and European Culture."

Eleanor was confused…taken aback. Her initial thought was a question…;

"What did he say? Did this young Indian…Native American; Indigenous Native, say that his mother taught English… taught American and European Culture?"

Seeing the look on her face… the confusion in Professor Winslow's eyes, Harry volunteered;

"My mother, was a young teenage, black-girl, taken captive by my people, the Comanche. My mother was given by my grandfather, the Comanche name "Pretty Buffalo Hair… she fell in love with, and married, my father; Running Eagle."

"My mother taught my father, Running Eagle, to speak English, as well as teaching him some, American and European…English Literature."

Eleanor sat dazed, silently listening… fascinated, mesmerized. She was about to speak…, to ask questions, when the door was opened.

The janitor, a young man, a "Negro", with a broom in his hand quickly sheepishly, apologized; *"Oh, Ise sory ma'am. I thoughts dat da room wuz empty."*

Eleanor looked at the clock on her desk. "Oh dear…6:05; no need to apologize Bernard, I had no Idea that it was this late. Bernard, if …, you could…, would you please give us another fifteen minutes?"

"Sho nuff ma'am. I gots me fo mo rooms ta do. Ise be cumin back lata."

Eleanor turned her attention to Harry, who upon the janitor's entrance, had stood. She motioned for the young "Native American", to sit.

"Harry, to say that I am intrigued, would be a gross understatement. I definitely want to help you. I will therefore, advocate for your inclusion, as a student, in one of my classes."

"Oh, by the way Harry, at what school did you receive your primary education?"

Harry responded; "I am a graduate of the Carlyn, Indian-Residential Vocational School."

Eleanor then asked; "At Carlyn… were you taught English, at the Carlyn School?"

Harry's response was; "My grandmother, Little Flower, taught me the English, that her adopted-daughter, her former captive black-slave, my mother, *"Pretty Buffalo Hair"*, had taught her."

"Carlyn… supplemented… improved and expanded, the rudimentary English taught me, by my grandmother, Little Flower."

Eleanor sat forward in her chair. She glanced at the sheet of paper on her desk, on which she had been scribbling, notes; She leaned across her desk and spoke; "Little Flower; Pretty Buffalo Hair, those are very colorful, descriptive…., I assume, "Native American" names?

Harry responded to Professor Winslow's declarative question, by nodding his head. Affirming the correctness, of her assumption.

Without having been asked, Harry volunteered. *"Comanche"* names are meaningful names. They often reflect the deeds, the visions, and/or the physical appearance of the person."

"My grandmother's name, "Little Flower", was given to her by her grandfather, when she was a child. He chose for her, the name Little Flower because her smile, when she was a baby, reminded him of a blooming field of flowers."

"My black mother, *"Pretty Buffalo Hair"*, was given her name by my grandfather, because, the texture of her hair reminded him, of the wooly- hair, of the mane of the Peoples' animal-brother, the "buffalo."

"Professor Winslow, your interest in *"Comanche"* names, leads me to believe, that you have probably surmised that; My *"Comanche-Name"*, is not, Harry Bird."

Eleanor did not speak. Harry, because she had not spoken, without having been asked to…, continued.

"When we arrived at the Carlyn, Indian Residential-Industrial-Vocational School, we were told, that we would not be allowed to keep our Comanche names. That our retention *of* those names, would hinder our assimilation, into "White-Society."

"We were given two lists of names, and told to pick a name; one from each list. We were told that failure to pick a name, would result in having a name, assigned to you, by your dormitory manager."

"The name that had been given me, by my grandfather, is *"Dark Eagle"*. **_Dark_** is to honor my black-mother, and **_Eagle_**, from the name of my father, Running Eagle."

"From the list of first names, I chose the name **Harry**. From the surname list, I chose the name **"Bird"**.

"The name Harry, will always remind me, of my black-mother, *"Pretty Buffalo **_Hair_**"*, who chose to live her life, as *"Comanche"*. And I chose the name *"**_Bird_**"*, to keep in my heart, my father, the Comanche Warrior, Running Eagle."

Eleanor glanced at the clock on her desk; 6:14. "Harry…personally, I would prefer…It would be my honor, to call you *"Dark Eagle"*, but alas; *"When in Rome, do as the Romans do!"*

Eleanor saw the confused look; that had suddenly appeared on Harry's face. Without explaining the meaning, or the relevance, of her use of that particular idiom", she rose.

"Harry, I will do, what I can to enroll you into one of our "Humanities", classes."

Harry stood; and smiled; "Thank you Professor Winslow… I can't thank you enough for your time… and, your help."

****

After returning to her room in the "Female-Faculty" building, Eleanor sat at her desk; and as was her longstanding-habit, opened, and began to notate, to document, today's *"Important"* observations, into her diary:

September 4, 1888

Subject: "Harry Bird"; Alias "Dark Eagle"

This afternoon-evening, during my "Office-Hours", I became re-acquainted with a young "Native American" student, Mr. Harry Bird.

Mr. Bird had been the sole "Native American Student" that I met and talked to, during my brief-stint as a member of the faculty "Meet & Greet"; during, Freshman-Orientation.

Mr. Bird (Harry) was seeking my help. In summary, the reason for his seeking my assistance was; He wanted to "drop", a particular class, and replace it with another; A very common student-practice, at most colleges.

However, Harry had attended and graduated from the Carlyn, Indian Residential-Industrial-Vocational School, a school established and run by, the United States Government. Thus, that school's philosophy, its' regimen, is patterned after those of the U.S. Military Academies.

Suffice it to say, Harry was not familiar with the student's ability to, choose "elective", classes.

Within the first five minutes of our conversation, I knew what needed to be done to resolve his problem. Yet for some reason, that I still can't explain…

I sat and listened, and conversed… for more than an hour, with this very interesting, young man.

Harry Bird's innocence… the way that he had cleverly complied, with the school's mandate, that he abandon his tribal name "Dark Eagle"; and replace it with a more Anglicized name (Harry Bird), I thought to have been, quite impressive.
How he Dark Eagle had chosen, from the lists of names; the names "<u>Harry</u>" and "<u>Bird</u>", in order appease the school, while
keeping alive in his heart, the memory of his mother "Pretty Buffalo "<u>Hair</u>", and of his father "Running "<u>Eagle</u>".

Harry Bird, honoring, his mother and father; to survive in this white culture, while retaining, his Native American culture, reminds me of; still to this day… it reminds me of one of my two, all-time favorite students, Mandy Billings.

I am confident that by his dropping, one of his "Vocational" classes, Mr. Harry Bird… A.K.A, Dark Eagle, just
might become possibly, become… dare I say, one of my favorite students.

****

Chapter 28

Hampton Institute - Classroom of: Professor E. Winslow; October 8, 1883

The sixteen students that comprised Professor E. Winslow's "English-Literature 101" class, were mulling around in small groups of students.

Eleanor, stood in the hall, outside of the classroom. She stood on her "tip- toes", while she looked through the panes of glass; peering into the class- room.

Eleanor instantly noted the *"self-segregated"* composition, of the clusters of students.

1) A group of eight Negro-males;
2) A group of four Negro-females;
3) A group of two Native American-females;

And that over in the corner, engaged in what appeared to be serious, animated conversation, were two students that she recognized; The young Native American, that had earlier asked for her assistance, and an older Negro…, the man who during freshmen Orientation Day, had caught her attention, the older, mature, gentleman, with the "Salt & Pepper hair.

Eleanor was unable to make-out… to isolate, the substance of the various conversations.

However, she was able to clearly discern that the almost universal topic of conversation, was first; how lucky they were at having been accepted in this class.

And second; speculation, as to the nature and the subject matter, that the *"Chair of the Department of American and European Literature"*, Professor
E. Winslow, would be teaching.

Professor Winslow opened the door to her classroom. Sixteen students; thirteen Negroes, and three Native Americans, immediately took their seats, and gave Professor Winslow, their full, undivided, attention.

Sixteen pairs of attentive eyes, were all focused on Professor Eleanor Winslow, the "Chair-person" of the Department of American and European Literature.

Ordinarily, Eleanor limited her class-size, to no more than fifteen students. This class of sixteen, was the first time that she had exceeded her well known maximum of…fifteen students.

This class had "swelled" to sixteen, with the late admission of, Mr. Harry Bird.

Eleanor made note, of the fact, that the *customary,* segregated-by-race, seating, apparently, did not apply for Mr. Harry Bird and Mr. Justin Gulliver.

These two gentlemen; one, a nineteen-year-old Native American; the other A forty-two-year-old, Negro, were seated next to each other, amicably conversing, apparently enjoying each other's company.

****

Professor Winslow, as she usually did, had picked for the class's first exposure to English Literature…Shakespeare's Classic Play-Othello.

Eleanor had several reasons for choosing "Othello" to launch, the students journey into European Literature.

These were the *salient points,* that she had delineated in the lesson-plan, that she had written, last night, in her journal.

1. 1. Before the war, I first taught "Othello"; In the South, to an audience of three; Two white teenagers of privilege… members of South's slave- holding Planters' society; the third to a "literate", black-teenager.
2. 2 Then during the war, when I was an instructor at Gettysburg College, I introduced fifteen white northern young adults to "Othello".
3. Now I am introducing to this—my most diverse, racially-integrated, and throwing into the mix, one middle-aged Negro, Mr. Justin Gulliver, sixteen students; to— Shakespeare's "Othello".
4. It is my intent to compare the reactions, of these three disparate groups of students, to Shakespeare's Classic-Tragedy.
5. I am personally (academically?); Albeit a very small number of students; very much interested, in comparing my students', reactions, over the span of more than two decades; 1860 to 1883 (23 years), a period of social change, the likes of which this country has never before…, never seen.

****

Chapter 29

Professor E. Winslow's Office (Office Hours) Friday- October 12, 1883 3:55 P.M.

Eleanor sat at her desk, staring at her desk-clock. She could not explain it…, could not answer the question; "Why was she anxiously awaiting the arrival of this particular student?"

An unshakable…an eerie feeling, about her "adult" student, was haunting her thoughts.

Something…she couldn't quiet put her finger on what it was…, but Eleanor, could not dispel the feeling that they had met…, that she had met Justin Gulliver, before.

At precisely 4:00 P.M. Eleanor was snapped out of her, revery, by Justin's firm knock, on her office-door.

She quickly regained her composure; "Mr. Gulliver… please, come in. Please…be seated."

Justin sat. Eleanor looked at the clock 4:00 P.M. She then looked, quizzically…expectantly, at Justin.

For what seemed an eternity…to both student and professor, neither spoke.

Eleanor thought that this "awkward-silence", was ridiculous…, what was the mystery?

During her many years teaching…, teaching both elementary subjects, to students…, to both children and to adults; she had always, informally and formally, provided her students, the opportunity for "private-clarification."

To speak to her, one on one…, to ask relevant questions of the subject-matter…, that for whatever reason, they did not feel comfortable, asking in class.

"Well Mr. Gulliver, how may I help you? During that awkward moment of silence…, Justin, seated directly across from…, no more than three feet from the professor, their eyes the same level, leaned forward in his chair.

"Professor Winslow, I have read the entirety of William Shakespeare's classic *"Othello"*.

At first, Eleanor was surprised; She had divided her reading assignment for the five Act-Play into three distinct phases.

Professor Winslow had given the assignment to Mr. Gulliver's class, to first read; Acts I &II of *"Othello"*; She would then discuss daily…, discuss with the class, the characters, and the students' initial impression(s) of the *"Character"* … of the individual characters… with particular emphasis on, the main characters of the Shakespearean Tragedy, *"Othello"*.

The process would then, be repeated for Acts III & IV of _"Othello"_.

Finally, Act V; Professor Winslow would, using her adopted _"Socratic"_ method… Eleanor would guide the student's analysis of; the multiplicity, of "themes", "lessons" and the "morality", displayed by Shakespeare's cast-of- characters.

The fact that Justin Gulliver, this middle-age, black man, who by his own admission, has not until now… here at Hampton; has not been exposed to formal-education, should read in two days, Shakespeare's Classic;

"The Tragedy of Othello, The Moore of Venice"

And that he wished to _"critique"_ the classic, one-on-one, with the "Chair of The Department of American and European Literature"; will quite frankly, Professor Eleanor Winslow thought that, to be; extraordinary.

Genuinely curious, as to what motivated this "middle-aged man"…a man that she guessed was at least as old as, was she…to excelerate her assigned pace, for the class's reading and discussion, of the play, asked;.

Mr. Gulliver, while I am pleased, by your initiative, I can't help wondering, what motivates your obvious enthusiasm for this particular play; Shakespeare's _**"Othello"**_.

For a brief moment, Justin remained silent. Then… as the Professor, was about to repeat her question, he spoke;

"Professor, I was born in 1841…, a slave on a Southern Cotton Plantation. I spent the first nineteen years of my life, enslaved. Growing-up…being treated like an animal... treated worst, than a dog."

"In 1860 I went with my young master, as his slave-servant, when he enrolled at the Virginia Military Institute (VMI), which my slave-master said was the South's, preeminent, military academy."

"During the early days of the Civil-War, after the *1ˢᵗ Battle at Bull-Run*, I ran away…, I escaped from slavery."

After the passage of the Second Confiscation and Militia Act" in 1862, which allowed men of African Descent, to enlist…, in 1863 joined the Massachusetts 54th Infantry Regiment. I became…, as my grandmother Tilda used to sing, when I became;

"Ah soljah in da arm-mee, ah da lawd!" A combat-infantry- man, in the United States Army.

I advanced rapidly in the army. I believe that…no, I know for a fact, that my rapid advancement in the army, was because I was but one of a few, former southern-slaves *"contraband"*, in the army, that was literate.

From 1863—on and off—until 1883, a couple of months ago, I was a soldier, serving my country, in the United States Army.

After I left the army…, I decided to do at the ripe-old-age of 42, to do for my sister, what I knew, she would have wanted for me.

My sister would constantly repeat to me, what the most wonderful white woman that she had ever known, had drilled into her and her sister Rebecca's heads;

"Remember ladies; "Knowledge is Power!"

"Professor I was literate, because my brilliant sister, despite Southern-Law which prohibited the teaching of slaves to read and write… taught…, me to read and write'.

"*Othella*" was my sister's favorite classic. She said she was introduced to Shakespeare's Play by, and these are… were, her exact words; *"This classic was made known to me by the most wonderful white woman that I have ever known…my teacher my friend, Miss Eleanor Leary."*

My sister and her white sister, were being taught by and again, her exact words were…, *"The most wonderful white lady that I have ever known…my teacher my friend, Miss Leary.*

"My sister said that Miss Leary chose the play "Othello", in an attempt to build in her…, self-esteem…racial-pride; To show her what an educated black-man can accomplish, in a dominant, white-society."

Eleanor was dumbfounded, flabbergasted…, speechless. Her mind was racing. *"This can't be real, this can't be happening…this is impossible!"*

"This can't possibly be true. Is Justin Gulliver…, this tall, handsome, middle-aged…my age man…, is he Jason… Billings? The tall skinny slave- boy, Jason. Jason…Mandy's brother?"

Justin was so engrossed in what he was saying; that he was oblivious to Professor Winslow's reaction to his words. He continued.

"Over the years, I have read and reread *"Othello"*. The fact that he…a black man, was the General, commanding an army of white-soldiers, and that Othello was married to a white woman of the nobility, is undoubtedly the obvious, message…the image that Miss Leary, was attempting to use, in order to instill in my sister's self-esteem…racial-pride"

Justin was so engrossed, invested in what he had rehearsed…what he wanted, to discuss with Professor Winslow, that he failed to notice the expression on Eleanor's face. The look of incredulity…of disbelief, of wonder, in her eyes.

****

Concentrating…reading his carefully prepared thought-out, notes; Oblivious to the Professor's physically emotional reaction to his words, Justin continued:

"Professor Winslow, after having over the years, read _"Othello"_, many, many times, I've come to conclude that Shakespeare, instead of showing what a black man, can accomplish, I think that what Shakespeare actually showed, is that in spite of General Othello's accomplishments… that in spite of the Venetians'…the States' need for his military prowess, I think that what Shakespeare actually showed in his play _"Othello"_, is quite different from what I had initially thought."

I believe what Shakespeare underscored…whether intentionally or not; was…is, that white-society, will always think of black-men, even those black men as accomplished as General Othello; the commandant of the Venetian Army… of Othello, the provincial-Governor of Cyprus, as different.

I believe what Shakespeare underscored is that in white society, Othello and his ilk, may will be treated as an accomplished man, he will always be treated as Othello, the ***"OTHER"***.

Justin looked up from his notes. For the first time he noticed that Professor Winslow's eyes were glazed-over, …vacant.

"Professor Winslow", are you alright?"

Not comprehending Justin's words… but hearing the alarm, in his voice, Eleanor responded.

"Oh…oh, please excuse my manners mister Gulliver… Justin. I apologize. I guess I was experiencing…that I was in the throes, of a mental lapse."

"Please forgive me. I heard…your voice, but honestly, I did not quite comprehend the meaning of the words, that you were speaking. Again Mr. Gulliver…I ask that you, please forgive me."

Justin did not blink, nor did he speak. He instead… returned Eleanor's scrutiny.

Twenty years in the army… holding in his hands—practically after every payday—countless poker-hands, had taught Justin how not, to display his emotions…his feelings. Justin's *"Poker-Face"*, was unreadable.

Eleanor was the first to speak. She stammered; *"Jas*…ah Mister Gulliver… Justin, where were you a slave…in what State, … do you remember the name of the plantation?"

Justin could not believe that Professor E. Winslow, known and celebrated for her mental acuity apparently, had not been listening to a word that he had been saying.

Disappointed and dejected, Justin replied: I was born a slave on the Rosewood Plantation, in the state…, the State of Virginia.

Eleanor placed her hand over her mouth…and breathlessly, inhaled.

Before speaking she stared…scrutinizing…looking intently, at Justin.

"Jas…Justin, after graduating college, my first teaching position was in the state of Virginia. When I left Virginia, I met and married my husband, Paul Winslow."

"When I was teaching, the Billings sisters… one white the other black, my family name was Leary."

Justin's eyes immediately read the wooden-placard on Professor Winslow's desk; Engraved in the wood was; *'Dr. E. Winslow'*.

Justin looked up…their eyes met. "Prior to my marriage to Paul… to Dr. Paul Winslow— my husband Paul, was killed— he was a casualty of the Civil War. Prior to my marriage, my name… my maiden-name was… Leary, Justin, I am, Eleanor Leary".

****

Professor E. Winslow's Office; Friday 7:15 P.M

Eleanor's initial reaction to having found, an actual tangible link, to her past…to what she considered one of the most enlightening, remarkable, times in her personal…and her professional life, was that of both genuine glee and exultation.

The guilt for not having warned her two teenage students, her two friends that their father—Eleanor had long suspected that Rebecca's father, Henry Billings, the Master of the Rosewood Plantation—was also the slave-girl, Mandy's father—that her employer, Henry Billings knew that his property, the slave-girl Mandy, could read and write.

Thus, that they…Eleanor, Rebecca, and especially, the slave-girl Mandy, had broken the South's most inviolable, sacrosanct, law; the prohibition of the teaching and/or, the learning of a slave to read and write.

The feelings of guilt…of possible repercussions, especially punishment to be inflicted upon Mandy, the slave-girl, had never left Eleanor…had plagued her conscience, for nearly two and a half, decades.

When Justin was asked by Eleanor; "What happened…had Mandy, and had he or his mother, suffered any adverse consequences, for her having taught his sister, Mandy?"

Justin had assured Eleanor, that other than harsh words, neither Rebecca (Mandy's white-sister), nor had Mandy or any member of her family, suffered punishment, for Mandy's having *committed the Cardinal-Sin, the acquisition of the ability, to read and write.*

Upon hearing this, Eleanor's face had lit-up. It was as if a large "boulder of guilt", had been removed lifted, from her conscience.

Although Justin instinctively knew that she would eventually ask; that she would ask; "How is your sister… how is Mandy and her sister Rebecca? How is your mother? After the war, did you return to Rosewood?"

Justin dreaded having to answer those as yet… still, unasked questions.

Luckily, Eleanor looked at her desk-clock. She saw that the time was 7:30 P.M.

It was then that Eleanor realized that she, and her student, Justin Gulliver, were the only ones left, in the building.

Professor E. Winslow exclaimed, "Oh dear…the time has flown. We've been at this for more than 2½ hours."

"I'm sorry Justin…I've inadvertently, reversed our positions. Instead of my providing answers to your questions…it's been you, answering… my torrent of questions. For that…I apologize. If you would like, we can reschedule?"

When Eleanor saw the hesitant look on Justin's face, she added emphatically, … "Justin, I would very much like to reschedule…not only to attentively listen to, and respond to, your "*Othello*" comments, I must confess, that I have selfish reasons…motives for wanting to reschedule."

"I have a slew of questions to ask you, about the lives of my former students…my friends, Rebecca and Mandy Billings."

Eleanor stood and began to gather her personal items from her desk. Justin remained seated. Eleanor noticing that her student had not moved, asked; "Justin, is there something else?"

Justin hesitated, then replied, "Professor Winslow… he looked over his shoulder towards the door, it's late… it's dark outside, …Professor, I ask that you please allow me… no I insist that for your safety, that you allow me to … I insist on walking with you…seeing you safely, to your quarters."

Eleanor was about to decline…to assure Justin that, while she appreciated his concern…that she felt perfectly safe in walking alone, the short distance, to her residence.

Instead, she remained silent, gathered her papers and her handbag, and followed Justin, locking her office-door, as the departed.

For the first two-minutes, of their five-minute walk, neither, the student nor did the Professor, speak.

Then without warning, like floodwater cascading over a breeched-seawall, Justin in an anguished voice, blurted out; *"Mandy…my sister Mandy, is dead."*

In midstride, Eleanor stopped; she opened her arms, and enveloped the shaking with emotion, body of this tall, genuinely, grief-stricken, man.

As silent tears flowed down both their cheeks; They sat on the curb, and belatedly together, mourned Mandy's death.

****

Professor Eleanor Winslow's Home (SAME DAY) 7:45 PM

Justin was seated at the small kitchenette-table, in Professor Winslow's, off- campus, three-room, apartment. Utilizing the sleeve of his jacket, he was attempting to dry, the tears that had dampened his cheeks.

Eleanor, carrying a tray, on which were two cups of tea, sat the tray in the center of the small table.

She placed a cup of tea in front of Justin; she then sat down in the chair, opposite her guest, sipped her tea, and spoke: "Justin I appreciate how difficult talking about this must be. I'll understand if you don't… if you don't want to… Eleanor studied Justin's face…before continuing; "When…how, did Mandy…she stopped in mid-sentence.

Justin had abruptly raised his hand; indicating that she should stop.

Eleanor was about to apologize. Before she could speak, in a subdued but…firm voice, Justin spoke; "Professor Winslow… Miss Leary, I can only tell you what my sister, Mandy's white-sister…Rebecca, told me…shared, with me."

"I think that that should partially answer your questions. However, I feel it only appropriate…it best, that Mandy's… Pretty Buffalo Hair's son, Dark Eagle, tell you that which, I honestly do not know."

"If you would like Professor… I think that I can make that happen".

Instead of enlightenment, Eleanor was now, totally confused. She sputtered… "Mandy had a son… and what or who, is Pretty Buffalo Hair?"

"Justin smiled… "Yes professor, my sister Mandy- Pretty Buffalo Hair, had a son. As a matter of fact, you've met her son."

Mandy's son "Dark Eagle" … is one of your students… a classmate of mine, he is my nephew."

"Dark Eagle's" Angelized-American name is… Harry Bird. "

****

Justin, seeing on Professor Winslow's face, first a look of confusion, which had almost instantly morphed into that of shock and surprise. had decided to leave and give the professor time, to process the *"Treasure-Chest"*, of information that she had just received from him.

Earlier, during his "Office-hours" session, with Professor Winslow; and especially after she had admitted to, not having heard a word, of his assessment of *"Othello"*, Justin had stared in disbelief, at the Professor's face.

Justin's stare of disappointment, had turned into an intense, in-detailed study of Professor Eleanor Winslow's face; That reenforced his nagging feeling… his vague feeling, that until now, he had not understood.

Justin's now intense prolonged, scrutiny, *"took-in"* the physical features of Professor Eleanor Winslow.

Justin recalled that day at the orientation, when she had stood, he had estimated her height to be perhaps, five feet-five or six inches.

The color of the professor's hair was reddish-brown, with a few inter spaced, strands of silver-toned gray streaks at her temples. Her hair was swept-back from her forehead; gathered into a "bun", on top of her head.

Professor Winslow's eyes were blue…not your garden-variety blue eyes; Justin thought that the more accurate descriptive word, for the color of her eyes would be, dark-blue…violet.

Justin's feeling of *"déjà vu"*, bolstered by Professor Winslow's…, her earlier declaration, had now been confirmed.

In the South's antebellum world, a *"segregated-apartheid"* world, for a brief time in their lives he, and Professor E. Winslow; then *Miss Eleanor Leary*, had on …Virginia's Rosewood Plantation, in a sense, they had *"grown- up"*, together.

****

Chapter 30

Professor Eleanor Winslow's Office – Monday, October 15th 1883

Eleanor was seated behind her desk. Again, for the third time in the last five minutes, she stood…walked around her desk, and repositioned the two chairs, fronting the desk.

Normally, her student "Office-Hour(s)" meetings, were just that. Herself with one of her students.

The purpose of the student-scheduled-meetings was to—at the student's request—provide a venue, for a "one-on-one" opportunity for student/teacher scholastic-interaction.

This particular "Office-Hour(s)" meeting, was different. This time, instead of the student requesting the meeting…, this time, the teacher, Professor Eleanor Winslow, had requested the session.

Instead of a "one-on-one", student/teacher discussion of course work, this particular meeting would involve…would consist of the teacher, and simultaneously, with two of her students, events that were unrelated to their studies.

Additionally, instead of the student requesting the "Office-Hour(s)" appointment, and the student setting the agenda…, this time those two essential elements, were the "Teacher's", prerogative.

Today; Monday… three days following her extended "Office-Hour(s)" session with Justin Gulliver. Today, at the conclusion of class; Following a robust classroom discussion of; TOPIC: The "Theme" of *"Othello"*, which she had entitled:

"What…if anything, was Shakespeare attempting to convey, to his 17th century, Elizabethan audience?"

Today, after her very long, contemplative weekend, of self-deliberation and self-discipline…, today was the day, to get the answers…to fill in the gaps of; "What had become of her first… and her two brightest students, who she had left, without a word…had *"ABANDONED"*; her students…her friends and confidants; The Billings sisters…Rebecca and Mandy Billings".

As Justin and his fellow-student, his nephew Harry Bird, were leaving class, Eleanor had asked Justin to stay; "Mr. Gulliver…just for a moment, please".

After the students, including Harry Bird, had departed, Eleanor had "suggested" to Justin Gulliver, her middle-age student, that they "follow-up"…, that instead of rescheduling for some distant future date, that their previous "Office-Hour(s)" session, should resume today.

Before Justin could respond, Eleanor had hastily continued. "Justin, as you suggested last Friday, when I was on the verge of asking…, of asking you the circumstances attendant with, the "passing" of my friend… your sister Mandy, you said that Mandy's son… my student…, your nephew, Harry Bird, might be able to answer my question."

"Since both you and Harry are in my class, I would like you to convey to Harry, my request that he join the two of us, in my office, at 4PM."

"I apologize for the short notice; But considering that I have been waiting for more than two-decades, for information…for answers about the welfare of Rebecca and Mandy, I can't…, I simply refuse to wait, another minute."

"I expect to see you and Mr. Harry Bird, in my office…, tomorrow at 4:00 PM, for the continuation of our "Office-hours" session.

Professor Winslow repeated herself; This time placing emphasis on the phrase, ***"Tomorrow at 4:00 PM!"***

****

Professor Eleanor Winslow's Office – October 16th (Tuesday) 3:30 PM

Eleanor was seated behind her desk. Again, for the third time in the last five minutes, she stood…walked around her desk, and repositioned the two chairs, fronting the desk.
Normally, her student "Office-Hour(s)" meetings, were just that. Herself with one of her students.

The purpose of the student-scheduled-meetings was to—at the student's request—provide a venue, for "one-on-one" opportunity for student/ teacher scholastic interaction.

This particular "Office-Hour(s)" meeting, was different. This time, instead of the student requesting the meeting…, this time, the teacher, Professor Eleanor Winslow, had requested the session.

Instead of a "one-on-one", student/teacher discussion of course work, this particular meeting would involve…would consist of the teacher, and simultaneously, with two of her students, answering *her* personal questions.

Additionally, instead of the student requesting the "Office-Hour(s)" appointment, and the student setting the agenda…, this time those essential elements, were the *"Teacher's"*, prerogative.

****

Once again, Eleanor looked at the clock, 4:00 PM. Although she had been anticipating the arrival of her students, Justin Gulliver and Harry Bird, she was startled by the sound of knocking, on her office-door.

Eleanor took a deep breathe; "Come In." Justin opened the door, and followed by Harry, entered Professor Winslow's office.

Eleanor smiled and waved towards the two chairs, fronting her desk. Please gentlemen…please be seated." As directed, Justin and Harry sat.

Eleanor, looking directly at Harry, with the fingers of both of her hands, clasped together…intertwined, on her desk, she spoke; "Harry… *"Dark Eagle"*, has your uncle Justin, told you the reason that I asked that you join us at this…at his, Office-Hours-Session?"

Immediately, when she addressed him, using his *"Real-Name, Dark Eagle"*

Harry Bird; A tongue-twisting thought, flashed-across Harry's agile, mind;

"Harry Bird knew;" "That Professor Winslow knew;" "That his uncle Justin knew;" That he… Dark Eagle knew;" precisely why he was here.

****

Saturday morning…the morning following his uncle Justin's Friday afternoon lengthy," Student Office-Hour Session", with Professor Winslow, as they were sitting in the cafeteria, buttering their toast, Harry had innocently asked Justin; "How did it go Unk?"

Justin had not immediately answered. Harry, thinking that perhaps his uncle had not heard him, asked again; "What did Professor Winslow think of your interpretation of *"Othello"*?

****

Friday night when he returned to his dorm, —Justin and Harry, were not assigned to the same dormitory; Negro and Native American students, did not live in the same dormitory(s)—, Justin lay in his bed thinking of the best way to break the news of his *"Office Hours"* session, to his nephew.

How to tell Harry that their teacher, *"Dr. E. Winslow, Ph.D."*., is the former *"Miss Eleanor Leary*…the teacher who had taught his mother Mandy and her sister…his aunt. Rebecca, when they lived on the Rosewood Plantation.

For their meals in the student cafeteria, although there were no official rule(s); the Negro-Students, and the Native American-Students; *"Self-Segregated"*.

Justin and Harry (*Dark Eagle*), had unabashedly, enthusiastically broken the students' *"Unofficial"* practice of *"Self-Segregation"*.

On alternating days, Dark Eagle ate his meals, sitting next to Justin in the unofficial *"Negro-Section"*; and the following day, Justin in-turn, ate his meals, sitting next to Dark Eagle; in the unofficial *"Native American-*
Section" of the cafeteria.

Last night, Justin was having difficulty falling asleep. He had lain in bed thinking…thinking about, what he would say at breakfast, to his nephew, when…not if, but when Harry would undoubtedly ask for details, about his "Office Hours Session", with Professor Winslow.

How should he tell Harry, that; Dr. E. Winslow, Ph.D., was… is, the same Miss Eleanor Leary, who had taught his mother, "Pretty Buffalo Hair"…his Uncle Justin's sister Mandy, and his aunt Rebecca, when they were both growing-up on the Rosewood Plantation.

What was keeping Justin awake, was how his nephew would react to that, completely, surprising, unexpected, revelation.

"Did you hear me Uncle Justin… how did the meeting with Professor Winslow go? Did she agree, with your analysis of *"Othello"*?

Harry's repeated question, caused Justin to refocus. Before speaking, Justin waited until his nephew had swallowed his fork-full of scrambled eggs.

When Harry put down his fork and reached for his glass of milk; Justin began to speak; "Harry, brace yourself. What I am about to tell you… just might shock you, as much as it shocked me."

Harry, without drinking, returned the glass of milk, to the table. His facial- expression was that of apprehension…concern.

Attempting to allay, his nephew's concerns, Justin quickly, definitively stated; "Professor E. Winslow…is the former *Miss Eleanor Leary*."

"The same Miss Eleanor Leary…the teacher that taught your mother Mandy, and her white-sister, your aunt Rebecca, when they…when we, were kids, growing-up…living on the Rosewood Plantation."

****

Professor Eleanor Winslow's Office – October 16th (Tuesday) 4:20 PM

Eleanor was looking intently, at Harry's face. She saw, at the corners of his lips, what she thought was a wry-smile…or, she thought; Was it a smirk?

Justin had been intently listening to… and watching, the interaction between, Dr. Winslow, and his nephew.

Justin understood, that while ostensibly, originally this "Office-Hours-Session", with Professor Winslow, had been requested by him to discuss Shakespeare's play, *"Othello"*; that in reality this session had-in-fact been, requested by Professor Winslow, in her effort to obtain from Mandy's son *"Dark Eagle"*, some sort of closure.

Closure for her inaction twenty-odd-years-ago…her not telling Rebecca and her black sister Mandy, that their father—Eleanor's then employer, Henry Billings, the Master of the Rosewood Plantation—that their father knew.

That Henry Billings, the Master of the Rosewood Plantation, the owner of more than one hundred slaves, knew that the three of them; his daughter Rebecca; his slave Mandy; and his employee, Miss Eleanor Leary—who he had hired to explicitly, to teach his daughter Rebecca and his son Jesse— knew that the three of them, Rebecca; his slave Mandy; and she, Miss Eleanor Leary…that (*That Damn Yankee*), had been actively, knowingly, breaking Southern Law; by fostering and contributing to, the increasing literacy, of his property, his slave, Mandy.

Justin understood, and was comfortable with the knowledge, that while ostensibly, this "Office-Hour-Session", with Professor Winslow, had been requested by him to discuss Shakespeare's play, *"Othello"*; that in reality this particular session, had-in-fact been, requested by Professor Winslow.

Eleanor was determined…fixated on her effort, to at long-last obtain information, about the consequences if any, of their *"heinous crime"; that of teaching…of educating, a slave.*

Justin recognized and enthusiastically accepted, his "role" as a facilitator, in this…Eleanor's "Office-Hour-Session" , her attempt to find closure, for a decades-long dormant…now reopened sore.

Because of his years in combat…of leading his men…, being responsible for their safety…for their lives, Justin could understand and relate to the mental anguish of what he called the *"Caudah-Woodah-Shoudah"* syndrome.

Dr. E. Winslow was first and foremost, a proponent and believer in science. She did not believe in coincidence… she did not per se, believe in "FATE".
However, the fact that at this time…in this place, she would be teaching the son of "Mandy"; And furthermore, that Mandy's son's identity would be made known to her, by Mandy's brother…yet another *"Act-of-fate"*?

Gave Dr. Eleanor Winslow, Professor and Chairperson of Hampton's Department of American and European Literature…, quite frankly…it gave her "*Pause*".

Professor Eleanor Winslow; (*Maiden name; Eleanor Leary*); Justin Gulliver; *(A.K.A., Jason Billings); (A.K.A., Jason Ruth);* and Harry Bird; *(A.K.A., Dark Eagle)*; the three of them sat for 15 seconds—which Justin thought, felt like an eternity—in total silence.

Justin cleared his throat, and broke the awkward silence. He turned his head and spoke to his nephew.

"Harry, when Profess…" he glanced at Eleanor, then looked back at his nephew…and resumed; "When then, twenty-three-year- old, *Eleanor Leary*, hundreds of miles from her Nebraska home; from her family; was summarily discharged by your grandfather; who also threatened her with going to jail, for teaching his slave Mandy…your mother *"Pretty Buffalo Hair"*, she panicked."

"She was threatened, warned… ordered by your grandfather; Not to ever again, speak to either his daughter Rebecca, or to his slave Mandy."

"Hence Harry, Miss Eleanor Leary, left the plantation without telling Mandy or your aunt Rebecca, why she was leaving. That she had inadvertently, revealed to your grandfather, that in violation of Southern Law, his slave…your mother…, my sister Mandy, could read and write."

"For twenty-three years, *Miss Eleanor Leary*…Professor Eleanor Winslow, has been struggling with guilt. Guilt for leaving, without warning your mother Mandy, and your aunt Rebecca, that *"He Knew"*."

For the first time, Harry turning his head, now he was looking directly at Professor Winslow, he asked a one-word question. *"Guilty?"* Then Harry *("Dark Eagle),* stood, walked over to Eleanor and said; *"Absolutely… NOT GUILTY"*.

Professor Winslow asked; "Harry, how old are…what's your age? Not waiting for an answer, she continued. The average age of our freshmen"; she looked at Justin and smiled, excluding your elderly uncle; the three of them chuckled, is 18 – 20.

"If I were to guess, just from looking at you…I would say that your age falls within those parameters."

Harry was about to speak; Professor Winslow's raised hand, stopped him.

"Harry…by the way, last Friday, at our initial "Office-Hours" session, was when your uncle Justin, shared with me your preferred, Comanche name *"Dark Eagle"*.

"I am not using your…, that beautiful, meaningful, name, simply because Harry, if I did, my referring to you as *"Dark Eagle"*, instead of as Harry Bird, that could very well, negatively-affect, your time here at Hampton and beyond."

"If you're curious as to why…the reason that I introduced your age, into this discussion; is to give you a time-reference, for what I am about to say."

Both uncle and nephew had attentive…but quizzical, expressions, on their faces.

Professor Winslow continued, by asking Harry; "Harry, when I speak of the "Civil War", as my father used to say; *"I'd bet you dollars to donuts"* that you'd probably say, or at least think…1860, that… that's practically, "Ancient History".

"Well to me…, and I dare say, to your Uncle Justin, 1860 to us… just 23 years ago, is by no means, that long ago."

"Before the Civil War; In the Antebellum Southern-Slave holding states, slavery—the ownership of, and the perennial-enslavement of four million persons of African descent—was vital for sustaining and maintaining, the South's economy".

"Therefore, the draconian laws prohibiting the teaching of slaves to read and write, which were created to reduce the problem of *"runaways"*— Slaves that escaped to the North—was vigorously, "religiously", enforced."

In 1860, I was a young woman…about your age, from "Up North…a Yankee"; when I inadvertently—to my employer, the Master of a huge plantation…, the owner of more than a hundred slaves—I "confessed" to teaching his slave…his property, your mother Mandy…, I was given the option of leaving, immediately or, of being arrested."

"Frightened, alone…hundreds of miles from my family, without telling your mother Mandy, or your aunt Rebecca, that their father—at the time…, though I suspected that they did…, I did not know if they knew…, that they were sisters—I left Rosewood".

"The very next day, I boarded the first train whose destination, was anywhere, as long as it was north, of the Mason-Dixon line.

"For two-decades, in my mind…my conscience, I have wrestled with the fact that I did not warn my two…my only friends in the South; that the Master of Rosewood, knew that Mandy was literate…that the three of us, in the eyes of "Southern-Law", we three, were felons.

Eleanor studied the faces of her two students. She and Justin, at least age- wise…were contemporaries. They were both, intently looking at his nephew.

Harry appeared to have been listening-intrigued…, captivated; respectful, and attentive.

Justin had been…, suddenly struck by an insightful thought…the revelation that, Professor Winslow, was not the only one in this room, interested in "filling-in-the-blanks", the void…the history—1860-1883—of Mandy and Rebecca Billings.

Harry' reaction… his obvious, attentive-interest when hearing Eleanor's description of her "Last day", at the southern plantation, lead Justin to believe, that Eleanor, was not the only one in the office, with a genuine "greed", a hunger for that information.

Although Justin had not, as of yet, shared with his nephew, details of his and his sister Mandy's time, growing up as slaves on the Rosewood Plantation, he felt that this…that this very moment, was the right-time, to at least, tell to Harry, as well as to Eleanor, the events following *"The Massa's"* learning that his sister Mandy…Harry's mother, could read and write.

Justin's eyes shifted from his nephew…to Eleanor. "Professor, if I may."
Both Eleanor and Harry, eagerly looked to Justin.
Eleanor nodded her head. "By all means Justin. The floor is yours."

Justin stood, picked up his chair, and placed at an angle, which allowed him to address both Eleanor and Harry, without turning his head.

He took a deep breathe before speaking: "I remember that day as if it were yesterday; Our mother Ruth, who was "Miztress" Margaret's personal slave, burst into the cabin…I was in our cabin instead of the fields, because I had ripped my breeches and was told by the Overseer to go back to my cabin and change."

"Mama burst into the cabin crying, and wringing her hands."

"She was weeping-hysterically, and trying to catch her breathe. I attempted to calm her. I asked her what was wrong. I will never forget my mother's answer.

"Mama's exact words were":

"Dat Yankee-teecha dun went and teech Mandy ta reed an rite."

"Massa Henry…Deys fixin ta sell Mandy an me." "Lawd Jeeesus, pleez, pleez help us".

When he was speaking, Justin had been looking directly at Harry, his nephew.

Harry's expression had not changed. Growing up "Comanche", he had witnessed captive-slaves who did not, or could not, contribute to the welfare of the tribe, be sold or bartered by their owners, to other tribes.

When he heard a soft, almost inaudible, sob, Justin's eyes swiftly shifted, to Eleanor. Eleanor was holding a handkerchief to her, red-rimmed, blue eyes.

Alarmed, Justin was rising to his feet, when Eleanor lifted her free-hand, indicating that he should remain seated.

Eleanor with her damp handkerchief, wiped her tear-stained cheek.

Justin, in a worried-alarmed voice, asked; "Dr. Winslow…are you alright?". Eleanor nodded her head.

Justin, a contrite expression in his eyes, spoke: "Dr. Winslow, I apologize. It was not my intent to upset you."

Eleanor replied: "I assure you Justin; your apology is not, necessary. If not for my selfish…cowardly, departure…if I had alerted Mandy and

Rebecca, perhaps…Harry, your mother and grandmother would have not been sold".

Justin was momentarily stunned by Eleanor's emotional reaction to his narrative.

He turned his head so as to look at Harry. He then looked at Eleanor, before again, speaking. "Dr. Winslow…Harry, every thing I said is true. However, what I say now, I should have said, first."

"Harry, your Aunt Rebecca, to no avail cried, begged… pleaded with, her father, asking him not to sell Mandy."

Despite Rebecca's histrionic-pleading…her father…your grandfather, Henry Billings, the owner and Master of more than a hundred slaves, was adamant.

"For breaking the South's economically-most-important law, the prohibition of teaching slaves to read and write, Mandy, and her mother would be sold."

"However, thanks to your aunt Rebecca's foresight, she prevented the selling of Mandy…your mother, and her mother…your grandmother, Ruth."

Justin's words had the effect on Eleanor, of dissipating decades of latent, suppressed feelings of guilt. To her, it was if a humongous weight had been miraculously lifted form her mind…from her heart.

Seeing the change in Eleanor's demeanor, Justin allowed himself to relax.

Harry's response to his uncle's discourse, was to ask Justin; "Were you, Pretty Buff…ah… Mandy's brother, in danger of being sold?"

Justin, now at ease…relaxed and smiled. "That's a great question Harry.

The answer is simple. At the time that all this was going on, I was no longer Henry Billings' property. Your grandfather, had gifted-me, to his son Jesse."

"Jesse and me…or is it Jesse and I? Justin looked at the Professor; she diplomatically smiled and said; "Right now…I'm okay. Say with "whatever rocks-your-boat'."

"Justin chuckled. Then he continued; "Jesse had enrolled as a student…a cadet, at VMI…, the Virginia Military Institute.

'Your grandfather, had "gifted" me to Jesse, to serve as his personal-slave…, his valet."

"In short… the answer to your question is I was no longer his to sell; I was no longer the property, of Henry and Margaret Billings, Master and Mistress of the Rosewood Cotton Plantation. I was the property of their son, Jesse Billings."

"I first met Dark Eagle… he reached over and squeezed his nephew's shoulder, and smiling continued; "I first met Harry Bird, some years back…when I was a corporal stationed at Fort Concho".

"My troop…, the Indians called us "*Buffalo Soldiers*", was assigned the task of escorting, a Comanche-village, to the Indian Reservation at Fort Sill.

"I met Dark Eagle…Harry, when I intervened, breaking-up a squabble between ah group of Comanche…, and a white family…, the McCloskey family."

Justin was interrupted by a soft tapping on Professor Winslow's office door.

Professor Winslow looked apologetically at the two students; excuse me gentlemen. She turned her head toward the door; "Come in".

Bernard, the Negro janitor, opened the door…just enough for him to stick his head in Dr. Winslow's office, while having his feet and the rest of his body in the hall.

"Ise sory ma'am. I wuz just wondren ifin …when can I cleans da room?"

Eleanor looked at her desk clock. "Oh dear, its six o'clock. I had no idea, that it was that late."

The janitor, nervously wiping his brow with his handkerchief, stammered;

"Ise sory ma'am. I saw dat you wuz busy, so I safs your oface for last."

"I wooden ah bothered you….but my wife's holden-up supper…ah waitin on me. Dem chillins of ours…dey gets mighty agitee, ifin dey don't gets ta eat dere vittles.

"Oh Bernard…I'm so sorry. We lost track of the time. Please…, give us five minutes to gather our belongings."

As Bernard withdrawing his head… closing the door, Eleanor said; "Bernard, please extend my apologies to…to Annie and the kids.

"Thank you ma'am. Ise gunna, shonuff, gunna tell hur dat."

Professor Winslow stood. And while gathering her belongings, she began speaking. "Gentlemen, in addition to Bernard, I owe you both an apology."

"I became so mesmerized, in what you were both saying, that I lost all track of time.

"I'm afraid that in addition to my having inadvertently, delayed "Bernard's- family's dinner", unfortunately I have done the same too you."

Eleanor once again glanced at her desk-clock. "If I am not mistaken, the student cafeteria has closed."

"Luckily for me… actually, luckily for us, the faculty-cafeteria is still serving meals."

She looked at Justin; "Justin, during your many years serving in the army, I am sure that you've heard this phrase, probably heard it many times; *"Rank has its' privileges"*.

Justin grinned. Harry looked confused…befuddled. Justin explained to his nephew… Harry, I do believe that Professor Winslow, has invited us to dinner at the faculty cafeteria.

****

Professor Winslow and her guests, after having finished a "surprisingly-delicious" meal; "Fried chicken Mashed potatoes and gravy; Collard-greens and hot-cornbread, were relaxing over apple-pie and coffee.

Justin slid back his chair; patted his stomach and jokingly sighed; "If only I had known."

Both Harry and Professor waited for the "punch-line". When Justin did not continue, Harry and Eleanor looked quizzically at each other. Eleanor shrugged her shoulder.

Justin contentedly sighed and said; When I was in the army, we heard that phrase ""Rank has its' privileges", banded around all the time."

With a broad smile covering his face from ear to ear, he patted his stomach; "If only I had known... that "Rank has its' privileges", meant eating like this, I would have reupped, and become an officer".

Both Harry and Eleanor laughed. Harry innocently remarked; "Fat chance of that happening. Buffalo soldiers don't have officers."

Living on the fort Sill Indian Reservation, *"Dark Eagle"* (Harry), when he had on occasion left the reservation; the reservation was *"Off-Limits"*, to the soldiers; he recalled seeing the "Buffalo Soldiers".

As a twelve-year-old, Dark Eagle remembered asking Gray Wolf, his grandfather; "Why among the black Buffalo Soldiers… at the fort, why are all of the "Soldier-Chiefs" white?"

Gray Wolf had continued to silently smoke his pipe, thinking before answering; "I do not know. Many of the of the ways…the actions of the white-man, remain a mystery to me."

Professor Winslow—who was by no means, an expert on the "Officer-Core" of United States Army—joined in the conversation.

"Harry, I think that times are changing. I remember reading in the newspaper…I believe it was in 1877, that a Negro… a Mr. Henry O. Flipper, a former slave like your uncle Justin, graduated from West Point, and was commissioned 2nd Lieutenant Henry O. Flipper, the first black commissioned officer in the United States Military."

Justin smiling, gave Eleanor an appreciative look. Then he added; "That's right young'un.

"I remember…at the time the 10th Cavalry was stationed in Texas, at Fort Concho…, when *"Flip"*, that's what the men called him…when Lieutenant Flipper, came a riding… sitting high and proud in his saddle, reporting for duty, through the fort's gates."

"That's one memory, that will forever…, let's just say, I'll never forget that moment." Justin "accidentally" dropped his spoon.

As he bent down to retrieve the spoon, he hastily grabbed the end of the table-cloth, and wiped a tear from his eye.

Harry asked; "Uncle Justin…how did you feel, seeing a black-man…a black officer?

Before answering…Justin paused, it was as if he was trying to remember what he had actually felt standing there in 1877… six-years-ago, with his fellow *"Buffalo Soldiers"*. Finally, Harry's (*Dark Eagle's*), Uncle Justin said, a solitary word ***"Hope"***.

Eleanor, who had been paying close attention to her *"Senior-Citizen"*, student, was moved when she saw, Justin quickly turn and bowing his head, reach for the spoon that had fallen to the floor.

She was moved, when she saw this veteran of more than twenty years of service to his country—many of those years as a hardened, combat-soldier—during and after the Civil War—attempting to hide his emotions.

Eleanor quickly changed the subject. "Gentlemen…as much as it distresses me to interrupt, this fascinating moment of "Male-bonding", I think we have about an hour left…, before they politely, ask us to leave."

"Justin, before we left my office…I believe you were about to tell me, how you first met Harry… met *"Dark Eagle"*. Something about you stepping-in, to prevent an altercation between Comanches… and a white family?"

Justin now, fully-composed, spoke; "Ah yes, the McCloskey's…the white family, that had asked for, and had been given permission, to visit and to assist the Comanche, in their move from the plains…to the Fort Sill Indian Reservation."

"I met *"Dark Eagle"* … Harry, when I intervened, breaking-up a squabble, between a group of Comanches…, and a white family…, the McCloskey family."

"I had just been promoted to Sergeant, and was ordered to lead a squad of buffalo soldiers, to "protect the McCloskey's", and to escort the Comanches to the Reservation."

*"Turns-out that Mrs. McCloskey—Mrs. **'Rebecca'** McCloskey…Justin had deliberately emphasized the name **'Rebecca'**—was a wealthy lady, with considerable, political-clout."*

*"Well Mrs. **'Rebecca'** McCloskey —had asked that I… me, the recently promoted Sergeant Justin Gulliver, take her family…, Mr. and Mrs. **'Rebecca'** McCloskey's…, take her entire family, her husband William McCloskey, **'Rebecca'** McCloskey, their son Henry McCloskey, and their infant daughter, **'Mandy'** McCloskey, to visit the Comanche village."*

"The white family… that I mentioned earlier, were the McCloskey's, and the group of Comanches were Mandy's… my sister Mandy's, Comanche-family".

"There standing between Rebecca McCloskey, and his grandmother…, Mandy's adoptive Comanche mother, was a tall skinny young brave, my sister Mandy's son… mine, and Mrs. Rebecca McCloskey's nephew, … "Dark Eagle".

Justin's looked at Harry and smiled. His eyes then came to rest, on the now tear streaked face, of Professor Eleanor Winslow…, of Miss Eleanor Leary.

When he continued speaking, Justin once again deliberately emphasized the name **_Rebecca_**, and then the name **_Mandy_**. Impulsively… involuntarily, Eleanor's hands, "flew-up" to her face, covering her suddenly pale-cheeks.

Stunned, her eyes bulging…, in a subdued, excited reverent-voice, Eleanor whispered; *"Is Mrs. Rebecca McCloskey, …is she…is she your sister Mandy's, sister?"*

"Yes Miss Leary, Mandy *was* my sister…Mandy *was* Rebecca McCloskey's,… formerly Rebecca Billings', sister.

While listening to his uncle's narrative, Harry… *"Dark Eagle"*, as was Professor Winslow, was experiencing a bout of fond nostalgic, memories.

Dark Eagle remembered, that during his one solitary encounter with his white aunt Rebecca on the plains…at their Comanche encampment, he remembered…, her speaking with solemn, respectful-reverence, …, of her and his mother, Pretty Buffalo Hair's *("Mahn-dee's)"* teacher, Miss Eleanor Leary.

****

Chapter 31

Carlyn Indian Vocational-Residential School July-1884 Female Infirmary

Dark Eagle's, sister *'Golden-One'* lay alone…shivering, burning-up with fever. Her wet, mucous-blood encrusted blanket, was clutched in the bony fingers, of her hand.

The tips of *'Golden-One's'* fingers…her finger-nails were "clubbed", and had a bluish hue.

"Golden-One", whose name had been changed to; Rose Grant, lay shivering in her sweat drenched bed.

Elsie Smith, the infirmary nurse on duty, bent down and pulled back the blanket, which was being tightly clutched in the bony hand of yet another one, of her many patients.

Rose Grant…*("Golden-One")* was shivering. She moaned; and began spasmodically coughing.

In her confused state of delirium, she looked-up at the face of the tired nurse hovering over her, *"Golden-One"* extended her hand toward the nurse.

Golden-One *("Rose Grant")*, weakly, feebly…uttered *"Never Weeps"* …

"Dark Eagle", I am not well.".

"Rose'… *("Golden-One's")* emaciated face, was flushed. The tired, weary nurse, put her hand on the forehead of yet, another of her many, *"Consumption-stricken"*, patients.

The emaciated girl's forehead was hot and wet, with her perspiration.

The infirmary nurse—a portly, middle aged matronly-white woman, stood helplessly at *'Golden-One's'* … A.K.A, *"Rose Grant's,* bedside watching, as the emaciated girl's frail body, struggled… then lose, her fight for life.

With her right-hand, the matron made the sign of the cross. She then gently unfurled the little-girl's bony fingers, from her *"death-grip"*, of the filthy blanket…and pulled the blanket, up over the face of six-year-old *"Golden One"*.

The matron then turned and murmured, *"Go with God"*. She then turned, to the next bed… two strides to her left, and sadly performed the same… the very same… identical task.

****

Chapter 32

Carlyn Industrial-Technical, Indian School – The Home of the Superintendent December, 20th,1883)

Franklyn Schmidt, The Superintendent of the Carlyn Indian School, was engaged in a heated conversation with his nineteen-year-old daughter, Sarah.

Sarah, a freshman student at Ohio's Oberlin College, was home on "Christmas-Break".

Before they had both left Carlyn, to attend college…Sarah at Oberlin in Ohio, and Harry at Hampton in Virginia, Sarah had promised her best-friend *Harry Bird*, a former student at Carlyn, that she would ask her father, to… *"look-out"*, for Harry's three siblings, who were students…in residence, at Carlyn.

"Father, how could you? Harry's sister Rose, died in July, and you didn't write to him…, inform him of his sister's passing? Daddy, how could you!"

Sarah's, father…, Franklyn Schmidt, the Superintendent of the Carlyn Industrial-Technical, Indian School, bristled, and in the authoritarian voice that he had used when leading troops in "The War", calmly, rhetorically asked…stated; "Young lady, do you know to whom you are speaking? I am your father."

Sarah lowered her voice. "Daddy, I apologize…for raising my voice."

Sarah then— the volume of her voice lowered—, in an exasperated tone-of- voice, dripping with incredulity, again asked; "Daddy…, how could you?

"How could you not, have told Harry of his sister's passing?"

Franklyn Schmidt, the Superintendent of the Carlyn Indian Industrial-Technical School; Franklyn Schmidt, Sarah's father, walked over and sat- down, next to his beautiful, "Native American", of Cheyenne-Parentage, daughter".

Franklyn Schmidt…, Sarah's father, in what his wife Ingrid, Sarah's mother referred to as; "My Franklyn's reasoned, normal, tone-of-voice", Sarah's father explained.

"Sarah…sweet-heart…, although…; Franklyn stopped and started again, you came into our, your mother and me …you came into our lives when you were an infant. The doctor said that you were three… maybe four months old.

"Although your biological parents were Native American, Cheyenne-Indians, you've been raised…you've been raised white."

"You've not had to learn, to "assimilate to living in a white society, because being raised…brought up in a white society, is all that you have ever known."

For Harry Bird, having been born and raised Comanche; not having been exposed to civilized, white society, until he was a teenager…well honey…assimilation…, adapting to our ways, and thus being able to have a successful, life…well honey, that can be very difficult."

"Carlyn's alumni…your friend Harry Bird, is our…is a shining example, for Native Americans."

"Harry is excelling at Hampton Institute. I…, The Bureau of Indian Affairs, have been following Harry's thus far, successful time at Hampton. In an effort not to hinder his progress, I made the decision not to, at this time inform Harry, of his sister Rose', passing."

Sarah did not speak. Silently…she stared in disbelieve…not disbelieve in what her father had just said, she was staring because she could not reconcile, what he had said, with the man she adoringly all of her life, loved and called; My Father.

****

This week, the week before Christmas, as did most schools, Carlyn suspended classes for the Christmas Holidays. However, at Carlyn, the students…Native Americans, were not allowed to return to their reservations…to their homes.

The reason given for not allowing the students to return to their homes, was what was said, to be the fear of *"back-sliding"*. That the students would abandon the *"civilized"* language, practices taught them at Carlyn, and would revert to the *"uncivilized lifestyle"* and *"heathen"* practices, of their tribal elders.

Bright and early the next morning, Sarah left home, and walked the short distance to the campus of her father's, Indian-Industrial-Residential-School.

She opened the door and walked into the large gray, Administration Building. The usually bustling with activity building, was eerily quiet. Sarah, with the palm of her right hand, gently smacked her forehead. She muttered "Of course no ones here. Its' Christmas week."

Suddenly, one of the office doors opened, and a middle-aged-white woman, wearing horn-rimmed glasses, stepped into the hallway.

Sarah's back was to the woman. The white lady saw only Sarah's coat, and the copper-tone-colored legs, of what she assumed was one of Carlyn's female student.

In a harsh, abrasive, authoritative voice, she asked; "What are you doing here, you know…

As Sarah turned, to face the woman, the woman abruptly stopped what she was saying. Her demeanor…her tone-of-voice, changed. "Oh Miss. Schmidt, I'm so sorry. I didn't recognize you."

Most of the staff at Carlyn, at various staff receptions, had met or at least had seen "The "Boss's" mixed family; his Swedish-Wife, and his adopted *"Injun"*, daughter.

Every member of the staff was aware of the fact, that the Superintendent and his foreign wife, had adopted an "Indian daughter. "How can I help you?"

Sarah extended her hand. "Good morning, Miss…the middle-aged woman quickly spoke. Miss Abrams, ma'am, Miss. Francis Abrams.

Sarah smiled. "Miss Abrams. I was hoping that you could tell me, the dormitory of one of your female students

Miss. Francis Abrams, with a huge-gratuitous smile on her face, responded; "Why certainly, Miss Schmidt. Please…, follow me".

When Sarah opened the door of Female Dormitory "C", she was greeted by the cacophonous, girlish-sound, of multiple young female voices.

As she walked down the center-aisle which bisected the dormitory; towards the back of the room—Miss Abrams had shown her a chart of the bed assignments for "Female Dormitory "C", and had pointed out the bed assigned to Harry's sister, Brenda Johnson—the noise in the dormitory, had ceased.

The boisterous chatter, had been replaced by whispered, inquisitive, conversations.

Sarah distinctly heard whispered; "Who is that?" "Look at that at that gorgeous coat." "Who is she?"

When Sarah reached the last bed, she caught her breath. Her initial impression of the strikingly beautiful young woman. seated on the bed was; that there's no mistaking it; Brenda Johnson, looks like a softer-feminine version, of her brother, Harry Bird.

Brenda stood. Sarah asked; "Are you Dark Eagle's sister?" Sarah, turned to survey the room when, inexplicably, what had been a silent room, became filled with anxious murmuring.

Brenda—as was every student in the room— was aware of the "Strict rule", which prohibited; *"All Things Indian"*, quickly, guardedly, answered. My name is Brenda Johnson. I have two brothers, neither of whom are named, *"Dark Eagle"*.

Instantly, Sarah realized her mistake. Sarah was fully aware, that in the school's effort to help with the students' assimilation into "white-society", Carlyn's policy was to have the students replace their tribal names, with "American-Names".

Sarah hastily rephrased and repeated her question. "Are you Harry Bird's sister?

Brenda's concise and precise…one word reply was, "Yes".

Sarah smiled, removed the calf-skin glove her right-hand, and extended her hand toward Brenda. "I am so very pleased to meet you. My name is… Brenda interrupted; Sarah… "Your name is Sarah".

"Whenever I see Harry…or now read his letters, he mentions your name-the name of his *"Best friend-Sarah"*.

Sarah tried…but failed to smile. Sarah instead, pointed to the bed, and said; "May I sit?"

Brenda Johnson *"Never Weeps",* scooted over, making room on the bed, for her unexpected visitor.

Sarah reached for, and gently took Brenda's hands into hers. "Brenda, your sister Rose, has succumbed to her illness…Rose is no longer with us…your little sister…, Rose died."

Sarah had anticipated that the news of her sister's death, would be by Brenda, followed by tears-of-grief; Sarah opened her arms, ready to console Harry's sister.

Sarah was not prepared for Brenda's immediate reaction.

Brenda's facial-expression, had gradually changed from that of being politely inquisitive…to that of stoic-resolve…, of her acceptance, of the inevitable.

****

Chapter 33

Hampton Institute – Office of Professor. E. Winslow; Chair; Department of American and European Literature" (December, 29th,1883)

The sound of the soles of Harry's leather-shoes striking, the recently waxed and polish floors of the empty Faculty-Building, bounced and echoed off of the walls of the practically empty building.

As he stood in front of the Professor's office, Harry once again wondered why he was being summoned, to Dr. Winslow's office.

Due to the holiday-break, Hampton's campus was nearly deserted. Most of the college's faculty and student-body, had not returned from their "Holiday- Vacation".

Harry inhaled deeply…then firmly knocked on the closed office-door. In her clear, warm voice, Dr. Winslow said… "Harry…is that you Harry?"

Harry opened the door…and without entering, exclaimed; "Although belated; "Merry Christmas", Dr. Winslow."

Eleanor made an effort…and was successful, in producing a smile. "Thank you, Harry, and a belated "Merry Christmas" to you."

Harry had not missed the strained…almost miserable tone…the sound, in Professor Winslow's voice. He entered the office and remained standing.

"Dr. Winslow spoke; "Please…please Harry, be seated. She placed the paper that she had been reading, back onto her desk.

Harry was apprehensive. His eyes shifted to the document, that Dr. Winslow had been reading. Was it an official letter from the Bureau of Indian Affairs, revoking their financial support? If so…, if he no longer had the scholarship, he could not afford to attend "Hampton".

The withdrawal of Bureau of Indian Affairs support, would mean the end of Harry's academic aspirations.

Harry had been exceedingly diligent in his studies. His first semesters grades had placed him on the college's "Deans-List"; the list that officially recognized the individual-student's, academic excellence.

Dr. Winslow stood and slowly walked around her desk. She stopped directly in front of Harry…put her right hand on his left shoulder.

Harry's reaction to Professor Winslow's words and actions, was to sit-up…straight in his chair, and to resolutely face…and deal with, whatever came next. He reminded himself that he, "Dark Eagle", was the son of Stone Fist.

Eleanor squeezed Harry's shoulder. "Dark Eagle", turned his head, and his unwavering gaze; looked directly into the now reddened-blue eyes of Professor Winslow.

"Harry…your sister Rose, became very ill. The letter states that Rose fought the illness, valiantly. Your sister lost her battle with the illness. Rose passed away of *"Consumption"* in the Carlyn School's infirmary."

Harry I am so…so very sorry, for your loss."

"Dark Eagle's" …shoulders sagged. Despite his earlier resolve, he slumped- down in his chair.

Eleanor stood…she pulled the vacant chair over…flush against the chair occupied by her grief-stricken student.

Eleanor leaned over and put her arms around Harry. She remained silent, as Harry Bird's shoulders shuddered, as he clung to Eleanor; As the son of Stone Fist, unabashedly wept, in her arms.

Harry asked the college for permission to travel to Carlyn Pennsylvania so that he could attend the funeral services and the interment of his beloved little sister Rose…permission was denied.

Harry persisted. He asked for Professor…; he asked for Eleanor's help; And subsequently, when Professor E. Winslow, inquired as to why; Harry Bird…, why was "This particular student… why was he being denied a "routine" bereavement, leave-of-absence"; It was then that the professor was informed that funeral services and the interment of Harry Bird's sister Rose Grant, had occurred…had taken place in July.

Professor Winslow— who at this time in her life, had convinced herself that she was apolitical— was told that the Bureau of Indian Affairs'… that former President Grant's Peace Policy, was dependent upon the assimilation of "Native American Youth", into "Mainstream American" society.

Professor Winslow was told that her student; Harry Bird was one, of but a few, Native American students currently enrolled in accredited United States colleges, who were nationally thought of, as potential living-proof, of the success of the country's *"Native American Peace-Policy"*.

It was for that reason…that in order for the Bureau of Indian Affairs to…continue receiving congressional support for the program, that Harry was not, and would not, at this time, be given the full details, surrounding his sister's death.

****

Chapter 34

Professor E. Winslow's Office Friday-4:00 P.M

Once again…Justin Gulliver stood at the door of Professor Winslow's office. Again, Justin knocked on the door.

This session, the third "Office Hours" session, the Professor found to be, both interesting, and enlightening.

At this their second session, with his nephew Harry Bird in attendance, in an attempt to have her student relax…compounded with, her genuine curiosity, as to why a middle-aged man would, at this point in his life, chose to enroll as a freshman at Hampton, and what had led to his taking an elective course in the Department of American and European Literature, had peaked the professor's curiosity
Dr. Winslow opened the session by asking; "Well Mr. Gulliver…, my I call you Justin?"

Justin did not speak, instead he nodded his head. "Very well then; Justin, first I want to once again apologize, for my inattentiveness, at our last formal Office Hours session.

"Justin…before we discuss _"Othello"_, I am fascinated by your intense interest in Shakespearian-Literature. I was hoping…that perhaps, you could assuage my curiosity."

****

Chapter 35

Hampton Normal and Agricultural Institute; Office of the Vice Principal Friday, October 28, 1883 1 PM

Professor E. Winslow Eleanor; Chair of the Department of American and European Literature was seated in the anteroom of the Vice Principal (*Chief Operating-Disciplinary-Officer, of the college*)

Her presence in this office— the first time in her more than a decade of teaching at Hampton—was in compliance with the request…, directive…, the order, of Mr. Julius R. Henderson, the Vice Principal of the "Hampton Normal and Agricultural Institute".

Eleanor had received, via inter-office-mail, a terse, cryptic, note from the Vice Principal, *"requesting"*, that she meet with him, in his office, October 14th, at 1 PM

Upon receipt of the "Summons", Eleanor suspected…knew…, she just knew with almost absolute certainty, that her being "Summoned", to meet with the Vice-Principal was, because of "the rumors".

Justin's numerous, now almost weekly …often multiple-times a week *"Office Hours"* appointment, were beginning to "raise eyebrows among both the students, and the faculty.

Eleanor was looking at the clock, hanging on the wall of the "Office of the Vice Principal" 1:20 PM; when the Vice Principal's door, opened and a distraught, distinguished-looking, Negro faculty-member, whose name she could not recall, exited the Vice Principal's inner office.

With his head down, staring at the floor, walking rapidly…her beleaguered, dejected, colleague…, not acknowledging Eleanor's presence, opened the anteroom door, and exited the Office of the Vice Principal.

At 1:25 PM, The door to the Vice Principal's inner office swung-open.

"Professor Winslow…please… please, come in". Eleanor stood and followed the Vice Principal.

Eleanor was surprised by the size of the Vice Principal's, Office.

Relative to the size of her office, the office of Mr. Julius R. Henderson, Vice Principal of the "Hampton Normal and Agricultural Institute", appeared to her; to Professor E. Winslow, Chair of the Department of American and European Literature, to be if anything…slightly smaller than that of her office.

Hanging on the wall, equidistant apart; directly behind the Vice Principal's desk, were two photographs; The first of the schools' 'founder, General Samuel C. Armstrong, and the second photograph *hung four inches distant- parallel to that of the General; W*as of Booker T. Washington, Hampton's most distinguished; Negro-Former-Slave, graduate.

"Dr. Winslow..., I wanted to discuss with you, a serious complaint from several of your students".

Eleanor leaned forward in her chair. A perplexed, questioning, expression covering her face. Her initial thought...reaction to the Vice Principal's statement was that of total confusion.

Serious complaints...complaints by students? What student complaint(s), would rise to the level, of having a Department Chair, being literally... "Called into the Principal's Office"?

Eleanor took a calming breath, then spoke; "I'm sorry sir...I don't understand. What complaints? Who..."?

The Vice Principal held-up his hand. "Dr. Winslow, as to who or how these complaints came to my attention, is not important.

"What is of importance is if...are the complaints true; And if true, can they be..., by you...be justified.

The Vice Principal, picked up a sheet of paper and began to silently read.

Still holding the paper, he asked; "Dr. Winslow, several of your students have complained about their inability.to obtain...He looked down at the paper and read; "Their inability, to make *"Office Hours"* appointments, with Professor Winslow."

"Your students state that although you continue to hold "Office Hours", those sessions are now predominantly...almost exclusively with one student. Still holding the paper, he read; "A Mister Justin Gulliver".

The Vice Principal, seeing the confused look on Professor Winslow's face, asked; are these complaints true. And if true, do you have a plausible explanation as to why... you give, this particular student...this, he glanced down at the paper…is why Justin Gulliver, monopolizing your "Office Hours".

****

Friday, October 28, 1883 1 50 PM Dr. E. Winslow's Classroom

Following her return to her office, Eleanor was seated at her desk; lost in thought, concentrating. Mulling-over in her mind…, her meeting with the Vice Principal.

Although it was never stated by Vice Principal Henderson…Eleanor thought…, imagined that she had detected in the Vice Principal's tone-, an implicit accusation.

Eleanor, attempting to clear her mind, shook her head. She decided that whether real or imagined, the thought…the appearance of impropriety, between her and a student…especially a handsome, intriguing *(Age-Appropriate)* student, was unprofessional…, was unthinkable.

Eleanor decided that today…after today's class; she would speak to her student, "Mr. Justin Gulliver", and tell…inform said-student, that she had cancelled all of their previously-scheduled, future *"Office Hours,"* appointments.

****

Friday, October 28, 1883 3 00 PM Dr. E. Winslow's Classroom

At the conclusion of class…after a robust question and answer session with the students; Topic- "The Tragedy of Hamlet, Prince of Denmark"; as the students were filling out of the classroom, Eleanor's eyes were fixed on Justin.

When Justin with his nephew Harry in-tow, were about to pass-by her desk, Professor Winslow spoke; "Mr. Gulliver…a moment please."

Justin gave his nephew an affectionate shove, propelling Harry towards the door; "I'll be along in a minute…meet you at the cafeteria".

When Professor Winslow and Justin were alone, she spoke; "Jus…, Mr. Gulliver; While I've enjoyed…thoroughly enjoyed, and found fascinating, our *"Othello"* "Office Hours" Sessions... In mid-sentence, attempting to regain her composure, Eleanor, broke eye-contact with Justin, and turned away

Mr. Gulliver, while generally, I usually avoid clichés, this particular *cliché; "All good things must come to an end."*, this particular cliché I'm afraid; is apropos.

Then…in a whispery-soft voice, the "Professor of American and European Literature" said… "actually Mr. Gulliver…, that saying is actually, not a *cliché*, it's a proverb".

Eleanor abruptly turned, and hastily left the classroom. As she was walking, almost running, down the hall, Eleanor reached into her purse—pulled out her handkerchief—and blotted at the silent-tears that were trickling down her cheek.

The delighted-smile that had been on Justin's face, had disappeared; It had been replaced by a forlorn-look, of abject misery.

Justin Gulliver, retired Army veteran; Veteran of innumerable hand to hand combat encounters; As well as countless hands-of-poker; Justin Gulliver, had lost his, *"Poker-Face"*.

****

Chapter 36

Hampton Institute Male Student Dormitory Saturday-December 15, 1883

The Hampton campus was practically deserted. The vast majority of the student population, as well as the faculty, had left…gone home, to celebrate…to be with family and friends, during the Christmas-break.

Dark Eagle ("Harry Bird"). after weeks of soul-searching, had decided not to. spend time with his family on the Fort Sill Indian Reservation.

Harry Bird ("Dark Eagle"); had instead, choose to accept, Franklyn and Ingrid Schmidt's invitation, to be their guest…, to spend the holidays at their Carlyn Pennsylvania home, on the campus of his "Alma mater"; *The "Carlyn, Indian Residential-Industrial-Vocational School"*.

After his acceptance of the Schmidt's invitation. Harry wrote a letter to his Grandparents, Gray Wolf and Little Flower/via Mr. Terrence Lawrence, Indian Agent-Fort Sill Indian Reservation, Oklahoma Territory, USA.

When the Indian agent read the letter to Gray Wolf and to Little Flower, Dark Eagle's grandparents…Little Flower was initially disappointed hurt

Little Flower looked to her soul-mate, her husband of more than forty-winters. Gray Wolf's stoic, lined-weathered-face, was expressionless.

Having lived, more than forty-winters in a polygamous society, as the sole wife of Gray Wolf…after having giving this man four babies, Little Flower knew that the stoic face of her husband, was a façade. She knew that Gray Wolf was hurt.

Little Flower asked the Agent to please…once again, read "Dark Eagle's" words.

The Indian Agent complied:

> My loved and honored grandparents;
>
> I write to tell you that I have been invited by my best-friend, Sarah Schmidt, to spend my Christmas vacation, with Sarah and her family, here at the Carlyn School.
>
> My time back at the school, will be not only with Sarah; Sarah and I will also visit with your grandchildren, my brother
> "Under Foot", and my sister, "Never Weeps". Sarah and I, send to you, our undying love. Your Loving grandson,
> Dark Eagle

Each time that the agent read the name *"Sarah"*; From her lift hand, Little Flower, would extend a finger.

Little Flower held her left-hand, all of the fingers extended, up in front of her husband, Gray Wolf's face. In her soft, lilting, loving voice, she spoke;

"This many times in his letter, Dark Eagle, said the name *"Sarah"*.

"As did his father, our son Running Eagle…many winters past, when he was ill; fighting the evil-spirits, for his life. When instead of calling out to me, "Little Flower", his mother… our son, Running Eagle, Dark Eagles father, called out the name *"Mahn-dee"* the name of the girl who would later, become his wife; Dark Eagle's mother, *"Pretty Buffalo Hair"*.

"Though he was near death, our son Running Eagle chose to call for his woman…, not his mother. To embrace the future, not the past."

"My husband; Grandfather of Dark Eagle, I say with love flowing from my heart; "The Great Spirit controls the future.

"Dark Eagle's choice to be with this one named Sarah, to him…, she is the future.
"IT IS…, AS IT SHOULD BE".

First a twitch…then an almost undetectable smile, formed at the corners of the mouth, of Gray Wolf

****

Chapter 37

Hampton Normal and Agricultural Institute;

Home of Professor E. Winslow - November 7, 1883

For six weeks, Eleanor had thrown herself into her work. As the chair of the Department of American and European Literature, in addition to teaching, Dr. E. Winslow had many additional myriad, duties and responsibilities.

Although Hampton, was a relatively "New-Institution of Higher Learning", its faculty, especially its' "non-Tenured", faculty was acutely aware of their need to; *Publish or Perish*".

When Professor Winslow, had been a non-tenured, junior member of the faculty, she had been a prolific writer.

The vast majority of her published works, whereby she analyzed and critiqued the works of literary giants, were well received by the academic community.

It was during…and subsequently following, their (Professor Winslow and her student; Justin Gulliver's) second "Office Hours" session, that Eleanor began to realized, that she was becoming attracted, both mentally and physically, to her *"mid-life crisis-forty-ish"*, freshman-student, Mr. Justin Gulliver.

Eleanor after having been told by Justin, his history—the trials and tribulations, that he had faced and overcome—Eleanor had theorized, that her attraction was eerily, analogous to a paper that she had written and submitted for and been published, several years earlier, in the prestigious; "Journal of English Literature".

In that paper Eleanor had dwelled upon, and emphasized, Shakespeare's portrayal of Desdemona, in his classic work *"Othello"*. That the *"Bard's"* portrayal of Desdemona as an innocent, naïve, young woman; bored with the "Venetian-Gentlemen" that her father paraded before her...as potential suitors...as a rebellious young woman *"Looking for a Hero"*.

In that paper, Dr. Winslow had acknowledged the plausibility, that *"Teenage-Rebellion"*, may have been...probably was, undoubtedly, a major factor that contributed to, and for Desdemona's love of *"The Moor"*.

The paper was entitled; *"Othello"; Exploring the Physical and Emotional, attraction...that Desdemona, felt for General Othello"*.

Now lying here in bed...reflecting, trying to analyze her, attraction to Mr. Justin Gulliver; impulsively, Eleanor opened the drawer of her bedside night stand; removed her journal and as she had done, since she was a teen, Eleanor began to write.

Similarities between Shakespeare's General Othello and Mr. Justin Gulliver

1	Attribute-Traits	General Othello	Mr. Justin Gulliver
2	Worldly	Yes	Yes

3	Courageous	Yes	Yes
4	Accomplished	Yes	Yes
5	Maturity	Yes	Yes
6	Masculinity	Yes	Yes

Eleanor dipped her pen into the ink well, and then…continued writing:.

These are but a few of the admirable traits shared by the fictional Othello; and the real-life…, flesh and blood, Mr. Justin Gulliver.

"I will save my listing of Mr. Gulliver and General "O'.", possibly sharing, of undesirable- traits, for another day.

****

Chapter 38

Friday, October 19, 1883
3:05 PM Professor E.
Winslow's Classroom

Following today's robust discussion of; the American Novelist, James Fenimore Cooper's Historical-Fictional novel; *The Last of the Mohicans*, as the last students excited her classroom, Eleanor having gathered her notes and text, and was about to leave, someone was lightly rapping on the door.

Eleanor turned her head…thinking that one of her students had returned to retrieve a forgotten, or misplaced object, caught her breath.

Standing in the hall, with his hand on the knob of the half-opened door, was Justin Gulliver.

Unable to suppress her excitement at seeing him; Eleanor took one step toward Justin and stopped. 'Jus…Mr. Gulliver, I am delighted to see that you are well.

I was beginning to worry. Are you alright? Before Justin could answer, Eleanor stated. "I …we all, have missed your presence in class these past few days".

"I was prepared to ask your nephew Harry, if you were ill. Unfortunately, I was distracted…and Harry left before I could talk with him."

Justin did not speak. Instead, he walked over to one of the desks in the front of the room, and sat.

For a tense few seconds, neither the student nor did the Professor, speak.

Justin was the first to speak. "Professor, I've shared with you…told you…, given you a brief synopsis of my life. I've told you quite a bit of y trials and tribulations. However, there are a few gaps …that I have not shared with anyone, not even with Harry…that I would like…that I want to share with you.".

"You are aware of the fact that I spent more than twenty years of my life, soldiering in the United States Army."

"I bring that up as a preface…to explain what; With your permission I am about to say."

Eleanor., who had remained standing, took a step towards Justin. Justin stood…and as if he *was still in the army*… speaking to his Commanding Officer, said; "Permission to speak freely Professor"

Because of her time during the war, teaching runaway slaves, at Virginia's, "Fort Monroe" , Eleanor, was tangentially… vaguely familiar, with military protocol.

She knew that when a soldier of lower rank, wanted to convey to a soldier of higher rank his unvarnished opinion, he would before speaking, qualify his opinion with the words… the request; *"Permission to speak freely Sir"*.

Eleanor not knowing what Justin might say…but hoping that he would say, what she wanted to hear…what she wanted to say to him; not trusting her voice, merely nodded.

"Professor, I believe it's obvious to you, as it is to everyone on campus, that I am not your typical first year college student. I'm a full grown…a mature man."

Justin, paused. His mind was frantically searching for the right words.

Exasperated, he blurted our; *"Oh Hell Ellie, I'm gunna cut-to-the chase; Professor Winslow…I like you…I really, really… like you"*.

Having said, what he had come to say, Justin walked around Eleanor' s desk and reached for the doorknob.

Eleanor, momentarily speechless, found her voice.

"Justin, while I have been instructed…ordered by the Administration, and righty so; to make my "Office Hours Sessions, more equitably available to all of my students; However, that notwithstanding, sessions that I hold in my home, on my own time, is totally under my control.

"Having said that; I expect to see you tomorrow… at six O'clock; with your text, at my home.

****

Chapter 39

Hampton Virginia – Monday, Dec 10, 1883; Home of Professor E. Winslow (7:25 PM)

Professor Winslow and her *"Adult" middle-age student*, Justin Gulliver had ten minutes earlier, concluded their agreed-upon, final "Office Hours" discussion of Shakespeare's 17th century tragedy; *"Othello"* … *"The Moor of Venus"*.

Justin was seated in the living-room, on the professor's small "Victorian-Buxton Sofa". Eleanor had removed their text-books, and their notes, from the small coffee-table, that stood in front of the sofa.

Carrying a silver tray, on which sat two cups of coffee and a plate of cookies, Eleanor entered the room…she leaned over and sat the tray onto the marble top of the coffee-table.

Justin patted the space next to him. Eleanor sat at the extreme end of the small sofa. She picked up the coffee cup, nearest to her and sipped. She exclaimed; "Oh…Oh, that's hot."

Justin stood…he gently removed the cup from Eleanor's hand, and returned it to the table.

Flustered, Eleanor picked up the plate of sandwiches, and without speaking thrust the plate toward Justin.

Justin, reflexively, stepped back. The plate of sandwiches slipped from Eleanor's hand, and broke into three pieces on the floor.

Eleanor was mortified. Both she and Justin, simultaneously together, kneeled down and picked-up the three fragments of what had been a beautiful piece of chinaware. A white plate, whose border consisted of hand- painted ripe-red cherries.

Eleanor looked at the fragment that she held in her hand, as did Justin. Justin, with an incredulous look on his face began to chuckle. Eleanor joined in.

Justin was the first regain his composure… he, still staring at the pieces of broken-dish in his hand asked. "Ellie, are you thinking what I'm thinking?"

The sexual tension which seconds ago, had hung in the air…had intensified.

Eleanor initial thought was he called me *"Ellie" …, Oh my God…that sounded so wonderful. "Ellie…from his lips. It sounded oh, so, …so, good!"*

Justin's worried voice, interrupted her reverie. "Ellie…are you alright?"

"This time her thought was; *"I did it again"*. She immediately, chided herself… *"Eleanor Winslow…get ahold of yourself. You're acting like a teenage-girl in the throes of her first crush."*

"What was it he said after he called me Ellie? Oh yes…, it was are you thinking what I'm thinking?"

"Of course, my white dishes, lined with the cherries; They are analogous to…the white handkerchief, with the embroidered strawberries in the play; "Othello". The lost handkerchief, that. was to Othello, proof positive, that substantiated the villainous Iago's trumped-up, spurious-charges, of Othello's wife Desdemona's, infidelity.

"Justin, seeing the confusion in Eleanor's eyes, decided that; *"Enough is enough"*. He reached out and took the piece of broken-china, from Eleanor's hand. With her hand in his…Justin led her to the sofa.

When they were seated. Justin was the first to speak; "Do you remember two months ago…, when I confessed…when I stood in your deserted classroom; and like an eight-year-old boy speaking to an eight-year-old girl, blurted out…, said to you; *"Professor Winslow…I like you…I really, really… like you?*

Before, she could respond, Justin continued; "Well now Ellie, here I am… sitting in your home…; A forty-two-year-old black-man, speaking to a mature…, might I add, a beautiful mature white-woman… here in the state of Virginia, the state that housed the capital of the "Confederacy", about to say to you, words that I thought I would never say again.

"Eleanor Winslow…Ellie I love you…I am in love, with you."

Eleanor sat motionless. She did not speak. Justin, crestfallen by her silence stood and walked toward the coat-rack next to the door, on which was suspended, his woolen-winter-coat.

Ellie who had been transfixed upon hearing Justin's word; words that she had in her imagination, heard spoken by him, to her, countless times, stood.

Justin, his back to Eleanor…his hand on the doorknob, froze when he heard Eleanor's soft-whispered words.

"Justin… don't go."

****

Justin took two hesitant steps towards Eleanor. Eleanor unabashedly, rushed to Justin, and threw her arms around his neck. Their lips met. Their first kiss.

With their lips meshed together Justin, withdrew his arms from around Eleanor's waist, as he attempted to remove from his shoulders, his heavy winter

Eleanor…her eyes closed, her lips maintaining contact with Justin's, lips, assisted Justin in the removing of his coat, from his shoulders.

Justin's tongue found its' way pass Eleanor's lips…into the warm wet cavern of her mouth.

Between the two of them, they managed to slide Justin's coat from his broad shoulders; The overcoat fell to the floor.

Justin's arms encircled Eleanor. He lifted her and kicked the coat at his feet, creating a clear path, to Eleanor's bedroom.

With Eleanor's head nestled in the space between his head and shoulder, Justin, carried Eleanor to the bedroom; And with the tip of his shoe, pushed open the bedroom door.

Justin gently lowered Eleanor to the floor. Staring into each other's eyes, they kicked-off their shoes and once again, kissed.

Eleanor's lips, closed around Justin's tongue… welcoming his appendage, thus… partially fulfilling, Eleanor's long awaited… unrequited, constantly fantasized-entrance, of Justin's body, into hers.

Frantically, still locked in a lingering kiss, Justin and Eleanor undressed each other. The naked couple fell onto the bed, both gasping for air.

Eleanor shyly ran her hand over Justin's still rock-hard, muscular, practically hairless, chest.

Despite her having been happily married for three years, Eleanor realized that this…this…minute, was the first time, that she had ever seen the body of, a naked, fully aroused, man.

Sheepishly, she averted her eyes…and became conscience of the fact that, she too was naked—During her marriage, neither she nor did Paul, actually see each other, naked—, and that her naked body, was for the first time…, being seen by a man

,
Eleanor quickly turned and got into bed, pulling the bedsheet up to her chin.

Justin was confused. What had happened? Although his confusion had in no way, affected his libido…his desire to make love to…not to merely have sex, but to love, and make love, with this beautiful, erudite, woman…, Eleanor's sudden mood-swing, had genuinely, confused him.

Justin, feeling stupid, standing in the middle of the room… "butt-naked", with —what he thought was the "*Hardest…Hard-On*", of his entire life— self- conscientiously, slipped under the sheet, now literally "*deflated*", next to Eleanor

For several awkward minutes, they lay…both naked inches apart, both staring at the ceiling; neither Eleanor nor did Justin speak.

Finally, Justin sat-up in bed; turned his head, looked at Ellie who had pulled the bedsheet under her chin, and asked; "What's wrong Ellie? Did I say or do something that upset you?

Eleanor did not answer. Again, Justin asked; "What's wrong Ellie?"

Eleanor, still clutching the sheet to her chin, turned her back to Justin, and faced the wall.

Justin, at a loss for words…and not wanting to prolong Eleanor's obvious discomfort, slowly picked up the edge of the sheet, and swung his legs over the edge of the bed.

Justin wordlessly leaned over to retrieve his shoes and socks, which had somehow, been kicked under the bed.

With both socks in his hand; Justin heard Eleanor, in a whispery voice, speak.

"It's I, whole should apologize. You did nothing wrong…; In fact, it's just the opposite. You…you Justin…, you did everything…everything right. I'm so ashamed."

Justin was now totally confused. "You're ashamed, ashamed of what? Ashamed of yourself… for having feelings for me?"

Eleanor, still holding the sheet…, covering her breasts, sat bolt-up-right.

"No…no Justin I…I…when I saw you standing there, your beautiful body… you looking like…like a Bronze-Greek; "*Adonis*", I was reluctant…ashamed for you to see my naked, forty-two-year-old body".

                                    Precious In His Sight

Justin turned; their eyes met. "Ellie, I've lived…, I lived an active life. You know about my growing-up a slave. I've told you some…. suffice it to say, not everything, but I have told you, of my life in the Army.

Still naked, Justin stood. "Ellie, look at me. His back was to Eleanor. With his right arm, he reached over his left shoulder and touched two dark-raised scars on his shoulder blade. These I got when a slave working in the fields when, the overseer…, *my white biological father,* lashed me with his long snake-whip. Berating me for what he perceived, was my not picking-cotton, fast enough.

He then bent-over, and pointed to a small indentation in the cheek of his right buttock.

"This one …I call it my *"little beauty"*, was when I was…pardon my "French" …, when in the Massachusetts's 54th, I was shot in the-ass, when during the battle of Fort Wagner', back in '63, we were ordered to "Fall- back", to retreat."

"Ellie, what I'm trying to say is that time…and life's experiences, takes its' toll, on all of us.

The fact that, at age forty-one, I don't have a paunch...a "beer belly" is probably because, I've led a very active...you might say strenuous, physical life. And I should add...I don't drink a lot of beer."

Justin walked over to the bed and slid in under the sheet. He turned his head to face Eleanor who was still sitting up, her back against the headboard of the bed...still holding the sheet...covering her breasts.

Justin raised himself in the bed...his back against the headboard. He gently...placed his hand on Ellie's and looked into her eyes.

Eleanor placed her hand that was not holding the sheet. onto Jason's.

Justin and Eleanor's eyes locked. Justin slowly lowered the sheet. He looked lovingly...appreciatively, at Eleanor's naked body.

"Ellie...; You're beautiful."

With his thumb and forefinger...Justin touched...then gently squeezed the pink-erect, nipple of Eleanor's right breast. Eleanor moaned.

****

"Af-tah the Loving"; That blissful period of time, post-physical expression, of their love, wrapped in each other's arms, Eleanor innocently asked; "Justin, what are your plans for the "Holiday Break? Will you be spending the holidays with your family?"

Justin shrugged his shoulders... "Other than my sister's son, my nephew Harry, who will be spending time with his brother and sister at that Indian school in Pennsylvania; I have no family.

"Rebecca, my sister's sister, invited me to spend Christmas with her family".

"However, a trip across country, to the McCloskey cattle ranch in Lost Springs Kansas, is a bit…, is a lot, too expensive for me".

"Besides, I don't want to spoil their Holidays. I'd probably stick-out like a sore-thumb."

During the Holiday-Break, I plan to just hold-up in the dorm. It'll be nice and quiet; And I can catch up, on a whole lot of reading.

"How about you Ellie, are you planning to go home to that small-town in Nebraska… to spend time with your family?"

Eleanor snuggling even closer to Justin, lifted her head and lightly kissed Justin's chest.

She sighed and resting her head on his chest said; "Nebraska is so far away…and besides my brothers are married…raising their own families."

"Usually, during the holidays, I spend time with my in-laws Sanna and Willem Winslow, at their home in Gettysburg Pennsylvania. They're Quakers, and although they are devout Christians, they don't "celebrate" religious-holidays

Sometimes at Christmas, I feel uncomfortable, at their home. I guess it's because I feel, that they feel, that they are depriving me of my customary "Christmas Celebrations"."

Eleanor sat-up. "Justin, instead of you spending the holidays alone in that deserted dormitory; And my "infringing upon the tranquility of my In-Laws, why don't you…why don't we, you and I, spend the Holiday Break, here…together?!

****

Eleanor, born and raised, Irish Catholic, had —when she and her husband Paul, who was born and raised, a member of the Religious Society of Friends *(Quakers)*, when they were essentially *"newly-weds"* —; during their first December as a married couple; Had asked Paul, "Does your family observe and celebrate Christmas?"

Paul had responded by saying; "We do not participate in religious festivals.

We observe the *birth*; acknowledge the *crucifixion*, and rejoice for the *resurrection*, of, Jesus Christ, our saviour, each and every day of our lives".

"Eleanor I, as do my family, know that you are Catholic. And as my mother adamantly insisted, when I told her that you and I, were going to marry, and that you are Catholic; She said "That, by no means…., nor should it."

"The fact of you're not being a Quaker, does not diminish the fact, that you are a good, virtuous person…, a person of faith".

"My parents have welcomed you into our family. And as I just said; "We "*Friends*;" observe …and hold dear in our hearts; *"Christmas", "Good Friday," and "Easter"*, and celebrate them, each and every day of our lives".

"Therefore, it's logical and reasonable to conclude that; Since the 25th day, of the twelfth month, is "A Day"; That that day, and on all days, you are and will always be; welcome in their home".

Eleanor had shaken her head. Although she had never taken a formal course in "*Scientific-Logic*" nor did she quite really grasp the concept of "*Circular- Logic*", she had wisely decided not to ask…nor to challenge, her husband, Dr., Professor Paul Winslow's "Logic".

 Precious In His Sight

Eleanor had reasoned that, the fact that Willem and Sanna Winslow, had unconditionally welcomed her…with open arms, into their family… well that, was as she had often heard sung by the slaves, in the fields of the Rosewood Plantation's cotton fields…; *"Dat bees Good nuff foo Me!"*

A second smile lit up her face, when she also remembered one of her mother's— Molly O'Leary's —favorite saying; "Sometimes honey…, you've got to know when; *"To let Sleeping Dogs lay."*

****

Chapter 40

Hampton Virginia – Wednesday, January 2nd, 1884; Home of Professor E. Winslow

Lying together, naked in her bed, Eleanor read to Justin, the text of the telegraph message that she had, before the holidays, sent, to her in-laws; Sanna and Willem Winslow:

"Mom and dad." **STOP**

"Won't be able to visit." **STOP**. *Something came-up.* **STOP**

As she was reading to him, Justin was planting little kisses on Eleanor's neck; alternating gently nibbling her earlobe, and blowing his warm breath, into her ear.

.

Apparently not listening …, oblivious to what she was reading, Justin abandoned her ear, and with his left hand reached over her body; and blindly groped for the paper that she held in her hand.

As Justin positioned himself between her thighs Eleanor's hand reached for him and loving, gently, squeezed Justin's pulsating, engorged member.

Eleanor dropped the paper onto the bed, she reached for that *"Something"* that had *"Come-up"*; Justin's stiff throbbing manhood, that she now guided to the entrance of her moist, welcoming vagina.

Along with the love she felt for this man; Eleanor could not help smiling at the accuracy of the wording of her telegram;

SOMETHING had indeed..., COME-UP!

****

Hampton Virginia – Friday , February 22nd , 1884; Home (Bed) of Professor E. Winslow

The phrase…the proper-appropriate words that, would express what Justin felt…, was feeling at this moment, was how he had felt, that night, December 17, 1883, the first time that he and Eleanor…had shared their bodies…had sanctified, their commitment to each other… their love".

Justin turned his head. To his surprise instead of being asleep, Eleanor was staring at him.

When she saw the embarrassed, startled look in Justin's eyes, spontaneously… together they, both Justin and Eleanor, began to laugh.

Justin was the first to speak: "I'm sorry Ellie—Eleanor loved it… that, when they were alone—he called her "Ellie", or sometimes "Honey"— "Honey, I'm sorry… I was lost in thought. Reliving the past two months…the best two months of my life."

Eleanor reached for…and gently, tugged at Justin left arm. She then slid over, resting her head on Justin's practically hairless chest.
Justin wrapped his left arm around Eleanor.

They lay together, in each other's arms until Justin, hearing Eleanor's soft, regular breathing, gingerly removed his arm, and gently broke contact with Eleanor's body.

Eleanor, asleep with a blissful smile on her face… turned her back to Justin.

Justin snuggled up against Eleanor's back. With his right-hand, he reached, for the down feathered-comforter…and pulled it across their bodies.

Justin and *"Ellie", snuggled together, fell asleep…,* their juxtaposed-bodies, resembling two priceless-spoons, at "rest", in a velvet-lined, silverware-tray.

****

Earlier that week, lying in bed, happily exhausted, following their lovemaking, Justin had sat up and nudged Eleanor.

Eleanor had drifted into that foggy-state of being; *"half awake… drifting on the threshold of sleep".*

"Ellie…Ellie, are you asleep? Eleanor had drowsily responded; "Not any more my love".

"Ellie…sweetheart, I have to tell you something…I have to confess.

Now alarmed, Eleanor was wide-awake. In a trepidatious voice, she asked; "What is it Justin…what do you want to confess?

Justin, hearing the concern in her voice, had quickly clarified. "Well sweetheart maybe my use of the word confess is not…is not, in this instance, the right word.

Now fully awake, Eleanor said; "Justin, you now have my undivided attention. I'm listening."

Justin took a deep breath, and *"confessed";* I am not a fan of Shakespeare.

Eleanor, let out her breathe, as relief washed over her. "Justin Gulliver, don't you ever do that to me again!"

"I thought you were about to confess to being *a mass murderer*…or…or a *Confederate Spy*…, or that you were about to say the most horrendous thing, that you could ever, ever, possibly say to me…Eleanor started to whimper…as tears welled-up, in her eyes.

Justin threw his arms around her joining them together. He began to gently rock her back and forth; "Shush, shush honey, I didn't mean to upset you".

With her head pressed to his chest, Eleanor wrapped her arms around Justin's torso, pulling him even, closer. "Justin, I thought you were about to say…, to say that you no longer loved me."

An incredulous expression spread over his face. Justin gently pulled away from Eleanor, looked into her red-rimmed blue eyes and in a throaty raspy voice, filled with emotion, said; "Ellie; ***"I'll Always, Love You"***.

Wrapped in each other's arms, after their latest, physical expression of their love…, with Justin lightly snoring, Eleanor…, suddenly sat-upright.in their bed.

She nudged Justin. "Justin…Justin…Justin, are you awake? Justin moaned… "go to sleep Ellie. Eleanor persisted; Justin, are you awake?

Justin rolled over and faced Eleanor. "Okay …okay…I'm awake. What is it?"

Eleanor asked; "What did you mean?" Justin now fully awake, answered; "Ellie my love, you'll have to be a little more specific."

Eleanor, with a confused look on her face, responded. "I thought…the way that …since you had read over and over…over in the span of two decades, _"Othello"_, I thought that you were an avid fan of the works of William Shakespeare, the "*Bard of Avon*".

Justin, realizing that he would not be allowed to go to go back to sleep, until and unless, he explained his earlier statement, sat-up, his back, as was Eleanor's, was against the bed's head board. He took a deep breath.

"When we were kids…slaves on the plantation, my sister Mandy and I…I, as did everyone…at least every slave that I knew, had come to accept our situation…our plight-in-life, that had been drilled into our heads by the *"white Massas"*, as well as by the *Massas'* minions…the black-slave preachers."

"We were worked like animals…treated like animals. We had no knowledge of as a people, who we were…or where did we come from. We had no past, no future…only the present. We had no self-esteem."

"Ellie, you gave my sister Mandy, "Self-Esteem". What you gave her …and what she in turn… my kid-sister transmitted to me; was Racial-Pride.

One of the tools that you used to accomplish that, a "tool" that Mandy shared with me, was Shakespeare's fictional play **_"Othello"_**.

"It was your intent... *"Miss Leary"* ..., to show my sister Mandy— the little precocious, black-slave girl— that a black man, can be successful…can advance and prosper, in white society."

"Unfortunately, your untimely, abrupt, departure from Rosewood, occurred before my sister Mandy…and her white-sister Rebecca, had the chance to read the entire play."

"As I sit here thinking about it…I guess you might say that I became obsessed with my need to understand the mindset of the author…a white man, Shakespeare, who two hundred years ago, wrote _"Othello"_.

"I have to admit, that twenty years to read a "Play" …, even one written in that archaic 17th century, "Elizabethan" English, is an awfully long time.

Truthfully Ellie, it didn't take twenty years for me to read _"Othello"_, however it did take twenty years… off and on… for me to understand _"Othello"_.

"After having read and reread, countless times the play _"Othello"_, my opinion as to what I thought the author, William Shakespeare was trying to say, would invariably change, after each reading."

"My initial thought was what was he…what was Shakespeare attempting to show his 17th century, white Elizabethan audience."

"Was his message actually, what Mandy and I believed it to be? Was Shakespeare _"spreading the word"_; That a black man, can be successful in white society?"

"As time passed…as I excelled in the army, on the battle-field; in the classroom; Excelled at literally, running Richmond's "Freedmen's Bureau", when I would over and over again, reread _"Othello"_, each time that I came across… that I encountered, the many racial epithets, that the _"Bard"_, put into the mouths of the plays character; the white racist-Venetians— who incidentally, in the play, never get their _"comeuppance"_—, the more I became convinced that what we thought…you, me, Mandy and Rebecca, thought motivated Shakespeare to write _"Othello"_, may not have been, the case."

"Now..., Professor Winslow... "Chair of American and European Literature", I'd be the first to admit, that I..., by no means, am I even remotely, qualified, to judge Shakespeare's work, or his motives."

"However, as of January first, 1863, when President Lincoln issued the *"Emancipation Proclamation"*, I became by law, *"**FREE**"* to read... and to express... my opinion, of anyone...anything, including the works of William Shakespeare."

"I came to the realization that in real-life ...at least in my *"Real-life"*., a black man...Justin paused, then he made a fist and thumped his chest... "A black man...me, this black man, cannot... could not until 1877, become a commissioned officer, in the United States Army".

"It was after having reread for the umpteenth time, *"Othello"* ... it was when I thought that Shakespeare's message was that... *"Jealousy, lying and scheming, ultimately, results in tragedy"*. It was then that I had an epiphany; I am now of the opinion, that Shakespeare's play *"Othello",* ... is a Racist Play."

"It was here at Hampton, after reading and discussing with you the play, that I have come to conclude that; while there are multiple *"themes"*, messages, take-aways; including "A black man can succeed In White Society, I... Justin Gulliver, a 42-year-old-freshman at Hampton Institute; am of the opinion that, essentially, William Shakespeare's *"Othello"*, is a racist play.

"I believe that contrary to my...to Mandy's ...yes even to *"Miss Eleanor Leary's"*, initial assessment of *"Othello"*, I believe that the *"Bard"* was showing, was in fact, reiterating a fact of life that existed in the 17th century...which still exists today, here in the 19th century."

"That ultimately, irrespective of his intellect, his achievements, despite his acknowledged strategic, value to the "State", in a white society, the black man will always, be looked upon…treated as, the *"**Other**"*.

Eleanor reached for and held Justin's hand. She managed to smile and said; "Justin it won't always be that way. We…our children, their children…, we can change it."

****

Lying in Justin's arms— Justin had fallen asleep—Eleanor. was smiling as she was remembering hers' and Justin's, conversation, that night three months ago, when they were in bed, celebrating their third night of blissful, *"Christmas-Week's"*, cohabitation.

The couples third night sleeping together, had just concluded following that night's, third "round of making love".

As they lay in each other's arms, Justin had begun to stir… he opened his eyes and had jocularly exclaimed; "Not bad Ellie…not bad at all!".

Eleanor sat up, smiled…and with a mischievous smirk at the corners of her mouth had said; "I beg your pardon kind-sir; are you grading the teacher?"

Justin laughed. "Not at all Professor". I was not speaking of the quality, which by the way is [A+] … I was marveling at the quantity. Three times, in two. hours!?" Wow!

"Not bad …not bad at all, for two *"middle-aged"*, relics."

Eleanor had picked up a pillow and thrown it at Justin. She then, in what she thought, a stern voice had said; "Speak for yourself "old-man".

With his left arm, Justin had deflected the pillow…while with his right hand, he had pulled Eleanor to him.

Laughing, their bodies intertwined, Justin and Eleanor, rolled on the bed.

Eleanor disengaged, and abruptly, stood. "Seriously Justin… we have to talk."

Naked, Eleanor stood and had walked across the room, to the room's only chair on which was hung her terrycloth-bathrobe. She put the robe on, then turned the chair, so that it faced Justin. Eleanor sat and began to speak.

"Justin, do you remember…do you recall that cliché…that proverb that I quoted when I canceled our scheduled "Office Hours"?

Before Justin could answer, Eleanor quoted; *"All good things must come to an end."* Well, whether cliché or proverb, that sentence is definitely, apropos when applied to us…to this Christmas-break."

"This…this romantic…physical relationship between the two of us, between you and me…between me your teacher-Professor E. Winslow, and you…my student Justin Gulliver; In the eyes of this college…, in the eyes of any college, our relationship would be considered as being both unprofessional, and unethical."

Justin sat-up…his back was against the bed's headboard; the bed sheet covered his waist and his lower extremities.

"Ellie…, Professor Winslow, I have a confession. While I do actually love the play <u>"Othello"</u>, I hate… well not literally hate…, that's a bit strong, let me rephrase, I am not interested in pursuing a career teaching American and European Literature.

"However, I would very much like to teach disadvantage kids, math, engineering, and physics.

I plan to teach Engineering. That being said, when I return from Christmas Break, I intend to…no offense Ellie…Professor E. Winslow, I intend to drop "American and European Literature".

"My intense interest in _"Othello"_ … was and still is, genuine. My sister Mandy is responsible for my becoming a huge fan of that play.

"When we…the three of us…you, myself and Mandy…; Justin stopped, and amended his statement…, I forgot to include a very important person in my narrative. I'll start again."

"When we four, I neglected to include Mandy's white-sister Rebecca… when the four of us… you, myself, Mandy and her sister Rebecca were living on the Rosewood Plantation…; my sister and I black-slaves, you and Rebecca white slave-owners, —seeing Eleanor bristle…Justin quickly apologized, I'm sorry, of course you didn't own slaves.";

"However, Rebecca…, Mandy's sister, because she was the daughter of the _"Massa"_ of Rosewood, as defined by Southern-Property-Law, Rebecca owned slaves…Rebecca owned her black-sister, Mandy."

"I'm sorry Ellie, for a moment there, I got offtrack. Oh yes, I was explaining my interest in… that one particular Shakespearean play, _"Othello"_."

"Ellie, before you came to Rosewood…Mandy was suffering…she was depressed…she was struggling with her self-identity issues."

"When she and her white sister "Becky" were together alone, playing school or having little "Tea-Parties", my sister Mandy and her white sister Rebecca, were a gregarious, happy… kids."

"However, when she was not with "Becky", Mandy would mope around… her head hanging down, like a mistreated, whipped hound-dog."

"After I escaped from slavery and was working for the Union Army as a Contraband-Civilian-Scout/Interpreter—when I escaped slavery, blacks were not permitted to enlist in the United States Military—I would often hear the white-officers, saying that this or that soldier had no self-esteem."

When you came to Rosewood to teach the *"Massa's"* children, you put your-self in danger by defying… breaking the law, by teaching Mandy…a slave to read and write.

You deliberately chose to have your students (The two white kids; Rebecca; her brother Jesse and clandestinely, my sister Mandy) read *"Othello"*.

"Mandy told me that you…Miss Eleanor Leary, that you chose the play *"Othello"*, in an effort to instill in her, "Self-Esteem…Racial-Pride.""

"Mandy said that you wanted to show her that there are places outside of the South, where Black Men, can achieve great things. Where black men can become Generals, commanding and leading, thousands of white-men."

"Unknown to you…and for that matter, to anyone, Mandy taught me everything that you taught her. That is how as a black slave boy, forbidden to learn to read and write, I became aware of *"Othello"*.

"And I became aware of… of the existence of, and I quote the words of my sister; the existence of; *"My Friend, Miss Eleanor Leary…the most wonderful white-lady, that I have ever known."*

"It's been twenty-three years since I last had a glimpse of you. Then when at Orientation, I first saw this strikingly-handsome, academician sitting at one of the tables...I thought she...you, looked vaguely familiar."

"However, in the past twenty years I've been a lot of places and seen a lot of men...and a lot of women."

"On orientation day when I saw you *"Manning"* one of the tables, my curiosity, got the better of me; I decided to stand in your line...to get a closer look."

"When I read your name on the placard; *"Professor E. Winslow"*, needless to say, to me, that name didn't mean anything...didn't ring a bell."

"I had never met you. I knew the name of the "Yankee" teacher who taught my sister, was *"Miss Leary"*; But I never knew, nor did I ask..." What is Miss Leary's first name?"

Eleanor had sat listening, ... mesmerized, not wanting to interrupt Justin's discourse. Then he stopped talking.

Eleanor waited to see if he would continue, before she spoke; "Justin I remember...in fact I don't think that I will ever forget; Mandy and Rebecca...Rebecca and Mandy Billings."

"When the girls and I, held our Saturday and Sunday, "All-Day" teaching sessions, during our break for lunch, we would often talk about our private lives...our families".

"I do recall Mandy mentioning to me that she had a *"Big Brother"*, but I think...if my memory hasn't failed me... in fact I'm pretty sure that her brother's name was ... is, Jason."

Justin was impressed. He smiled and said; "Ellie, I do love you…not only do I love you for who you are…I love you for who you've always been."

"As we have both stated…or at least, we both agreed, twenty years is a long time. Tell you what…he then chuckled….

At Freshman-Orientation, when I first saw you…I thought you looked familiar…and that I might have seen you before."

Eleanor wondered; *"Why is smiling…why is he laughing?"*

Justin, still chuckling, and as if he was psychic… without her having asked, Justin answered Eleanor's unspoken, questions.

"Ellie…in my time soldiering, there's been many a time when I've been in situations…standoffs, when I have…or, my antagonist, found it necessary to say;
"You show me yours…and I'll show you mine".

Eleanor looked quizzically at Justin; She did not. respond. Justin's chuckle, turned into a bonifide belly laugh.
With the knuckle of his right index finger, Justine wiped a tear of glee from his eye.

"Professor Winslow, your academic achievements are numerous and might I add, most impressive.

"However, Ellie I suspect that your naivety in worldly…non-academic, matters is probably not on par, with your academic brilliance."

"Okay…here goes". Over time, due to circumstances…events that I've had to face, in order to survive, I've had to change my name.

"Jason Billings; Jason Ruth; Justin Gulliver. Ellie you're the first…the only person that I have ever told; my many aliases.

"Professor E. Winslow, it is my intention to enroll as a student in the school's department of Mathematics and Engineering."

"I will therefore, no longer be your student. I hope with all my heart and soul that I will be …considered by you, to be the man in love with Eleanor Winslow.

****

Justin Gulliver, Professor E. Winslow's student…" Ellie Winslow's man had dropped…withdrew, from the college's Department of American and European Literature; And preferring courses in engineering, had switched majors.

During his time in the army, Justin had assisted in the design and the construction of pontoon bridges.

The bridges had to support, not only the weight of the soldiers and their mounts, the bridges had to support the weight of supply-wagons and field- artillery pieces.

Justin's experience in the army qualified, coupled with his proclivity for mathematics, made easy, Justin's transference from the Humanities, to his becoming a student in Hampton's Department of Mathematics and Engineering.

****

Chapter 41

Home of Professor E. Winslow - Hampton Virginia – February, 1884

Justin…as he always did when *"visiting"*, the residence of Professor E. Winslow, knocked on the door.

Eleanor opened the door, and in a formal voice, said… "Mr. Gulliver? Please, please, come in."

Justin entered the hallway and closed the door. Before he could hang-up his overcoat, Eleanor rushed over to him, threw her arms around his neck, and passionately, kissed him.

Justin was surprised… but delighted at Eleanor's enthusiastic…and by all means, welcomed, greeting.

Still standing hugging him, Eleanor could feel…pressing on her stomach, the result of Justin's body's, autonomic-physiological response, to her ardent, greeting.

Ellie…certainly not *"Professor E. Winslow, Chair of the Department of American and European Literature"*; removed her right arm from around Justin's neck…reached down, and gently squeezed Justin's expanding, erection

Justin caught completely by surprise, with both of his arms, encircling her waist, leaned back and stared at Ellie.

Still hugging him Ellie demurely smiled… and with a coquettish grin, looked up at Justin and said… *"Say mister…Is that a banana in your pocket…or are you just happy to see me?"*

Justin leaned over…Eleanor, all five ft-five and a half inch in height, standing on her tiptoes, put her hands on the back of six ft-three-inch Justin Gulliver's, neck.

Justin leaned over…Eleanor, on her tiptoes, put her hands on the back of Justin's neck, and standing in the hall…Justin and Ellie…, Ellie and Justin, kissed.
The two lovers… together; standing in the hall, locked in an embrace, that if the *Chair of the Department of American and Literature*, could have seen…, she would have thought, resembled a classic Michelangelo … or, perhaps a Donatello, Sculptured-Renaissance, work of art.

Ellie ended the kiss. She leaned back in Justin's arms…a radiant smile on her lips, her bright blue-eyes sparkling, she said… *"Justin…; We're pregnant"*.

****

Office of General Samuel C. Armstrong Principal Hampton Institute – February

22, 1884 (11:10 A.M).

General Armstrong was seated behind his desk, reading and then signing a document.

He placed his pen in the inkwell and smiling, looked up at what he thought was the serious-face, of Professor Eleanor Winslow, the "Chair of Hampton's Department of American and European Literature".

Leaning back in his chair, still smiling, the General spoke; "Good morning, Eleanor. If I may ask…not that I am complaining, it's always a pleasure to see you. what is the "urgent matter" that you wish to discuss?

Instead of speaking, Eleanor handed a sealed manila envelope to the General.

General Armstrong opened the envelope, removed the single sheet of paper, and began to read;

Sir;

For personal family reasons; I am resigning my position as "Chair of Hampton Institute's Department of American and European Literature"., effective, March 7, 1884

It has been my honor, and my pleasure, to over the years, have worked for, and with you, at Hampton.

Sincerely,

Eleanor M. Winslow, Ph.D.

****

Chapter 42

Gettysburg Pennsylvania, Home of Mr. and Mrs. Justin Gulliver July 9ᵗʰ, 1884

The downstairs living-room, and the adjacent kitchen, of the neat two-story home of the Gulliver's, was packed with the newly-wed couples, relatives and friends.

Justin's nephew Harry was in the living-room, standing in a corner, engaged in an animated conversation with Eleanor's closest friend, Elizabeth *("Call me Lizzie")* Jones.

Lizzie, was an active spokesperson for the *"The Suffragette-Movement"* — being led by Susan B. Anthony, and Elizabeth Cady Stanton—that was attempting to secure for women, the right to vote.

Harry…becoming overwhelmed by the passion and the vehement, conviction in "Lizzie's voice…was discreetly, looking for help.

Looking for someone…anyone, who would "rescue" him from this charming, but stridently-loquacious, woman, who was verbally, and rapidly, putting forth a long list of reasons for supporting an amendment… to the United States Constitution, giving women, the right to vote.

Harry suppressed a sigh of relief as a stunning, young Native American woman, approached.

With a huge smile of pleasure… and of relief, Harry took the young woman's hand, and with a tinge of pride in his voice, announced; "Miss Elizabeth…, *"Lizzie"* Jones, I would like to introduce you to my friend, my very special friend… Miss Sarah Schmidt."

Sarah, smiling, extended her free hand. "Hello Miss Jones, I am so very pleased to meet you."

With both of her hands, Lizzie took Sarah's hand… "My dear the pleasure is all mine. I am delighted to meet, my best friend Ellie's, nephew's…, very, very special friend…, his girl-friend?"

Both Harry and his beautiful "very, very, *special-friend"* Sarah, blushed.

****

Eleanor, supporting with her right hand, her "distended- with- child belly", waddled, over to Justin…her husband Justin, who was…, judging by their smiles— having an agreeable, interesting *"talk," actually a* mixture of sign, English, and Comanche, —with Gray Wolf and Little Flower, Justin's sister Mandy's, adoptive Comanche-parents.

When Harry, told his uncle Justin that— *Gray Wolf and Little Flower,* his grandparents, as well as his siblings, in residence at Carlyn, at the expense of Rebecca McCloskey— would be attending their wedding, Harry *("Dark Eagle"),* had volunteered to, and had taught, Justin and Eleanor, a few simple-rudimentary words of the Comanche Language.

When Eleanor, joined the group, Little Flower smiling turned to Eleanor and said; *"Ah at last we meet. Miz Lee-ree, my black-daughter Pretty Buffalo Hair's…Mahndee's, friend, her beloved, teacher".*

When she heard the words *"Mahndee"* and beloved, spoken by Little Flower, with such reverence and love, Eleanor turned her head, averting eye- contact with Little Flower, as tears welled-up in her eyes.

Little Flower seeing the tears, silently flowing down Eleanor's cheeks, took Eleanor's hand, and lead her away from group.

Eleanor mumbled; "Forgive me Little Flower …I don't know what came over me."

Little Flower softly, gently said; "There is nothing to forgive. You weep because you mourn the death of your friend… my daughter Pretty Buffalo Hair… *"Mahndee."*

For the first time Eleanor noticed Little Flower's left-hand. Two fingers were missing from her hand.

Little Flower seeing Eleanor's shocked, visceral reaction, at the sight of her mangled-hand, lifted, and examined her hand.

"This I did. I cut-off my fingers, to mourn the loss of the life of my daughter *"Pretty Buffalo Hair"* …*the loss, of…Mahn-dee*.; As I had done to mourn, the loss of life of my son, *"Mahn-dee's"* husband, Dark Eagles' father my son, Running Eagle."

Little Flower lifted her hand. "When I look at this hand, and I no longer see the missing fingers, I think of and mourn the loss of my two children.; Dark Eagle's parents, Running Eagle, and "Pretty Buffalo Hair…*Mahn-dee*"; who I will again see soon, when we together, walk the trail of our departed ancestors."

****

                                      Precious In His Sight

Chapter 43

Gettysburg, Pennsylvania –The Home of Mr. and Mrs. Justin Gulliver. September 19, 1887

Justin was lying in bed, fully awake. He looked at the clock on his bedside table: 5:30 AM.

Justin looked to his left, at his sleeping wife's back.

He carefully, gently slipped his left arm under his wife's peacefully, slumbering body.

He then wrapped his right arm around her waist, and snuggled-up to her lightly freckled, back, melding the couple together… forming a perfect pair of *"spoons"*.

Justin and his beautiful bride—the couple had just recently, celebrated their third wedding anniversary.

His wife, the love-of-his life…, now semi-asleep…and partially awake, with her left hand, removed her husband's hand from her stomach, and drowsily, reflexively, placed his hand onto her right breast. Still half-asleep, she pressed her still-firm buttocks against Justin's suddenly awakened, rapidly expanding, manhood.

With his arms encircling Eleanor's body, Justin placed his lips upon her ear and whispered… "I love you Ellie…, ***I'll Always Love You***."

Smiling, Eleanor turned facing her man; She sat-up and gently pushed his shoulders flat onto the bed; and wordlessly lifting her left leg, and straddled her husband.

As if it had a mind of its' own, Justin's now fully erect "shaft", found and slid, into his wife's moist, welcoming, vagina.

She leaned over making the pink nipples of her breasts, accessible to Justin's hands and his eager lips. It was at that moment, that their bedroom door flew open.

"An inquisitive, sleep-ladened, childish voice uttered, "Mommy…why are you on top of Daddy…are you hurting Daddy?"

At that moment of pre-ecstasy…hearing his daughter's voice, was to Justin's manhood, analogous to "sticking a pin" into a fully inflated balloon.

As his now limp-deflated "shaft" exited her vagina, his startled wife turned her head and exclaimed; "Becky, sweetheart, why aren't you in bed?"

After she had put on her robe, and had escorted their inquisitive, beautiful, daughter back to her bedroom…, Eleanor leaned over and kissed the child's forehead, and said; "Go back to sleep "Becky", daddy will take you to grandma Senna's for breakfast.

When she returned to her bedroom, she was disappointed to see that the bed was empty.

Eleanor looked at the clock on her bedside table: 6:20 AM. She was disappointed. Eleanor muttered under her breath "Why is it… that I just can't get enough of him. She sighed and under her breath, murmured; "Ellie Gulliver… act your age".

****

Unlike her husband, Mr. Justin Gulliver— who taught mathematics in one of Gettysburg's public schools—who's first class began at 9:00 A.M, Professor Eleanor Gulliver's—Chair of Gettysburg College's Department of American and European Literature—first class, started in the afternoon.

It had become a standing joke between Justin and Ellie that, when the alarm went off at 6:00 A.M. and Justin got out of bed to prepare for work, Ellie, before pulling the covers up, over her head, would say; "Remember soldier…, *"Rank Has Its' Privileges."*

Jason would dutifully chuckle. Their little joke; *"Never got Old".*

Chapter 44

Gettysburg Pennsylvania, Home of Mr. and Mrs. Justin Gulliver Monday September 19, 1887 (Pre-Dawn)

Justin was lying in bed, fully awake. He looked at the clock on his bedside table: 5:30 AM.

At least two more hours before he had to "rise and shine", Do his A.M care; dress little "Becky"; drop her off at Grandma Sanna's, then "go to work.

Try as he might…Justin could not get back to sleep. The harder he tried… the more awake and alert he became.

Not wanting to disturb Eleanor Justin, glanced at Ellie, and thought; "This woman that I am sleeping with, is the only woman in my entire life, that I have ever actually, more than once *"slept with"*.

Justin lying on his back, placed his hands behind his head, and let his mind wonder.

****

December 17th 1883. That was the date of the very first time that he had "slept with a woman". Invariably as he always did, Justin…in his mind had immediately rejected the euphemism, *"slept with"*.

Over the past twenty-odd years… in and out of the army, Jason Ruth… Justin Gulliver, had sex … had lain with many women.

However, during his life-time, Justin had only *"Made Love"*, with but two women.

In 1867, he had *"Made Love" to* and *with* his fiancé Maureen Montgomery; Who was murdered by a *"Lost Cause"*, White-Supremist-Bigot; And he had *"Made Love", on* that very special day, December 17th 1883, the day…the night, that he and Eleanor, had first *"Made Love"*. The night that he and Ellie together, *"created"* their" *Masterpiece"*, their beautiful, ecru- complicated daughter, Rebecca Ruth Gulliver.

Though he certainly did not consider himself to be a "Romantic", Justin's mind categorically rejected the phrases; *"Had sex" and/ or, slept together,* as being an accurate, descriptive phrase of his and Eleanor's, frequent physical expression, of their love".

He smiled as he thought; "I can't wait to see the look on Ellie's… on the face of my wife, Eleanor Gulliver, the renowned, erudite, Professor of American and European Literature's face, when I share with her, my perfect phrase to describe the night of December 17th 1883, the night that we first *"Made Love"*.

Justin smiled and thought; two more hours before I have to get up, take *Becky-Ruth,* to *Grandma Sanna,* and get myself ready for work.

Now, not wanting to fall asleep, afraid that he might oversleep and be late for work, Justin made a conscience effort to recall the *"small"*, wedding present, that his aunt, Rebecca McCloskey… his wealthy, aunt Rebecca— the owner of the largest cattle ranch in the state of Kansas—, had given the newly-weds, Mr. and Mrs. Justin Gulliver… she had arranged and paid for, their wedding reception

****

The smile on Justin's face broadened, as he recalled the conversation, that night— after the festivities… when he and Eleanor; *"Aftah the Loving"*, sat up in bed and talked and talked and talked, about their "Glorious Day".

The Gulliver family; Justin his wife Eleanor, who was holding their three- year old toddler, Rebecca Ruth, in her lap, leaned over and whispered in her husband's ear "Justin who are …who are all of these people?"

Justin, smiling with an appreciative laugh said; "Ellie, the vast majority of these people… our guests, are my…are our friends and relatives."

Justin spotted. His nephew Harry and his date the lovely Sarah Schmidt seated at one of the numerous small tables, throughout the room.

Justin extended his arms out to his daughter Rebecca-Ruth (*Becky), who happily reached out to her "Daddy"*.

Justin took Eleanor's hand into his, and together… the "Gulliver's walked over to Harry and Sarah's table.

As they approached, Harry, stood…Sarah remained seated.

Justin asked; "Harry…Sarah, may we join you? Sarah smiled; Harry answered; "By all means…please…please do.".

Sarah, a radiant smile on her face; commented, "Mrs. Gulliver, what a beautiful…beautiful, name. Mr. and Mrs. Justin Gulliver, we would be honored if you would…; please…please join us."

Eleanor smiled and nodded her head… "Ahh…Mrs. Gulliver…I do very, very much, like the sound of that very, very beautiful name."

"However, Sarah, since I think…I have a strong suspicion that we are going to become very close friends—Eleanor impishly smiled at Harry—perhaps even close relatives, I insist, that you call me Ellie.

"Besides—she first looked at Harry, then at Sarah—coming from you kids… addressing me as Mrs. Gulliver, is making me feel "Ancient".

Both couples, laughed. Seeing and hearing the adults laughing; the "Newly- Wed's" three-year-old daughter, Rebecca-Ruth too…began to laugh… joining in the merriment.

****

Justin pulled out one of the two vacant chairs at the table; Eleanor sat, and then after pulling out the last vacant chair; Justin sat.

Justin turned to Harry; his eyes taking in the panorama of the room "This is a fabulous reception."

"When your Aunt Rebecca wrote to me, and asked how many people would be attending, I …Ellie and I…gave her a very small list. In our wildest dreams…we didn't expect this kind of turn-out."

Harry, grinned; "Aunt Rebecca and I, also exchanged similar letters. I told her, that you had told me, that a couple of your friends, and Prof... Ellie's In-laws, would be attending the wedding."

"I knew...as did you Uncle Justin, that my Aunt Rebecca's Ranch, is not that far distant, from the Fort Sill Indian Reservation.

"The letter that Aunt Rebecca sent me in reply, said that she had visited the reservation; had met with, my grandparents...Little Flower and Gray Wolf."

"Aunt Rebecca told my grandparents that their daughter, Pretty Buffalo Hair's brother Justin...was about to be married, and that Justin, their daughter Pretty Buffalo Hair's brother, would very much like them, and all of Pretty Buffalo Hair's Comanche relatives, to come to the wedding of Pretty Buffalo Hair, *Mahn-dee's,* brother, whom they had previously met; Sergeant Justin Gulliver".

My grandparents, Gray Wolf and Little Flower, gave Aunt Rebecca a verbal- list of your sister Mandy's...my mother "Pretty Buffalo Hair's, Comanche relatives".

"In her letter, Aunt Rebecca wrote, and I quote...or at least, I will try to quote.

"Dark Eagle" ... he stopped to explain to Eleanor, "When my aunt and I first met on the Fort Sill Reservation...before I, my brother and sisters..., as were all of the reservation children between the ages of five and sixteen, were *"shipped"* via the rail-road, to attend "Indian Residential-Vocational Schools".

The children of the lodge of Gray Wolf, where sent East, to the Carlyn-Indian Residential-Vocational School, where we were forced to change our names.

"I chose from the school's list of names, the name *Harry Bird*, to honor, and to keep with me, the names of my mother; "Pretty Buffalo *Hair*" and my father; Running *Eagle*."

"At the Carlyn Indian Residential-Vocational School", where I was forced to change my name...; before I became Harry Bird, my name was *"Dark Eagle."*

Harry continued... "Anyhow, Aunt Rebecca wrote that she would "take care of everything".

"That the McCloskey's would pay the expenses for, and accompany her sister Mandy's brother's relatives...my, Comanche-relatives including my sibling's here in Pennsylvania..., here at the Carlyn school, round-trip and living expenses, to attend the wedding of *"Pretty Buffalo Hair's brother's* wedding."

Suddenly...inexplicably, Harry looked distraught...concerned. Justin seeing his nephew's troubled face, asked; "Harry...are you alright?

Harry, with an apologetic, sorrowful expression on his face, looked at Eleanor. "Prof... Ellie. I apologize. I neglected... forgot to mention that, at the bottom of her letter, Aunt Rebecca added a post-script."

"She wrote; "Please tell Miss Leary, that I cannot wait...I am so looking forward, to seeing her again."

****

Eleanor stood and anxiously...her eyes darting back and forth; she scanned the room.

She saw her best friend "Lizzie and her husband Theodore (Teddy), sitting at a table, sipping coffee...engaged in conversation.

Eleanor spotted her In-laws, Sanna and Willem Winslow, both were as usual, *"plain-dressed".* sitting at a table with Sanna's friend, the ex-slave *"Minty".*

"Minty" was an abolitionist- *"conductor"* on the "Underground Rail Road"; and a Civil-War Union Army Veteran, Miss. Harriet Tubman.

The rear of the rectangular shaped room, was populated by far, with the largest assemblage of guests; Justin's sister Mandy's... and by extension... Justin's, eight Comanche Relatives and what appeared to be a white family of four...two adults, one dark swarthy-complected, young man, and a little girl...a toddler.

Seated at the table were eight Comanches (All attired in *"White-Folks"* clothing); and what Eleanor correctly-guessed, were the McCloskeys and two Mexican Women..., Stone Fist's, the Warrior Chief who adopted Dark. Eagle...; 2nd wife *Juanita, whole Eleanor guessed was about her age;* her twenty-three-year-old, Mexican daughter, Chiquita, and a beautiful, petite Chinese woman; *Mai-Ling, the Comanche War Chief,* Stone Fist's 3rd wife.

Approximately, four feet removed from the three pushed together tables, that were occupied by the McCloseky family and their Native American, Mexican American and Chinese American guests, was a smaller gathering; (two tables pushed together), that Rebecca McCloseky had referred to as, the *"Kids"*, table.

Eleanor reached for Justin's hand, and breathlessly said; "Justin let's go over and greet our guests.

Justin and Eleanor…, both holding the hand of their three-year-old daughter, Rebecca Ruth Gulliver, walked toward the rear of the room.

As Justin and Eleanor rose and walked toward the long extended, pushed together tables, in the rear of the room…, so too did, Mrs. William (*Billy*) McCloskey, who had for five minutes, been staring at the table occupied by the newly-weds, stood.

Eleanor dropped Justin's and *"Becky-Ruth's"* hand, and ran towards Rebecca.

Rebecca at almost the same instant, began running toward Eleanor. The two women, met in the center of the room; and without saying a word, they embraced…joyously hugging one another

With tears welling up in their eyes and flowing down their cheeks, now holding each other at arm's length, Rebecca just could not resist,

She laughingly said to Miss Leary…to Eleanor, to her and her sister Mandy's beloved teacher, their coconspirator…, and most importantly, the "Billings" sister's best friend…, with a radiant smile spreading across her face, Rebecca McClosekey greeted Eleanor with the words; *"Dr.*
Livingston…I Presume?"

****

The two women laughing, and still holding hands; As they had done twenty- seven-years-earlier; when Miss Leary, Rebecca and Mandy… Rebecca's black-enslaved sister had frequently done, at the conclusion of their classes, under one of the Rosewood Plantation's, huge, leafy, Oak-trees.

****

Ten-year-old Mandy ("M-Cubed") McClosekey, while keeping her eye on her charges…, the four children at the "Kid's-Table"— Out of the corner of her eye, witnessed her mother and the stranger, whom she correctly assumed was "Miss Eleanor Leary".

The women…the lady who had; back in the bad…the very bad "Olden Days"; taught her mother when her mom and her namesake, her black Aunt Mandy, who was a "slave" lived, on that awful "Rosewood-Slave Plantation"— "M-Cube's" face lit-up.

Seeing the radiant smile on her mother's face, allowed her—the very- for- her-age, mature ten- year- old, 2nd Lady of the "New Rosewood Cattle Ranch"—focused her attention on the four "children" left in her charge;

"Huan", the nine-year-old son of Mai-Ling, the Warrior Chief Stone Fist's 3rd Wife; "Luz", the four-year-old daughter, of Chiquita and her husband Jose, a ranch hand who worked at the New Rosewood Cattle Ranch; Makah, the seven-year-old son of Spring Blossom, the Warrior Chief Stone Fist's 1st Wife; and finally, *"Rebecca-Ruth"*, the three-year-old daughter of Mr. and Mrs. Justin Gulliver.

The *"Three, now Two Musketeers"*, *sans* Mandy; This time instead of strolling to the plantation's "Big House", this time, they were returning to join and acquaint themselves with their welcoming, multi-racial;

Native American [Red]; Mexican [Brown]; Chinese [Yellow]; Ex Buffalo-Soldier; [Black] Kansas Ranchers; [White] …multi-ethnic, multi-religion family.

Billy and Rebecca's son, Hank, placed two chairs, next to his mothers. Rebecca, Justin, and Eleanor joined their extended "American Family".

They watched as Rebecca and Billy's "white" daughter; *"M-Cube's"*, lead her…their little group of five, to the dance floor; where the five children, joined hands, forming a circle; And sang and skipped to the children's song; "Ring Around the Roses…Pocket Full of Posies…

Seated next to each other, at their "long-table", watching their children skipping and singing; Justin clasped and gently squeezed, Eleanor's hand; who-in-turn, with her free hand, took the hand of Rebecca who took Little Flower's hand; Little Flower, extended her free hand to Chiquita, who clasped the hand of Mai-Ling.

Eleanor, watching her three- year- old toddler "Little-Becky", trying to keep-up with the older children, smiled and said; isn't she precious… aren't they all *"Precious"*.

Eleanor's Quaker mother-in-law, Sanna Winslow, who along with her husband Willem, quietly, reverently said; "As *thee* can surely see; that *thy* children are all;

"PRECIOUS - IN HIS SIGHT"

The End

Epilogue

(1) On Tuesday, June 15th 1887, Justin Gulliver, B.S., graduated, Summa Cum Laude, from; The Hampton Institute, with a Bachelor of Science Degree in Mechanical Engineering.

(2) Justin Gulliver and Eleanor Winslow, were married, July 27th 1887; their daughter, Rebecca Ruth Gulliver was born Oct 10th 1884

(3) Eleanor and her daughter *"Becky Ruth"*, for four years until her marriage to Justin, lived with her "Abolitionist-In-Laws, Sanna and Willem Winslow, in Willem and Sanna's converted basement apartment.

(4) The apartment had served, before and during the Civil War, as a *"Station"*, for the *"Underground Railroad"*, that assisted in the escape of runaway slaves.

(5) In 1910 the two cousins, thirty-three-year-old" *Mandy Margaret McCloskey"*; and her twenty-six-year-old cousin; *"Rebecca-Ruth Gulliver"*— who had both during their teen years, been volunteer-activists in the National American Woman Suffrage Association, headed by Susan B. Anthony— became, key (NAWSA-speakers), advocating across the nation, for an amendment to the United States Constitution… which would give women the right to vote.

(6) On June 4, 1919, The Susan B. Anthony Amendment to constitution…that allowed women to vote was, after decades of debate…was approved by the Senate of the United States of America.

When the United States Senate, approved the *"Susan B. Anthony Amendment"* …the 19th amendment to the United States constitution, which allowed women *(white-women)*, the right to vote… in the ceremonial-office of the President of the Senate…witnessing the signing of the passage of the *"bill"*; representing the suffragists; Stood forty-two-year-old, "Mandy Margaret McClosekey", and her cousin, thirty-five-year-old, "Rebecca-Ruth Gulliver".

As they were existing, the office; One of the older suffragists, smiled when she overheard her young colleague, Mandy Margaret McClosekey say to her cousin, Rebecca Ruth Gulliver;

"Next-up…we obtain the vote for all, of our sisters; Blacks-women; Native- American women; Mexican-American women; Asian-American women, all Americans, men and women".

The two cousins, hand in hand, walking down the steps of the Capitol Building, were singing.

"Jesus loves the little children…all the little children of the world;

Be they Yellow; Black or White…; We're all precious in his Sight. Jesus loves all the children of the World".

The *"Dynamic Dual"* of ***"Mandy and Rebecca"***, lives on.

www.ingramcontent.com/pod-product-compliance
Lightning Source LLC
Chambersburg PA
CBHW030911300726

48970CB00001B/112